THE RIVERCLIFFE LEGACY

DEE ERNST

225
ALEXANDER
STREET

To find more of Dee's books, go to
www.deeernst.com

Comments? Questions? An uncontrollable desire to just chat? You can reach me at
Dee@deeernst.com

ISBN#9780998033402

❀ Created with Vellum

For my father

THE RIVERCLIFFE LEGACY

CHAPTER 1

$\mathcal{I}$magine, if you will, a quiet, tree-lined street in Brooklyn, New York. Not *too* quiet — there's the pleasant rumble of traffic from the highway at the end of the block, and the occasional high-pitched yapping of someone's over-priced, designer dog. The brownstones on the street are all fairly uniform, until you come to one that looks, if not disheveled, at least more shabby than chic. The window boxes are filled with geraniums and sweet potato vine, two decidedly B-list annuals. The shutters are painted in a shade that was never, by any stretch of the imagination, a Pantone Color of the Year.

That would be the house where I grew up.

It's the house I moved back to, at the age of thirty-eight, when I realized I could no longer afford to keep the nice, suburban bi-level that had once belonged to my husband and myself.

You'd think that living in a brownstone on a residential street in the heart of a vibrant city would not be the worst thing in the world. And normally, it wouldn't. Normally, I'd be thrilled that my family and I were living there. Normally, I'd be grateful for the quiet, tree-lined streets and the lull of the traffic. I'd be glad that my kids could walk to a very good public school, as well as live only three subway stops away from the Brooklyn Botanical Garden. And I'd also be thrilled at my own decent commute to Brooklyn College, where I was taking grad courses while psyching myself up to take the CPA exam.

But.

There's always a but, isn't there?

The aforementioned brownstone still belonged to my mother, the smart, funny and decidedly strong-willed Marcella Castellano Harris. My children and I had moved into the bottom level. It was not technically the basement, but most of the square footage was below ground, and there was a noticeable lack of sunshine and cross ventilation. I slept on the foldout couch in what was ostensibly the den. The two girls shared another room, formerly called an office. My son made do with a large, windowless closet. We all fought over one bathroom.

It had not, as you can imagine, worked out well.

My daughter, Lily, was always a bit of a drama queen, but at sixteen had really hit her stride. Any slight, real or imagined, resulted in a performance. As an example, consider a simple shower, taken during an otherwise peaceful Sunday afternoon. She emerged from our single bathroom, wrapped in a towel, and dripping on the cold tile floor.

"I hate this bathroom, I hate this house, and I hate you." Her voice was a low, furious snarl.

I took a deep breath. "Did you run out of hot water again?"

"Running out of hot water is what happens every time you turn on the tap," was the answer. I could see her pale arms, puckered with goose bumps, trembling. "How could you bring us to this hellhole to live?"

Kira sank down into the cushions of the couch, her shoulders shaking with silent laughter.

"Is this really a hellhole?" I asked Lily quietly. I turned to Kira. "Is it?"

Kira shook her head. "No. But Lily's right, there's *never* hot water." Her voice was a giggly mess.

"Maybe if you didn't take such long showers?" I suggested.

Lily's voice was still low, barely a whisper. "Ten minutes is *not* an excessively long shower."

Kevin made a rude noise from the other side of the couch. "You were in there twenty-six minutes," he said. I didn't doubt him. Timing Lily's showers had become a favorite pastime of his.

"You are a miserable excuse for a brother," Lily hissed, and strode away, with all the dignity that a sixteen-year-old, wrapped in a towel, could muster.

"We're trapped in here like rats in a maze," Kevin said conversationally. "And with a woman who belongs on *Hoarders*."

"Grandma has been very generous," I reminded him. "She didn't have to take us in."

He shrugged. "She's the grandmother. Isn't that her job?"

Kira was still trying not to laugh out loud. She was six, and her normal state was mid-giggle. She had just turned three when her father left, and I don't think she remembered him all that much. She had, at least, shown no outward sign of anger or hurt at Ed's leaving, and tended to treat time spent with her father like a visit from some B-list celebrity —a reason to eat junk food and have fun, but nothing more.

Kevin had recently turned twelve, and was a complete mystery to me. He'd spent his time in elementary school practicing to be a perfect jock. He tried out for, and got on, every sports team available through school and the local Recreation department. I spent lots of time shuttling him to and from various practices and games. Since moving to Brooklyn last summer, however, he'd shown no interest in any activity aside from what he could play on his phone. Upon enrolling in middle school, he had joined nothing. He had also grown silent and judgmental, and he gained almost twenty pounds.

Lily was Kevin's age when Ed left. She went from a fairly goofy little kid to an intellectually and morally superior being who barely tolerated all those unfortunate enough to be around her. Since starting her new school, she'd latched on to no less than four Best Friends Forever. Those friendships, however, burned too brightly and flamed out quickly. Currently, there was no one she spent time with.

And she was a total bitch. I can't say I blamed her. She'd reveled in the role of Daddy's Girl and Ed's leaving hit her the hardest.

I looked at my offspring. "You guys do remember that this is temporary, right? And I'll be back on my feet soon?"

Kira rolled over and buried her little face into the couch cushions. Kevin made another rude noise, adjusted his earphones, and stalked out.

Lily came back into the room, still towel-wrapped, and stood directly in front of me. "I hate everything," she whispered.

Sometimes, so did I.

Ed and I had been divorced for over three years, and I was still reeling. I had thought my marriage was working. I loved my husband. He came home every night and played with his kids, gave me back-rubs and took us all on day-trips on the weekend. I had felt us moving apart, emotionally, but figured that was what happened when you were married almost fifteen years. His level of emotional detachment was much higher, however. By the time he physically moved out of the house, he'd sold his business and moved most of the money into a separate account, under his own name. He hadn't been a shrewd businessman for all those years for nothing. Then he moved to another state with another woman and filed for divorce, citing irreconcilable differences.

I felt like such a cliché—the wife and mother abandoned for the Hot Young Thing. So aside from my own broken heart and the equally broken hearts of my children, I had every eye in our affluent suburban neighborhood turned on my family, second-guessing every word and deed, past and present.

I could have stuck it out in the suburbs of New Jersey after my divorce, even with all the intense and unwanted scrutiny, but it took me less than a year to realize I couldn't sit on my butt all day lamenting my poor choice in husbands. When my family became my unemployed self and my equally unemployed children, I quickly saw whatever savings I had salvaged being frittered away on things like food and electricity. One cannot live on child support alone. I needed to get out and find a well-paying job. Since I'd stopped working right before my daughter Lily had been born, and hadn't gone back, I quickly found out that, even with an accounting degree, being a full time wife and mother was not the kind of experience corporate America was looking for. Granted, the Principles of Accounting were written in stone, but the software I had become proficient at in the brief years I had worked was obsolete, and no one seemed interested in re-training a woman in her late thirties whose most recent skills were carpooling and secretary of the PTA. I needed more than a quick brush-up on my accounting skills.

I hadn't liked college the first time around. I chose accounting as a major because a book about it came first, alphabetically, on my guidance counselors' bookshelf, and when she asked me what my interests were, it was the first thing I saw while desperately trying to find an appropriate answer. My real interests, at the time, were drinking after school and trying to be popular, so I lied. Accounting served me well, and I earned a degree in something that, if nothing else, got me a job. And I'd been fairly successful at it for the twenty-eight months I'd worked before giving up my glamorous life as a staff accountant for the equally glamorous life of mother.

That was then. This was now. Now I needed an MBA/CPA kind of salary so my very smart children could go to good schools and have their own well-paying careers. I wanted my son to be happy and successful. I wanted my daughters to be happy and even more successful, so they would never be left high and dry by a lying husband who fled in the middle of the night with all the cash on hand and a waitress from Hooters.

I made a plan to go back to school and get my MBA. It would take two years. So the house was sold. After paying off the mortgage, giving Ed his half (New Jersey being a community property state) and paying the realtor's commission, I was not nearly as solvent as I thought I'd be. If I kept myself on a strict allowance the money would last just about two years, but only if I didn't have to worry about paying rent. That's when we all moved back to Brooklyn.

My mother kept asking why I wasn't looking for a rich husband. I kept reminding her that I'd already had one of those, and it hadn't ended well.

Now there was a light at the end of this tunnel. I'd have my MBA by next January. Then I could look for a real job and hopefully make enough money to get a place of my own. My personal goal was to *not* be living with my mother when I turned forty. I had nine months to make it happen.

My children had heard it all before. I think they stopped believing. I think they felt, in their deepest heart of hearts, that they'd be living with Grandma until they were old enough to move out and get *their* own apartments. Just like they felt their father was not coming by anytime soon to take them out to lunch and to the zoo. I tried not to think about it too much, but sometimes the burden of causing their disappointment was so hard to bear I'd just sit on the back steps, a juice glass full of wine in one hand, crying. My mother would deflect the kids, often treating them to the movies or ice cream, giving me the time I needed to pull myself back together.

Being a parent was rough.

Especially being a parent during a long, hot summer, when the kids were not in school and there was no pool or beach, or any extra money to *go* to a pool or beach. Last summer, our first since moving in with my mother, the kids and I spent the entire month of July camped out on Long Beach Island, in the cramped, noisy beach house of my once-upon-a-time neighbor, Chrissy Muller.

Chrissy and I were not particularly good friends. In fact, I had made no friends at all in the whole fifteen years I'd lived in New Jersey. I knew lots of women, mothers of the kids who went to school with mine, who were in the carpools, or helped with soccer. But no strong bonds were formed. I kept my family in a tight little circle, and was reluctant to let anyone else in. I'd learned that from my mother, and her you-and-me-against-the-world mentality.

So that made up for the long, boring August. Almost. But this year Chrissy was the one getting a divorce, and it looked like her husband was getting custody of the beach house, leaving me with nothing to occupy my children for ten weeks except a six-year-old Playstation 2. After all, there were only so many bike rides to be taken in a week.

"Why don't we know anybody outside of Brooklyn? Aren't there any long-lost relatives I can get re-acquainted with?" I asked my mother. "You know, with a boat or a country house with a pool?"

"Risa, honey, please," my mother said, taking a long drag on her cigarette. "It's really not my fault I was an only child." She tapped her ash into her pretty china saucer, then expertly swirled the tip into a sharp, glowing point. "And my father never fooled around, so there's not even a half-sibling we could suddenly discover."

We were sitting in her kitchen, frozen in 1972, but immaculate.

My mother was not an especially good housekeeper. Her rooms, except her kitchen, were filled with clutter. She liked to save things. She wasn't quite bad enough to have her own reality show, but that was a very close judgment call.

She was a great cook, and her homemade gravy with meatballs could please even my oldest and most miserable child. As a second generation Italian, my mother prided herself on her Sunday gravy, her good wineglasses, and her carefully waxed upper lip. She was now in her early sixties. She had married, at seventeen, a charming Irishman, spent a few tumultuous years being chased out of all five boroughs, and got pregnant the week before her husband got sent to state prison for a list of crimes and misdemeanors too long to remember. She moved to Brooklyn when normal people could afford to, got a job as a secretary, and raised me alone. When I asked to come back, she merely raised both eyebrows and said yes. She did not say I-told-you-so, for which I will always be grateful.

"What about my other grandpa?" I ventured.

My mother did not like to discuss my father. But she would occasionally give me glimpses into his family, tantalizing peeks into lives I had only imagined throughout my childhood.

"Your father did say he was raised on a plantation," she said.

"But I thought he was from upper New York State. Aren't plantations a southern thing?"

She nodded. "Yes. But he was never very good at geography. He

7

used to talk about feeding chickens and herding cows." She frowned. "His uncle did something with milk. He did not like country living, your father. He didn't like getting his hands dirty."

Since she was feeling expansive, I pushed, just a little.

"Is that why he moved to Queens?"

She smiled. "Yes." She got a wistful look in her eyes. "That's when he started stealing cars."

"And he met you?" I prompted. This was usually as far as she got in the Greatest Love Story of All Time.

"Yes. I was working at a hardware store. He came in for new crowbar." Her eyes got misty. "Love at first sight."

I could see where my father could have easily fallen. My mother, even now, was a beautiful woman. Creamy, flawless skin, high cheekbones, big dark eyes and glossy hair. Any good looks I had came directly from her. In fact, when I was in my twenties, I looked very much like the woman who smiled from her wedding picture, the only picture she kept of her and my father together.

And I could see also how she could have been swept off her feet. My father was everything a handsome Irishman could be—thick, curling hair, wide blue eyes, and smile that could melt the hardest of hearts.

"And he asked you out for coffee?"

She sighed. "We spent the whole night talking. We walked through the entire city. He was such a charmer. He asked me to marry him at dawn, in front of Radio City. I said yes without even thinking about it."

From there, the details became harder to pin down. I knew they moved around a lot. I knew her family never approved. I remember, as a small child, all the stories she would tell me of what our lives would be like "When Daddy Came Back". Somewhere between second and third grade, those stories stopped, and I realized later that my father had probably been released from prison about that time, but had not returned home. Eventually, my mother stopped mentioning him at all.

But it was during those years that I came to love my father. She talked about him constantly, and from the glow in her eyes and the smile on her lips, I knew how special he was. I had his face in my head, and my mother's words built the rest of him: clever and funny, full of dreams and plans for the future. As a child I believed in Santa Claus and the Easter Bunny. I also believed in my father. Because my mother made him so real to me, I continued to believe, all into my teen years, long after he was supposed to have come back and rescued my mother and I. And because he was real, I never got over his abandonment. Maybe my mother did the both of us a great disservice for giving me a real father instead of just the *idea* of a father. Losing an idea could be disappointing. Losing the real thing was completely devastating.

She tamped out her cigarette. She allowed herself five a day, and each one was a ritualized event. "So, what are we going to do with those kids? Cause I gotta tell you, honey, this summer is gonna be a hot one and I can't be babysitting every day."

She had retired the year before, after working for thirty years in a small plumbing supply company that actually paid her a pension. She still worked, weekends only, doing data entry for a small law firm. She also kept herself busy by volunteering for a few choice organizations and had a brisk dog-walking business that was strictly an under-the-table enterprise. I think she welcomed us because she was somewhat lonely, but I also knew that she had enjoyed her life, and my family and I had really thrown her off her game.

"I'm not taking any classes this summer," I told her.

"Fine, fine, but what are you going to *do* with them?"

"Lily wants a summer job," I told her.

"Then she should have been applying back in January. Just because everyone around here looks rich, that don't mean those kids aren't going to work anyway."

"I was thinking about camping."

She leaned forward and looked at me with interest. "And what, exactly, do you know about camping?"

"It's cheaper than trying to rent a house somewhere. Campsites are, like, ten bucks a night?"

My mother patted my hand. "Good idea, honey. And how much do you think it will cost you to rent a tent, sleeping bags, and all that other camping crap you're gonna need?"

"Can't I borrow all that stuff?"

"From whom?"

My shoulders slumped. "You don't know any campers?"

She pushed herself away from her kitchen table. "Nobody in Brooklyn are campers, honey. Nobody I know, anyway. Didn't any of your fancy Jersey neighbors camp?"

My neighbors in New Jersey were not, by the way, fancy. But because my former home had been surrounded by a green lawn, and I could park my car in the garage instead of having to move it from one side of the street to the other, my mother always thought of my neighborhood as on a par with 90210.

I sighed. "No. Nobody camped. I'll never be able to go away. Where was this plantation? Does the Harris family still own it? Maybe we could pay them a surprise visit."

My mother raised a carefully plucked, then back-filled eyebrow. "Well, I know his mother died before Billy and I even met. He did mention his brother's wife, who hated him and forbade him from ever setting foot on the old homestead again. The farm is upper New York State somewhere. Maybe you could find something on your computer. See if it's still owned by the aunt. You could drive there and see if anyone in the family has changed their mind."

I narrowed my eyes. "That's sarcasm, right?"

She drained her coffee cup and pushed away from the kitchen table. She smiled. "Why, yes, dear. It is."

"What was the name of the farm?" I called after her as she swept out. "I'm a desperate woman."

"Forget it," she called back.

I sighed. She was right. I was going to have to figure something out, and fast.

But then the family found me.

.   .   .

The envelope was creamy white, with an embossed logo, Butterfield and Butterfield, and a return address on Park Avenue.

Inside, a thick, single sheet informed me that the firm of Butterfield and Butterfield, representing the Cliffe Trust for sixty-three of the past one-hundred and eighty-six years it had been in existence, had important information for me, a direct descendant of the Cliffe family. The information needed to be discussed in person, and when would it be convenient for Mr. Butterfield to come by?

"Mom? Who are Butterfield and Butterfield? And what the hell is the Cliffe trust?" I yelled.

She came flying into what she called the upstairs parlor. It would have been a very pleasant room, with bay windows and a high ceiling, but every horizontal space was covered with something — books, papers, magazines, empty pots where green plants once lived. I insisted that there be room to sit on the sofa, and the coffee table be kept clear so I had a place to read my mail and occasionally put my feet up.

"Who?"

"Butterfield and Butterfield."

"They're lawyers."

I looked up at her. "I know. It says so right here on their stationary. You know them? You hate lawyers."

"These are the family lawyers. Your fathers' family. He told me about them."

I stared at the letter. "What could they want? They mention the Cliffe trust. Was that his family? Do you think he died?"

She snatched the letter from my hand and read it quickly. "No, they'd notify me. After all, I'm his wife."

"Ex-wife, you mean."

"No." She handed the letter back. "He sent me divorce papers, about thirty years ago, but I never signed. We're still married."

"WHAT?"

"Oh, don't be so dramatic."

I struggled to get my jaw off the floor. "You and Daddy never divorced?"

"Don't call him Daddy. You never knew him. He never meant a thing to you."

"Well, he obviously meant an awful lot to you if you're still married to him."

"Good Catholic girls don't divorce," she said, trying to look nonchalant.

"Oh? When was the last time you went to mass?"

She turned and walked out. I followed her through the dining room. Because we ate in the kitchen, the long, mahogany dining table was covered in several piles; magazines (select pages carefully removed, creating *other* piles) catalogs (appropriate pages dog-eared) and coupons (some dating back to the '80s).

"Then what do you think this is about?"

She shrugged. "Call and find out."

I did call, but the woman on the phone was not very forthcoming with information. She did tell me that Mr. Alan Butterfield was available to drop by to see me the following Thursday, and I agreed to be home.

My children were intrigued by varying degrees.

"Maybe its Dad's lawyer, and he's cutting back on child support," Lily suggested.

"Maybe you've won the lottery," was Kira's guess. Her understanding of what lawyers did was hazy, at best.

Kevin actually took the letter and read it very carefully. "You're probably being sued," he said at last. "For lots of money. Did you do anything really dumb lately?"

I took the letter back. "No, Kevin. At least not anything dumber than usual."

Alan Butterfield, when he arrived, looked exactly the way a lawyer was supposed to look. He was fairly bland-looking, with a calm, reserved air about him and a very soothing voice. He sat down across from me in the upstairs parlor, in a chair cleared of debris especially for his use, pulled a file from his briefcase, and opened it. I liked him for that. Paper always seemed so reassuring to me. I hated people who read off of their laptop screens. That may have been because of my on-going fantasy about tiny people living inside computers and making things up. But — whatever.

"Theresa Anne Harris Armitage, my information states that you are the only child of William Henry Newsome, also known as Billy Harris, and Marcella Castellano. Is that correct?"

I frowned. Also known as? What did *that* mean? I nodded.

He looked at a few more papers. "I regret to inform you that William's mother, Catherine Hamburg Newsome, passed away three weeks ago."

My head exploded. I had a grandmother? Where had she been all my life?

"How did she know about me?" I asked. "And more important, why didn't she get in touch with me while she was alive?"

Mr. Butterfield cleared his throat. "I believe she had, in fact, tried to find her son William's family. Unfortunately, William got married under one of his many, ah, professional names. His real name was not, in fact, Harris. His real name was William Henry Newsome. But he was married under Harris, so that was his wife's name, and yours." He leaned forward and dropped his voice to a confidential whisper. "Finding you was a real bitch. We didn't even have your mother's correct maiden name. Cathy thought it was Costello, not Castellano. The only real facts we had to go on were a wedding date and your birthdate. Luckily, we had a very inventive clerk who found William's rap sheet and started looking under all his known aliases. She found a marriage license issued at the right time, and we started really digging from there." He sat back. "Without her, we might have *never* found you."

I stared at my mother, who was white as a sheet and had fire in her eyes. She had been standing in the doorway, trying not to look like she was bursting with curiosity, but had come over to stand behind Mr. Butterfield.

"His real name was what?" she growled.

"Newsome."

"Were we even married? Legally?"

He shrugged. "Well, it doesn't really matter as far as the trust is concerned. He told his mother that he had married, told her your name, and acknowledged that Theresa here was his daughter. That's all that's important here."

"Maybe to you," my mother said, her voice shaking, "but what about me?"

He looked sympathetic. "I'm sorry."

"So," my mother continued slowly, "he lied to me about his real name, his family... he told me his mother died before we even met. He told me he grew up on a farm. Was anything he ever told me the truth?"

My heart jumped out of my chest at the look on my mothers face. She had carried something of a torch for Billy Harris, because she had loved him in spite of his unlawful ways. She had excused and forgiven his various illegal activities, but I knew lying was something she could not forgive so easily.

"Yes, there was a farm," Butterfield said in a soothing voice. "There still is. That much is true."

I glanced at my mother. That one kernel did not seem to salve her anger.

"Mom," I whispered. "I'm so sorry."

She turned to me, still seething. "He didn't just lie to me, he lied to you. You had a friggin' grandmother. She could have been in your life. We could have had real Thanksgivings. Summers on a farm. She could have come to your First Communion. What a snake!"

She was right. As much as he'd lied to her, I had also paid a price. "I guess I'm sorry about her dying," I said to Butterfield. "But I never knew her."

"That may be, but she knew you. Or, she knew of you, which makes my job easier. Under the terms of the Cliffe Family Trust, at Catherine's death, the entire Cliffe estate passes on to the next female related by blood. That's you." He closed the file and folded his hands. "Any questions?"

Hundreds. I was in a quandary. On one hand, I had long ago stopped being curious about the man who absented himself from my life all those years ago. Finding out now that his lies had added another layer of pain to my mother's life made me want to add even more distance between us. But Mom had been very tight-lipped when I *had* been curious, and here was the possibility of answers.

"Wasn't there any other family?" I asked.

Butterfield opened the file again. "Catherine had three sons. He was the youngest."

"Aren't any of them in line to inherit?"

"The two older boys are both dead, and neither had children." He closed the file and shook his head. "The Cliffe Family Trust is very old, and has never been broken. Only a female can inherit. Catherine Newsome was the eleventh, or possibly thirteenth woman to take ownership of RiverCliffe. Now you are the oldest living female in the family line. After you, it would fall to your oldest daughter, and so on."

I sat back. "What exactly does the Cliffe estate consist of? You said it was a farm?"

Butterfield folded his hands together. "The name of the property is RiverCliffe. It's located about two hours from here, along the Hudson River. There's the main house, several outbuildings, and almost three hundred acres, most under cultivation or being used as grazing land. Right now, there are four leases attached." He opened the file again.

Two hours away. All that, and a possible family, had been just two hours away. I looked up at Mom again. Her jaw was clenched so tightly I was surprised I couldn't hear her teeth cracking.

He shuffled through some papers. "Daniel Rugg runs his cheese factory from the main barn, and keeps all his animals on about one hundred acres. He also has hay and barley growing. Mackenzie Sutton farms almost one hundred fifty acres. Corn and winter wheat. Martha Newsome rents a cottage and has about twelve acres for her herb business."

"Wait. She's a Newsome? Why isn't she getting anything?" I asked.

"Because she married into the family. For that reason, her lease is one dollar a year until her death. Then, there's the cemetery. That is leased to Woodmark and Sons, funeral directors."

"A cemetery?" I asked. "I own a cemetery?"

"Yes. The entire property is, of course, owned outright. There are currently no mortgages or loans against the property. Between all the leases, your income is roughly sixty thousand dollars a year. That goes directly to you, by the way. It is not in any way tied back into River-Cliffe House."

My ears, had it been physically possible, would have pricked up. "Sixty thousand dollars?" That was more more than three times what was left of the house sale money, and I'd worried about how I was going to make it stretch. Now, I didn't have to worry about buying books for the next semester, how I was going to replace the air-conditioning in the mini-van, or if I could get Kevin braces.

He nodded. "Yes. And the house itself has been run, very successfully, as an inn for the past twenty years. The staff is very, ah, concerned about your plans going forward."

"An inn? And a *staff?*" I had a sudden vision of myself, dressed entirely from the Land's End catalog, sipping brandy by a roaring fireplace while my smiling and very well paying guests gathered around me.

He pulled something from his folder. It was a brochure for River-Cliffe House.

I looked at it cautiously. Whoever put this together was a pro. The picture of the house itself was almost storybook: a soaring clapboard building with welcoming porches, surrounded by flowering shrubs and lots of green. The interior of the brochure highlighted a few beautifully decorated bedrooms, a great room, complete with my fantasy fireplace, and a pool pretending to be a woodland pond. There were even a few pictures of guests enjoying a picture-perfect countryside.

"Wow," I said. This was not for the economy-minded, I could tell. "So, I take it this is worth a boatload of money, right?" I tried not to sound too eager.

Butterfield nodded. "Yes. Boatload is a very appropriate word."

I looked at my mother. "He told you it was a farm. Did he tell you anything about all this?" I asked her.

She shook her head. Her coloring and breathing had returned to normal, but her eyes still glittered. "I knew that Billy was from upstate, and he mentioned cows, but I had no idea he was from some-place like this."

Butterfield cleared his throat. "To be honest, it wasn't always like this. In fact, at one point, it was a decrepit, failing mess. Catherine was quite a visionary. And a very strong personality. She built her little empire from nothing."

"And now it's mine?" I asked. "Why would she leave it to me? I still don't understand."

Butterfield shrugged. "She had no choice. I told you, the trust is very clear. Only a female may inherit. It's been that way for almost two hundred years."

My mother was still obviously in shock, but she narrowed her eyes and twisted her lips, a sign of deep thinking. "Billy would never let a moneymaking opportunity like this one go untouched. Is he up there?"

Butterfield shook his head. "Not now. He's shown up briefly now and again over the years. As far as I know, Catherine hadn't been close to her sons. To be honest, they were not very loyal. Or loving. I gather that Catherine was not sympathetic to any of their life choices. William is the only one still living, and, as far as I know, is not pres-ently incarcerated." He cleared his throat. "He was there for her funeral, and lingered for a while. A sheriff finally had to ask him to leave."

My mother rolled her eyes. "Figures," she muttered. "What a family."

He nodded. "Indeed." He handed me his card. "Have your attorney contact me as soon as possible, and we'll transfer the property and funds."

"Funds?" There was cash too?

He finally smiled. "Yes. A boatload."

After he'd gone, Mom and I poured a bit of wine and sat on the front stoop. She lit a cigarette, an extra one for the day.

"Right up the Hudson," she said at last.

I nodded. "Apparently."

Her hand was steady as she tapped her ashes into her saucer, but her voice shook. "I can't believe he did that to me. He knew...he knew I could have used all the help I could get."

I waited as she inhaled, then blew the smoke from her nostrils in two thin and furious streams. "My dad hated Billy, and cut me off from everything after we married. Billy knew that. If it hadn't been for the one life insurance policy my father forgot about, you and I would have been living on the street. Literally. That's what I used to buy this place. And all the time, right up the river was his mother. Your grandmother. She could have helped us."

I nodded, trying in my own mind to visualize how different my life would have been. My mother did everything she could to shield me from whatever problems she faced, but I grew up knowing we didn't have any money, that her paycheck was stretched so thin that any small misfortune became a disaster. As I got older, and babysitter costs went away, things got easier, but I spent the first twelve years of my life on tiptoe, trying not to cause any trouble, keeping to myself so I didn't have to share what little we had with anyone else. There were no sleepovers or parties with friends, because some weeks Mom could barely feed the two of us, let alone any extra mouths I may have brought along. It was only after I got a job in high school was there suddenly a few leftover dollars every week for something extra—a movie, coffee after school, an illicit bottle of wine with a few of the girls from the bakery where I worked. But by then I was known as a loner, and I could find no one to share my sudden, newfound extravagance. It took me until college to finally feel comfortable with friendship, and even then, I was slow and cautious.

"So, what are you gonna do," Mom asked. "Sell it all and live a life of leisure?"

I glanced at my watch. I had to leave to pick up Kira from school in ten minutes. "That sounds good. Take the money, buy a new house somewhere, try to get the kids back into a routine like we had..."

"With Ed?" Mom shook her head. "Listen to me, baby. You're never gonna get back to a life like you had with your ex-husband, because he's your *ex*-husband. And a new house isn't going to change that. Your kids need to get used to a new routine, 'cause from what I can tell, the one they got here isn't going too well."

I nodded. "We're not in an ideal situation right now," I agreed.

My mother pulled back her head and looked at me in astonishment. "Not ideal? Risa, this is the pits, for your kids *and* for you. I wish I could do more for you all. I hate that all I can offer is my crummy basement."

I reached both of my arms around her and hugged her tightly. "Mom, every day I thank God for your crummy basement. Otherwise we'd be living out of a mini-van."

"At least Kevin would have a window," she said, wagging her finger. "I think lack of sunlight has affected his weight."

"Eating bags of chips and spending hours playing games on his phone has affected his weight," I countered.

She shrugged. "Still, he could use a little sunshine."

"We all could, Ma," I said. "We all could."

CHAPTER 2

I didn't have an attorney. But I did have my best friend from college, Beth Calder, who was currently practicing patent law in Buffalo, NY, and she said she'd have one of her colleagues give Butterfield a call.

Beth called me back the week before the Memorial Day weekend. "So, Risa, you've inherited an inn with a four-and-a-half star Yelp rating. What are you going to do with it?" Beth asked.

I sighed. "Sell it?"

"No. You can't sell it. This is a trust. The property must be handed down through the women only, and cannot be sold until there are no living relations left. If you don't want it, fine. Then it's Lily's."

"What if she doesn't want it?"

Beth sighed. "I gather that all those Butterfields take this very seriously. They would probably start going back, maybe hire a genealogist, and see if they could track down some distant relation. And if they found one, everything would go to them, not you."

Whoa. "In that case, I don't know. I guess I could just let it continue on without me. All I really want out of this is enough money to buy my own place with sunshine, fresh air, and no meth labs down the street."

Beth clucked. She did that. I found it annoying after a while, and she knew it, so she always tried to keep it at a minimum. "You live in a fairly nice residential area, Risa. Not exactly meth lab country."

"True. I need to check out how much money is really involved here. Even if I couldn't get a big chunk of cash, a steady income would be such a relief. And who knows, maybe I wouldn't have to finish this damned MBA that's sucking the life right out of me."

She laughed outright. "I never could figure out why you went for a degree in something you hated so much."

"It seemed like a good idea at the time," I told her. "And I don't hate accounting. In fact, I find a great deal of comfort in all those rows and columns, and everything adding up just right. It appeals to my sense of order. And it should come in useful right now. I'll be able to tell if someone is cooking the books."

Beth went on. "Your grandmother had a small personal fortune, cash and stocks, that she bequeathed to her employees and a few close friends. Her son got nothing. The trust is very interesting, but looks legit. The account for the estate is very healthy. In fact, with the leases, and a salary from the inn, you could be comfortable, provided you didn't splurge too often. The inn is very highly rated, and is financially sound, as are the businesses that lease from you. You stepped in it, Risa. A win-win."

I sank back onto the couch. "When can I see it?"

"Anytime. But they're usually booked on the weekends, so I'd call rather than drop by. What are you going to do?"

As it was the end of May, my kids were counting down the hours until the last day of school. I hadn't told them about RiverCliffe yet, mainly because I wasn't sure what to say to my kids. How would they react to a sudden windfall which included a great-grandmother who could have been in their lives had her son not been such a lying snake? And RiverCliffe itself? Would they want to see what was their legitimate "home place"? Kira would welcome the adventure, I knew, but Kevin? Would he even bother lifting his nose up from whatever was playing on his phone?

Lily, I didn't want to think about. She was without any current companion, and constantly complained about how lame her high school was. But I knew that even if I picked her up and placed her in a certified Eden, she would hate it, for no other reason than it was my choice. She did not talk to me about, well, anything really, but I knew that she blamed me for her father's leaving. I was sure she had pinpointed something I did or said to make him leave, and therefore, any and all of my decisions going forward from that point were, by the simple fact that they were *my* decisions, very bad.

I sighed. "It's a long, hot weekend coming up. I'll see if there's room at the inn."

I hung up and found the brochure that Alan Butterfield had left. I went to the website. The pool would be open. Would the hills really be that green? Were the cows that clean and pretty?

I dialed the number. A real person answered the phone.

"Ah, hello. My name is Theresa Armitage, and a Mr. Butterfield—"

"Oh, Mrs. Armitage, we've been so hoping we'd hear from you." The voice on the other end was low-pitched, female, and a little breathless. "Let me put you through to Winston right away."

I heard a click, then classical music. I spent a few seconds humming tunelessly, when another voice came on.

"Mrs. Armitage, I'm so glad you called. I'm Winston Talvert, acting manager. What can I do for you?"

Winston had a deep, throaty voice, the kind that conjured up lumberjacks swinging axes and roasting whole oxen in a fire pit.

"Well, I was trying to figure out when I could come up and meet you all," I said.

"Any time," he said at once.

"But I understand that you're a very popular place. Will there be room?"

He chuckled. At least I assumed that what it was. It could have been a nearby train rumbling through. "The owner's suite is always available," he said.

"Owner's suite? Oh. That sounds lovely, but how big is it? I'd like to bring my kids."

"The suite is actually the family home that was built in 1847, after

22

the original cabin was destroyed in a fire. It's quite substantial and comfortable. It's attached to the main building, of course, but in it's own little world. You've got a bedroom on the first floor, along with your own living area, and a small kitchenette. Two bedrooms in the second-floor attic."

"Really?" Hmmm… "How many bathrooms?"

"Two. Should I get it ready for you?"

I felt myself starting to smile. "How long will that take?"

"By tomorrow."

Wow. "How efficient of you. We'll be there Saturday morning."

I clicked off the phone and stared at it. Could it really be that easy? Of course not. Now I had to tell my kids.

I took them out for pizza. I found them less likely to pitch a fit when out in public. We ordered, and as we waited I looked at their happy faces. Kira was scribbling on the placemat. Kevin was plugged in and fixated on his phone. Lily sat, head bowed, staring into her hands.

"So, guys, I have some news," I began. "We're going away for Memorial Day weekend."

Lily lifted her head, and Kevin scowled. Kira seemed oblivious, happily coloring.

"Where?" Kevin asked.

"An inn. Upstate. It's also a working farm, and there's a pool."

"So, what would we do there?" Kevin asked.

"Well, we can swim, hike, go down by the river and maybe rent boats. What do you think?"

Kira looked up. "Are there pigs and chickens at the farm?"

I tried to remember the livestock on their website. "I think so."

"Cool," she said, and went back to coloring.

"Is there Wi-Fi?" Lily asked.

I nodded, on surer footing. "Yes. And cable. But you can get that here. There will be fun things to do and all sorts of little towns we can explore."

"Can we go to Sleepy Hollow?" Kevin asked.

"Maybe. Why?"

"I want to see that headless guy," he answered.

Lily rolled her eyes, her all-time favorite method of expression. "Don't be stupid, Kev. You do know that's not real, right?"

"Of course I know it's not real," he shot back. "But there are all sorts of headless horseman stuff there. Don't you know anything?"

Lily's eyes narrowed. "How could we afford that? You keep telling us we're broke."

"We're not so broke anymore. Remember I told you about a lawyer? Well, it looks like I inherited this place. It's called RiverCliffe."

"Are we going to have to *live* there?" Lily asked, her voice rising an octave. "I bet there's not even a *mall* there."

"No, Lily, we're not going to live there. In fact, now that I have some money, we can look for our own house. Maybe over the summer."

Kira frowned. "We'd have to leave grandma?"

"Baby, we'll never *leave* grandma, we'll just be in a home of our own. But for the long weekend, I thought it might be fun to go up and see what it's like."

Kira sat back. "Can I get a horse?"

"I think they already have a horse," I told her.

"It'll be better than hanging out around here," Kevin grumbled.

I nodded. "My thought exactly."

Lily slumped forward, burying her head in her hands. "Nothing but country hicks," she groaned.

"'I don't know about that," I said brightly. "After all, people like us will be visiting there too"

She raised her head and gave me the Look Of Death. "That's even worse."

Well, alrighty then.

It took us less than three hours to get there, but we spent some time in traffic. When we finally exited the highway, no one in the car was speaking to anyone else in the car. Road trips, I had found, were not the bonding experience in my family that they may have been in other, more normal families. My three children could argue over anything—who sat in the front seat, what the standard space allotment was for those doomed to the backseat, who opened the CheezIts first, the color of the sky…

It may have only been a two hour and forty-nine minute trip, but it certainly *seemed* longer.

We breezed past Hyde Park, and Kevin went into navigation mode, taking directions, of course, from his phone.

"Next left," he called out.

"Now?"

"No, *next* left. See, this I why I should have gotten in front."

"Now?"

"YES!"

We arrived at RiverCliffe just before noon.

The brochure didn't do it justice. The house was huge, and quite beautiful. I could see where sections had been added and improved, as the wooden siding changed size with each addition. But it was painted a soft yellow, and the porches, balconies and banks of windows made for a warm, inviting whole. We pulled up before the broad front porch. There was a silence as I shut off the car, and little by little, sounds came to us—distant voices, the mooing of a cow, and…clucking? Quacking? Somewhere, a farm fowl was making noise.

Kira grinned. "Can we see the animals?"

Kevin got out and narrowed his eyes. "Looks clean."

Lily could find nothing bad to say, and kept mercifully quiet.

A young girl came hurrying up from a gravel parking lot at the foot of the hill.

She smiled. "Hi. Welcome to RiverCliffe. I'm Jessie. Are you checking in? Can I help you with your suitcases?"

"Hi, Jessie. I'm Risa Armatige. Yes, we'll be staying, but we'll get our own things, thanks. Do I park down there?"

She nodded. "Yep. See you later," and disappeared through the double front door.

It took us a few minutes to get the suitcases out, and as we climbed the few stairs to the porch, both doors swung open. A very short, thin young man beamed at us.

"Welcome to RiverCliffe," he boomed, in a voice that sounded so far removed from his physical appearance that I glanced behind him to see if there was a seven-foot-tall bearded Viking lurking anywhere.

"Winston?" I asked. There could not be two people in the world with that voice.

He stepped aside with a sweep of his hand. "Yes. Please, come in."

I stepped into the foyer, and there was a row of people standing, most of them wearing tan polo shirts with a red insignia where the pocket should have been. They were all smiling nervously, hands clasped, heads nodding. Very Downton Abbey.

I smiled back. "Hello everyone."

"Mom..." Lily said in a high-pitched voice.

"These are my kids," I said, setting down my overnight bag. "Lily here, and Kevin, and Kira. And, look, you all have nametags. That's easy."

I had to take a few deep breaths. Meeting new people always pushed my anxiety level up. But...these were the inn employees. I didn't have to make an impression on them. I was the new owner. And, after this weekend, I probably wasn't going to see any of them again. I felt my shoulders relax.

Kira pushed her way forward. "Who's in charge of the cows?" she asked.

The girl who introduced herself as Jessie stepped forward and knelt down in front of Kira. "I can take you out there. Danny is in charge of the cows, and he's really excited to meet you all."

Kira grinned and looked up at me expectantly.

"Why doesn't Winston show us where we're staying," I said, "and we can *all* go meet Danny."

Lily leaned up against a long library table in the middle of the foyer. "Really? Meeting cows?"

"Whatever," I breathed.

Winston nodded briefly to his staff, and they faded away in seconds. "This way," he said. He looked slightly odd for a moment, and then I realized — he was the kind of guy born with a clipboard in his hand, and without one, he looked almost naked.

He tried to take my bag, and when I said no, thanks, he did not try to wrestle it away from me. He led us through the foyer, and the charming room that had been in the brochure. We went past a staircase, then took a left into another century. The ceilings were lower, the windows smaller, and the plaster walls darker. Winston opened a heavy wooden door. "Welcome home."

The room was old, no doubt. A huge stone fireplace stood at one end, the ceiling low and beamed, but the walls were smooth plaster and there were lots of windows. It could have been a charming room, but the furniture was obviously from an era of fake leather and chrome, and had not aged well.

It didn't matter, I kept telling myself. It was clean, it was private, and it was only for the weekend.

"Are you friggin' kidding?" Lily whispered.

Woven rugs covered wide plank floors and a long narrow table flanked by benches sat under the rippled glass windows.

"There's a small kitchen to the left, and the steps are right here," Winston said, pointing upward.

The steps were narrow. "I'm betting this isn't up to code," Kevin said loudly as he trudged upstairs.

Winston laughed, which sounded like dropped stones echoing in the bottom of a water barrel.

"One bedroom is here," Winston said, opening a door tucked under the stairs.

This was a bit more my style. A large, four-poster bed. A comfy reading chair by the window that looked across to the Hudson River. A fireplace. A small but exclusively MINE closet. A bathroom with a spacious claw-foot tub, obviously tacked on as a late nineteenth- or possibly early twentieth-century afterthought.

I turned to Winston gratefully. "This is fabulous. Really. I never expected anything like this."

He looked relieved. "Whenever you're ready, I'll show you around.

We have eighteen guest rooms, and we're full this weekend, so you'll have a chance to see us in action."

I'm not the kind of person who enjoys living out of a suitcase. Even if I'm just staying overnight, I unpack everything. I even put out my toothbrush and deodorant. So it was a few minutes before I had a chance to check on the kids.

Upstairs was not as cramped as I thought it would be. Two equally sized bedrooms with high ceilings and a large bath.

Kevin was at his open window, his suitcase thrown on one of two twin-sized beds. "I can see boats," he said.

I stood behind him and looked over his head to the scene before us. "What a gorgeous view."

"Yeah. Did we bring the binoculars? So I can watch the boats?" There was a rise of excitement in his voice I hadn't heard in months. I gave him a quick hug.

"I don't think so, but we'll see if we can get some in town. Unpack, please, and put your stuff away, okay?"

The girls' room was on the other side of the hall, also with two twin beds. I peeked into the bathroom, which Lily was already in, lining the narrow shelf above the sink with various bottles and brushes.

"Mommy, look, we can see the animals," Kira called.

I crossed the narrow hallway and looked out. Their window was on the other side of the house, away from the river. Spread before me was the whole of RiverCliffe, gently rolling hillsides dotted with herds of sheep and cows, small, white outbuildings and carefully cultivated fields. It could have been a postcard.

"There's no TV up here," Lily pointed out.

I looked around. "No, there's not. I guess you can watch with us downstairs in the living room."

She looked at me as though I had just suggested she walk down the stairs and into the farmyard, naked.

"I don't think so," she said succinctly.

"Unpack, and meet me back in the lobby. We'll check everything out," I told them, and headed downstairs.

I peeked into our kitchen. Fine for just me, impossible for two people trying to cook at once, which was perfect.

I went out the back door and into the sunlight.

The sounds of the animals were louder, and there were voices, muffled and low. The main barn was to the left, along with a few long, white buildings. To the right, farther up the sloping ground, was a small house and a long, roofed, open-sided building. I could see clusters of plants hanging upside down, obviously drying. I crossed the yard for a closer look.

The drying shed was cool and dark. I did not recognize any of the hanging plants but they smelled lovely — earthy and fresh. I wandered around for a few minutes, taking in the sounds and smells. I may have spent most of my adulthood in the suburbs, but this—this was the country. The real country.

"You must be Billy's kid," a voice said.

I turned around. Behind me stood a white-haired, dark-skinned woman, who could have been anywhere from fifty and eighty, wearing very faded jeans and a man's white button-down shirt.

I nodded. "Risa Armitage."

She held out her hand. "I'm Bernadette Miller. Martha and I are partners. We were wondering if you'd show up."

I shook her hand. It was rough and warm. "How could I resist?"

She grinned. Her teeth were large and square and stained from too many cups of coffee. "You alone?"

"No. My kids are here. We're getting ready for the big tour."

She nodded slowly. "Winston likes giving the big tour. He's very proud of the place. We all are. Cathy did a bang-up job. You'd better not screw things up."

"Well, my plan right now is to make sure nobody's cooking the books, and then letting everything continue to go along as it's been. Why fix what isn't broken?"

She shook her finger at me. "Glad you're not stupid. When you're done with Winston, come by our place. Martha made cookies." She turned and walked away, toward a small white cottage. I watched her as she turned the corner, and headed back to the main house.

Winston and my children were waiting for me in the lobby. It was more like a very large hallway, with windows open to the porch, a long narrow desk at one end, and a very high ceiling. Kira was lit up like a Christmas tree. Kevin was interested enough to have left his phone elsewhere. Lily looked as though her next steps were going to be off the gangplank.

"I was just telling the kids about the original owner," Winston said. "Andrew Cliffe." He pointed to an oil portrait hanging over an antique dresser. Andrew was a handsome if stern-looking man, dark-haired and dressed in a black coat and frilly white shirt.

I took a closer look. "When was this done?"

"Seventeen seventy-eight," Winston said.

I looked around. "And Mrs. Cliffe?"

Winston beamed. "This way."

He led us back to the large great room. Over the fireplace was a much larger portrait of a beautifully dressed, smiling woman.

"She's pretty," Kevin said. She was more than pretty. Her auburn hair was drawn up, revealing a slender neck. Her face was a perfect oval, with high cheekbones and large, shining eyes.

I looked at the portrait closely. This woman was my blood. I searched for something familiar, a curve of the cheek, something in her smile—anything I could see in her that I also saw in myself.

Nothing.

"Andrew and Gemina were said to be very much in love," Winston said. "As she lay dying, she begged him to bury her in her favorite field, so she could always be near him, and watch over her family. That's how you came to be the owner of RiverCliffe Memorial Park, Ms. Armitage."

I couldn't take my eyes off this woman. My great-great-great-grandmother? Maybe more greats? I hadn't known of her existence a few months ago, but she was the reason I was standing here, on the cusp of change, on the edge of something better for my family and myself. "Call me Risa, please. How long were they married?"

"Almost twenty years. They had four sons. Then, very late in life, they had a daughter. The birth weakened Gemina, and she died when Elsbeth was not even four years old. All very sad."

Lily stood beside me, looking almost interested. "Were they rich?"

"Yes, they were. Andrew owned almost all of the valley, and Gemina came from a wealthy Boston family. Ship-building."

Kira was on tiptoe, leaning into the painting. "Cool."

Kevin frowned. "Did you say cemetery?"

Winston grinned. "Yes. On the other side of the dairy. Gemina had the best view of the river you could imagine."

"Gross," Lily muttered.

"No, it's quite a lovely place," Winston said.

Lily shuddered. "Whatever. I'm more interested in the pool," she said. I could see the flicker of bright blue water through a set of glass doors, and Lily and Kevin moved toward it.

I watched them, then turned back to the painting. "Her poor little daughter," I said, gazing up at Gemina's face. I looked down at Kira, who was also looking at the picture. "All alone with a bunch of grown men."

"Oh, no," Winston said, matter-of-factly. "We have her letters, as well as her diary. She claims to have had a very good relationship with her mother."

"But," Kira said, her little face wrinkled in a frown, "I thought her mom was dead."

Winston smiled broadly. "She was. But Elsbeth would frequently visit her mother's grave, and the two of them would talk. That's why the farm was left to her. That was the beginning of the Cliffe family legacy."

He moved outside, toward the pool. I stood there, mouth slightly open. What had he just said? That the two of them would talk? Did he mean Elsbeth and her dead mother? Was he *kidding*?

Kira tugged at my hand. "So, Gemina is a ghost?" she asked, her eyes wide.

"Of course not," I muttered, and hurried after Winston.

The rest of the property was stunning. The pool looked cool and inviting, surrounded by trees and looking like it was plunked down in the middle of a forest. He took us past a clay tennis court, and gave a quick tour of the barns. Yes, there were cows. And horses. A thin, slightly stooped man of about sixty, introduced as Tim, offered to take us trail riding any time we wanted. Kira was more than ready, but I talked her down by mentioning lunch.

There was a low, white building that Winston identified as the cheese factory, and there, off past another barn, was a low stone wall, lined with towering oaks. Beyond that was a meadow. The cemetery.

The kids took off back to the house, motivated by hunger, which gave me a chance to grab Winston's arm.

"Ah, Winston, the thing about Gemina and her daughter?"

He looked at me. "Yes?"

"You almost made it sound as though they talked even *after* Gemina was dead."

He nodded. "Yes."

"Yes what? Was Elsbeth…touched? I mean, claiming to talk to her dead mother is just a little crazy, right?" Just what I needed. I finally found out about my family, and they were bonkers.

He frowned. "Didn't Mr. Butterfield explain things to you? About the Cliffe trust?"

"Just that only women can inherit. What else is there?"

He took a long breath, held it, then exhaled noisily. "I thought you knew. Well, awkward."

"What?"

"I know this is going to *sound* crazy, but it isn't. After Gemina died, little Elsbeth would visit her grave. And one morning Gemina showed up. And every time Elsbeth visited, her mother would be there. No one else could see Gemina, and for years, yes, everyone thought the little girl was…odd. But she convinced her father that Gemina was still around, so he left the farm to her. She had children, and over the course of the years, more and more people were buried next to Gemina, and it was Elsbeth who formed the trust. It seemed that the female offspring could see them, which is why only females could inherit."

"Female offspring could see who? Gemina?"

"Yes. And all the others."

I was getting more and more confused. "What others?"

Winston rolled his eyes. "The cemetery people, of course. Everyone who's buried there."

I felt my jaw drop. "Elsbeth said she could see and talk to *everyone* who was buried there?"

He nodded. "Yes. And her daughters could, and their daughters." He looked at me. "And since you are a direct descendant, and a female, you can too."

He began to walk away. I looked back to the cemetery. It looked green and peaceful in the sunlight. "I can what? Are you saying I can see and talk to the dead?"

He stopped, turned around and shook his head. "Not all the dead, of course. Haven't you been listening? Only the ones buried at RiverCliffe."

Oh.

"And by the way?" Winston added, "not all the staff knows. I mean, everyone knows the legend, but not many people know it's *real*. So you may want to keep this under your hat."

Of course.

By the time I got my jaw up off the ground and started breathing again, Winston was back at the house. I walked slowly, periodically looking over my shoulder, waiting for a host of bodies to rise from the ground and wave.

No, I wasn't waiting for anything. The whole idea was ridiculous.

But not really. I grew up believing that the spirit or soul of a person can last forever, and that it was possible, by the few and special, to cross the line between here and beyond, and communicate with that spirit or soul. My mother believed, strongly, and I grew up listening to her talk about people who claimed to reach into the void. Mom was also a believer in her "feelings" and claimed to know things before they happened. I wanted to be like her, of course, and have "feelings" too, or better yet, be one of the few who could do more than just remember the dead. I wanted to reach out and communicate with them, if for no other reason than to prove that her belief was real. Now, faced with the absurd possibility that I was, perhaps, one of the few and special, I went into total denial mode.

"There's no such things as ghosts," I muttered as I went through the lobby of RiverCliffe. "There are no such things as ghosts." Oddly enough, I found the voice in my head singing the old theme song from *Ghostbusters*.

I followed Kira's laughter into the dining room. My kids were sitting at a table by the window, and a tiny African-American woman had them in stitches over something. Even Lily was smiling.

"Is this your momma?" The woman asked, turning to me. Her voice dripped southern honey, and her smile was brilliant white against her very dark skin. "Your kids are telling me what a terrible cook you are."

"They're many things, my children," I said. "But they're not liars. I'm Risa." I held out my hand.

She shook it. Her fingers may have been tiny, but they were strong. She could have been any age between twenty and forty. "I'm Serena Book. I cook around here most days. We're closed, usually, at this time of day, but I figured y'all might want a little something to eat after your trip up here."

"That would be great," I said, sinking into a chair next to Kevin. "But these guys only eat grilled cheese. It's the one thing they trust me to make for them that might actually taste okay."

"Well, that's fine, because we have homemade bread, and cheese from Danny, and house-cured bacon. I also have tomato soup simmering, made with my canned tomatoes, and fresh basil. How does that sound?"

She asked the kids, but my mouth was watering so much that if any of them had said no, I would have probably thrown them out the window. But they all nodded happily, and Serena went through a pair of swinging doors at the end of the dining room.

"So Mom," Kira said, "what's with the ghost?"

Lily's head shot up. "Ghost?"

"Winston said Elsbeth could talk to her dead mom," Kira said matter-of-factly. "That makes Gemina a ghost, right?"

"There is no ghost," I said. "There's no such thing as ghosts."

My kids had enough to deal with — the divorce, living in Brooklyn and now another change in their fragile routines. This weekend was supposed to be a time for them to relax, not worry about ghosts rising from the cemetery next door. I had no idea how much of my mother's beliefs had penetrated into their psyche, but I didn't want to test anything right now.

"Then why did Winston say that? About Elsbeth and Gemina talking?" Kira asked.

I wrinkled my nose at her. "I'm sure that's just something they tell all the tourists. Keep them intrigued, you know?"

"So, no ghosts?" Kira asked, her little face falling.

"Nope," I said. "We'll have to make do with farm animals, and the swimming pool, and the river, and horseback riding, and good cooking. Do you think you can deal?"

Lily sighed and slumped down in her chair. "Good. This place is lame enough without ghosts."

Kevin, without ear buds, heard what I said the first time and shrugged. "Can we get a kayak or boat to take on the river?"

"We'll ask."

"When can we see the animals?" Kira asked.

"After lunch. And I met someone who maybe knew your grandfather."

Lily looked up. "*Your* dad?"

I nodded.

"Wasn't he a real jerk?" she asked, watching me closely.

I hadn't talked to them much about Billy Harris, just that he had been a crook who went to prison and divorced my mother. They all knew I'd been raised without him, but had never been curious about him. I don't think I'd ever referred to him as a jerk.

"Is that what you think he was," I asked her. "A jerk?"

She shrugged. "Well, yeah. I mean, he *abandoned* you, right?"

I kept my voice even. "Do you think *your* father is a jerk?"

35

Kira looked up. She was not just my happiest child, she was also the child who wanted everyone else to be happy, too. "I think Daddy's neat. He takes us cool places," she said, smiling.

"Yeah," Kevin mumbled. "When he bothers to show up."

I looked at Lily. "Well?"

"He thinks that just sending money is enough," she said in a low, angry voice. "Your father didn't even do that, did he?"

I shook my head. "No, he didn't."

She looked around. "He lived here, and he didn't send you anything? Jeez, he was rich, and his mother was rich."

I cleared my throat. "Apparently, this," I gestured around at the quiet, elegant room, long windows overlooking the pool, fresh flowers on every table, "wasn't around when he married grandma."

She shrugged. "Whatever. I don't know why you're interested in talking to *anyone* around here. They left you and grandma all alone in Brooklyn, didn't care about you, didn't care about *us…*"

What could I tell her? She was right. Had Cathy Newsome even tried to find my mother and I? Granted, we were living under one of my fathers' fake names. But had she even tried? Or had she sat back, building her little empire, not thinking about us at all?

Serena came back through the swinging door, a huge tray balanced on her shoulder. She set it down next to us and served steaming soup in white stoneware crocks, and thick, golden sandwiches on a platter. She also set down a pitcher of water.

"Here you go, unless you want something else to drink?"

"Coffee," Lily said, looking at her soup with interest.

Serena glanced at me.

"Make it two?"

She grinned, grabbed the tray, and was gone.

We all dipped into the soup.

"This," Kevin said in a hushed voice, "is better than Campbell's." He took another spoonful. "It's awesome."

I had to agree. Even Lily found nothing to complain about.

Kevin was done first, of course, and started on the sandwiches when Serena came back, this time with a smaller tray and coffee things.

"Do you mind if I join you?" she asked as she poured. "We're all very curious about y'all."

"Have a seat," Kira said. "We're from Brooklyn, where we live with Grandma Marcie. We used to live with Daddy in Morris Plains, but he's with someone named Alicia now."

"Oh, well," Serena said, sitting down slowly. She glanced at me, her eyes dancing. "That's interesting."

"Grandma belongs on *Hoarders*," Lily said, taking a tiny bite off of a corner of a sandwich. She chewed carefully, then took a bigger bite. "We're sleeping in the cellar."

"I don't even have a window in my room," Kevin contributed. "And there's only one bathroom and it has a really tiny shower."

I sighed and closed my eyes. All true, but did they have to make it sound so bad?

"And does this Grandma feed you bread and water?" Serena asked innocently.

I had to laugh out loud over that one. I opened my eyes and saw that Kevin was giving the question some serious thought.

"No," he said at last. "She's really a good cook. Lots better than Mom."

"Her only saving grace," Lily muttered.

Serena glanced at me again, grinning. "So, kids, what do you think of RiverCliffe so far?"

"I love it," Kira said. "There are *cows* here."

"Yes," Serena said. "And horses and goats and chickens."

"Is the pool heated?" Lily asked.

"Yes. And it's supposed to be hot this weekend. Did y'all bring your suits?"

Lily shrugged. Kira nodded excitedly. Serena poked me with her elbow.

"How about you?"

I swallowed a mouthful of sandwich. "I stopped wearing bathing suits in 2012."

Serena tut-tutted and shook her head. "Risa, nobody up here's gonna care what you look like in a suit. This is *not* New York City. We're normal."

I thought about Winston and the ghost. "We'll see." The grilled cheese sandwich had to have been the best thing I'd eaten in a week. And the coffee was delicious too. I'd probably gain twenty pounds in the long weekend.

"You just cook breakfast?" I asked.

Serena sat back and sipped coffee. "Breakfast and happy hour. Not a real happy hour, exactly, but about five o'clock we put out wine and cheese, coffee and finger sandwiches. Out in the great room, not here. That gets the guests mingling. For about an hour. On weekends and holidays, the dining room opens at six for dinner. We get lots of town people here. We've got a pretty good reputation, food-wise."

"Then you're not going to be cooking for *us* all the time?" Kira asked, her face a mask of tragic disappointment.

Serena shook her head. "No. Sorry. But if you want, you can help me in the kitchen, and then *you* could cook. How 'bout that?"

It was Lily who lifted her head. "Really?"

Serena nodded. "Sure. I'm always cooking up something back there, bread or cookies or soup. I'd love the company."

I dared not look at Lily. She was actually interested in something? Even the slightest hint of approval on my part would completely change her mind, so I kept my mouth shut and my face neutral.

"Where did you train?" I asked Serena.

"C.I.A.," she answered.

"You're a spy?" Kevin asked, his eyes lit up.

Serena laughed. "Nope. Sorry. Culinary Institute of America. It's right here, you know. You can take a tour, if you like. Big tourist spot. I was so glad to stay up here. As much as I don't love the snow, it beats the Mississippi summers."

"Is there a ghost here?" Kira asked abruptly.

"No," I said.

Kira sighed. "Mom, I'm not asking you. I'm asking Serena. After all, she *lives* here."

Serena leaned toward Kira. "I can honestly say I have never seen or heard a ghost in this house." She settled back. "Ever."

Kira looked disappointed.

I breathed a sigh of relief. Maybe Winston was pulling an elaborate joke. Maybe it was some sort of hazing. Maybe he was crazy. Or maybe he was trying to scare me off. He'd been running things for a few months now, and seemed like the kind of guy who liked being in charge. Was he worried I might muscle in on his territory?

I'd have to let him know that was *not* my plan. Then he'd stop with the heebie jeebie stuff.

I sat back and sighed. "I got an invitation for cookies with Martha," I said.

Serena grinned. "Yes, I bet you did. Those are two of the craziest old ladies you're gonna meet, but we all love them."

"If they're crazy," Kira asked, "why do you love them?"

Serena stood and began to gather cups and dishes. "Once you meet them, you'll know. And Martha's cookies are better than mine. Y'all just go out the side door here, past the pool, and they're in the little house with the big porch." She looked at me. "Good luck." She took the loaded tray back through the swinging doors.

I stood. "Ready?"

Kevin made a face. "Who are these people?"

"Relatives of your grandfather. Aren't you curious about him?"

Lily straightened slowly. "No. And I really don't get why you are."

I didn't quite understand it either. I had spent lots of time when I was younger, trying to imagine my life with him. During college, I'd actually tried to find him. But for the past almost twenty years, I'd managed not to think about him much at all. But I was curious. After all, it was he who brought us all to this place.

I sighed. "What do you want to do instead?"

Kira jumped up. "See the animals."

"Yeah, Mom," Kevin piped up. "Can we see the barn?"

I looked at Lily. She shrugged. "That's fine. I'll take them."

I nodded. I doubted anything would happen to my kids, but it was a strange place with strange people, and I didn't want them wandering. Lily could be trusted to keep an eye out.

"Okay, then. We'll meet back here in half an hour. If I finish up early, I'll meet you over at the barn. How does that sound?"

Kira was off like a shot, Kevin behind her, out the dining room door. Lily rolled her eyes.

"You owe me," she muttered, and followed them out.

I ran my fingers through my hair and went out the side door. I walked past a thick hedge, bright green and shoulder-high, and found myself poolside. I skirted the pool, went out the gate, and turned toward the small white house with the big porch.

CHAPTER 3

*B*ernadette was sitting on a rocking chair on the porch, moving slowly, a steaming mug in her hands. I could smell the coffee, and something else, something sweet and chocolate. I came up the steps and she smiled broadly.

"Martha, she's here," Bernadette called out over her shoulder. "And she looks just like Marcella."

I stopped. "How do you know that I look like my mother?"

"Billy showed us pictures, of course. He was a handsome devil, your father, and Marcella was a beautiful girl."

I sat down on a rocker across from her. "My father came here? When? How often?"

A very tall woman came through the door, holding a tray with more steaming mugs and a plate of cookies. She looked to be Native American — dark-skinned, with straight graying hair, a flat nose and black eyes. When she smiled, her teeth were very white.

"Last time he stayed for any time was right as Cathy was getting the inn going. He was sniffing around for money, so she chased him off," Martha said. Her voice was low and musical, with no discernible accent. She set the tray on a small table. "He'd show up, off and on, usually for a day or two. He'd always manage to rub Cathy the wrong way 'bout somethin', and she'd run him off. I'm Martha Newsome. I was married to your uncle, Claymore Newsome. Welcome." Her hand was large and wrinkled, and when I took it, she had a grip like iron. She stared directly at me, and after a few seconds, smiled. "We're glad to meet you. Sit. Coffee's fresh and so are my cookies."

My mind was going in so many directions I could barely breathe from excitement. They knew my father. He'd showed them pictures of Mom. Had he talked about her? About us? He had been willing to share us with these people, but he did not want Mom to even know of their existence.

Who did that? What kind of a person did that?

I grabbed a mug of coffee with one hand and a thin, warm chocolate cookie with the other, staring from one hand to another, trying to decide what to do first. I finally looked up.

"He told my mother that Cathy died fifty years ago. He also said that you," I pointed the cookie at Martha, "hated him and told him never to come back here."

Bernadette made a noise. "Billy was the smoothest liar I ever come across."

"Mom said he was a charmer and a crook," I blurted.

Martha sat down and held her coffee mug in one hand, the other tugging on the ends of her long hair. "They all were. All those boys. My Claymore could talk the birds from the trees, but there wasn't an honest bone in his body. At least your daddy made it back here for the funeral. He was the only one left."

"How long ago was that?"

"About three months now," Martha said. "Cathy died on Valentine's Day."

"And how was he?"

Martha and Bernadette exchanged a look.

"The same," Bernadette snorted.

I sipped the coffee, thinking that the extra caffeine would keep me up all night, but I had a feeling I wouldn't be sleeping too well anyway. "I'm sorry, but can you be more specific? I don't really know what 'the same' means."

Martha took a cookie and chewed it slowly, her eyes never leaving my face. I could see that this was a woman who thought about things very carefully, and she was trying to get it right.

"Billy was the handsomest of the three. And I knew them all. Clay was the oldest, you see, and he brought me out from Wyoming almost fifty years ago. We moved into this little house and I never left. I saw all his brothers grow up and out, and none of them lifted a finger to help Cathy get this place into any kind of shape. Billy was spoiled rotten, and his mother's favorite, so he came back most often." She took another cookie. "While he was in prison, the place finally started making some money, and of course when he got out he thought he could help himself. Cathy got tough. Threw him out. But Billy had a warm heart, and he'd come back, just to see her."

He'd had a warm heart for his mother. Why hadn't he had a warm heart for me?

She smiled. "He never offered to help her, of course, but he'd make her laugh. Her dyin' hit him hard, I think. But being cut out of everything hit him harder, and when he realized he couldn't do nothin' about it, he left."

"Did he talk about us?" The cookie was perfect. I ate the thing in three bites, reaching for another.

"He talked about Marcella," Bernadette said. "He was in love for sure. And he had a picture of you, just one, sent to him right after you were born. He used to go on about seeing you some day, but as the years passed, he stopped mentioning it."

Until that moment, I thought I'd stopped feeling the hurt and resentment I'd felt as a child. But it all came rushing back on hearing that he had, in fact, cared enough at one point to tell others he wanted to see me, to know me. If he had thought enough about me once, what had changed? Why had he chosen to forget me?

Martha sipped her coffee. "I always asked him, of course. I kinda liked to see him squirm."

Why, thank you Martha. I would have liked to see him squirm, too.

"What was Cathy like?" I'd been so fixated on my father's absence in my life, I never stopped to consider any other relations. Here was my aunt, who knew my grandmother, all my uncles and possibly their wives as well. I settled back in my chair and drank some more excellent coffee, willing myself away from the cookies. Could I get a whole family history right here and now?

Bernadette sighed. "She was a hardworking woman who loved this place with all her heart and soul. She had a worthless husband and three equally worthless sons. She made a success of herself in spite of them." She shifted in her seat. "I came to work here on the farm as a kid. My folks were dirt poor, but Cathy put us up and we all worked for her. She had a good heart, that woman."

Martha snorted. "She was also one tough bitch. She hated me because I was Lakota. Didn't speak to me at all for the first two years I lived here. Our first real conversation, other than about my working the farm, was when Clay got himself killed and we had to discuss the funeral. I suppose she could have made me leave, but she didn't."

"Clay was killed?" I said. "I'm so sorry."

Martha shrugged. "I wasn't. I knew by then he was a liar and a thief. Got himself shot in a robbery up in Boston."

"Oh. What about the third brother?" I reached for another cookie.

Martha sniffed. "That was James. Poor James. Everything the messed-up middle child was supposed to be, and then some. He wanted to be a painter. Clay said he had talent as a kid, but his daddy didn't want no sissy artist son, so James got all the art beat out of him and ended up running drugs across the border into Canada. Got his throat cut somewhere up in Toronto. I only met him once, but Clay always said he was a good one."

Bernadette laughed. "One hundred or so years ago, those boys would have been a famous outlaw gang. The Newsome Brothers. Probably would have had songs written about them. As it was, they got killed off 'cept your daddy. Guess he spent too much time behind bars to be in the line of fire."

Well, this was unexpected. Instead of coming fine, upstanding farm stock with the one black sheep, I was instead descended from a long line of crooks. I wondered if my mother knew. "And my grandfather? Cathy's husband?"

Martha finished her coffee. "He never worked as far as I knew. Spent most of his time making illegal hooch. Apparently, *his* daddy was a well-known bootlegger, and Old Harry just carried on the tradition. Got killed when the still fell on him. Spent a whole night bleeding out in the barn. 'Course, some say Cathy heard him hollering for help and just rolled over in bed, but, well, you know how people talk."

"Of course," I said faintly. This was getting more interesting by the minute. Martha must have read the expression on my face, because she reached out her foot to give my ankle a nudge.

"Now listen here, Risa. Cathy Newsome was born on this place. She spent her whole life here, and managed to take a bad situation and turn it to gold. Not such a bad legacy, is it? She fell in love with the wrong man is all. And we've all done that, right?"

I thought of Ed and nodded. "Yes, we certainly have." I gazed wistfully at the plate of cookies. If I ate another one, I'd have to roll myself off the porch. "My kids are down at the barn right now, but when you see them, could you maybe, I don't know, lie about the family history?"

Martha laughed. "Now, Risa, come on. You know them kids will *love* their family history. In fact, they'll probably blab it all over the Facebook or whatever they've got going on these days."

I stood up. "Yes, you're right. And they'll also love telling my mother all about it. God knows *I'm* not going to be the one to tell her."

The two women stood and both hugged me tightly. Martha, when she drew away, had tears in her eyes.

"We're so glad you're here," she said. "And we both think you should stay. RiverCliffe needs a woman at the helm. It's been that way for over two hundred years."

"I'm not planning on it, to tell the truth. I want to take the kids back to New Jersey, maybe get them back in their old school. They... didn't do too well in Brooklyn. I think they need to go back to something more familiar." I told her.

"Maybe they need a fresh start," Bernadette said. "Maybe they need clean air and lots of sun, and a good river."

I shook my head. "I don't think they're really country kids."

"They'll love it here," Bernadette said. "I know they will. Send them this way. If nothing else, Martha's cookies will convince them."

I went down the steps back toward the house, thinking they were probably right.

My children were surrounded by chickens.

I'd spent a few minutes walking around two large barns, carefully avoiding a large paddock filled with cows. I finally found them beside a building, playing with chickens. I never knew that chickens were all that playful, and maybe they weren't. Maybe they were actually running in terror from the three young people who were chasing them, but the chickens didn't sound all that afraid. In fact, they sounded downright cheerful.

But then, I was born in Brooklyn. What did I know?

Kira ran up to me, all smiles. "Daniel says we can come out every morning and collect the eggs for breakfast."

"Good. It's about time you started pulling your weight around here," I said. "Where's Daniel?"

Kevin, squatting two feet from a largish, rather spectacular looking bird with scarlet plumage and bright eyes, pointed in the direction of the building without his eyes ever leaving the chickens face. "In there."

Lily looked almost happy, an expression I hadn't seen in a while, so I averted my eyes from her general direction and went inside.

The first room was an office of some sort—concrete floor, white walls, a few desks and chairs and a wall of filing cabinets. I went down a short hallway, following voices, until I came into a large, lofty room where four people, dressed in what looked to be white spacesuits, were making cheese. I knew they were making cheese because I'd seen a few documentaries in my time, and was an avid watcher of the Cooking Channel. There was a huge vat of something that the people were standing around, using wooden rakes to move the liquid back and forth. Yep, making cheese.

"Daniel?" I called out.

The tallest figure came toward me and motioned me to follow him back down the hallway I just came through.

He was very tall, and when he pulled off his white hair net, a long, bushy mane fell past his shoulders. He grinned and held out his hand. "I'm Daniel Rugg. Your kids are a hoot. Welcome to RiverCliffe."

He was old enough to have several gray hairs running through all that hair, but his eyes were bright blue and his smile genuine. I shook his hand warmly. "I'm Risa. Give them ten minutes. Believe me, they'll start to drive you crazy."

He nodded. "Yeah, got a few of my own. Pretty much the same age. We could have the makings of a few good friends here. Just checking us out?"

"Yes. The place is beautiful. I'm not used to all this green, and the cows. And chickens. Quite a place."

"Yes, and it's been here such a long time. Things that last as long as RiverCliffe are special. And we all kind of just move along you know, just like the river."

"You've been here...?"

"Almost thirty years. Back before Cathy got the inn on its feet. Organic was the craze then, and I found a good market for my cheeses. Once the inn started going strong, I saw no reason to leave, and Cathy kind of liked me staying. There's a rhythm to RiverCliffe, and its good to stay true." He looked sideways. "I hope you're not thinking of changing things up too much."

I shook my head. "I'm probably not going to change a thing."

He nodded. "Good to hear."

I thought about Winston, and his ghost story. "I suppose Winston is pretty good at running things?"

Daniel nodded. "Oh, yes. Winston is a man who likes to be in charge."

"So, I guess he's going to be happy with my being an absentee landlord?"

He ran both hands through his hair and made a face. "Is that the plan? Well, yes, he'll be very happy with that. But...RiverCliffe has always had a woman at the head."

I shrugged. I wasn't interested in what RiverCliffe always had. I was just interested in what it could do for my family and me. I was tired and starting to feel cranky. "Well, thanks for giving my kids something to do. I'm sure I'll be talking to you later."

He grinned. "Probably. I'll be here. When the inn is full, everybody works. Winston runs a very tight ship. He's big on meetings and schedules and those sorts of things. In fact, he'll probably ask you to his Sunday morning staff meeting."

He has meetings on Sunday morning? "Winston and I were going to have to have a long talk, and soon."

Daniel nodded. "Yep. Sooner the better. Winston loved Cathy, but I know he was chaffing a bit under her. I'm sure he's going to bursting with all sorts of new ideas."

I tilted my head. "What about that rhythm?"

Daniel shrugged. "You're going to have to be the one to tell him no. This place has survived a lot, and I don't think there's much that can bring it down. But change can be disruptive." He narrowed his eyes. "Don't let Winston's ideas bring us down, Risa. This is your place now. It will feed you, and house you, and give you strength, but it needs something in return." He nodded his head and turned, walking away.

I heard a shriek from Kira. I ran back outside and found Kevin chasing her, holding a chicken in both of his hands, attempting to stab her with the poor bird's beak.

"Kevin," I yelled. "Are you kidding me?"

He stopped, looked slightly guilty, and released the chicken, which ran, clucking angrily, to the other side of the yard. Kira stopped making a 'help me' noise and went into a fit of giggles. Lily was actually smiling.

"You realize," I said firmly, "that birds are actually pretty smart, and soon every chicken on this place will know what you did and will label you 'Chief Chicken Grabber'?"

He ducked his head. "Sorry, chicken," he yelled toward the general direction of the flock.

Lily came up to me, her eyes narrowed. "Is that true? About chickens?" she asked in a hushed voice.

I sighed. "What do I know? I'm a stranger here myself. Let's go into town, pick up some food, check things out. What do you say?"

Kira face fell. "But there's still lots of stuff here we haven't seen."

"True," I said. "But we have two more days. Come on. I need to buy some things."

We walked back to the inn and I made a list in my head. Orange juice. Milk and cookies. Stuff for sandwiches. Premade chicken salad. Good bread.

Vodka. Tonic. Limes.

More vodka.

I wasn't usually a big drinker, but my brain was on overload, and I knew I'd need something extra to soothe all the voices in my head.

The trip into town was short and sweet. Kira spent the entire trip chattering non-stop. She loved the chickens. She loved the barns. She wanted to ride a horse. She wanted to pet the pigs. She thought Winston was cute.

Lily had less to say. In fact, when I casually asked what she thought so far, I didn't even get a grunt.

Kevin lifted his head from his phone to ask about the river. Three times. He wanted to see the kayaks.

So much for my children's burning curiosity about their family history.

We returned just in time to troop through the lobby at Happy Hour. Winston hurried over to me, ignoring the shopping bags in my arms, and suggested I have a glass of wine and meet some of the guests. Before I could protest, a young man in a RiverCliffe shirt whisked the packages from my arms and herded the kids through to the back of the house. As the young man was tall and very cute, Lily followed with a smile, and Kevin and Kira trailed silently in her wake.

Winston looped his arm through mine. "We have some regulars here this weekend. You should meet them."

I sighed. I was still wearing the clothes I'd put on early this morning, and I knew they were wrinkled and possibly sweaty. Whatever makeup I had put on had vanished, and my hair was sticking to the back of my neck.

"A bit of a warning would have been nice," I muttered out of the side of my mouth.

Winston grabbed a glass of wine off the center table and pushed it into my hand. I pushed it back. Wine on an empty stomach would not end well for me.

"You look fine," Winston said. "Let me introduce you to David and Alison Ferrell. They've been coming up here for what, David, thirteen years?"

The Ferrell's were a handsome older couple who dripped money and charm. They expressed regret at Cathy's passing and wished me luck. So did the other ten or twelve people I was introduced to. I didn't remember a single name. I was hungry and tired and sweat had dried all down my back. I snagged a few finger sandwiches, which were delicious, and a hunk of cheese, and eventually my blood sugar rose to an acceptable level and I felt almost human again. By then I'd already spent forty minutes smiling and alternating between trying to connect the faces and names and wondering vaguely what my kids were doing. Finally, Winston made polite 'we're done now' noises, and the lobby emptied in less than a minute. Serena appeared with a large, empty tray and began to clean up.

"Everything was delicious," I said to her.

She beamed. "Thanks." She squinted at me. "You okay? You look a little pale."

I sighed. "It's been a long day."

"Well, not to worry. I put together a chicken potpie for y'all. It's in the warming oven in the kitchen whenever you want it." She loaded the tray with empty plates and glasses, and lifted it to her shoulders. "I figured you'd want to eat someplace quiet. Unless you want me to save you a table in the dining room?"

"Oh, Serena, thank you! The potpie sounds like a great idea. And you're right. I don't think I could face the dining room tonight."

She smiled and vanished around a corner. Winston materialized at my shoulder.

"She's a great cook. I envy you that chicken potpie."

I looked at him. "Why don't you join us? Bring it on back in about half an hour. You and I should talk a bit."

He cleared his throat. "Sure. That's probably a good idea."

I wound my way back to the owner's suite and found Lily actually chatting to the cute young man who had taken my groceries. She'd even put things away, and was leaning against the counter in the kitchen, smiling rather giddily.

Lily was a beautiful girl. This was not just the mother in me talking either. She was tall and slender, with a soft oval face, large, brown eyes, and dark hair that fell in perfect waves down almost to her waist. She often pulled her hair up into that messy bun look, but she also knew how she looked when it was down and around her face.

Kira looked just like her, only smaller, of course. They both took after me, or rather, my mother. Kevin, on the other hand, was a minia-ture of his father, and looked like he belonged in another family altogether.

Lily looked up as I entered, and didn't even stop smiling. "This is Trent. He works here on weekends."

I held out my hand, and he shook it firmly.

"Pleased to meet you, boss."

I shook my head. "No boss, please. Risa. And thanks for helping."

He ducked his head. "A pleasure." His eyes shifted to Lily. "See you later?"

Her smile faltered. "Maybe. I'll text you"

Oh my. Later? To do what? And she'd *text* him?

He backed out and I eyed my daughter with suspicion. "What did he mean, later?"

"There's a dance in town," she said airily, liked we talked about dances all the time. "He invited me. To, you know, meet some kids and stuff." She shrugged. "But it'll probably be lame. A bunch of country hicks."

I sighed. "Just as well. We don't know anything about him. I wouldn't let you go off with a total stranger."

She straightened, and her eyes narrowed. "So I'm just supposed to sit around *here* all night? And do what? Watch the cows sleep?"

I should have known better. Now that I thought it was a bad idea, it was all she wanted. "Winston is having dinner with us. I'll ask him about Trent. If he can vouch for Trent, then you can go. If you really want to."

"Winston's is having dinner with us? Why?"

"We need to work a few things out, that's all."

She glared. "He's weird."

"Only because his voice seems to be coming out of a completely different body."

She choked. That was her idea of laughing at something I said. "That's it all right." Then she flounced away, and I heard her footsteps on the stairs.

I mixed my vodka-and-tonic on autopilot. According to Daniel, Winston would want to make changes. I had it in my mind to let everything continue as it was, and just sit back and collect a nice paycheck while getting back to the serious work of being a single parent in the Jersey suburbs. How was I supposed to keep Winston on track if I was three hours away?

I drank on autopilot as well, and fairly quickly. I was mixing another, making a conscious effort not to put in more than four shots, when Kira appeared.

"We're hungry."

"Who?" I looked around her. "You and your imaginary friend?"

"Me and Kevin."

"Kevin and I. Winston is bringing a chicken potpie for dinner. A few more minutes."

"Can I visit the chickens tomorrow?"

"I don't see why not, but I thought we'd go down by the river."

"Kevin wants to learn to sail a boat. Can I learn with him?"

"I think tomorrow will be more about a kayak."

"Can we ride the horses?"

I nodded. "Sure. Maybe Monday before we head back home."

"Is there a ghost in the graveyard?"

See, it's important to pay attention. "There are no such things as ghosts."

"So is Winston a liar?"

"Winston is an expert storyteller. It's probably a very important part of his job."

"Okay."

And she was gone.

I stared at my second drink. Was it rude for me to greet my first guest blotto? Thankfully, there was a loud knock at the door, and I could smell chicken and baked piecrust.

Dinner, and my dinner guest, had arrived.

Winston came through the door carrying a tray that looked and smelled like heaven. Directly behind him was the young woman, Jessie, lugging two canvas totes. She dumped them by the door and grinned.

"You are so lucky. That potpie is legendary." She turned and shut the door behind her.

Winston set the tray in the middle of the table. "She's right. This is huge. Like a coronation dinner."

I noticed him eyeing my drink. "I'm having a vodka tonic. Would you like to join me? And maybe we can sit outside and enjoy a bit of the evening before dinner?"

He nodded and followed me to the kitchen, where he did not blink at the vodka/tonic ratio. We then went out the back door and stood quietly in the fading sun, drinking.

"Why aren't there a few chairs for right here?" I asked. "This looks like an ideal place for the evening cocktail."

"Cathy liked the river view," Winston said. "But I love looking out into the hills, too. Very peaceful."

"Please don't mention the ghost thing to my kids again," I said. I didn't mean to sound so blunt, but that's vodka for you. "I don't care if there is or is not a haunted cemetery next door. They've had a rough year, and I want them to be relaxed this weekend, not worrying about…ghosts. And things."

He sighed. "Of course. If that's what you wish, I completely understand. But it's as close to urban myth as we've got around here. Half the people believe, and the other half just like the idea of it. If they're here long enough, they'll be hearing stories."

"We're just here for the long weekend, so they shouldn't hear anything. Especially not from you."

"Fine."

I glanced at him. "But?"

"If either of your daughters walk through the graveyard, chances are they'll see or hear someone. That's how it works."

"Oh, God, really?" Was I supposed to believe this? I walked around the side of the house and stared.

The cemetery lay peaceful in the fading light. Past the row of oaks, all was still. No wisps of suspicious-looking smoke, no mysterious glow, no sorrowful echo.

I was beginning to think that Winston was trying to scare me off. "So, where are they? These restless spirits?"

"You can't really tell from here," he said. "You have to be *in* the cemetery. And they can't leave. Apparently, there are rules."

Yeah, right. I sipped. "Did Cathy tell you this?"

He nodded.

"Did she tell you all the family secrets?"

He shrugged. "My parents disowned me when I told them I was gay. She basically disowned her sons because they were all such terrible crooks. We were kind of made for each other, so, yeah."

"Did she tell you why she never bothered to try and find her only granddaughter?" I stared straight ahead, almost afraid to hear his answer.

"But she did, Risa. But…didn't Butterfield tell you? We didn't know your real name."

"We?"

"I helped her, of course. It was a yearly ritual. On Billy's birthday. But we never knew you were in New York. Billy had told her years ago you both moved out west. We spent years looking for Marcie Newsome. In California, Oregon, Montana...we tried." He shook his head. "She called it her biggest failure, not being able to find you."

I felt my throat close up. She'd tried. At least she'd tried. I cleared my throat.

"Do you miss her?" I asked.

"Very much. She was a very...forceful character, but I loved her. This place is my family, and she helped make it that way."

"You say this place is family. Does that mean you want to stay on?"

He turned sharply. "Of course. Why? Do you want me to leave?"

I shook my head. "No, not at all. I know nothing about being an innkeeper, and quite frankly, really don't want to learn. My management approach would be strictly hands-off. I was thinking I'd just head on back home and let you run things. How would you feel about that?"

He grinned. "Risa, I'm honored. Really. And I know I could do a good job. Cathy had every faith in me. You can too."

I sighed. "Good. RiverCliffe is lovely, it really is, but, well, we're not exactly used to this sort of thing." I gestured, vaguely. "You know, green. And I'm a Brooklyn girl. I'm more the concrete type." I turned to him. "And I don't think keeping the girls on this side of that stone wall will be too hard. All I have to do to keep Lily away is suggest she go in. And Kira is a scaredy cat. So that part should be easy."

"And you? Aren't you at least curious?"

"Not at all." I turned back. "My kids have probably eaten half that potpie already. Kevin has an acute sense of smell and no manners."

We walked back. The original house had been square and utilitarian, with a center door and small windows. The awnings and shutters had added charm, though it was still a plain dwelling from the outside.

As I had suspected, my children had settled themselves around the small table and were happily eating.

"What, you couldn't wait?" I scolded. "We have company and everything."

Kira giggled. "Hi, Winston. This pie is really good."

Winston sat next to her and reached across for a plate like he'd been eating next to her for all her short life. "This potpie is what wars are fought for," Winston said. "What causes brother to turn against brother. Why a husband would betray his wife."

I almost had to agree with him. It wasn't just about the chicken and potatoes and carrots. There were mushrooms, and tiny sweet peas. And was that sherry in the gravy? And that crust...

"Mom." Lily interrupted my oh-so-pleasant thoughts. "Trent?"

I had to think for a second. "Oh, right. Winston, it seems that one of the employees, Trent, has asked Lily to a local dance. Even though it might be lame, she says it would be more fun than staying here with me. I say he's a total stranger and how can he possibly be trusted. What do you say?"

Winston swallowed. "Trent is Bernadette's grandson. He's going to be a high school senior next fall and grew up with Martha and Bernie right here at RiverCliffe. The dance is fully chaperoned. In fact, Bernie will probably be there. He wants to go to Cornell after he graduates. Right now, besides school and work, he volunteers at the local library two nights a week." Of course. He also probably rescued kittens in his spare time.

"Well," I said, "I guess that's about as good a recommendation as anyone can get. What time were you going to leave, Lily?"

She pushed herself away from the table, shooting daggers at me with her eyes. My guess was that she really didn't want to go at all, but would now walk through fire, or a dance full of country hicks, rather than admit it. "In twenty minutes. I'll send him a text. Thanks, Winston."

Kevin reached for another helping. "Can I learn about boats?" he asked.

"Sure," Winston said. "In season, we have someone full time down at the river."

"But that's during the summer," Kevin said. "What about now?"

"Now you can take a kayak or canoe, of course. But that's about all. We don't need somebody down there until the season starts. We have guests who sail up every summer."

"Sail?" Kevin stopped eating. "Mom, can we come back so I can learn to sail?"

"Wait a minute," Winston said, "First of all, you'll need your own boat. RiverCliffe doesn't have its own sailboat."

"Mom, can you buy a boat? Please?"

I stared at my son. "Kevin, I wasn't planning on coming back here. Whatever—"

Kira began to jump up and down in her chair. "Please, Mommy? I could feed the chickens every day. And learn to ride a horse. Can I learn to sail with Kevin? Please?"

I sat back. "Guys, I thought we'd spend the summer looking for a house, our own house. Wouldn't you like to go back to Morris Plains to live?"

Kevin scowled. "That place sucks."

"What? I thought you loved living there." I said.

He shrugged. "It was okay when we were with Dad, but…"

Of course. I hadn't been the only one to hear the whispers, catch the looks of curiosity and, worse, pity.

I looked at Kira. "Do you want to go back there?"

She shook her head vigorously. "No. I want to come back *here*."

I looked up at Winston, whose expression was completely neutral. "How would that work, exactly," I asked. "Could we stay here?"

"Of course," he answered immediately. "But I thought you wanted to be, well, hands-off."

He didn't want me here, I thought. He wanted to run RiverCliffe himself, without interference. I guess I couldn't blame him. After all, he worked with Cathy for years. I knew he would resent my stepping up and into her place from virtually thin air.

But this was my place now. Whatever forces had kept RiverCliffe from me my whole life were now giving me a chance to…belong.

"I'll have to think about it," I told Kevin. "It's a big step, you know?"

"It would just be for the summer," Kevin said.

True. And hadn't I been wishing to spend the summer visiting a relative with a country place? And a pool?

"We'll see," I said. I looked at Winston. His eyes gave him away. He wasn't at all happy with the way things were going.

"Winston, perhaps we can buy something for RiverCliffe? Some sort of sailboat? You know, just in case?" I had no idea how much a sailboat cost, but I didn't care. I had money, and my son wanted to do something that would keep him outside and away from video games all summer. "Who would I talk to about that?"

Winston smiled automatically. "I'll have Wayne give you a call. He teaches at the high school, but he's been working every summer on the river for years. He'll know what to get."

"Perfect."

"And if you decide *not* to come back, it would still be a valuable asset. We often get guests asking to sail. Cathy never thought it was worth the expense, but..." He shrugged. "We didn't agree on everything."

"Can I learn too?" Kira asked.

"If this Wayne person thinks you're old enough, yes. Otherwise, you might have to do with chickens and horses."

She rolled her eyes. "Okay, I guess. So, Winston, what's in those bags? Can I look?"

Winston shot me a look. "Well, I put together a little bit of River-Cliffe history for your mom. There are some old diaries, and Cathy's scrapbook."

Diaries? As in, Elsbeth writing about how she and her dead mother sat around and chatted in the nearby graveyard? Then another concern hit me.

"What happens if I rip a page or spill something on one of those diaries? They've got to be, what, over two hundred years old?"

Wilson shook his head. "These aren't the originals. They're in the county library. No, periodically, the diaries would be copied and hardbound, the originals locked away. Cathy actually took the whole lot of them to some guy in New York City and had them turned into these lovely little volumes. Easier to read and pretty indestructible."

Thank God.

Kevin, it seemed, was finally done eating. "Were there cookies?" he asked cautiously.

"Yes, there were," Winston said, and both Kira and Kevin scurried into the kitchen, emerging with a plate of what appeared to be home-made chocolate chip cookies.

"Can we watch TV?" Kira asked.

I nodded, and began clearing the table. Winston helped, and as a reward I made us two more drinks. Lily came down, her hair curled, a bit of makeup, and a mini dress that made my heart skip a beat until I remembered wearing something just as short to my dances.

"He's meeting me out front," Lily said. "Can I go?"

"Winston and I will go with you," I said. "We'll have our drinks in the great room."

I told Kevin and Kira where I was going, and they grunted in acknowledgement. Winston and I followed Lily out, and into the great room. It was empty, so we sat in front of the fireplace, which had been obligingly lit. I watched as Trent met Lily in the lobby, and she turned and gave a quick wave as she left.

"You're sure he's not a maniac?" I asked.

Winston sighed. "Are you kidding? Bernie is driving them out there. And she's a chaperone. She'll be watching like a hawk."

"What's her story?"

Winston settled further into the wing back chair. "She worked here when it was just a farm, and helped Cathy turn it into what it is today. She and Martha are a couple, totally devoted, and Trent is the product of Bernie's short and unhappy marriage that produced one daughter, who got pregnant as soon as biologically possible, had Trent, and left town."

I looked at my drink. "I'm not sure having another one of these was a good idea."

"Of course it was. After all, today was a big day for you, I imagine."

"Are you going to have a staff meeting at the crack of dawn tomorrow?"

"Yes. The dining room opens for breakfast at eight on Sundays, and our regular weekly staff meeting is always right before. Did you want to come?"

I shrugged. "Should I?"

"You'll probably be bored to tears with details."

I took a long drink. "I'm an accountant, you know. Working on my MBA. Details are kind of what I do."

We sat in silence.

"And the books?" I asked.

"Everything is on Cathy's desktop. Any time you're ready."

A couple I'm sure I spoke with earlier wandered through and smiled. I smiled back. "I probably won't have time to take a good look. After all, I'm with the kids, and we're on a mini-vacation. So, I might have to come back after all."

A bright, fake smile appeared. "Excellent. May I ask, will your husband be joining you if you do return?"

"No more husband, thank God. And if a Mr. Edward Armitage *does* happen to show up, at any time, feel free to shoot him for trespassing."

Winston chuckled. Very Entish. "Yes, ma'am."

"Did you know my father?" I'm not sure where that came from. The vodka, probably.

"Yes." He looked uncomfortable.

"Look, I never met the guy myself, so don't think you're going to hurt my feelings by being honest. What was he like?"

He swirled the bits of ice left around in his glass. "Oily."

"Interesting word."

He chuckled. "He was every smarmy used-car salesman in the world. Charming and quick with the compliments, but always looking for a crack to squeeze into. Cathy had a soft spot for him, but she had his number and never gave him an inch of slack. I wouldn't be at all surprised if he showed up here looking for you."

I'd been feeling very comfortable, but that was like a splash of cold water on my happy place. "Really?"

"Sure. He came here for the funeral, and stayed a few days, trying to get someone to tell him where all the money went. I finally called Alan Butterfield, who contacted the local sheriff, Scott, who came by and spent an hour with Billy behind closed doors. Billy then packed up very quickly and left. But I know him, and I'm sure he'll be back."

I sighed and drained my glass. "So, it looks like I'm descended from a long line of scum-of-the-earth types."

Winston stood up so he could look down at me with authority. "No, Risa. You are not. You're descended from a long line of strong, extraordinary women. Who happened to have incredibly bad taste in men."

I cracked a smile. "Well, at least I know where *that* came from."

He handed me his glass. "I have to get home. I have a very early meeting tomorrow."

I stood up, took the glass and sighed. "Yeah. Me too. Good-night."

He walked off, and I headed back to the suite.

Kira and Kevin were watching a Harry Potter movie, one of the few things they both enjoyed. I sat with them for a few minutes, but curiosity got the better of me. I carried the tote bags into my bedroom and settled into the chair in the corner. I began with Cathy's things.

All the material was separated into large manila envelopes, carefully labeled. In 'Personal - 1948-1962', there was her birth certificate. She was born, via midwife, right on the property in 1931. So were her two brothers, whose stiff, shadowed faces appeared in one photo, along with an infant Cathy. Her high school diploma. Her mother's death notice. Nothing, on paper at least, of her father. Then came a marriage license to Harry Newsome, birth certificates for three boys and a girl, the death certificate for three-month-old Loretta Elise Newsome. Like Elsbeth Cliffe, Loretta had come late into her mother's life. The one picture showed a sweet-faced baby surrounded by ruffles and frills. There were also death certificates for her husband and her two oldest sons.

There were pictures, small, square, black and white photos of Cathy, a lean, plain woman who looked tired and was invariably holding one child or other. Her husband did not look tired at all.

Harry was tall and handsome and was always smiling. Probably because he wasn't too busy working.

In the envelope marked 'Clippings-Harry 1966 ', yellowed news-paper articles told the story of Harry's death, in an accident involving the possible illegal distillation of whiskey. By the dates, I could see that the boys were all almost grown, my father about twelve. Harry died a month after baby Loretta. I couldn't even imagine the burden of grief and, if Martha's story was true, guilt Cathy must have been carrying.

'Legal stuff for Inn' held building permits and contracts that traced the evolution of an old relic to an inn. Harry must have had one whopping insurance policy, because the before and after pictures showed lots of boarded up spaces being made into light and gracious guests rooms. Cathy must have worn out her Instamatic camera. I don't know when all the bedrooms and additions were added, because they were already in place when Cathy started renovations. It looked to have taken almost four years.

RiverCliffe House appeared to have been fairly successful from the start. There were copies of all the brochures through the years, and I could see the inn becoming brighter, more sophisticated, and, I imag-ined, more expensive. There were lots of promotional shots that had been saved, and it was there I finally caught a glimpse of the remark-able woman who had put this all together. It must have been taken shortly before her death, but Catherine Hamburg Newsome, in her mid-eighties, didn't look nearly as tired as the twenty-something version. She was poised and smiling, snow-white hair in a casual, tousled bob, wearing a simple sheath dress on her slim and straight body. The staff was around her, and I recognized most of them. I flipped over the picture and there, scrawled in red ink, were the words "85th B-Day" I flipped the picture again and stared long and hard. She looked happy.

I put the picture carefully back in its envelope.

She had made a good life for herself from a bad circumstance. I admired her for that. And I felt glad that, at least in the end of her life, she seemed happy. I felt a bit of a spark, a slim thread connecting me to a woman I had never knew existed. She had carved out something from the wreck that had been RiverCliffe to give over to me, without even knowing for sure I could ever take it.

In the other tote bag were also manila envelopes, but these were much older. The papers and documents were not as well organized, but I pieced together the tale of Henrietta Jacob, who built the main building as, yep, an inn. It was a time when the Hudson Valley was becoming a mecca for the newly rich. One faded article was about all the new mansions being built up and down the river, financed with money made during and after the Civil War. Henrietta must have been smart enough to figure that maybe the not-so-wealthy would like a taste of all that natural beauty, because she added on to the farmhouse, built the two- story building, and also had a dock and boathouse constructed across the main road that had, by now, cut through the original property. Sure enough, there were photos, showing a very stiff but smiling staff, dated 1882, commemorating the opening of the RiverCliffe Inn in its first incarnation.

Here was another story. The depression caused the inn to fold, and for years it remained boarded up. There were marriage certificates and more photos, mostly of smiling brides and handsome husbands who looked completely disreputable. Was that another thing all these women inherited? Lousy taste in men?

"Mom, she's asleep." I looked up, startled, to find Kevin leaning against the doorjamb. I glanced at my watch. Almost eleven. I'd been lost in the history of a place I had never imagined existed. As a story of success and failure, ruin and rebirth, it had been compelling enough. But to know that this was *my* story as well...I'd been captivated. And I'd never even gotten to any of the diaries.

I got up, went into the living room and peeled Kira off the couch, carrying her upstairs. I pulled off her shoes and socks and tucked the quilt around her. By the time I was in the hallway, Kevin's light was out and I heard a muffled, "G'night."

I went back downstairs, got a glass of water from the sink, and walked outside the front door, turning to look at the river.

It was glorious. There was no other word for it. The surrounding hills were all bathed in the moonlight that reflected off the water. The air was filled with night noises that belonged to another time and place — crickets and tree frogs, rustlings, the bark of a dog, and the hooting of owls.

I took a few steps and looked over into the cemetery. It looked tranquil and...asleep. Of course, asleep. What else would it be?

I saw the beams of a car coming down the main road, and heard it as it swung into the drive. There were faint murmurs, and a few minutes later, Lily came into the kitchen.

"Mom?" she called.

"Out here."

She stood beside me. "This is pretty."

"Yes, it is."

I wanted to put my arm around her shoulder and draw her tight against me, kiss the top of her hair and ask how the night went. But I knew better.

"Good time?"

"Yeah. These kids aren't too bad."

"Think you could hang with them for the summer?"

"What?"

"Kevin and Kira want to come back here. Kevin wants to learn to sail. Kira is in love with the chickens. What do you think?"

She shrugged. "It would be better than Brooklyn, I guess."

"I had planned on looking for a house. Maybe go back to Morris Plains." I waited, looking sideways at her.

She shrugged again. 'This place is closer to Daddy," she said, in a very small voice.

I sighed. I had finally spent all of my anger about the way Ed had treated me, but I still held a fierce resentment for the way he had treated his children. He had moved to Massachusetts, some small town in the western part of the state where his new wife had been born. It was far enough away from Brooklyn to give him as excuse for not seeing the kids on a regular basis, and granted, it had been quite a distance. RiverCliffe was closer than Brooklyn, and much closer than anything we would find in New Jersey.

"Do you think if you lived closer to your dad, he'd visit you more?"

"Maybe. It doesn't matter."

"Yes, it does. You haven't seen him since, what, winter break?"

She nodded.

"So…is that a 'yes' or a 'no' about staying here for the summer?"

"Yes. I guess."

She went back inside and I stood for a few more minutes.

It looked like we might be back.

CHAPTER 4

I awoke early and could smell coffee. And baking. Had Serena started baking at the proverbial crack of dawn to fortify the staff? And was there going to be enough left for me if I was late?

I showered quickly and threw on what I hoped was an appropriate meeting-the-staff-outfit — denim skirt, a linen button-down blouse and my Bass loafers. Too preppy? Was that even a thing anymore? And did I even care? I took a breath. No time for middle-school insecurities to come creeping back, as they usually did when I found myself facing a large group of strangers. Yes, these people were my employees, but even if I did decide to come back, why was I worried about impressing them? Shouldn't they be impressing *me*?

I made it out to the dining room just as the meeting began. Winston introduced me, formally, while I drank my coffee and salivated over freshly baked sweet rolls. I sat behind Serena and whispered, "Do you, like, live here?"

She cackled. "They rose all night in the fridge. Just had to throw them in the oven this morning."

The meeting, as Winston had promised, was a bit dry. Forecast for the next few weeks, one of the rooms was being painted, a new canoe.

"Risa," Winston said, his voice rising a bit, "wants a sailboat, so I'm going to have her talk to Wayne about that. I know some of our guests have asked in the past, so yay, Risa, for your first executive decision!"

Everyone actually turned to me, clapping, while I tried to smile with my mouth full of roll.

There were about twenty people in the room, and I was beginning to think that RiverCliffe was a bigger operation than I had first thought. Winston went on to talk about three weddings at the end of June, plans for the long 4th of July weekend, and 'the usual Carson week', which set everyone smiling again.

It was like he was speaking in a foreign language. If I did come back to RiverCliffe for the summer, would I want to be a part of the business side of running the inn? I didn't think so. I'd be happy with checking the bank statements and writing checks.

Winston rattled off some facts about checkout-times, and then began a rather detailed housekeeping discussion. Yes, I was into details, but the sweet rolls and sugar ran up against the coffee, and the room became very stuffy, so I got up quietly and walked right through the lobby and out the main door.

Once again, the river view was amazing. I wondered if the people who worked here, and saw this every day, ever got tired of so much beauty. I walked down the steps and across the gravel drive, and before I even knew it, I went through the break in the low stone wall and was in the cemetery. After all, if I was going to come back for the summer—and I still hadn't decided—I needed to be able to throw the entire outrageous ghost story back in Winston's face.

It was dark and cool beneath the long row of trees that ran parallel to the wall, all the way down to the road. I walked on further, and the shade lessened. No disembodied voices greeted me. No mysterious points of light. No lone woman in a long dark dress stepped out from behind any of the oak trees that were scattered about. I walked on, noting the smell of fresh-mown grass and the faint whine of a car as it passed below.

The view here was, if possible, even more beautiful. As I looked across the river, pale white and pink blossoms dotted the landscape. I made my way down to a simple stone bench and sat, looking across the river, watching the far-off trees ripple in the sunlight.

"Best place on earth," a voice said.

I was afraid to turn around. I think I was actually holding my breath. Oh, my God… was it…

It was a man, dressed in jeans and a beat-up denim jacket over a Grateful Dead t-shirt. He had longish, dark hair and eyes that looked as though they'd been squinting into the sun for years.

"For thinking, that is," he went on. "Sitting here, looking across the river at that little orchard there. Why, you'd think whoever planted those trees did it as a favor, you know?"

So much for ghosts. I breathed in grateful relief. "Yes, I was thinking the same thing."

I looked at him. He was attractive in that bad-boy sort of way I had, in my dating days, tried to avoid like the plague, with a small hoop in his ear and a scruffy shadow of a beard. He pushed his hands into the pockets of his jeans and grinned at me. His teeth were small and very white.

"I'm Caleb."

"I'm Risa." I glanced around, looking for a car. "Did you walk here?"

He gestured behind him. "Walked down. The view is worth it."

"So," I asked, letting a bit of tease into my voice, "do you come here often?"

He threw back his head and laughed, and the gravestones seemed to sing along with the sound. "Well, I guess. I…know some of the folks here. And like I said, it's the best place on earth for thinking." He looked down. "Mind sharing?"

I shook my head and he sat beside me. He wasn't a big man, not too tall, and slender. He leaned forward, his forearms resting on his thighs, his hands clasped together. His hands looked rough, and there was a leather cord tied around one wrist.

"Then I take it you knew Cathy?"

He grinned. "Hell, yeah. Everyone hereabouts knew Cathy. She was one fierce old lady. Determined. And fearless. Not like my old lady, not at all. Linda was a pretty thing but afraid of her own shadow. Cathy was a warrior. Never saw her back down from anyone or anything." He glanced at me. "What about you? You afraid?"

Good question. "I try not to be, but I spent a lot of years with just my mom, and we were kind of the only game in town, you know? I relied just on her. That makes it harder to step out and rely on yourself, and that's it's own kind of fear. Now that it's me and my kids, well, I'm trying to be bolder. In fact, I may actually take a big step in an unknown direction." I looked at him. His eyes were a warm brown and he seemed to be about my age, his dark hair streaked with gray around the temples, the lines around his mouth not from just laughing. "I'm trying to be less rigid, I guess. I had a plan, and I'm the kind of person who really needs a plan. I like to see how things going to line up in the end. That makes me feel safe. So stepping away from that plan, for someone like me, does take courage."

"Well, good for you for trying. Can't ask too much more than that from anyone, now, can we?" He shifted his weight. "The thing about fear, though…it's sometimes hard to figure what you're really afraid of. Are you scared of falling, or maybe hurting yourself if you land too hard? Scared of flying? Or the plane crashing. It's a tricky thing."

There was something in his voice. A twang that made me think of cows being herded along a winding, dusty trail. "You're not from around here, are you?"

He shook his head. "Nope. Texas born and bred. Left the day I graduated high school. I took my bike and headed to Canada. Got sidetracked in Michigan, spent a few years in the army, and when I was discharged I got back on my bike and rode some more. I fell in love with New York State, I gotta say. Lots of green. And I've always loved me a river. I been up and down the Hudson a dozen times or so."

I looked out at the river as a car drove by. Could I imagine myself on the back of a motorbike, my hands around the waist of someone like Caleb, watching the hills and the water rushing by as the road unwound beneath me, no destination in mind?

I shook my head slightly. No. Not in a million years. "And Linda?"

He sighed. "Linda was like one of them country songs, all passion and heartbreak and good love gone wrong. We had a time, she and I, but…well, no matter now."

The wistful note in his voice struck something in me. I wish I had struck someone like a country song. Any kind of song, really. Ed would never remember me with anything resembling plaintive regret. Ed would remember me with no regret at all.

"Kids?"

"A boy." His tone shifted. I immediately heard the pain in his voice and I backed away quickly.

"I'm a city girl myself," I said. "Brooklyn. New Jersey for a while, and that's a beautiful state. But hills like these…"

"I know. They just take away your breath. Texas has hill country that's lovely," he said, his voice soft and relaxed again. "And Southeast Asia is probably the greenest place on earth. But this place puts everywhere else I've ever been to shame. And the people are real friendly, you know? New Englanders, well, they can be standoffish. And Southerners are downright clannish. But folks here just let you be and don't judge."

"If this is the best place you've been, what was the worst?"

"A jail cell in Detroit," he said immediately. My eyebrows shot up, and he grinned. "I probably deserved to be there, but talk about a nightmare. 'Course, the drugs I was on at the time didn't help."

Yep. Bad boy. Was that why I leaned in closer?

"Caleb, I have a feeling you lived a sinful life."

He chuckled and shook his head. "Yes, I surely did. I have tried very hard to make amends, but the past, well, there are always scars, you know? Even the good times leave a mark." He looked sideways at me, his eyes bright. "How 'bout you, Risa. Any scars?"

I had so many. Where was I supposed to start with a question like that? With my feelings about my father I had thought dead and buried? The closed and tightly wound life with my mother? My failed marriage? My unhappy children?

But I wanted to find some sort of an answer, for no other reason than I didn't want him to stop talking.

I reached over and pointed to his t-shirt. "When I was thirteen, I lied to my mother, took a train to Connecticut all by myself, and saw the Grateful Dead. I smoked pot for the first time and almost got raped. It was the best and worst experience of my life. And when my mother found out, she grounded me for six months. I got over the grounding. Never got over the rest." And I hadn't. Those moments of recklessness had given me a sense of freedom I'd never had before, but I never again stepped outside of the carefully drawn boxes my life eventually became.

He sighed. "Saw them in San Fran. Another best and worst experience. Yeah, a Dead concert will do that to you." He shifted, and his legs stretched out before him. He was wearing scuffed ankle boots. "Now, I get my kicks sittin' in the sun, talkin' to beautiful ladies."

I laughed. "Caleb, I bet you've spent a lot of time sittin' in the sun, talkin' to beautiful ladies."

He gazed up at the sky with feigned innocence. "Now, Risa, that'd be telling, and a gentleman never tells."

I wanted him to tell me. What was it about this man?

I had not gone out for so much as a coffee with a man since the day Ed left. Part of it was, of course, being so hurt. Then, I was angry. By the time I'd moved to Brooklyn, I'd at least stopped hating all men in general, but had met no one that sparked even the tiniest bit of interest. But Caleb... he looked at me and as our eyes met I felt a little jolt, something I hadn't felt in a long time, and the warm air between us shimmered.

"Mommy!"

I stood up and saw Kira. She was outside the stone wall, almost hidden in the shadows of the oak trees. She waved and began to run toward me.

"I gotta go," I said. "It was good meeting you, Caleb."

He stood and nodded, pushing his hands back into his pockets. "Good meeting you, Risa."

I started walking toward Kira, then broke into a run.

Suddenly, I didn't want her in this place. Winston's words came back to me, and I felt a surge of panic. What if Winston *wasn't* lying?

Why, Caleb could have been a ghost. Right now, there could be hundreds of spirits, waiting to rise up in front of my little girl... she was inside the wall, and paused, and my heart leaped in my throat as I looked frantically for a ghost.

No ghost. Of course not. She stopped to bend and pick up a dandelion that was puffed out like a cloud.

She held it out to me. "Look!"

I grabbed her hand and turned her. "Very pretty baby. What are you doing out here?"

"Looking for Gemina, of course. Who was that man? Is he a ghost?"

"No. He's a motorcycle man."

She looked over her shoulder as I dragged her along, and she waved, scattering the dandelion puffs behind her.

I glanced over my shoulder. Caleb grinned and waved back. The panic faded. How stupid was all that? There were no ghosts here, just a peaceful field with a lone man, sitting and thinking. The only thing that had found Kira was the puff of dandelion.

I crossed out of the graveyard and tugged Kira's hand. "Race you."

She ran. We both ran, away from the quiet headstones and towering oaks, back into the sunlight.

I brought the two tote bags full of RiverCliffe history home with me. I asked Winston if it would be all right, promising to bring them back if we returned for the summer. He looked puzzled.

"Risa, those are yours. You don't need to ask me. Everything here belongs to you, remember?"

I'd had a hard time with that. I spent Sunday lying by the pool, watching my kids enjoy themselves, then out on the river before dinner, paddling in the cool water. Monday morning we'd taken a trail ride through green and sunlit fields. All the while, it never occurred to me that everything I saw and touched was mine.

I had spent the first half of my life in my mother's house, where everything we had, everything we did, had a price-tag. When I married Ed, money flowed freely, but it was never money that *I* had earned. It was always his, and he was always careful to remind me. After the divorce, I finally had control of my own finances, but they were so pathetic, I felt like I had gone backward in time, where, once again, everything had a cost. Child support was just that—it fed my kids, kept them in nice clothes and good shoes, paid for the cell-phones for Lily and Kevin, and covered what was owed after Ed's health insurance paid the basics. But there was no real money for me.

Until now. Now I had leases that provided income, and I could draw a paycheck from the inn without even having to work for it. I had a lump sum from Cathy that was sitting in my bank account, enough to buy a house, maybe even two houses. And I had RiverCliffe, with all those rolling hills and beautiful views.

It was hard for my brain to get used to the idea that I would no longer have to check my bank balance every morning before deciding what to do during the day.

Mom listened patiently while the kids chattered about how wonderful everything was—especially the food. She even pretended to listen to me when I tried to explain when and how we'd be moving there after school let out. But as soon as there was a break in the conversation, she dove into the tote bags and began to examine the life her husband never told her about.

"My mother-in-law looks like she never got a good night's rest," Mom said.

We were at the kitchen table, the kids having gone downstairs, each of us with a glass of red Chianti, my mother's favorite.

"She actually looks much better in the newer pictures," I said. "The older she got, the more successful she became, and she began to look happy and relaxed."

Mom held up a picture, a black-and-white square. "Billy was a cute kid," she murmured. She handed me the picture. It was one of the few of all three brothers together, my father in overalls, squinting at the camera. I had seen only one picture of Billy, the wedding picture where he smiled happily down at his adoring wife. As a child he had the same line of the jaw, the same heavy eyebrows.

"And the aunt? Clayton's wife. Billy told me about her." Mom scrutinized another picture. "Clay brought her back from some reservation out West. Billy never liked her."

"She wasn't a fan of his, either. But she never told him to stay away. He told them about you. About us. His family knew who we were." I felt the rise of anger. "He just lied to them about our names, and where we lived, and how to find us."

Mom nodded. She had lit a cigarette, an extra one, but this was an occasion. It wasn't every day a person got to look back into the past of someone they had loved and lost, no matter how much other baggage was attached.

"What are you going to do about this place?" She was carefully examining the brochure for RiverCliffe House. "You're really going back?"

"Ma, look at this place. It's a resort. I'm thinking about going for the summer."

She shrugged. "There's so much to do *here* in the summer, you know that, there's stuff for the kids…"

"A month ago you were practically kicking me out of the house."

She sniffed, took a drag of her cigarette, and carefully tapped the ash away. "I don't want you with his people."

I stared. "What other people do I have?"

She shrugged. "My cousin."

"Dora? Who you haven't spoken to in fifteen years? The one you refer to as 'That bitch in Hartford'?"

She waved her hands, a thin trail of smoke making curlicues in the air. "You don't know them!"

"No, I don't. This will give me a chance to *get* to know them. Besides, the only one I'm directly related to in any way is Martha, through marriage. So she's not even "his" people. I'll be living with strangers I have absolutely no blood ties with. Does that make you feel better?"

She shrugged again, inhaled, then dramatically exhaled out her nose. "You never know what kind of weird genetic thing you could inherit from that family. I'm just being cautious is all."

I sat back. Was this the time to tell her about the weird genetic thing I supposedly already inherited? "So, Ma, listen. There's this thing."

She rolled back her eyes. "I knew it."

"I'm supposed to be able to see the dead."

Her cigarette froze at her lips, and her eyes narrowed. "Says who?"

"Says Winston. According to him, it's a whole thing. All the women of the family are supposed to be able to talk to the dead in the cemetery next door. It started with the first Cliffe, Gemina. Apparently, after she died, her and her daughter had quite the conversations. And, legend has it, all women descended from Gemina have the same... talent. Gift. Whatever. That's how I inherited in the first place. I'm the female descendant." I took a deep breath. "But he wants to run River-Cliffe, and he wants to run it by himself. I think he just made the whole thing up just to, I don't know...scare me off?"

She blew smoke and glanced around the room. "Can you see any dead people now?"

My shoulders slumped. "No. I told you, it supposedly only works with the dead people in the cemetery up there."

She pursed her lips and nodded. "Interesting. You know I have always felt very strongly about this particular subject."

"Yes. I know."

"I'm a believer."

"Yes, Ma, I *know*."

"So?"

"So what?"

"Did you see anybody? Oh, Risa, don't tell me you didn't go to the graveyard to check it out!"

"I did go. And the only person I saw was a very nice man who drove his motorcycle up and down the Hudson River."

Her eyebrows shot up. "Was he cute?"

I shook my head. "Stop."

"No, seriously. Those biker boys can be *very* attractive. Was he?"

"Yes, he was. But unless he makes a habit of hanging out in the graveyard, I don't think he's going to be on my radar much."

"Still, you should try to find out about him. Where he lives. How old, do you think?"

I stood up. "Ma, stop. I can't believe you're still trying to fix me up. Last week you practically assaulted that poor man in Starbucks."

"He was very nice and polite. And obviously interested in you."

"He asked me to move my purse."

"See!"

I threw up my hands. "Forget it. One thing I did learn is that all my ancestors had crappy taste in men. It looks like Gemina was the first and last one to be happily married. You can look at this stuff, but keep it together, okay? I want to go through it all myself."

Then I called Ed. I hadn't spoken to my ex-husband in over a year. Our communication had been mainly through text and e-mail. The kids had seen him since then, of course, but not on any kind of regular basis, and the last time had been in February.

He answered on the third ring. I was surprised. I had expected my call to go directly to voicemail, he would never call back, I'd call again, and we'd play phone tag for a few weeks. That had been the usual routine every other time I had tried to reach him. Could it be he'd actually be interested in hearing from me, for one reason or another?

Not really.

"Hello, Risa, I'm glad you called," Ed said. "We need to talk about child support."

I sighed. "I'm not the one you talk to about that, Ed. My lawyer is the one you talk to."

He chuckled. "Do we really want to pay them to settle something you and I can talk out ourselves?"

"Yes. Listen, the kids and I have a chance to spend the summer in the Hudson valley, near Rhinebeck."

"Did you inherit a vast fortune there, Risa? Or have you finally found yourself a full-time job?"

I closed my eyes and fought the urge to scream. "Raising your children *is* a full-time job, Ed, but as a matter of fact, I did inherit something. My grandmother died and left me her place. The thing is, they'd be much closer to you. And it's a pretty place. With a pool. Good for a summer vacation, you know? But I'm not going to go up there unless we set up some sort of schedule for you to see them."

I could hear him on the other end of the line sigh, and pictured him getting ready to assume his 'on-the-phone' position—leaning back in a chair, cigarette burning, a can of Diet Coke close by.

"That's still a bit of a drive."

"'These are your kids, Ed. I seem to remember you fighting pretty hard to get weekly visitation, and once the ink was dry on our settlement, you stopped mentioning it."

"I'm a little busy, here, Risa."

"Fine. The kids are out of school in two weeks, and we'd go up there that weekend. How about the weekend after that?"

"I'll check my calendar."

There was silence as we listened to each other's angry breathing.

"This child support thing is a real pinch in the wallet, Risa. I just bought a new place, and the business is in a little slump."

"Why would you buy a new place if the business wasn't doing well?"

"Alicia–"

"I don't care, Ed. When are you going to get back to me about picking up the kids?"

"Picking up?"

"Yes. As in, driving here, getting out of your car, putting them into your car, and then taking them somewhere, for lunch, or a picnic, or for a walk along the river. Anything, just as long as you're showing them that you are, in fact, their loving and concerned father."

"I talk to Lily all the time."

My head started to hurt. "When was the last time you talked to Kira?"

Silence.

"I remember you with her, right after she was born, Ed. You called her your happy little mistake. You doted on her."

More silence.

"Did you ever ask Kevin why he stopped playing sports? Did you ever ask him how he spends his time instead? He gained almost twenty pounds last year, Ed, and only grew one inch. He's a young boy. He shouldn't be spending all his time playing on his phone and eating too much crap. Ever talk to him about that?"

Finally, "I'll call you next week," he said, and hung up.

I spoke with Winston at least once a day. I gave him the authority to get Wayne the River Guy to buy a sailboat, something that was safe enough for a beginner but wouldn't embarrass RiverCliffe's more experienced sailing guests. FYI, you can spend a whole lot of money on a boat. Luckily it was a sound investment in my business rather than a careless personal extravagance I could barely afford.

The last day of school, I took the kids to Applebee's.

"We need to decide what to do this summer," I told them. I'd been putting off their constant queries while I thought about what I wanted to do. "We have a few choices." I took a deep breath. "We could start looking for a new house. Now, maybe not Morris Plains, but we could live someplace nice, you know? We could be like those people on *House Hunters*, going from place to place. And then we would have a new place to live."

Kevin scowled. "You do know that show is a set-up, right?"

"How long would it take?" Lily asked. "Could we be out of grand-ma's soon?"

I shrugged. "I don't know how long, Lily. We'd have to look, and put in an offer, and there's paperwork…a few weeks maybe? A few months."

Lily's mouth flattened to a thin line. "And we'd have to live in Brooklyn the whole time? No thanks, Mom. Really."

I looked at Kevin. He lifted his eyes from his phone. "That sounds like a bad idea."

"I want to go to RiverCliffe," Kira said clearly. "We could swim all day, and I could play with the chickens."

Kevin sat up. "Did they get a boat? A sailboat?"

I nodded.

"Serena said she'd teach me to cook," Lily said. "I'd like that."

I sighed. "Well, that *was* one of our options."

Lily narrowed her eyes. "You talked to Daddy?"

"Yes. He agreed that it would be easier for him to see you guys up there."

"Then I want to go," Lily said. "That's my vote."

"Mine too," said Kevin.

Kira waved her hand happily. "Me too. So, when are we going?"

"We need to pack, and get rid of some stuff, because at the end of the summer, we're still going to have to find a place to live, okay?"

They all nodded in agreement.

We spent a few days going through the basement, deciding what to bring, packing a few boxes, and agreeing that, while we were gone, all of the furniture could be donated to the nearest shelter. I packed the minivan with suitcases and a few shoeboxes. Finally, I put the two tote bags in the back seat and drove back to RiverCliffe, without ever reading Gemina's diaries, or those of her daughter, or *her* daughter, and so on.

I probably should have made the time.

We arrived on a Tuesday, just after lunch. Lily immediately went into the kitchen, threw her arms around Serena, and announced that she was ready to cook. Serena laughed and got her an apron. I watched for three minutes, and left.

Kira stopped in at the barns and Daniel put her to work feeding the chickens. He waved me away after about seven minutes. His own daughter, who looked to be Kira's age, was showing my daughter the ropes. I figured she was set for the summer.

Kevin and I walked down to the river. The main road that ran parallel to the river was busier than when we'd been there a few weeks before, but once you crossed the highway and walked for two minutes toward the water, you were in another world, and the noise of the cars and everything else faded away.

Wayne De Graff was tall, thin, and bald, with a wide smile and laughing eyes. He was, I knew, a few years away from retiring, but he looked ageless. He shook hands with Kevin and I, showed us the new sailboat, and told Kevin there was plenty for him to do at the boathouse. Winston had told me that Wayne occasionally asked for help down at the boathouse, but because there were long stretches of time with little or no activity down there, Cathy had never agreed. Now, Wayne pitched to me his need for an assistant. Some days, every single guest wanted a canoe or kayak, and they would have to wait. With an assistant to help guests get out on the water, distribute life jackets, sort out oars and fishing poles…

I looked at Kevin. "If you want you can help Wayne, and during the downtime he can teach you to sail. But you have to commit, Kev. Seven days a week. Not all day, or every day, but when Wayne needs you. And you can't be in the middle of Minecraft and blow him off. He's going to be counting on you."

Kevin looked just like my ex-husband, with a square jaw, straight, sandy-colored hair and thick brows. He nodded. "It's a deal. And Mom? Maybe RiverCliffe could use jet skis?"

"I don't think so," I said.

Wayne grinned. "Ah, Mom, come on," he said, laughing.

"One thing at a time," I said. "Kevin, you good here?" He nodded and I gave him a quick hug. "If Wayne complains, you're out. Don't forget to come up for lunch."

I walked up the hill, crossed the highway, and back up to River-Cliffe House.

Winston was sitting in the office behind the front desk. He looked up as I walked in and smiled brightly.

"Unpacked?"

"No, we aren't. The kids were very anxious to dive right into things. We'll have plenty of time tonight." I said the words lightly, but was inwardly cringing at the thought of all my things stuffed into the suitcase instead of being put away where they belonged, but the kids had been so excited, I went along with them.

I sat on the edge of the second desk, the smaller desk that, I guessed, had once been his. "I told you I was going to be hands-off, and I still mean it. I'm back because it's summer vacation, and I needed someplace to take my kids."

He nodded. "Of course. They don't like the beach?"

I lifted an eyebrow. "Lily gets burned too easily. " I picked up a file from the desk and waved it. "Since I *am* here, I'd like to look over the books, see where things stand and, you know, familiarizing myself with the process."

"Of course." His mouth was a thin, tight line. "After all, you are the boss."

"Yes. I am." I glanced around the room. It was small and cramped, but well-organized. "Listen, Winston, I realize that a large part of running RiverCliffe is interacting with the guests, and I'm guessing you're really good at all that."

He was more than good at that—he was a marvel. He knew their names, and made index cards of them all, recording their likes, dislikes, and any comments they made, so that the next visit could be even better. In our phone conversations over the past weeks, I could hear in his voice where his passion lay as he explained what he was doing and why.

His mouth relaxed just a bit. "Thank you."

"I'm not a big people person. I'm happy when I'm surrounded by lists and chores to do, not so much strangers wanting to make small talk. So, if you did want any help, I can take over some of the administrative stuff. Accounting and paperwork. That would free up more of your time to spend with the guests." I shrugged. "But only if you think I could be of any real use."

He sniffed. "I could use the help, actually. This accounting isn't my strong suit. I didn't realize how much Cathy did on a daily basis, and it's starting to catch up with me."

"Good. Let's start with signing me on to the computer, and we'll go from there."

I spent an hour looking at Profit and Loss Statements. The MBA classes I'd been taking had refreshed my accounting knowledge, and I actually knew what I was looking at. And RiverCliffe seemed to be on sound financial footing.

Then I got up and checked on my children. Lily and Serena were in the kitchen, making finger sandwiches. Lily glanced up, smiled briefly, and went on with her work.

Kira was in a large garden behind one of the barns, weeding. Daniel's daughter, Haley was at her side. Kira showed me her basket of green things, and she was careful and patient in explaining the names of each.

Kevin was scrubbing down a bright orange kayak. His t-shirt was soaking wet, and I could see the back of his neck turning red in the sun. I went back up to the suite, dug out sunscreen, and brought it back down. Kevin was mortified when I suggested I put some on the back of his neck myself. Wayne saved the day by assuring me he'd be responsible for the any and all applications, on the back of the neck and anywhere else needed.

Back up to RiverCliffe.

I glanced towards the cemetery. Just curious, of course. There was a newly dug grave right by the entrance, flowers piled high, and a small American flag fluttering. Who, I wondered. A visit to the Woodmark and Sons Funeral Home was on my list of things to do. But not quite yet.

I went around the back of the inn and up to Martha and Bernie's drying shed. They were both there, standing in either side of a long work table, stripping dried rosemary from tough stems.

Martha grinned. "So you're back. Good for you."

I gave her a quick hug. "Yes, I'm back. Just for the summer. It was actually the kids who wanted to come back here. They each found something they wanted to do, so here we are."

"What are you going to do?" Bernie asked, her grin wide and wicked. "I'm betting Winston didn't want you around, butting into the business."

I laughed. "We've agreed that I can help with the accounting and payroll, so he can spend more time with the guests. But you're right, he didn't want me back. He even concocted an elaborate ghost story to keep me away."

Martha and Bernie exchanged looks.

"Ghost story?" Bernie asked.

I nodded. "Yes. He told me that there were ghosts in the cemetery, and only I could see them. Well, my daughters too, because we were descended from the original…" I watched their faces. I expected them to look amused or surprised. Instead, these were two faces of two women who had heard this all before. "What?"

"Well, honey, that's all true," Bernie said.

I folded my arms across my chest. "What's all true?"

Martha pushed her rosemary branches off to the side and leaned her strong hands against the rough tabletop. "All women descended from Gemina Cliffe are born with the ability to speak to those souls buried in that meadow." Her voice was quiet and calm and she spoke with absolute authority. "That is not a ghost story. That is the River-Cliffe legacy." She looked at me, her eyes gentle. "Do you find that hard to believe?"

I swallowed. No, I don't find it hard to believe in *theory*. I was just wildly uncomfortable with the idea it could actually apply to me. "That seems farfetched," I managed at last.

She shrugged, and pulled the rosemary back in front of her. "I imagine you'll have to find out for yourself. See, it's been easier for all the women here at RiverCliffe in the past, because they were born here, and grew up knowing. Take all the time you need, Risa. Just be prepared."

A cell phone noise sounded, and Bernie pulled hers out of her pocket. "Winston's looking for you," she said.

"Okay. Thanks."

"Come to dinner Friday," she said. "Bring your kids. We want to meet them."

I nodded and went back to the inn.

In the lobby, Winston was standing and talking to a tall, broad-shouldered man. When he saw me, he waved me over.

"Risa, here's someone you should know."

The broad-shouldered man was wearing a khaki uniform, with a badge on the breast pocket. "Welcome, Mrs. Armitage. I'm Scott Van Wyke. Sheriff. Good to meet you."

I knew that sheriffs didn't always come with a Stetson and a Colt strapped around the hips, but he was kind of a surprise. With fair hair and blue eyes, not to mention the fact that his shoulders were as wide as a Buick, I would have pegged him as, at least, a lumberjack. Or a Viking. His hand completely swallowed mine as he shook it. It was warm, and I felt a tingle go all the way up my arm, a physical reaction to an attractive man, something I hadn't felt in a long time.

"Hello," I said. "Are you here in an official capacity?"

His smile was wide and genuine. "Not at all. Just wanted to meet you. We're kind of between a few municipalities here, so if the need arises, I'm the man to call. Got it?"

"Got it. Does the need arise often?"

"Well, your daddy had to be escorted off the property back when Cathy died," he said. "I want you to know that if he comes back, I'd be more than happy to do it again."

"Ah, well that's good to know, Sheriff."

"Scott. Please." His eyes held mine for a moment, and I felt a small glow.

"I'm Risa."

His smile broadened. "Risa it is."

Winston looked from at me, then at Scott, then back to me again.

"Scott here," he said, in a very credible talk-show-host voice, "Is a divorced outdoorsman with a fondness for good food. Risa is a city girl who enjoys vodka tonics and lists of things to do. Can these two crazy kids find happiness together?"

I laughed so hard it was almost a snort. Scott threw his head back, and his laughter echoed against the ceiling.

"Good one, Winston," he said, his shoulders still shaking. "That's a good one."

I finally stopped laughing enough to begin to blush. Scott leaned down and dropped his voice. "The problem with small communities like this is that everyone thinks they're a matchmaker." He straightened. "They've been trying to fix me up for years now."

"Got it," I said. "I'll take the warning."

He nodded as he backed off, and walked out.

I turned to Winston and glared. "Don't ever do that again," I said, trying to keep the down giggle in the back of my throat.

"Just so you know—"

I held up a hand. "I mean it."

"But—"

"Stop. Not another word about that man. Now. Where were we?"

I turned and marched back to the office.

When I got back to the apartment, I found the very first diary, that of Elsbeth Cliffe Hawkins. The introduction explained that all the entries were word-for-word from the original, but that some spellings had been changed for the modern reader. I flipped forward to a random page. What, exactly, had Elsbeth been writing about?

Sunday, May 12th

Today I finally discussed with Mother the question that had been lying most heavily upon my mind. Jonathan has declared his love for and his intent to marry Caroline Wilkerson, a most vain and unhappy woman. Although I have great love and respect for my oldest brother, her own situation across the river must be dire indeed if she finds in Jonathan a better opportunity.

Father, in an unexpected show of generosity, agreed to hand over the farm to Jonathan, as he is the oldest son and first to marry. Father seemed to think that Jonathan and his new bride would continue to allow our entire family to live at RiverCliffe. However, I am certain that Caroline will turn us out immediately.

My most pressing concern is how I can continue to visit Mother once Jonathan has taken control of RiverCliffe. Caroline, I am sure, will not be happy here, and may press Jonathan to sell our most beautiful home. If that were to happen, I would no longer be able to walk across the great meadow and visit Mother in the most sacred place where she is interred. So it was with an anxious heart I visited her today. After our usual greetings, I put to her my worries.

"Mother, Jon is *finally* getting married in two months, and Father has promised him the farm. If that happens, Father and I will likely get thrown out of the house, and may very well end up living in the woodshed. As for the rest of my brothers, they will have to go out on their own. Can you imagine David away from the farm? He'll probably end up in prison. So will Marcus. And Seth—"

"Elsbeth," Mother chided gently. "You are being harsh. Your brothers may not be of strong mental capacity, but they are moral and upright men."

"Yes, Mother, but they only know two things; fighting for General Washington, and farming. Now that there is no longer an army, and they have shown little desire to seek decent and honest work outside of the farm, how else would they occupy their time?"

Mother shook her head. "Jon would not do all that. Woodshed indeed. You are his family."

I once again struggled between the love and respect I felt for Mother, and my total impatience with Her attitude toward Her sons. "Mother, please. I know he's the firstborn, and your favorite son, but you don't know him anymore. Besides, he is besotted, and you've never met that witch he's marrying. She does not understand the value of family, nor the blessings of a generous heart. She cares more for money than kin. In fact, she may want to sell the farm altogether, and take the money to live in town. What would happen then? If this falls into the hands of strangers, I may never be able to see or speak with you again."

Mother thought. "Then we need convince your father to leave the farm to *you*."

I sighed in frustration at her continued belief that all would be right with the world. "I'm the youngest and the only girl. Father's word is law, and his decision would be honored by all of my brothers. But what could I possibly say or do to convince him that I, the least valuable of all his children, should be given his largest asset?"

Mother frowned. "Are you sure you're the only one who can see me?"

"I have brought all of your sons out here to stand with me at your graveside. I know that they have come by themselves. And father still visits you early mornings, does he not? Have any of them been able to answer you when you spoke?"

Mother had to concede my point. No one else had acknowledged her presence, while I had been coming and chatting for over ten years now.

"What you have to do is prove to your father that we are meeting, and that he cannot separate us, " She said, as though that were the simplest thing in all the world.

"And how, dear Mother, can I do that? I am at a loss as to what to tell Father. After all, it was he who buried you, and continues to this day to mourn you. How can I tell him that, every Sunday morning, we meet and converse like this?" I shook my head.

She smiled. "Tell him the truth. How we began talking, that day after your fourth birthday. Then, if he doubts you—"

"Not *if*, Mother. When." I interrupted.

"Yes. When he doubts you, simply tell him that his wife wishes that you inherit the farm just as she once wished for a small, white mare."

I stared. "Is that all?"

Mother nodded, smiling. "Yes. It is hard to keep secrets in so large a family, but Andrew and I managed. He will know that it is truly his wife, speaking from beyond this world, who makes such a request."

Knowing that she was the most wise of women, I chose to believe her and threw my arms around her neck and kissed her. "Thank you."

She patted my hair lovingly. "Of course. After all, I could never let anything come between us. If death could not, what chance has any wife of Jon's?"

And so I departed the meadow, walking through the low stone wall, which separated it from the rest of the farmstead, to speak with Father. Upon hearing my words, he turned quite pale and stared at me in disbelief, then dismissed me and shut the door of his bedroom, leaving me alone in the front parlor. Now I must wait to see if my Mother is indeed still wise, and if her words, coming from beyond this world, will save us.

. . .

I closed the little book slowly. By pure coincidence, I opened to the single entry that laid out the beginning of the RiverCliffe legacy. Now, all I had to do was believe in it.

That night, over hot dogs and beans, I told the kids about Bernie's invitation to dinner.

"Will Serena cook?" Kira asked.

I shook my head and looked at the sad dinner on my plate. "No."

"Will one of them cook?" Kevin asked.

I nodded.

"Thank God. I'm in." He finished his plate, took another, then announced that his first day of work tired him out, and he went upstairs.

Normally, Lily would have sighed, rolled her eyes, dragged her feet, and feigned blindness or leprosy rather than agree. But she asked if Trent would be there, and when I said probably, she nodded.

On Friday, she even put on a little makeup before we walked over.

Martha was a great cook. She roasted a chicken with, she explained, carrots and potatoes she'd grown herself and stored in an old-fashioned root cellar. Kevin told me, with a very serious face, that if the vegetables in New Jersey had tasted this good, he would have eaten much more of them as a child. That's right *as a child*, because now, apparently, he was a full-blown adult.

Lily, thank God, did not gaze longingly at Trent as though he were the last cute boy on earth, so I felt much better about them leaving to see a movie in town. Kira, for all her interest in vegetables and gardening, had not asked Martha where the chicken had come from. I had a feeling it came from the same yard that Kira visited every day. In fact, we may have been eating Fred, as she had recently named them all.

After dinner, as I was thinking about getting to bed early, like, in half an hour, Bernie sat beside me and nudged me with her elbow.

"Let's go get a drink. There's this great little place, not on the river, 'cause that's for tourists, but just down the road a ways. We can get a beer and maybe watch a game of pool. What do you say?"

I was going to say that I was exhausted. I was going to say that I didn't drink beer and thought pool was the most boring thing you could possibly watch, right after golf. I was going to say I felt like a tourist, so couldn't we sit in a cute place by the river?

But then I thought that it sounded just like the kind of place a guy who rode his motorcycle up and down the river would go to.

"Do I need to change?" I asked. I was wearing jeans and a cotton pullover sweater.

"Are you kidding? You're overdressed. I'll drive. Martha can walk over and sit with the kids, or they can just hang out here. She hates going out. But you and I? We could be great drinking buddies, I can tell."

I wasn't sure I wanted to be anyone's drinking buddy, but suddenly, the idea of actually going out somewhere sounded perfect. "Let me walk back and get some money."

"Nah, this time it's on me." She raised her voice. "She's coming with me to the Bear Claw. You got the kids?"

Martha made some sort of noise of agreement from the kitchen. I looked at Kira and Kevin.

"Are you guys okay staying with Martha? I know you don't know her very well, so if you'd rather I stay home…"

Kira rolled her eyes. "Mom, she's *family*. Of course it's okay."

I glanced at Bernie, whose eyes got suddenly bright. "'That's right, baby. We're family." She nudged me with her elbow, hard. "Right?"

I sighed. "Right." I kissed the kids good-bye and we were off.

The Bear Claw wasn't just down the road a ways. It was down the road, off to the right, up the mountain and through the forest. And over another mountain. Bernie drove an ancient Volvo like it was an all-terrain Range Rover, chattering over potholes and around hairpin turns.

It was a warm and welcome sight, however, a low, cabin-type structure with lights blazing from every window. The parking lot was a rather unorganized affair, with no rhyme or reason to the lines of cars parked there. It looked to be a full house. As we hiked from our spot near the tree line, I noticed several motorcycles, and my interest lifted even more. Would Caleb be there? It seemed the kind of place he'd fit right in to. The possibility gave me an unexpected jolt.

Inside was crowded and noisy, with a jukebox blaring Buddy Holly. This was not like the hipster bars I'd pass through in Brooklyn. This was very much a place for the locals to hang out; the people who spent their days waiting on and watching the tourists throw lots of money around. Bernie nodded to several men and women, pushed us up to the bar, and waved down the bartender.

He was polishing a shot glass and was wearing a dark green apron. He could not have looked a more perfect barkeep. He nodded at Bernie and fixed his eye on me.

"You the new owner?" he asked.

Bernie answered. "Yes. Risa Armitage, this is Henry Hollister, owner of the Bear Claw and all-round asshole. I'll have a beer. Bud. Risa?"

I wanted to ask for a Cosmopolitan, or maybe a Moscow Mule, just to see the reaction, but decided not to press my luck. "White wine? Pinot?"

Henry nodded and set to work.

I looked around, half expecting to see deer heads and antlers on the walls. Instead, there were lots of landscapes. Of course. The Hudson Valley School of painting. I would have to watch myself. I was often guilty of jumping to conclusions.

"So," I said in Bernie's ear, "I guess my inheriting RiverCliffe was kind of a big deal?"

She nodded. "Oh, yes. Tourism drives the economy up here, and we're very careful to protect what we got. There's a slew of B&Bs and hotels up and down the river, and they keep lots of people employed. We're not nearly as big as some, but between the inn and the farming, me and Martha's little herb business, and the cheese factory, we keep more than thirty families fed." She looked past me and waved. I glanced back and saw a huge man in a white button-down shirt shouldering his way toward us.

"On the tab?" Henry asked as he put down our drinks. Bernie nodded.

"People run tabs here?" I asked, sipping tentatively. The wine was perfect, cool and slightly dry.

"This ain't the big city," Bernie said, slurping the foam off the top of her beer. "Ah, Scott, good. This here is Risa."

I recognized the sheriff. He looked more relaxed and quite handsome out of uniform. He shook my hand and smiled warmly.

"We've met," he said to Bernie. "And I believe Winston is planning our engagement party even as we speak."

Bernie cackled. "I bet he is."

"Good seeing you again," I said. "Bernie here must know all the VIPs?"

He threw back his head and laughed. "Well, she knows a lot of folks who are interesting, if not important. So, yeah, I guess." He looked around and gestured with an open hand. "So here you are, at the Bear Claw. Must be quite a shock from what you're used to. Brooklyn, right?"

I nodded. "Yep. Born and raised. Took a short detour into Jersey, but I ended up right back where I started."

He nodded. I was expecting the usual, "Never been to the big city myself" but instead...

He signaled Henry. "Got my Master's at Columbia. Loved city living. I'd go down to Chinatown and walk all the way back, eating everything in sight. Still miss the food. Henry here is a pretty good cook," he said, grinning and taking his beer, "but can't get him to put Thai or Vietnamese on the menu."

"Now, that's a shame," I said, laughing.

"It is. But not to worry, there are plenty of great spots to eat around here, if you know where to look."

Was that some kind of invitation? Or, at least an opening?

I took a mental step back. I had met Caleb, and my interest had been piqued. And then Scott. Was the universe trying to tell me something? Here I was, in a totally unfamiliar place and not feeling too freaked out about it. Maybe it was time for me to take another baby step in a new direction.

"You'll have to take me on a tour," I said, trying to sound sophisticated and totally nonchalant.

"I'd love that," he said at once. "And I can fill you in on all the local legends." He sipped his beer. "Your father, for instance."

My mind sharpened. That's right. He'd met Billy. "You knew him?"

Scott shrugged. "Not really. I escorted him off of RiverCliffe back after Cathy died. He didn't put up much of a fight. He just seemed a tired old man. I'd heard the stories, of course."

Bernie nodded. "They had quite a reputation when they were younger, them three," she said.

"That's right," he said. "They were before my time as sheriff, but I remember as a little kid they were the number one hell raisers in the valley. Your daddy was a piece of work, if you don't mind me sayin'."

I drank off more wine. "I don't mind at all." I filed it away, another scrap of information. I kept waiting to hear about the sweet, charming rogue who swept my mother off her feet. That was another Billy. Here, no one knew that man.

I looked around. The pool tables were at the other end of the long, narrow room, and there were four games going, all of them looking fairly serious. "I bet you break up a lot of bar fights?"

"Some. These guys are pretty well behaved, mostly, although there are a few I like to keep an eye on."

"Do you know of a biker named Caleb? Said he rode up and down the whole Hudson River a few times."

Scott pursed his lips and frowned, thinking. "Can't recall, sorry." He turned as someone called his name, and nodded to someone back in the crowd. "That's my cue. Good seeing you, Risa. Later, Bernie."

He lumbered off and Bernie got us another round. The bar was a warm, happy kind of place, for friends and talk and a few drinks at the end of a rough night. If I could remember how to get here, I'd come myself, and wouldn't feel awkward walking in alone.

Bernie grinned at me over the top of her beer. "So, who's this Caleb? You met a fella already?"

"What? No, not really." Since coming back to RiverCliffe, Caleb had been pecking away at the corner of my brain. I had liked him. Just as I had liked Scott. Maybe it was being away from Brooklyn, and out of my mother's house, but the Hudson valley air had seemed to awaken an interest in men. "I actually ran into him back during Memorial Day Weekend. In the cemetery. We had a chat, is all. He said it was a good place to come and think, and he was right. It was perfect."

"Ah, Risa?"

I turned to her. "Yes?"

"Dontcha think that maybe he, well, you know..."

"Know what?"

She drank, then set the mug down, positioning it in the center of the small, damp napkin. "He might have been a resident."

"Well, I figured. He said he came from up over the hill."

"No." She stared at the beer mug and moved it a quarter of an inch to the left. "You know, a *resident*."

I put down my wine glass and stared at her. "Like, of the cemetery? You mean..." My voice had been rising, and I looked around quickly and dropped into a whisper. "A ghost?"

She pushed the mug away. "Well, it happens. Especially to you Cliffe women. Just sayin'." She stood up. "You want another wine? Mebbe watch them play some pool?"

I shook my head. All of my night-out good feelings had been ground into the wood floor. "I can go. Ready?"

I followed her out and didn't say a word until she had jock-eyed her car out of the parking lot and had it back on the paved road.

"So, you think Caleb was a ghost?"

"It's possible."

"Well, you're wrong. For one thing, he didn't look like a ghost."

"And how, exactly, *does* a ghost look?"

She had me there. "He was solid. And he wasn't bloody or anything. He looked like a real person."

"Well, since I've never seen a spirit myself, I couldn't say if that described one or not. So I guess I'll just take your word for it," she said reasonably.

"And he was dressed, like, modern. He had on jeans, and his ear was pierced."

"Not everyone who's there died in the 1800s, you know. Why, Jimmy Metcalfe was buried just last week."

We continued down the winding road in silence, while I tried to remember every single thing I'd ever learned from *GhostHunters* on TV. Or the *Long Island Medium*.

"I suppose," I said at last, "the funeral home has all the records?"

"Since 1936. Or seven. That's when they took over. Until then, people just kind of, you know, asked the family and bought a plot. Woodmark came along and offered to manage the whole operation, and Cathy's mom said yes. Saved her the mowin' of the grass and such. Cathy remembered back, though, when her family did the buryin'."

Note to self: visit Woodmark and Sons, and see if there was ever a Caleb buried in RiverCliffe cemetery.

CHAPTER 5

*S*aturday morning was busy. Noisy and busy. The dining room was full, coffee drinkers were on the broad, front porch, umbrellas were up by the pool and I felt lighter than I'd felt in months.

Lily was in the kitchen. Breakfast was a big deal at the inn, and Serena arrived at four in the morning to start her baking, along with her silent, somber-looking assistant, Glena. Every day was a different menu. Sure, standard items like eggs and oatmeal were always available, but the selection of baked goods and omelets depended on what Serena had available that morning.

Lily had been getting up at six-thirty to begin her day. I expected her to sleep in on the weekend, but she had slipped out while I dozed a little later than usual. By the time I made my way to the dining room, she was already there, her apron on, hair pulled back, bringing hot dishes out from the kitchen.

I made my way over to her. "Do you guys need help?"

She looked around the dining room. "Table six needs clearing," she said. "And we need a few setups."

"Got it," I told her, my heart bursting. She was working! And taking it very seriously! And she almost smiled at me!

Kevin and Kira came by a bit later, Kira fresh from the barns, with a basket full of eggs and a few bunches of parsley. They had both eaten back in my own kitchen, cereal and strawberries from Daniel's garden. Kevin told me he'd be down at the river. Kira asked if she could play with Daniel's daughter, Haley. They vanished into their lives, leaving me to smile, pour coffee, and hopefully not be drawn into any conversation.

By ten thirty the dining room had cleared, and Serena came out, saw me re-setting a few tables, and grabbed my arm.

"You're not supposed to be doin' this, boss. You're supposed to the on the porch. Holding court."

"Holding court?"

"That's what Cathy did on the weekends." She led me out of the dining room. "Sit and talk to folks. She knew all the RiverCliffe stories."

I stopped halfway through the lobby. "Look, I don't mind helping out. In fact, I enjoyed it. But mingling with the guests is Winston's job, not mine. Besides, I don't know any RiverCliffe stories."

She shook her head in disgust. "Well, you better learn some. And RiverCliffe is yours, Risa. Not Winston's. I can see that maybe you have to grow into this role, so why don't you start by going out and sitting in the porch."

"What I really want to do," I told her, "is to pay a visit to Woodmark."

Her eye widened. "Oh? Getting curious?"

Yes, I was. Mainly, I was curious to find out if anyone named Caleb had ever been buried there. I nodded.

"Well, can't do it on the weekend. We're too busy. I know Garth," Serena said. "I'll call him and let him know you're coming. Monday morning?"

"Sounds good," I said. I looked around the lobby. She was right, we were busy. Because I checked reservations every night with Winston to see what the next day was like, I knew we had another full house.

I could have gone back into the office, where I could have been quite happy with my ledgers and numbers. After all, Winston and I had made a deal. But Winston wasn't scheduled to come in until after eleven. Maybe I should at least try to be more social with the guests. But what on earth was I going to talk about?

Another note to self — read those old diaries.

The front porch overlooked a wide sweep of green lawn, the main highway and, of course the river. The graveled parking lot was to the side, as not to obstruct the view. Good planning on Cathy's part. The porch itself was wide enough for comfy wicker chairs and mismatched side tables, the painted floors scuffed and worn, the bead board ceiling painted a pale blue. I found an armchair and settled in, waiting for my captive audience to flock around me, eagerly awaiting whatever pearl of wisdom might spill from my lips.

I waited some more. Maybe they all knew that Cathy was the teller of tales, and I was just the rookie and probably worthless in the story-telling department. Maybe no one recognized me as the owner, and just took me for a guest, or maybe one of the kitchen help on a break. Maybe I didn't look like someone who deserved a court to hold. Whatever the case, I had a very peaceful and quiet spell there, watching people come and go, and looking at boats on the river.

"May I?"

I looked up, hoping for an audience at last. It was Scott Van Wyke, wearing his khaki uniform and holding a mug of coffee in one hand.

I patted the chair beside me. "Have a seat. I'm supposed to be, as Serena put it, holding court out here, regaling my spellbound guests with tales of the Cliffe family legacy. I think all my guests have figured out I'm not the regaling type."

He grinned. "Well, you *are* new around here. Maybe you can work on your regaling skills and try again in a few weeks." He leaned back, settling his shoulders. "Bernie tells me you're divorced."

I hadn't told Bernie I was divorced, but I should have realized that any information shared with one member of the RiverCliffe gang would be immediately shared with all. "Yes. It was not what you'd call cordial."

"Mine was. In fact, Serena and I get along better now that when we were together."

My eyebrows shot up. "Serena? My Serena?"

His grinned broadened. "Well, she was *my* Serena first. I met her when she was still a student, talked her into marrying me, and then talked Cathy into giving her a job here. I'm an all-or-nothing kind of guy. Things didn't exactly work out between us, but that's life." He raised his coffee mug. "That's why I get all the free coffee I want."

I was puzzling this out in my head. Scott looked to be older than I, possibly close to fifty. Serena seemed, well, ageless, but I would have pegged her for late twenties, early thirties at the most. "Was there cradle robbing involved?" I asked.

He nodded. "Oh, yes. When her mama came up for the wedding and saw the cranky old white guy her daughter was marrying, she was not happy. But we were, Serena and I. For a while, anyway." He cleared his throat. "But the reason I brought up the subject at all is because I was thinking, well, how about dinner some night next week? I know you can't get away for a big Saturday-night date, but maybe something, you know, smaller? To get started on your tour?" His eyes twinkled. "After all, you did ask."

Date? He actually said *date*? Did men even do that anymore? I'd spent a whole lot of years not dating, and it seemed to me that things involving men and women had changed course a bit. Of course, I had thrown out the bait, but he'd taken it, and here he was, this very nice, undeniably attractive man, asking me out for a good old-fashioned night on the town.

I felt a bit of a grin trying to fight its way up, but I managed not to look too eager. "You're right. I did ask. And that sounds just lovely."

He stood. "Good. I'll find you sometime early next week, and we'll make plans."

I stood as well. He was close to a foot taller than I was. "Well, finding me will be easy. I'm right here."

"Yes." An awkward moment, then he nodded briefly and went back into the inn.

I sat back down, watching the river, thinking about dinner some night next week, and how nice it felt to have something to look forward to that was all mine.

. . .

I had been back at RiverCliffe only five days, but I felt it tugging at me, drawing me in. I woke up every morning after a deep night's sleep, feeling not just rested, but revived. Fresh air? Serena's coffee? A decent mattress? I wasn't sure, but I felt grateful. I also realized that RiverCliffe was my responsibility. In just a few short days I understood the scope of what it took to run a place like this, the time and energy that the employees put in to making RiverCliffe House worthy of four and a half stars on Yelp. I sat behind the smaller desk, across from Winston a few hours every day, and played with payroll and accounts payable. But there was much more to running a successful business, and if I wanted it to stay successful, I thought I should think about a larger role.

Part of that larger role, I knew, was knowing everything I could about RiverCliffe. Not just what was happening in the next few weeks and months, but also what had happened in the past.

Sunday morning I went to the graveyard again.

No, I was not looking for Caleb. My rational brain told me that he was on the road, going up the Hudson. He might even be in Canada. He might be living with a lovely woman who let him fly as free as he liked and always welcomed him home. He might have realized he was gay and had a young, virile stud holding on to him from the back of his motorcycle. He may have decided to never come down and think on a Sunday morning again, just in case he ran into that crazy Risa woman.

I found Gemina's grave. It was carefully tended, with a lilac bush behind the tall, worn stone that read, simply, Gemina, Beloved. No dates, no platitudes, no pat wishes for a good afterlife. Just Gemina, Beloved.

I had a diary with me. I had pulled it from the stack on my bedside table. I had no idea who it belonged to, or where it fell in the River-Cliffe timeline, but each diary was a different color, and this was bound in sage green. I sat in the cool grass, my back against Gemina's stone. The lilac cast a dappled shade, and I began to read. If I really wanted to know what the past RiverCliffe had been like, I had first-hand accounts to inform me.

Dimity Whitehall was born on the farm during the Civil War, and her diary began sometime in the mid-1870s. She was not very good about dates. She was also not very good about consistency. One entry would be all about how mean so-and-so was at her country day school, and the next was about how in the world she was going to get through her wedding night.

Apparently she got through it just fine because suddenly she had three children, all boys.

There was one entry, just a single line. "If I don't have a girl soon, who will keep the farm?"

Luckily, her number one son married and had four girls in a row, and Dimity took the oldest under her wing.

Another one-line entry sent a bit of a chill down my back. "Today little Lucy met my dear Robert for the first time and she was not afraid."

Her dear Robert, I knew, was her husband who had died before little Lucy was even born.

I closed the diary. Well, that was enough heebie-jeebies for one day.

I stood and stretched, and there, on the bench, sitting in the sun, was Caleb.

I looked at him, squinting my eyes against the sun. He looked solid. There was no dapple of light across his shoulders, no shadow from an invisible tree. I thought back to our last meeting. I'd pointed at the Grateful Dead letters on the front of his shirt. Had I actually touched him? I walked across the graveyard and sat beside him. "Weren't you going to say hello?"

He grinned at me. "My momma raised three kids in the hill country on her own, and barely had a minute to herself. She loved to read, and that was her private time, and none of us kids dared bother her if she had a book in her hand. If I learned only one lesson from her, it was to never interrupt a woman reading."

I nodded. "Well, that lesson will take you far, my friend. How have you been?"

He shrugged. "The same. Things have a way of settling in around here, you know? Patterns. You fall into a pattern."

"Doesn't that get a little dull?"

"Maybe." He grinned again. "Guess it depends on if your pattern is a simple stripe or a woven tapestry."

My jaw dropped in delight. "Yes, that's true. So I guess you've had a tapestry life?"

"Gold brocade, baby. With all those little seed pearls sewn in."

"Caleb, I seriously would not have taken you for a gold brocade kind of guy."

He leaned into me and whispered in my ear. "It's all part of my mysterious charm." He straightened. "How 'bout you?"

I had felt the warmth of his breath in my ear. Surely if a ghost had any breath at all, it would be cold.

"I think I'm striped," I said.

"When you have kids, striped is a good thing to be."

"Stripes are boring," I said.

"No. Stripes are a true thing. Straight and strong, with a clear line ahead. You can count on them. Sometimes, they're the only things you can count on."

I felt good hearing that. "You're right. Stripes *are* good. And I like that, having a clear line ahead. I'm very much a person who wants to know what's coming."

"And what's ahead for you?"

"We're here for the summer," I told him. "My children made the decision. They liked it here."

"How could they not? The river, the farm, all this fresh air and open space to breath in?"

"My kids grew up loving malls and video games. All this open space is not necessarily a big draw."

"What do you think did it, then?"

I thought. "I think they each saw someplace at RiverCliffe where they could fit in. It's been a rough few years for them. I got divorced, moved...I think they saw something here that could be just theirs."

"And you? Have you found something just yours?"

"Maybe." Just the day before I'd been so pleased to be thinking about dinner out with Scott. That was something just mine. So was my job behind my cramped desk, all those numbers, adding up so neatly. "Yes. I'm finding my place. I'm getting to know people, and that's important too. I don't make friends too easily, I never have, but I think there are folks who treat me like I'm part of the family, and that feels good."

"I never had too much luck making friends either," he said, a wistful note in his voice. "I think that comes from having my daddy run off. It's hard to trust, you know?"

I stared at him. "Yes, as a matter of fact, I do." Trust—in my own abilities, in people around me, in what the universe might throw at me — I'd never had that. I had spent years on the edge of my seat, waiting to take off and run. Something else I owed to Billy Newsome. "I never knew my father."

"Well, I knew mine," Caleb said, a hard edge in his voice. "He was a son-of-a-bitch drunk." He stopped, shrugged, and looked apologetic. "That was a very long time ago."

I didn't know what to say, so we sat in silence. It was a nice, warm silence, the kind that happens between two people who have nothing to prove to each other.

Finally, I stood. "I should help with breakfast."

He nodded and stretched his legs out in front of him. "I'll just sit here awhile longer. Don't forget your book."

I picked up the diary and walked away, looking back over my shoulder at his solitary figure, sitting still and peaceful in the sunlight. By the time I crossed through the low stone wall, he was gone.

Woodmark and Sons was in a modern-looking building right off the main street in New Hyde Park. Serena had told me that Garth would expect me between nine and ten on Monday morning. My kids declined to come with me, surprise, surprise.

I'd attended lots of funerals, mostly because my mother had considered going to a funeral as an acceptable form of recreation. Having no family of her own, even the slightest of acquaintances took on importance to her and, upon passing, received her complete attention. I was the only kid in the eighth grade to have a different black dress for each of the four seasons. But I had never met a funeral director quite like Garth Woodmark. He was short, very round, and wore a bad black toupee. He was also quite cheerful, even, dare I say it? Bubbly? Whatever the word, he had none of the seriousness and gravity of most funeral directors I'd come across.

"Well, now, Risa. Can I call you Risa? So sorry about Cathy's passing." We were in his office, thickly carpeted, heavily draped, with somber, dark furniture. He seemed totally out of place. "She was a lovely woman and a real pillar of the community. A pillar." He folded his hands in front of him. "What can I tell you about Woodmark and Sons, and our long and, may I say, satisfying relationship with River-Cliffe House?"

"Well, I guess I'm curious about the...residents?" Winston and Bernie rambling on about ghosts was one thing. After all, they were part of RiverCliffe, and may have been brainwashed early on to the whole idea that Cliffe women could speak to the dead. With Garth Woodmark, I was counting on a...professional opinion.

"Of course you are." He clapped his hands together. "After all, you could run into one of them at any time, am I right? Best to be prepared."

Oh dear. Him too?

"So," I began, "you've heard about the Cliffe women..."

"Of course! After all, my family has been doing business with your family for *quite* a while, eh? I always envied Cathy, you know. Imagine, being able to have a conversation with someone who lived a hundred years ago!"

"And you didn't find it...creepy?"

"Oh, my goodness! Of course not! Now, I have a list here of all the folks we've interred there, since 1937. Quite a lot of names! Quite a lot of souls." He opened a manila file, looked at it briefly, then turned it so that I could see the long and neatly printed out list of names.

I picked it up and scanned the names, looking for a Caleb.

"You'll notice, of course, that Cathy's sons are *not* there," he said. He dropped his voice. "She told me she didn't have anything to talk to them about while they was alive, and certainly didn't want to hear from them once they were dead!"

"Mr. Woodmark—"

"Garth! Please, why, we're practically family." More family? I was beginning to think that too much family was as bad as none at all. Especially since mine now seemed to include every Cliffe buried in RiverCliffe Memorial Park since the late 1700's.

"Yes. Well, Garth, I'm a bit thrown by your casual acceptance of the idea that the living can just…talk to the dead. Because I'm having a pretty hard time with it."

He smiled at me kindly. "Risa, I've been around dead people practically all my life. I started working here with my father when I was not even ten years old. There are bodies, and there are souls. I believe that, as strongly as I believe in the sun and gravity and the rising tides of the oceans. I know exactly what to do with the body, because it is a cold and static thing that can be both seen and touched. But the soul, well, that is a thing of the ether, of the fourth dimension, beyond the sixth sense. But that doesn't make it any less real. It just makes it something invisible to the eyes and ears of most of us. But to those who can reach beyond, into that other sense, why, how amazing must that be!"

I sat back. "I wouldn't know."

He smiled. "But you will. Now, is there someone in particular that you're looking for?"

I looked down at the list. "Yes. But I don't see him here."

'That doesn't mean much, I'm afraid. The Cliffe family kept records of who they buried before we took over, but, they let anyone in. Meaning, lots of nameless, lost folks who died around these parts were laid to rest there, because no one else would bury them without payment. The RiverCliffe Memorial Park, on the other hand, welcomed all, even those folks who could not pay their way in."

I closed the file. "That was very nice of them."

"They were, and still are, a kind and generous family." He smiled at me brightly, and I had to smile back.

"How are the Woodmarks about those sorts of folks?" I asked.

"We have never turned away anyone who the Cliffe family has asked us to inter. I can think of at least three nameless souls that we were asked to care for. It is an honor to serve the dead, you know. No matter who they are."

I decided then and there I would want Garth to take care of any and all of my family members. "Garth, it's good to know that my cemetery is in the hands of someone like you." I stood and held out my hand. "This has been a real pleasure."

He stood and took my hand in both of his. "Yes, it certainly has been. A pleasure."

I tucked the folder under my arm and followed him through the dim lobby and out into the bright morning air.

I got in my car and drove, but away from RiverCliffe, farther down the highway until I found a little cafe, where I sat and had a cup of coffee and a late breakfast. I opened the folder and looked at the names.

Garth had been right. No Newsomes were listed. I ate my scrambled eggs, which were almost as good as Serena's, but the toast was a disappointment. I was getting spoiled by her cooking.

I turned to the second page. I tried to remember some of the names in Dimity's diary, but imagined they had all moved on before Woodmark had taken over.

I almost missed it. There, at the bottom of the page, three John Does were mentioned.

The first was in 1946, a soldier found hanging in the bus depot in Poughkeepsie. He had removed his dog tags, and had no wallet or identifying papers on him. A janitor had found him, and the county sheriff's department had him for three months, waiting for someone to claim the body. When no one did, Cathy's mother, Bea, took the soldier and had him buried in RiverCliffe Memorial Park.

In 1956, the year my mother was born, a body washed up on the bank across the river from RiverCliffe House. Once again, after a month, Bea stepped up.

And finally, on December 18th, 1975, a biker, coming down the mountain from the Bear Claw, skidded on the ice, went off the road, and was killed. The bike burst into flames, and the body was burned beyond recognition. One month later, yep, Cathy took the body laid it to rest in RiverCliffe Memorial Park.

A biker.

In 1975.

I let my eggs grow cold and my coffee stale and bitter before I roused myself enough for the ride back home.

After dinner, I walked over to Martha and Bernie's house. They were both on the porch, each with a beer, a bowl of chips between them. Martha stood as soon as she saw me coming up the path.

"Let me get you a beer," she called, and hurried into the house. By the time I'd climbed the steps and sat in one of the rockers, she was back, and handed me an icy cold bottle.

I wasn't a big beer drinker, but boy, that tasted good going down. "Thanks. This is just what I needed."

Bernie grinned. "Ain't nothin' like a cold one after a hot day's work. How those kids of yours?"

"They're good. Listen, were either of you here in 1975?"

Bernie nodded. "We both were. Clay was still alive, he and Martha were living here, right in this house. I was working the farm, so I still lived with my family. What happened in 1975? That was a bit before you were born, no?"

I nodded. "Yes. A biker was buried here." Maybe a biker named Caleb. Hopefully not, because if it was him, then I was, in fact, one of those Cliffe women who spoke to ghosts, and I wasn't sure I was ready for that.

Martha nodded slowly. "It was right before Christmas, and it had gotten really cold. He skid comin' down the mountain. Burned to a crisp. Cathy had him buried on the top on the hill there." She nodded to the graveyard, lying on the other side of the house and barns.

"They never knew who he was?" I was trying to keep my voice casual, but Bernie was a sharp old bird.

"Is this your fella?" she asked, eyes twinkling. "I knew it."

"What?" Martha asked.

"Little Risa here met a gentleman in the graveyard. Thought he was something enough to ask about. Guess he was a ghost after all, eh?"

"Listen, Bernie, I don't know who he is. I just...well, I sat with Garth Woodmark today— "

Martha let out a whoop. "I bet that was a real treat," she cackled.

I had to grin. "Yeah. It sure was. But he gave me a list, of all the... interred, and there were three John Does, and I was curious, that's all."

Martha twisted her mouth, thinking. "Well, the Claw was being run by Stevie Guthrie back then. He's across the river in Kingston now, in a nursing home. He's blind as a bat, but I hear he still's sharp as he ever was."

" 'Course, he wasn't too sharp to begin with," Bernie said. "But he might remember, 'cause it was a big deal, that poor man dyin', coming down the mountain like that." She took a long drink of beer and burped loudly. "Scott been around to chat?" she said, looking sideways at me.

"Why, yes, Bernie, as a matter of fact, he dropped by Saturday morning. For coffee."

"Why, that's nice," Martha sighed.

"What else?" Bernie asked slyly.

I drank slowly and licked my lips deliberately before answering. "He mentioned a possible date." I felt the smile on my lips. I remembered his bright eyes, and the strength of his shoulders, and I found myself wanting to find out more.

She grinned, threw back her head, and let out a little shriek of laughter. "Good for Scott. He's been in need of a good woman. I sure hope you two hit it off. Serena might have been his passion, but a man needs steady and calm, someone to count on, and that little girl was never that."

"She was his passion?" Really? That's what *I* wanted to be. Someone's passion.

Bernie nodded. "Oh yes. My goodness, the minute he laid eyes on her, he was gone. He chased that girl all over this valley. She told him the truth, I'll give her that. She loved him, but not the way he loved her, and she knew she'd disappoint him. Scott didn't listen, of course." She snorted. "Men. Never do. She broke his heart." She looked at me critically. "You and he would make a good match, I think."

"Oh? So I guess I'm the calm and steady type?"

Martha reached out with her foot to knock Bernie's ankle. "Don't listen to this old bitch, she's just jealous. If she'd been any younger, she'd have made a run at him herself. 'Course, by then she figured out she really didn't like men all that much, after bein' with me, how many years?"

Bernie snorted. "Too many. Scott's a good one. If he comes knocking, open that door, little girl."

"Scott," Martha said dryly," has a Lancelot complex. Just know that. He'll try to make everything better. He lives for the rescue. 'Course, some women like that. Serena didn't."

Bernie shook her head. "You're too hard on him, Martha. He's just a naturally good and caring man is all." She finished her beer and gave me a hard look. "And don't put him off for no dead biker."

"Caleb," I said loudly and distinctly, "is not a dead biker."

"Yeah? Better check with Stevie first."

I shook my head and was thankful when the conversation shifted to more general things. I finished my beer and by the time I got back to my little corner of RiverCliffe House, Kira and Kevin were asleep in front of the television, and Lily was curled up, reading in a corner of the couch.

"Whatcha got?" I asked as I came in.

She held it up and I recognized it immediately as Dimity's diary. "I found it on the back of the couch," Lily said. "She says her granddaughter met her husband. But her husband was dead." She looked at me steadily. "Mom, can we really talk to ghosts?"

"Well, honey, so far the only person I've talked to in the graveyard was a cool biker wearing a Grateful Dead shirt," I said truthfully. "Does that sound like a ghost to you?"

She shook her head. "No, but have you read any of these?"

I sat next to her. "Yes."

"Do you believe them?"

I had to think about that. "Yes, I think I do." Her eyes widened, and I hurried on. "Lily, listen to me. There are so many things in this world we don't understand, and what lies beyond what we can hear and see is a huge mystery. You know that Grandma has always believed in a spirit world, right?"

She nodded, her eyes huge.

"Well, maybe there is something to that." I picked up the diary, running my hands over the smooth leather. "The women of River-Cliffe also believed. That was *their* truth. I'm trying to keep an open mind. You should too. If you're really that curious, go on over to the cemetery and find out."

Lily moved her shoulders, as though easing an ache. "I don't want to know. The whole thing is stupid." She stood up suddenly. "When are we seeing Daddy?"

"Ah…" That threw me. "I'll call him again. Tomorrow. Remind me."

She practically ran upstairs. I roused Kira and Kevin, herded them upstairs to sleep, and went to bed.

Scott and I had dinner across the river, in a quiet little restaurant with less than twenty tables where, apparently, there was no menu. You got fed what the chef felt like cooking, Scott explained. It was all farm-to-table, and all amazingly delicious. Scott was known there, and not just as the sheriff. Apparently he was a regular.

I had spent twenty minutes on my hair, ten on makeup, and tried on four different outfits in preparation for this date. I was ready fifteen minutes before he picked me up, and was forced to sit while my three children tried, unsuccessfully, not to laugh at me. Now that we were finally seated, I began to relax. He was a easy-going man who had mastered the art of small talk, so during the ride over and the first course (a spring roll made of shredded duck with mushrooms and leeks) conversation was all about the weather, the river, and the current political climate. Luckily, he and I were pretty much on the same side of the fence as far as politics went, or it could have gotten ugly.

After the third bite of spring roll and my fifth sip of wine, I slid from the general to the personal.

"Have you always been a foodie, or was that Serena's influence?"

He raised an eyebrow and thought. "Always a foodie. In fact, with the C.I.A. so close, I almost became a chef. My mother is a good cook, and I guess that helped. She was always leaving her cookbooks around, and since I'd read anything as a kid, I would occasionally sit back and read me a bit of Alice Waters."

"Well, I admire a man who appreciates good food. My ex thought Applebee's was a gourmet experience."

"I also like foreign films, 60's folk rock and walking on the beach at sunset," he said, grinning.

I help up my wineglass. "Sold! Where do I sign?"

He sat back as plates were exchanged. A small salad, with so many shades of green and yellow and red that it could have been an abstract painting. "How are you liking us so far?" he asked.

"Well, it's good to have something to do every day. I'm giving Winston a free rein to keep on doing what he's always done, and I'm sticking to the numbers, the details—it all makes my slightly OCD micro-manage-it-all brain happy. So far, my kids are still in the honeymoon phase of their summer break, so no complaints of extreme boredom or too much work to do—it could go either way. I'm not staring at the ceiling all night worrying about how I'm going to pay for my healthcare. And the scenery is spectacular." I drained my wine glass, thought a moment, then signaled the waiter for more. "Of course, we've only been here a few weeks, not long enough for the kids to mutiny, the economy to fail and bankrupt me, or one of the guests falling, suing me, and taking everything I've got."

He nodded. "I see. And are you always this optimistic?"

"I was raised by a single mom," I explained. "Italian. She lectured me daily on the cruel world, and how God may love you, but that doesn't mean you'll have a nice life. She struggled for a lot of years, doing for me. To this day, she saves coupons for disposable diapers, because you never know when disaster may strike, and you'll need to take them apart to stanch the blood flow. She made a big impression."

"I see."

"Then my husband left me, and I had to salvage what he left behind, which wasn't much. I went from being an affluent soccer mom to living in a basement with three kids and one bathroom, driving a used minivan. So, I look at my life, count my blessings, and stay prepared for the worst." I shrugged. "Even now, with such a windfall, I still wait for the phone call in the night that overturns everything." I saw the expression on his face change slightly, and held up my hand, palm out, as to stop the pity I could see rising in his eyes. "I love my kids. I've got my heath. And my life is really fine right now. It's good."

He shook his head. "I was raised by a loving couple who are still married, had two brothers and a sister, a dog, a few cats, we had horses...pretty storybook. Dad was an engineer and mom taught, so we had money enough for whatever we needed, plus some spectacular family vacations. I count my blessings, too. But I guess I always think about the next good thing that's bound to happen in my life."

"But you're a cop," I said. "You see the worst in people all the time."

He nodded. "That's true. I've held babies that have died because their crack-addicted mothers just forgot they were there. I've rescued tortured animals, talked down jumpers off a few bridges, and arrested men who've raped their ten-year-old daughters. But I've also seen the resilience of the human spirit, and the innate goodness in people. Sure, there is evil in the world. But there is also generosity and kindness. That's what I hold on to." He shrugged. "I have to, to do my job. Otherwise, I'd go home every night and drink myself blind."

I ran my fingers up and down the stem of my wine glass. Scott was a good man, a person of strength and integrity. Here was something real, I thought. Here was something I hadn't known before.

The main course was a small skirt steak, perfectly cooked, and tiny potatoes, shiny and tender and tossed with herb butter.

"You obviously eat here all the time," I said when I stopped chewing enough to come up for breath. "Why aren't you big as a cow?"

"I run," he said.

"Oh no, you're not one of those people, are you?" I'd never been very good at flirting, and here I was, joking and teasing an intelligent, attractive man who was flirting right back. "Please tell me you hate it."

"I do," he said at once. "Every mile of it. And each time I finish, I swear I'm never going to do it again."

"Liar," I said coolly.

He grinned. "Maybe. But at least I don't smile while I run."

"No one smiles when they run," I said, wanting to keep up the conversation. "You all look miserable and tired and ready to punch someone in the face."

He laughed. "Actually, sometimes I do feel like that. But being a sheriff and all…"

I nodded. "Yeah. Point taken."

"So I gather you're not one of those gym rats?"

I shuddered. "Please. To change clothes and go somewhere just to *sweat*? I never did get that." I pointed my fork at him. "I walk."

He laughed. "And I'm sure you're very good at it."

"As a matter of fact, yes."

The empty plates were whisked away. A small plate with a few wedges of cheese and plain crackers appeared.

Scott sat up. "See this on the end? That's Daniel's cheese. It's soft and sweet, and tastes just like fresh-mown grass smells."

It sounded so improbable, but he was right. It was the best cheese I'd ever eaten.

"I haven't paid much attention to the farming side of things," I said. "I probably should. Daniel is a genius."

"Yes, he is. He's also a savvy businessman. You've got good people there. Winston is a treasure. The man loves that place. And Martha and Bernie have a small goldmine in their herb business."

"You know an awful lot about RiverCliffe."

He shrugged. "Cathy liked me. She was a quiet and reserved woman, but she trusted me. We spent long nights, drinking good bourbon and talking about life."

I looked at him across the table. He would be a good man to do that with, I thought. Drink and talk. Then something else tugged at the corner of my brain. The stretch of the fabric of his shirt across those shoulders, and the faint fuzz of dark chest hair peeking out from the vee of his button down shirt seemed to reach out to me, like a small hand, fingers curling, urging me closer.

I hadn't had sex in a long time, and, on a purely primal level, I enjoyed sex. I hadn't been a virgin when I married Ed, but he, older and much more experienced than the other partners I'd been with, had been a careful and thorough teacher. Finally there was nothing left to learn from him, and at that point sex became a big part of my marriage, maybe the best part, because I felt like I was doing every-thing right, and was, at last, an equal.

A thought came, quick and very clear. I wonder what I could learn from Scott? I drank off my wine and signaled the waiter again.

"Be careful," Scott said with a teasing smile. "If you drink too much, I might take advantage of you."

"If I drink too much I might let you," I shot back.

Dessert was a slice of lemon cake, not frosted, surrounded by fresh berries and silky whipped cream. I ate in complete silence, savoring every bite. When I was done I sighed from pure bliss. "That was just about the best meal I've had in, like, years."

"Yeah, Cyrus does a good job. He's particular as hell, and pretty much refuses to do anything that would increase his business beyond the locals and a few well-informed tourists. He says it's all about the creative process."

"The creative process is a concept that is totally beyond me. I like things planned out, lined up, and very neatly done. The creative process sounds…messy. And spontaneous. Not me at all. But I'm very appreciative of artistic types. Especially those who can cook like this."

"As a point of information," Scott said. "I make a mean scrambled egg."

"I'm not sure that brings you up to this level of expertise, but I'll keep that in mind."

Was this a soft sell? Because I had to admit, it was working.

I met Ed while I was attending Brooklyn College. I had dated, slept around a bit, and even had a semi-serious boyfriend until that point. Ed was my Marketing 101 instructor. I should have been a bit more careful about him, as he was just divorcing wife number two, but when an older, accomplished man tells you that he loves you, and that he'd never cared about his other wives like he cared about you, you believed him. Especially if you've never had a father and had a real older-man complex.

So we were married, and he quit teaching and started up his own marketing firm, and did very well. He was a fairly good husband and father right up until he left, moving me into the wife number three slot.

So I hadn't had a whole lot of experience with men, compared with some other women my age. I had not even thought about dating or looking for a relationship until just now. Here was a seriously datable man, obviously making a pitch. And from where I was sitting, in an admittedly wine-induced haze of good feeling, he seemed just about right.

I firmly pushed away my glass of wine and pointed my finger at him. "You're a very nice man, Scott Van Wyke."

He smiled. "Why, thank you, Risa."

"And I've had kind of a lot of wine."

"I hadn't noticed."

I sat back. "Good. I'm not a very good drunk. My friend Beth can really put away the vodka, but with me, even just a little wine…"

"Changes your voice?" Scott suggested. "Just a little?"

"I'm slurring my words? Oh, God…"

"No." He reached over and grabbed my hand, patting it reassuringly. "Not at all. But your tone has changed. You're sounding... happier, I guess."

"Maybe that has nothing to do with the wine?"

He squeezed my hand. "That would be just grand."

Grand. What kind of man said "grand" anymore? Obviously, my kind of man.

He paid the check and we walked outside and spent a few quiet minutes watching the river. There was moonlight, and the sound of birds, and when he kissed me, he tasted like wine and berries and promises to keep.

CHAPTER 6

I had a dream that night about Caleb.

We were in the cemetery, and the sun was low in the sky, and I felt at peace with myself, relaxed and happy, and Caleb was sitting beside me on the bench —our bench—and I realized that he was the reason for my feelings. I reached out and grabbed his hand, and felt a jolt again, a warm, tingling feeling that went up my arm and spread like sweet honey to my soul. This was what happiness felt like, I thought. He was a friend. Maybe, in time, he would be more than a friend. But for now, for that moment, it was enough.

I stood and tugged at his hand. I wanted to go down to the river, to stand by the shore and feel the water lap at my feet. He followed me, laughing, and when we got to the end of the long drive down at the edge of the highway, he stopped and shook his head. I tugged at his hand again, but he let go.

"I can't, Risa," he said sadly.

"But I want to see the river," I argued.

He took a deep breath. "So do I, but this is as close as I will ever get, Risa. From here you have to go alone."

I felt a pinprick of anger then, just like when I was a kid, and told, no, you can't have that, and I'd start to argue…

"Mom."

I jolted up in bed. The sun was shining and Kevin was standing beside me. "Should I let you sleep? It's late."

I glanced at the clock beside my bed. Almost eight. Yes, it was late. I glanced around. I was wearing my tattered sleep shirt. My clothes from last night were in a heap on the floor. I sat up and reached down, grabbing the linen shirt I'd worn the night before. I stared at it, confused.

I had dinner with Scott. We'd kissed by the river. Then he'd brought me home. Then I dreamed about Caleb. It was an important dream, I knew. I remembered the feeling of happiness. But I also remembered that he could not leave, could not go beyond the end of the drive.

He couldn't leave the cemetery.

"I'm up, honey. Thanks. I've got something to do, okay? Just watch your sister."

I pushed him out of my room, pulled on clothes from last night, and practically ran out of the house to the cemetery. I needed to talk to Caleb.

Mornings were always peaceful at RiverCliffe, with lots of birds singing and the farm animal noises at top volume. Crossing into the cemetery, however, was like walking through a curtain—the sounds were softer, muffled, and even the sunlight was less intense, as though seen through a gauze curtain.

"Caleb!" I called. I looked around. Why on earth would he be in the graveyard? Unless, of course, he did live there.

"Risa? Hey, you're here pretty early."

He was beside me, and I reached out and touched the denim of his jacket. It felt just the way a denim jacket was supposed to feel. So maybe he was real after all. I allowed myself a small sigh of relief.

"I dreamt about you last night," I said.

He grinned. "Well, I'm flattered." There was a twinkle in his eye. "Was I any good?"

I had to laugh. "Not that kind of dream."

He managed to look incredibly disappointed. "Damn, why does that never happen with women I meet?"

I laughed again. "Sorry. But listen…we were here, sitting on our bench, and I wanted to go down to the river."

He sighed and looked past me, down to the water. "I love me a good river."

"But you couldn't come with me."

He shook his head. "No, I couldn't."

I heard the slow tick of time as I formed my words. "Because you're a ghost."

He nodded. "Yes."

Something inside clicked, very quietly. Everything he had said to me suddenly meant something entirely different.

Okay. I just had to pull up my big girl panties and admit that ghosts did exist and I could speak to them. Winston hadn't been crazy. Neither had Bernie. Garth Woodmark had been right.

So had my mother.

This was real. This was now a part of who I was.

He was watching me carefully. "You okay? Sometimes, it's a real shock to folks."

"Oh? A shock? Imagine." I kept looking at his face, the crinkles around his eyes, the half-smile on his lips. "My mother had high hopes for us."

"What?"

"She is on a perpetual search for my next husband. When I mentioned to her that I'd met you, she started seeing wedding cakes."

He was fighting a smile. "I'm not really good husband material."

"I see that now. She's going to be very disappointed. I need to sit down." I took a few steps to the stone bench and sat, looking down at my hands. "I always thought this was possible, you know. I just didn't believe it would happen to *me*."

He sat beside me. "We're not very scary."

"No," I agreed. "You're not scary at all. I think maybe I'd believe this more if you were. You're so real. That's what's hard. It might be easier if you were, I don't know, transparent?"

He lifted his shoulders, "Sorry." He let them drop.

'No, don't be sorry, it's just that I think I need some time to digest this."

"That makes sense."

I stared at the river. "You're easy to talk to."

"Thank you."

"I feel like we're connected somehow. Like you know me already."

He shook his head. "I feel the same, but there's no rhyme or reason to it. Maybe we were together in another life?"

My shoulders slumped. "Oh, God, is that a real thing too?"

He half-smiled. "I don't know. Honest. I've been here for almost fifty years. And I've been beyond here. It's downright amazing the things I don't know."

I looked around me, taking in the quiet green meadow, marked with stones of varying heights. "So, where is everybody else?"

"They're here."

"Will I see them?"

"In time."

"Why did I see you first?"

He shook his head. "That's one of the many things I don't know."

"If I want to talk to you again, you'll still be here?"

"Risa, I got nowhere else to go."

I walked away, past the quiet gravestones and into the dark coolness of the long line of oaks, through the low stone wall and back to the land of the living.

I called Beth Calder.

She was the closest thing I had to a BFF. We'd met in college, and had become good friends. We had kept in touch through the years, and not just the Christmas card kind of in touch. We called and met when we could, and spent at least one weekend a year together, someplace fun, where we could drink and eat and talk and be ourselves. She'd raised a daughter by herself, and had been great at it, right up to the day a drunk driver hit the two of them head-on. Beth spent six weeks in the hospital, got out, buried Erin, and then went back to work. She was one of the most resilient people I'd ever known.

She was the godmother to all my kids. Because I hadn't cared about that sort of thing, she and my mother had formed some kind of unholy alliance, and had worked it all out. I was grateful that she and my mother were so concerned about the spiritual lives of my children. Besides, I was glad of anything that helped fill the incredible void that had opened up in her life.

I called her on her cell phone and went straight to voicemail. I had spoken to her right after I decided to come up for the summer, but had not filled her in on all that I'd learned about my father and my new-found family. I was brief. "You have to come here. I've met a… man. And another man, and it's really complicated. Plus, I've learned stuff about my father." I clicked off the phone and stared at it. Then I took a shower, got dressed and pretended this was like any other day.

Winston didn't raise an eyebrow when I slipped into the office an hour later than usual. He was still sitting in the big desk, and I was fine with that. It made him happy and discouraged me from trying to settle in too deeply. Normally, I would have rearranged the desk, re-organized files, and changed everything until it was exactly like I wanted. Sitting in a smaller space, with less options, kept me from doing that. It made me uncomfortable, but I kept telling myself it was only for the summer.

"This afternoon Larry from the insurance company will be here. Did you see my note?" he asked.

I always saw his notes. They were written on hot-pink three-by-five note cards and taped to my computer screen. Not seeing them would involve total blindness.

"Yes, I saw. You want me to meet with him? Just routine, I guess?"

He nodded. "Yes. He wants to introduce himself, explain things, and probably check you out. He's notorious for hitting on women. This entire side of the river has the word out on him."

I made a face. "Whatever."

"But I don't suppose he'd have any luck with you. I mean, now that Scott's in the picture."

"We had a very nice dinner," I told him, "And a very nice good-night kiss." I felt a smile start. It had been a *very* nice kiss, and I was looking forward to quite a few more.

He let out an exaggerated sigh. "And here I'd been hoping for some really hot sex."

My cell phone rang. It was Beth. I stood abruptly and headed for the door. "I need to take this," I called over my shoulder.

I stood in the middle of the lobby. I could not think of any place to go where I could have a quiet conversation. I answered. "Beth? Thank God. Listen, I'm looking for a place I can have a little privacy, so you talk first."

"Jesus, Risa, really? Okay. I can come down and see you, but not this weekend. It's the 4th, and I have stuff going on. And the next weekend is bad 'cause I have depositions first thing Monday morning. But the week after? I can get there on Friday and stay until Tuesday afternoon. Sound good?"

The dining room was still crowded, as was the great room. The porch had a couple sitting and rocking, and they waved me over. I held up my phone and shook my head at them regretfully, walking down the steps. "That's perfect. We're probably full up, but you can stay with me. Do you mind?"

"Not at all, as long as I can do some rowing. You have canoes and kayaks, right?"

"I forget you actually like that outdoor stuff. Yes, we have both." I headed toward Daniel's barn, but heard Kira and Haley singing together, so I veered off in the direction of Bernie's drying shed.

"What about Billy?" Beth asked. She always called him that, probably because of all the conversations she'd had with my mother. She referred to him casually, like someone she'd known slightly in the past.

"Well, he told people here about us, about me and mom." The drying shed was cool and, more important, empty. "He had pictures of us and everything."

"So, he wasn't such a bad guy?"

"Yes, he was. He lied to Mom. We always thought his mother had been dead for years, and she'd been living just a few hours away from us. He also told Mom that we wouldn't be welcome here."

"But they were your family," she said. "Why didn't his mother come after *you*?"

"Because he lied to her too. And then there's the whole mess with the fake name."

"Fake name? What are you talking about?"

"I'm talking about my father, the snake. After his mother died, he hung around and tried to cash in. It took the sheriff to chase him off, but word on the street is he'll be back."

"See! You'll finally get to meet him."

"Beth, I love you, but your Pollyanna, gee-ain't-life-grand attitude can be a little hard to take sometimes. I don't want to meet him."

"Of course you do. I remember you spending hours in the library, entering his name in all of its possible mutations, just trying to find something about him. In fact, finding Billy was your main preoccupation in college, right after sex and white wine."

"But now I know that he wasn't just a wayward con man who just left us. He deliberately sabotaged any chance mom and I had of connecting with his family, and he did the same to them. He was evil. No, not evil, but… mean. It was a mean thing he did."

I heard her sigh. "Maybe that's an even better reason to finally meet him, you know? To tell him how much he hurt you? And maybe have him apologize?"

I sighed and looked around the drying shed. It was quiet, cool against the summer sun, and smelled of lavender. If I did meet him, is that what I'd do? Pour out my heart and hope that he'd tell me how sorry he was? "I hate you, Beth Calder, and never want to see you again."

"Yes, until I get there in two weeks. Now, what about these men? Two? How did you manage to find two? What did you always say?"

"I know. All of the good ones are married or gay. Or dead."

"What?"

"Never mind. I told you, it's complicated. I'm just glad you're coming. I really need to talk all of this new information out with someone, and try to make sense of it all."

"What about Marcie?"

My mother and I had talked several times in the days I first came up here, but I could see us heading back to the ritual Sunday-morning briefing that we'd established once I'd married and moved out of the house. "I can't talk to Mom about my father. She has also found new and amazing things to be angry with him about. Get this—she never divorced him. They're still married. But she didn't want me up for the summer because I'd be around 'his people.'" I ran my fingers through my hair. "And you know her, if I tell her I met a man, she'll start picking out centerpieces. If I tell her about two, she'll send a priest."

Beth laughed. "You're right. Okay, babe, gotta go. Right now I'm tight between meetings, which isn't nearly as much fun as it sounds. But I'll be there in two weeks. Warn the kids. I've got stuff."

"You spoil them."

"It's my job."

I clicked off the phone and closed my eyes. I could hear the sounds from the barnyard. I never stopped delighting in the clucks of the chickens. It was a sweet and comforting sound. I opened my eyes and Martha was standing in front of me, so close I probably could have touched her if I stuck out my tongue.

"I'm not going to make a 'walks-silent-as-an-Indian' joke, but I could," I told her.

She grinned. "All of the good ones are dead?"

"Martha, it's rude to eavesdrop."

"You happen to be standing in the middle of my office."

"Yes, I guess you're right there." And with, I thought, a considerable amount of dignity, I walked back to the inn.

I went back to the office and put on my best, hey, I'm the boss face, and turned off my desktop.

"I'm going to spend some time at the pool," I told Winston.

He lifted an eyebrow. "When Larry gets here, should I send him out to see you?"

Damn. No, I did not want Larry, the horny insurance guy, to sit next to me while I sat in my bathing suit. Where else could I go where I could quietly sit and read Elsbeth's diaries?

"Ah, never mind. I'll just be back at my place. I just need to...I need a little me time. Call me when he shows up, okay?"

Winston nodded. There was no significant look, an "a-ha, you're finally getting it" look, or a "goofing off already" look. There wasn't even a "whatever" look. Winston obviously had no interest at all in my motivation.

Good. Because explaining would have exhausted me. Even though Winston had been the first person to mention my unusual gift, I was not about to tell him that he'd been right, and that I had just received verification from a very reliable source. I needed to find out as much as I could from all the other women who'd been so accepting of a legacy that I was just now struggling to understand.

I went back into my little part of RiverCliffe, and dug through the diaries. Then, because I didn't really want to start something that would probably shake me up even further, I arranged them all on one whole bookshelf, moving down my Nora Roberts and Martha George mysteries. Cathy had done a great job when she had them rebound. Each volume was a different color, shaded faithfully to the color wheel, with the name of the author and the relevant dates on the spine. Lined up, in chronological order, they all looked like a rainbow on my shelf. I could have sat and looked at them all day. Instead, I took down the first one by Elsbeth Cliffe Hawkins and began to read.

Her first entry was as a ten-year-old, and she had already been visiting with her mother for over five years. It was Gemina who asked her to start writing down what was said, and Elsbeth kept it up faithfully until her own death at fifty-six. Some parts I skimmed through, some sections I skipped completely. Yes, I know. Here was a hand-written account of a life lived in a time and place I could not even imagine, and I swore that, at some point, I would go back and read every word. But right now, I just wanted to read about who Elsbeth spoke to, and how they interacted. I wanted to know what—and who —to expect the next time I set foot in the cemetery. And yes, I would set foot in there again. I may have been freaked out, but I was even more curious about what would happen next.

Thank God I didn't have to squint and try to decipher the hand-written diary. Although the original, hand-written diary was reproduced faithfully, there was also a transcribed version in regular print. Reading lines like "I was fearful of meeting again our faithful servant Raoul, as his death had been prolonged and bloodee, but he appeared to me as whole and cleansed," seemed less surreal as a conventional line of New Times Roman type.

Elsbeth was very careful in her descriptions of her mother. Gemina looked and acted as she had in life, warm and solid. At times, Elsbeth confessed to forgetting that her mother was really dead, because when they were together, Gemina was so...real.

I sat there, thinking about how Caleb had felt, until the house phone rang, and Winston announced that Larry had arrived.

Larry looked like every bad date I had in college. He was tall and slender, with wavy hair combed back off a high forehead, squinty eyes, and a moist handshake. His lips were full and very red, and he kept smiling at me even as he explained the dullest and most inane details of the RiverCliffe insurance policies. Every few minutes he'd stop talking and look at me expectantly, as though giving me the opportunity to gasp with pleasure, simper with delight, or coo about what a big, smart man he was.

This all took place in the office, so I had the chance to turn on my computer, pull up a few numbers, point out a few errors, and argue a few points in the fine print.

"I didn't realize you were so knowledgeable," he said, his enthusiasm dampened.

"I'm an accountant," I explained. "I live for the details."

That crushed it. He packed up his laptop and left.

Winston, who sat silently at his desk throughout the meeting, clapped politely. "I could see his erection deflate from here," he said, which served to lift my mood considerably.

I found myself working until Happy Hour, and as I walked through the lobby, a guest waved at me, and I waved back. I glanced around. Usually Winston was there, mingling and keeping the small talk going. He had gone to the barns to talk to Daniel, and was obviously not back yet. I squared my shoulders and walked toward the guest. I could do this, I thought. These people were *my* guests, and I owed it to them to make sure someone was here, making them feel welcome. Besides, the cheese puffs looked yummy, and Lily had been raving about them the day before.

As the wine was uncorked and guests started moving around the great room, Scott came in, in uniform, hat in hand. I went over to him at once, pleased to see him, and suddenly there was a…ping. A little shock that was a simple reaction to him as a man, an attractive man, relaxed and attentive that maybe, just maybe…

"Hey," I said, standing on tiptoe to give him a quick peck on the cheek. "Good to see you. Just cruising, I hope?"

He grinned, and his eyes went around the room. He saw Serena and gave her a nod. She lifted her hand in a quick wave. Then he looked back down at me.

Right. She had been his passion.

"Did you have fun last night?" he asked.

"Dinner with you? Why, yes, sir, I certainly did."

"My regular day off is on Wednesday. How about a quick turn on the river next week?"

He ran, and now suggested a "turn on the river". If he was one of those outdoorsy types who liked activities involving sweat, there could be an issue.

I raised an eyebrow. "Would a turn on the river call for changing clothes and going somewhere just to sweat?"

He chuckled. "Right, right. I'll cross that off my list. Permanently. Have you been to the Culinary Institute? We could spend the afternoon there. It's a fascinating place, and the afternoon snacks are amazing."

Now, that was more like it. A little walking, a little eating. "That sounds perfect."

He ducked his head. "Good. Then I'll pick you up around one?"

"I'll be here." I let my eyes linger on his lips, which looked very soft and full. "I know it's a busy weekend for me, and probably you have lots going on as well, but if you manage to find a few free hours..?" I could not have imagined myself suggesting something like that a few months ago. But I felt drawn to this man, and desire gave me courage.

He grinned. "I will absolutely give you a call."

He turned and left, and my eyes sought out Serena. She was busy pouring coffee for a very attractive couple from Germany.

She saw me watching and walked over, picking up a few empty glasses and a crumpled napkin along the way. "So," she said with a sly smile, "you and Scottie?"

I was in unfamiliar territory here. Was it acceptable to ask her about her ex-husband? Was that a break in the employer-employee code of honor? The woman-to-woman code of honor?

"You have a very nice ex-husband," I said, thinking I'd be fairly safe with a statement like that.

"Yes, I do. He was also a very nice husband-husband, just not for me."

"Oh?"

She shrugged. "Some women love the idea of a big, strong man swooping in and taking care of them, doing every little thing. That's what Scott did, and he was very good at it. But some women like to do things for themselves. That's all I'm saying. He's still a friend, and he still tries to take care of me, but we have gone very separate ways."

"So, I won't be sewing the seeds of discord and dissention if he takes me to the C.I.A for a tour?"

She shook her head. "Nope. Not at all. After all, I have moved on, and I'm pleased as punch that he has too."

"Pleased as punch? Serena, what century were you born in again?"

She laughed. "That's a throw over from my momma. You can take the girl out of the south, but..." She shook her head. "Lily is coming along really well. I want you to know that. Girls that age can be ornery, prickly things, and she's up there with the best of them, I can tell. But she's doin' just fine in my kitchen or, believe me, she wouldn't be there at all."

I breathed a heartfelt sigh. "That's good to hear, Serena. This week I've barely seen her at all, so our arguments are down to a record low. And she does seem happy."

"Trent is a good boy. A good influence. But she's not crazy over him, so that's a good thing."

I allowed myself a sip of wine. "Yes, I imagine inter-office romances can get tricky."

She made a noise, like a dainty snort. "I don't know about that. Me and Daniel are managing just fine."

I raised an eyebrow. "You and Daniel? Really? I didn't know. Damn, what's the point of being the boss around here if I don't get to hear any of the really good stuff?"

She smiled. "You just got here. Give everyone a little time to get to know you and you'll be drowning in gossip." She lifted her head and I followed her look. Lily was carefully carrying a large tray of what looked to be tiny fruit tarts. "Gotta go," she said, and scooted off.

Winston appeared so quickly I thought he might have been hiding behind a chair. His face was flushed, and he was out of breath.

"Sorry, things with Daniel took longer than I expected," he said, then smiled brightly at a guest. "Thanks for stepping in here."

"God, Winston, wear a bell next time! " I watched him as he smoothed his hair and adjusted the collar of his shirt. "To be honest, I haven't done more than smile and nod."

"That's a start. I know you're not too comfortable with the front of the house. Which is something we need to talk about. A big weekend is coming up, and I might need some extra help."

"Of course," I said. I knew how to check in guests, and had learned the floor plan of RiverCliffe House. "Front desk or housekeeping?"

He grinned. "Probably both. The entire staff is on, but every little bit helps." He cleared his throat "You were talking to Serena? Anything about you and our big, brave sheriff?"

"Not a thing. She was just happy he was moving on."

"Yes, well, she certainly has. Did she mention our tall, hippy-dippy cheese man?"

"Finally," I said. "Gossip!"

"What?" he asked, frowning. "Did I say something wrong?"

"Not at all, Winston. You got this? Good." I smiled at my guests and edged my way through lobby and the hell outta Dodge.

Daniel Rugg had three daughters. The oldest. Maya, worked with him making cheese. The middle daughter, Jillian, was around Kevin's age, and her main job seemed to be weeding the garden and keeping an eye on the youngest, Haley. Since Haley and Kira had become best friends in a few short weeks, she spent time watching my daughter as well. I offered to pay her for her time, but she just shook her head shyly. When I spoke to Daniel, he shook his head as well.

"No, that's okay, Risa. She likes being the mom. Let her be."

Daniel's wife, I now knew, had died two years earlier of cancer. It had come on very suddenly, and taken her in just weeks. Daniel moved his family from their house in town to RiverCliffe, at Cathy's insistence, rehabbing the top floor of the long garage that housed the farm equipment. Living over a garage may not sound all that appealing, but rumor had it that the interior was something out of a magazine, as Serena had helped with finishing the space after all the renovations had been done.

As a result of Jillian's watchful eye, I barely saw my youngest daughter during the day. Between the chores in the garden, collecting eggs and swimming in the pool, she was as busy as she was happy. After dinner, she and I would walk to the barns to settle all the animals in for the night.

Kevin, after being at the riverbank all day, came home smiling. He was exhausted from the work, and was usually in bed before ten. Because he could not walk to a grocery store for the chips and other junk food he'd craved in Brooklyn, he'd lost some of the roll around his waist. In fact, in just two weeks his jeans were starting to sag.

Lily was not only learning to cook, she was actually doing the cooking back in our own little kitchen. She and Trent had gone out a few times, but she had also become friendly with a vague, thin girl her own age, Mia, who drifted in and out of our house like a gypsy, in a swirl of long skirts and floaty tops.

The point was that none of my kids had bothered much with the cemetery. I tried to imagine how my two very different daughters would react to meeting someone, then realizing that someone was a ghost. I had played over about three different scenarios, each with a very different result. All of those involving Lily ended badly. But with Kira, I really had no idea how she would react.

But then, of course, I found out.

"Mom!" Kira banged through the back door, shouting. She was running for the door to the main part of the inn when I stopped her.

"I'm here. What's up?"

Her face was flushed and she had a grin that spread from ear to ear. Had she figured out what the lottery really was, and won? Gotten to name another chicken? Climbed up on her favorite pony, Mountain Dew, all by herself?

"Haley and I were in the graveyard just now, and guess what? I saw a ghost! Isn't that really cool?"

I forced myself to keep a benign smile on my face. "What did you say?"

She hurried to sit beside me, taking my hand and looking concerned. "It's okay, Mommy. It wasn't scary at all. In fact, it was really neat, except that Haley got scared and ran off. But she was *so* nice."

"Who?"

"Bea."

I wracked my brain. Wasn't Bea the name of Cathy's mother? "Honey, how do you know she was a ghost and not just a person visiting someone's grave?"

Kira let go of my hand, obviously assured I was not going to collapse entirely. "She told me she was. See, Haley and I were reading the old gravestones, and we were in front of Bea's and Haley said her name out loud, her whole name, Beatrix, and she pronounced the x on the end, and this nice lady appeared and said that you *didn't* pronounce the x, and she said the name different, and I thought Haley could hear her, but she couldn't, and when I said, but this lady is right here, Haley ran away, and then Bea and I had a nice talk."

"I see." I took deep, cleansing breaths. "How...interesting." The good news was I wouldn't have to hold my breath through the next seven weeks waiting for something like this to happen. And Kira seemed perfectly accepting of the whole idea. Good for her. The bad news was, of course, that there was still the other shoe to drop. Lily. Her reaction, I knew, would not be as smooth.

Kira continued, very matter-of-factly. "I told her who I was, but she said she already knew, and that she was my great-great-grandmother."

I counted back in my head. If Cathy was my grandmother, then Bea would be my great grand, so..."That's right."

Kira rolled her eyes. "Of course she was right."

I cleared my throat. "What else did she say?"

"Just how happy everyone was that there were now three Cliffe women around, and how Cathy really worried about that."

Well, at least *someone* was happy.

"Kira, honey, I don't think I want you to play in the graveyard anymore."

Her face fell. "But Mommy! Bea said she couldn't wait for me to visit her again." She tilted her head and slammed me with logic again. "I don't think we should piss off any ghosts."

"Don't use that phrase, please," I said automatically.

"Sorry. I don't think we should get any ghosts angry. Do you?"

"Good point. Okay. If you want to visit, that's fine. But you probably shouldn't talk about this to anyone else. Just me. Because you don't know who would understand what's happening, and who wouldn't. Okay?"

She nodded. "Yeah, Bea said something about that too." She pointed her index finger to her temple and twirled it. "No loony bin for me, Mom." She frowned. "I think we should warn Lily."

"I'll worry about that. Now, how about some dinner? I have Daniel's tomatoes, we could have sandwiches."

Her face lit up. "Lots of mayo?"

God, how I loved that kid. I gave her a quick squeeze. "A ton of mayo. Let's eat."

Kevin had asked to have dinner with Wayne. They had gone fishing, and were going to clean and eat whatever they caught, and I had, of course, said yes. Lily had gone off with Mia earlier and texted me they were having pizza together. So my baby girl and I sat in front of the rippled glass window and ate, chatting about chickens and how she didn't think she wanted to sail boats after all, but was seriously thinking about riding for the U.S. Equestrian team, and how did I feel about getting her a horse that could jump things? I was so grateful for the normality of it all I almost said yes.

She snagged two oatmeal raisin cookies and wrapped them carefully in a paper towel. "I need to find Haley. What should I tell her?"

"Honey, I have a feeling that if she ran to her daddy and told him you were talking to no one at the the cemetery, he probably gave her the whole rundown. I'd just give her a cookie and head for the barn. Don't the chickens need to get put to bed?"

She nodded, stuffed the cookies into the pocket of her shorts, reducing them, I'm sure, to cookie crumbs, and headed out the door. I cleaned up, put away Elsbeth's diary, and went out the back door toward the drying shed.

Martha and Bernie were both there, working at the long table that ran down the center of the building. It was where they sorted and packaged their dried herbs. One wouldn't think there was much money to be made in something so simple as dried oregano, but the local farm stands, markets and restaurants kept them in the black. Martha looked up when she saw me and grinned.

"Any more dead ones?" she cackled.

"I was just wondering if either of you two ladies would come with me to visit that guy who used to run the Bear Claw? Steve Somebody?"

Bernie smacked the tabletop with the palm of her hand. "I knew it. It's that biker feller. He's the one you're askin' about, right?"

Why fight it? "Yes, it's that biker feller. I'm curious. Do you really think this Steve person will remember him?"

Martha placed a clump of rosemary, so fragrant I could smell it from the end of the table, on an old-fashioned scale, marked the label, and wrapped it in brown paper. "I ain't seen him in a while, but Ruthie at church goes every couple of months, and she said he's still pretty sharp. When you thinkin' of goin'?"

"I guess evening would be good?" I ventured.

Bernie shook her head. "Nope. Old folks get real confused as the sun goes down. First thing in the morning is probably best. This weekend is gonna be crazy for you, so next week? Next Wednesday? Wanna go then?"

I thought. "Scott is taking me to the C.I.A on Wednesday afternoon," I told them.

Bernie cackled. "We could go early. Right after breakfast."

"Sure. Your breakfast or mine?"

Bernie grinned. "I won't make you get up at dawn, you're still too much of a city girl. How 'bout nine? Martha, you comin' too?"

Martha nodded solemnly. "Wouldn't want to miss a chance to see Stevie. He was a pistol when he was up at the Claw."

"Okay then, it's a date." I left them, and set out for the barns.

I had to hunt for Daniel. I knew he spent evenings bringing in his stock, and I finally tracked him down in an empty stall, sitting in the straw, scrolling through his phone while the remains of a slice of pie sat in his lap. "Am I interrupting?"

He looked up and broke into a smile. "Just dessert. I had a feeling I'd be seeing you this evening. Haley told me about Kira in the cemetery. Is she okay?"

I nodded, and slid down the rough wall of the stall to sit in the straw beside him. "She thought it was cool. Not freaked out at all. How about Haley?"

He took the plate and remains of his pie off his lap and set them in the straw. "My girls were raised on all things RiverCliffe, so they know about you Cliffe women. Suzie loved talking to Cathy about it." Suzie had been his wife. "Haley *was* freaked, but not scared. Heck, when Kira came by, Haley was asking her all sorts of questions. I think if there hadn't been cookies and chickens involved, they'd be back in that graveyard right now."

I leaned my head back against the wood. "This is very strange, Daniel."

"I'm sure it is."

"Kira says she met Bea, Cathy's mother."

"Cathy had nothing but love for her mother. Bea is probably a great woman."

"She's a great woman's *ghost*, you mean."

He nudged me with his elbow, and I turned to meet his eyes. "All you have to do is stay out, Risa. No one is obligated to take a gift."

"Too late, Daniel. I met one of the, ah, residents already."

His face lit up with interest. "Really? How'd it go?"

"I haven't quite decided."

He stood, held out a hand, and pulled me to my feet. Then he bent to pick up his plate.

"You don't have to go back, you know."

"Yes, actually, I think I do. I'm glad Haley's okay." We walked out of the barn together. "I had some of your cheese last night, by the way. I had dinner across the river at Cyrus' place. It was delicious. I think you and I should go over some sales figures, see what we can do to ramp this operation up."

"The problem with going big is that you risk losing quality control. Small batches are the key to keeping everything just right."

"You're right, I suppose. Scott said you were a genius."

"At making cheese, yes. As for the rest of my life..." He lifted his shoulders then dropped them in an elaborate gesture. "Just trying to keep my head above water."

"With three girls, that's about the best you can hope for," I told him. "See you later."

. . .

I went directly to the cemetery, stood by Gemina's gravestone, and called Caleb's name. I listened, but heard only the birds and the faint sound of cars on the highway below. I walked over to my bench, our bench, and sat, waiting.

"He thinks maybe you and I should get to know each other."

I took a deep breath and twisted around to look. "Hello," I said.

She sat beside me. "Hello, honey. My, but it's a pleasure to talk to you. You look so much like your momma. I sorely wish I'd met her."

Cathy Newsome appeared to me looking like she did in her later pictures, when the tired and lost look had gone from her eyes. She looked strong and confident, and when she smiled, I could see that my father had gotten his smile from her, warm and full of charm.

"Grandma." My voice cracked, and I felt a rush of something so strong and powerful and loving and confusing I couldn't say anything else.

She took my hand in both of hers and patted it, and we just sat there for a while in the sun, two women, bound by a single, wayward man who had managed to bring heartbreak into both of our lives, thereby binding us forever.

I finally cleared my throat. "I wish you'd been able to find me. I needed you. Mom needed you."

She sighed. "I know, dear. I know. I wish that too, more than anything in the world."

"Do you know what he did?" I felt angry tears and I fought back a choking sob. "Do you know how he kept us apart?"

She nodded sadly. "Of course. We know everything here." She put an arm around me and pulled me close. "And once you're here, you'll know everything, too, including how wasteful and empty things like anger and hate really are. But I know you're feeling those things now, and it's okay. Use them, Risa. Use them and get stronger. Use them and learn."

My grandmother felt warm and strong, and smelt of lavender and spring grass. I sobbed like I hadn't since I'd been a child, when I first realized that my father was never going to come home and make my life happier. Finally, I pulled myself away from her and wiped the tears from my eyes with the back of my hand. "Caleb said it was amazing the things he *didn't* know."

She laughed, low and rippling. "Yes, well, it's not like the answers to every question in the universe are laid at our feet. It doesn't work like that. But with the people and places that have been ours, well, the connection still exists. And truths are revealed here that we'd never know otherwise. I know, for example, that Billy had no other children with the other women he'd been with. I'd asked him, but he never gave me a straight answer. But now, I know."

I drew back. "Did you know that Mom never divorced him? She never signed the papers."

She made a little sound of surprise and pleasure. "No? How wonderful. Of course, the three women he married after Marcella may not agree, but I think that's just ...perfect". She dropped her arm from around my shoulders and took my hand in both of hers. "My sons were all such curious creatures. Selfish and mean."

"Martha said that James was the good one."

She squeezed my hand. "Martha didn't know everything about James. If she did, she never would have said that. I really don't know how I managed to raise three such disreputable sons. Although I suppose having a thoroughly disreputable husband had a lot to do with it."

"Did you really hear him calling, turned over in bed, and let him bleed to death?"

She sighed. "I didn't hear him. We'd had a fight, and I'd drunk a bit. I was...passed out." She shook her head. "I was sorry the next morning, I truly was. But, I'll admit, I got over grieving pretty quick."

We sat for a few minutes in silence while I tried to figure out which of the six hundred questions in my mind I should ask next. "So, this place. I suppose there are rules?"

"Many. First, there are boundaries. There's the wall along the highway, of course, that continues up the hill there. Andrew and Gemina carried all those stones and built the original wall themselves, before the highway, to keep the sheep out. This was her favorite place, you see, and she let the cows here, but sheep eat down to the root, and would have spoiled everything. There used to be a stream, see, there to the right? It's long dried up, of course, but the boundary still exists for us. And behind us, the land used to belong to someone else. It was bought by the family back in the late 1880s I think, but again, the line had been drawn and we've never crossed it."

"And I guess you can choose how you...look?"

She grinned. "A real perk, I can tell you. You do not want to see how some of these folks looked when they were buried."

"Like Caleb."

She sighed. "Yes. And he could have shown himself as a younger man. But Caleb is an honest soul. Blunt, even. But he's easy to know. There's a reason, of course, that he saw you first. And you may never know what that reason is. But it's there. Believe it."

I sighed. "It's probably the universe showing me that my soul mate really exists, and sticking out its tongue, laughing."

She squeezed my hand. "That is not true. The universe is not cruel, just some of the people in it."

We sat in a comfortable silence while I sorted out more questions in my head. This was not what I expected, this connection to a woman I didn't even know had lived just six months before. But I felt happy and comfortable with her, believed her, and knew that she wanted the best for me. This was family, I thought. This was what I'd been missing my entire life, this warm and solid strength. My own mother loved me fiercely, and I knew it, but in Cathy there was a strong and steady peace that I know would have eased me through my life, and I felt the anger against my father rise again.

"Every year, on Billy's birthday, I would try to find you," she said, as though sensing my feelings and trying to deflect them. "Poor Winston. He knew so much more about the computers and the Internet than I did, and when he started helping me, I know he thought I was just a crazy old woman who dreamed up a family. He'd say, very quietly of course, that maybe, just maybe, I didn't have all my facts straight. He was right, but at the time I couldn't believe that Billy would have deliberately misled me. I knew he was a liar, of course, but..." She shrugged. "Was your mother as angry as you were?"

I nodded, then stopped. "I'm not sure. At the time Butterfield told us, yes. But she stopped referring him as that snake I married right before I came up here, so I think she's already forgiven him. She loved him then, and she's loved him for forty years since."

She sighed. "Yes, Billy's like that."

I looked around at the headstones. "How many of you are here? Do you know?" I asked.

"Of course I know. You want an exact number?"

"No, but…where is everybody?"

She looked around. "They're all here. Most times, they need a really good reason to be seen. Just as you need a good reason to see them." She glanced sideways at me. "Do you want to see them?"

I cleared my throat. "Not right now."

"And we know that. We can see that. You need more than an open mind, here. You need an open heart." She was dressed in slacks and a simple cotton sweater, and she brushed an imaginary something from her shoulder. "Your little Kira is a delight. Why, I almost jumped out myself, but didn't want to scare her off."

"I think, by the time she's my age, she'll know each and every one of you here, and will have heard all your stories."

"Good. We need someone like that." She looked at me. "How about you? Given a little time?"

I shook my head and stood up. I loved this woman, a pure and instinctual feeling that I knew was as true and real as anything else in my life. But I'd spent too many years on tiptoe, waiting for a blow to fall. Simple trust was anything but simple for me. "I don't know, Cathy. I'm not sure I can be like that at all. Sorry."

I walked away from her, past the oaks and back to RiverCliffe House.

CHAPTER 7

The Fourth of July was a really big deal in the Hudson Valley. According to Winston, we could expect three nights in a row of fireworks, drunken revelry on the river, and a long line of celebrants coming down from the Bear Claw, roaring past RiverCliffe House in trucks, cars and motorcycles, possibly shooting firearms into the air in joyous recognition of our country' s independence. The dining room would be jammed, especially on Saturday and Sunday night, when fireworks would be going off directly opposite us, and the view from the porch was considered a prime viewing location. Luckily, our paying guests could go up to the second-floor balcony, narrower, to be sure, but private and higher up, thus avoiding bloodshed over who was entitled to sit where on the porch. Several guests would be arriving by boat, all part of a glorious days-long regatta up and down the river.

Winston and I had agreed the day I arrived that one of us would be on property at all times on the weekend. Since I lived there, it made sense to take the Saturday shift. There wasn't any actual work involved, it was just a matter of my being there in case of an emergency. Winston showed up early on Sunday, which was a heavy check-in, check-out day, allowing me to wander off and spend time with my kids. But since it was a holiday weekend, he would be on property during the day for both days. We were usually fully staffed on the weekend anyway, but employees who would normally have a shift off were expected to be on duty.

My ex-husband, after several missed phone calls and awkward messages, had finally said he could visit the kids over the 4th, but they had all balked. There was so much going on that they did not want to be off with their father somewhere, missing the excitement. Kira flatout said she'd rather watch fireworks than be with her father, and I believed her. Kevin argued that Wayne was going to need him, and I realized that Wayne was giving him much more attention and, quite frankly, affection than Ed ever had, and it wasn't just Kevin's devotion to his work that was keeping him down at the river.

Lily had wavered. "What does he want to do?" she asked.

I read Ed's text. "He'll pick you up early Saturday morning, drive you out to his place, take you to lunch, and—"

"Never mind," she said, cutting me off. "Why do we have to go *there*? Alicia's there. Why can't he just spend the day with us?" She shook her head violently, and I could see the hurt in her eyes. "Tell him not over the 4th. I need to help Serena. The dining room is going to be crazy busy."

My heart ached for her, and I texted Ed back, suggesting they spend the day together, but at RiverCliffe. He said no. Ed managed to conceal his disappointment as the visit was pushed off yet again.

It was my first holiday weekend, and it was exhausting. Even though the dining room took reservations, people were lined up to the porch steps waiting to get in. But that was not particularly bothersome. What were were the guests, who were particularly needy and irritable.

The typical guest at RiverCliffe House was over forty, drove a very expensive car, and tended to be conservative in dress and attitude. After all, a typical three-day, long weekend stay cost about what I paid for my first car.

Usually our guests had been here before, knew the staff, had a plan and were very gracious. On a holiday weekend, however, a different kind of guest checked in, still affluent, but, as Winston described them, "Very touristy."

"What does that mean, exactly?" I asked him. "And before you roll your eyes, remember that I am new at this, so be kind."

He folded his hands together, like a schoolboy. "Of the eighteen rooms occupied this weekend, half are returning guests. They will probably arrive by boat, and will spent most of their days sailing up and down, checking out other people's boats, and generally leaving us alone, unless they happen to remember Happy Hour and pop in for a snack. The other guests will hang around the lobby, ask us where to go and what to do, complain the horses aren't all Lipizzaner stallions, the pool doesn't have a fountain in the middle, and get really pissed off because we have no gym facilities. In other words, they will have arrived with unreasonable expectations. Sure, they'll read the brochure, go online, read Yelp reviews, and probably go into a chat room somewhere and ask a thousand questions. But still, they'll show up and want to know why we don't have a bar, or where the hot tub is."

"We don't have a hot tub? Put that on my to-do list. And what is a Lipizzaner, exactly?"

He harrumphed. "Risa, this is serious. You have been in a honeymoon period for the past few weeks. But let me tell you, the shit is about to get real."

He was right. They started arriving Friday midday, before all the rooms were ready. Check-in time was three o'clock, and returning guests hung out in the great room or dropped off their luggage and headed to Hyde Park for the afternoon. But first-timers got cranky and wondered where they could get a drink. When told they had to drive six miles, they got even crankier.

I did not even get a chance to mingle during Happy Hour, because one of the guests arrived in his powerboat and clipped off a tiny piece of our dock. Drinking may have been involved, but after I assured him there would be no actual blame, he insisted on giving me a tour of his boat. Then he wanted me to cruise with him over to Kingston for dinner, even as his stony-eyed wife sat, perched on their luggage.

Wayne and Kevin were scrambling, and I was so proud of my son for him calm and professional air amidst the hubbub, I almost hugged him in public.

Finally, around nine o'clock, I turned to Winston and said, "I quit."

He laughed. "Yes, I know. Well, tomorrow should be much easier."

"Does it suck giving up your day off?" I asked.

He shook his head. "Not really. Like I said, Saturday is easier. No check-ins, so we can just help with housekeeping and in the dining room. Dinner will be crazy, like tonight, and afterward, there's a great view of the fireworks from here. Most of our dinner guests will sit right on the porch, watching, fighting over rocking chairs, and wondering why there are no waitresses bringing them drinks. The fireworks are down-river tonight, so we can't see them, but tomorrow and Sunday they'll be right outside the front door."

Bernie and Martha had taken Kira out earlier to drive down to see the first night's fireworks. Kevin had dragged himself in just after dark and said he was going to bed. Scott called me, saying he'd be on duty, he was just checking in. That had been the end of my exhausting, exciting Friday night.

An hour later, Serena came by, looking tired but happy. "Another successful holiday Friday," she crowed. "Did you see those smiling faces?"

I smiled. "Yes, I did. Lily still in the dining room?"

Serena shook her head. "No, Trent came by for her. I think they're heading over to Daniel's. I am too. Wanna come?"

I was bone tired, but my brain was still percolating. Winston poked me in the ribs. "That's where I'm staying tonight," he said. "I'll be over there in a bit. Why don't you go?"

I tilted my head. "Is this my official invite to the Cool Kids Club?"

Serena slipped her arm through mine and tugged me away from the desk. "Well, I guess. We don't do too much 'cool' round here, but we do sit and talk and solve the problems of the world."

"That sounds lovely," I said. "After you."

We climbed the stairs that ran up the side of the long garage where all the farm equipment was stored. There was a narrow deck that ran the whole length, looking over the treetops and the river.

My daughter was sitting next to Trent, and I breathed a small sigh of relief when she didn't have to scramble off his lap or untangle herself from his arms and legs when she saw me. She just looked up from where she was sitting, next to him on her own plastic Adirondack chair.

"Mom? What are you doing here?" Her voice wasn't even hostile.

I waved. "I got invited," I told her, and followed Serena into the apartment.

It was kind of a shock. Daniel had struck me as your basic hippy-dippy kind of guy. I was expecting milk-crate shelves and lots of macramé and tie-dye. Instead, the whole space was painted a very trendy gray, with white trim, sleek hardwood flooring and, at one end, a kitchen of stainless steel and white marble.

Daniel was sitting with Maya at a narrow dining table with black iron legs and a distressed wooden top that was at least eight feet long. He had his laptop open, and there were what appeared to be invoices spread around him. He looked frustrated, Maya bored.

He saw us and grinned. "Saved by the boss. I hate this business part of my life. Thank goodness Maya here has a head for numbers."

"Scott told me you were a savvy businessman," I said.

Serena made a rude noise. "He said what?"

Maya rolled her eyes. "The man is helpless," she muttered, gathering up the papers and stacking them neatly to one side. "Completely helpless."

Serena came up behind him and kissed him on his ear. Maya, I noticed, did not even look at Serena.

"I am an accountant, you know," I said. "I mean, if you need help."

Maya lit up. "Really? Could you? Honest, Risa, he's the worst."

I laughed. "Sure, I'll be happy to help with this stuff. After all, you folks have taken over the care and feeding of my youngest child."

He waved a hand. "We love Kira, you know that. But help is always appreciated. Kira and Haley are back playing Wii. Grab some wine and go back outside. It's a gorgeous night. I'll be there in a few."

Serena had already gone to the refrigerator and found a bottle of wine that she waved at me. "Come on out. I'll pour."

I went back on to the deck, walked to the railing, and looked out. You could see the river, but barely. The garage was on a slight rise, in back of the barns, and would have had an amazing view if not for the trees, roofs, and outbuildings.

Serena handed me a glass of wine. "Nice night."

I nodded. It was. It was hot but not muggy, and the breeze was perfect. I leaned against the railing and sipped wine. "Too bad about all these trees and buildings. This would be a great spot to watch the fireworks tomorrow night."

"What? No." Serena shook her head, her dark skin glowing in the light of the lit tiki torches. "Daniel always watches the fireworks from the cemetery. So do Bernie and Martha. The view is perfect, and you can bring your own lawn chairs. That's where Cathy always watched them."

Lily popped up beside Serena. "Seriously? But what about all the dead people there?"

Serena raised her eyebrows. "The dead people don't bother anybody. Never have. Now, I know that Cathy would be having conversations with some of them, but everybody else just watched the fireworks in peace."

"The first day we were here, and Kira asked you about ghosts, you said there weren't any," Lily said.

"No, I didn't," Serena said. "I said I'd never seen any in the house. And that was the truth. I've never seen any *anywhere*. Kira asked the wrong question. If she had asked me if *she* would be able to see a ghost, I would have answered just as honest, and I would have said yes. But—" She shrugged her shoulders.

"Mom, I don't want to watch fireworks there," Lily said, her voice getting a little squeaky and high-pitched. "This is *so* stupid. Why do we have to go there?"

"You won't have to," I told her. I looked over at Trent. "I bet there are lots of places you can watch them, right Trent?"

In the darkness, all I could see was a shrug. "That's where I always go. Everyplace else is really crowded. Unless you can find someone to take you out to the middle of the river."

"There," Lily pounced. "We have a boat. We can sail into the middle of the river and watch."

I exhaled slowly. "I'm not going to let Kevin take the boat into the crowded river at night. He's too inexperienced."

"Then make Wayne take us." Her voice was ratcheting up to a whine.

"Wayne will have been working all day. I will not make him do anything of a sort. He has his own family."

I glanced down at Serena, who was concentrating on a spot somewhere off in the direction of the smaller barn. She caught my look and shrugged, turning to Lily. "To be honest, honey," Serena said, "I am usually still in the kitchen when they start. What time did you leave tonight? After ten? Well, the fireworks are usually over by then, so I don't see it will be much of an issue."

Lily tightened her jaw, and I saw a familiar look. Lily loved fireworks, and not seeing them, especially when they were right outside her door, would not make her very happy.

"You can probably run up to the second-floor balcony," I told her. "Just for a few minutes, anyway. It will be crowded with guests, and it will be up to Serena to let you take a break, but there probably won't be any ancestors up there with you."

She looked back at Trent. "Where will you be?" she asked.

I saw his shadow shrug again. "I'm on tomorrow morning, so I'll be off by six, and I'll probably stay with Gram and Martha. Sunday night I'm there 'till eleven. I don't think we'll see them together."

She made her most oh-life-is-so-unfair face, but it looked like the crisis was averted. She shrugged elaborately, pulled her hair out of its topknot, ran her fingers through it a few times, then twisted it back up to the top of her head. "Fine."

I sighed inwardly, looked around and sat on a grayed-out teak armchair. Daniel came out, and a few minutes later Haley and Kira, asking whether Kira could sleep over. Daniel nodded, as did I; then Winston came up the stairs, and we sat and talked almost until midnight about the weekend and the guests, and what to serve for dinner Sunday night. Then Lily and I walked back to the inn. I took a quick look around the now-peaceful lobby, checked in with Jessie, who had drawn the overnight shift, and headed back to the apartment with Lily.

"Are you going to watch from that graveyard tomorrow?" she asked.

"Maybe. Depends on how busy we are here. I have to work too, you know."

"Yeah, but…you like talking to them, don't you?"

I reached my arm around her and gave her a quick hug. "It isn't terrible. I'm giving myself the chance to get used to all of this, Lily. It's a hard thing to accept, but it's real. I need to give myself time. So should you."

She shuddered, and shrugged my arm away, then climbed the stairs to bed.

Saturday was much calmer.

The line to the dining room was roughly the same, but our guests had figured a few things out and weren't nearly as annoying. In fact, sitting out on the porch after breakfast, I enjoyed myself for the first time. Thanks to my reading of Dimity's diary, I finally had stories to tell about the Civil War that claimed three of the four sons at RiverCliffe.

Kira and Haley had been making themselves useful, ferrying the damp towels from the pool to the vast laundry in the more modern end of the basement, throwing them in for a quick wash and a power dry. They scurried up and down, smiling and happy.

I spent most of the day helping in the dining room and cleaning rooms. Guests at RiverCliffe paid lots of money for their rooms, and expected first-class service. They got it. Even with lots of dining guests, folks coming up from the dock to wander around and look, and with all eighteen rooms booked solid, including the four rooms with sofa-beds full to capacity, they had clean towels and sheets every day, fresh flowers, amazing breakfasts and smiling people everywhere they looked.

It was really hard work, and I was incredibly proud of my small but capable crew.

"Should we give everyone a bonus?" I whispered to Winston.

He looked shocked. "This is their job. If you reward them extra for doing their jobs, what signal does that send?"

"That I appreciate their hard work?"

"Working hard is what they're supposed to be doing, Risa." He shook his head. "Cathy was very particular about who she hired. She'd be upset if even one person gave less than one hundred and ten percent."

I'd have to ask Cathy about that, I thought, next time I saw her. And then I found myself smiling a bit. Seeing Cathy again hadn't seemed like something I wanted to do, but now, thinking about it, I was looking forward to it.

"So, Winston, you want to watch the fireworks tonight or tomorrow night? I figure one of us should be up on the balcony, keeping an eye on things. That means the other one of us could be relaxing somewhere, really enjoying the show."

He thought for a moment, his mouth twisted a bit, then shrugged. "I'll work tonight. You can go down with Bernie, Martha, and the rest. It's like a party over there."

I walked away, thinking how calmly everyone seemed to be about the fact that I could, and probably would, talk to ghosts while watching the fireworks. No one seemed to think it was unusual except me.

Kira was practically gushing. "Mom, do you think Bea will be there tonight? I really liked her. And how about other ghosts? How many will there be, do you think? Do ghosts even *like* fireworks?"

I gave her a hug and glanced around. There were a few guests walking by. They weren't close enough to hear us, but.... I knelt and looked her in the eye. "Kira, we aren't going to talk about this where other people could hear, remember?"

She looked guilty for a moment as she glanced around. "Sorry. I forgot." Then her little face lit up again. "Lily and I are reading about Dimity. Isn't that a really cool name? Maybe we could find her?"

I stood. "Maybe." Dimity? I knew that Lily and Kira were reading about fifteen minutes worth of RiverCliffe diaries a night, but didn't know how far they'd gotten. I myself was just now in the middle of the Civil War, and...wait? Wasn't Dimity a cousin? And if she was a cousin, were there even more Cliffe women out there, separated by years and generations and marriages and illegitimate births? How many of us were there, really, given this gift?

I'd have to ask Cathy about that, too, next time I saw her.

We marched out around eight thirty, Bernie and Martha each carrying a webbed beach chair, Trent dragging a cooler. Daniel and the girls were already there, as were half the people from Daniel's dairy, all sitting among the headstones, chatting happily. Kevin ran down to them, and sat beside Daniel's daughter, Jillian. I tried to keep myself from smiling. Jillian was a very quiet, pretty girl, and I knew for a fact she'd been putting herself in Kevin's way for almost a week now. Apparently it was paying off.

Kira and I had a blanket and a thermos of apple juice, as well oatmeal cookies that Lily had baked a few days before. Haley ran up when she saw us, and parked herself next to Kira.

"If your lady comes," she said solemnly, "don't tell me."

The weather had turned, and rain was coming in the next twenty-four hours, but that only meant a cool breeze coming up off the water that shook the leaves and kept away the bugs. Daniel came by and offered me some wine and cheese. I shook my head, waved at Bernie and Martha, and waited for the show to begin.

Right after the first starburst, Cathy came and sat beside me. "Oh, I love this," she said, smiling. I smiled back, and let myself enjoy the feeling of quiet happiness at her presence. She looked around me to peek at Kira, who froze, then smiled tentatively. "My mama says hi," Cathy said in a low voice.

Kira nodded happily then looked upward again.

"How's your first big weekend?" she asked.

"Busy," I told her. "The staff is working their butts off."

"That's what they're supposed to be doing," she said. "That's why I hired them. Sitting on the porch, weaving stories, well, that's your job. Everyone else should be jumping."

It looked like Winston was right. "Cathy, how do you know there aren't more of us out there? More Cliffe women?"

She shrugged. "I don't. Andrew and Gemina had four sons, and they all married. It's possible that all the women born from them share the same secret. It would take a genealogist to track us all down. You want to take that on?"

I shook my head. "No, I suppose not."

Three large rockets went up at once, creating a loud boom and illuminating the ground as though it were still daylight. The graveyard was a lot more crowded than it had been a few minutes before.

I leaned over to Cathy. "Hey, are all these folks... residents?"

She looked around and nodded. "Yes. Let's face it, it gets pretty boring around here." She grinned. "I told you. There are a lot of us here, Risa. Most times they just stay where they were laid to rest, cause there's no cause for them to be stirrin'. But when there are fireworks, well, it's a big deal."

"But you're like, what, the Welcome Wagon?"

She laughed. "Yes, I suppose. The last of us to arrive kinda gets the job by default. Someday it will be your turn."

My turn. I thought about that for a moment as I looked at the faces that now surrounded me.

Yes, Daniel and his girls were still there, sitting next to Bernie, who was drinking a beer and pointing up at a particularly delicate flower of fire in the sky. But there were faces I'd never seen before, men in long-sleeved shirts and buttoned-up collars, women with their hair tightly permed, or drawn up in a carefully braided bun. I glanced at Kira. Her eyes were wide as saucers, and as she looked up at me, she wriggled closer. I put my arm around her and continued to look.

They were not all related to me, of course, all these silhouettes standing and sitting around me. I knew from Garth Woodmark's list that more than two-thirds of the souls in RiverCliffe Memorial Park were not members of the Cliffe family. But I still felt completely relaxed. This, I thought with a bit of a giggle to myself, was the closest I'd ever get to a Cliffe Family Reunion.

Caleb was there, standing with a young boy, his hands pushed into the pockets of his jeans. I stared at him, trying to decide if I should call his name. No one would hear me, I reasoned, with the booming all around. But Cathy must have read my mind, and she called out to him loudly. He turned, saw us, patted the boy on the back, walked over to us and sat on the edge of the blanket.

"How are you?" he asked softly.

I glanced at Kira again. She was leaning over to Haley, giggling and pointing as the sky lit up again, this time with orange marigold petals

"I'm not sure, but I may be getting used to all this'" I said. Cathy stood gracefully and moved away. He moved up beside me, his knees propped up, leaning back on his elbows.

"Who were you standing with? That little boy?" I asked.

"He's Marcus Goode. He died of fever, way back when fever was a thing that could kill you. He's a funny kid. It took him a long while to be able to come out and watch with us. He said the noise was too much like cannon fire."

Cannon fire. "When did he die?"

"Seventeen ninety-something. When all of this was barely a state. Elsbeth let all sorts of folks get buried here. She said she didn't want her mother to be lonely."

"Is she here? Gemina?"

Caleb nodded and pointed.

The sky lit up and I saw a tall woman, in a full, sweeping shirt, her arm around the waist of another, smaller woman. I watched until the sky exploded again with light, and recognized the oval face, the smooth hair pulled back in a neat bun.

"She looks just like her picture," I whispered to him, leaning close to his ear.

He turned his head and our faces were so close. He was grinning.

"I never saw her picture. Most of my time spent around here was up at the Claw."

"Did you know Cathy when she was…you both were… alive?"

He nodded. "She came around to the Claw on occasion. She was a tough woman, but liked her good times. Her sons had all been regulars up there, at one time or 'nother. Including your father. Cathy liked to tell stories. She loved those boys, a mother's love. But she didn't like them much, you know?"

I shook my head. "No, I don't. I never knew."

He reached to give my hand a quick squeeze. "It must be a terrible feeling, to have been left behind."

"There are more terrible things, I'm sure," I said. I looked across the cemetery, all the way down to the road. They were standing, looking up, laughing at the bright colors that rained down like broken stars. As I watched them, some of them turned back and waved at me. Kira waved back as Haley sat beside her, unconcerned.

"What's your name, Caleb? Your whole name?"

"Caleb Josiah Fielding. My mama was Christian woman, can you tell?"

"And you? Were you a Christian man?"

He chuckled. "Not so much. In fact, for a while there my mama told me she wished she'd never taught me the Ten Commandments, 'cause I'd made it my life's mission to break every one."

"When you were alive, would you have believed this? RiverCliffe? Me being able to talk to you like this?"

"When I was alive I believed in very little. Vietnam took a lot from me. Having Henry gave me a few things back, but not enough, I don't think. Now I am able to see more, and no matter what you believe, if it's in your heart, then it's a true thing."

Kira leaned into me, and I bent my head to her. She cupped her hand around her mouth and whispered in my ear.

"Do you see them all, Mommy?"

I nodded. "Yes, I do. Are you scared?"

She shook her head. "No. Why would I be scared? They're happy we're here."

"Yes, I think they are."

We sat there together, among the living and the dead, and watched the fireworks bursting above the river.

On Monday night, peace returned.

Yes, we were still full. But after Happy Hour, the dining room remained dark, and a feeling of calm reigned. RiverCliffe knew what to do. We smiled, and worked, and we kept our guests happy.

Scott called and asked if I felt like a quick drink. I actually didn't, but I felt like I wanted his company. He picked me up late, after Kira and Kevin had eaten, and Lily and Mia agreed to babysit. Lily lifted an eyebrow.

"Do we get paid?"

I reached in and grabbed a couple of twenties from my purse. "Here. You can call for pizza, or just keep it. I won't be late."

"It's already almost nine."

"Okay then, I will be late. Is that going to bother you?"

She shrugged and shook her head. "Mia and I will be fine."

We went up to the Bear Claw, shared a plate of nachos and I had a glass of wine. It was much more low-key than the last time I'd been there. The crowd was quiet, the jukebox played soft classic rock, and the nachos were much better than I'd have thought.

"Was the weekend crazy?" Scott asked.

I nodded and tried to maneuver a nacho into my mouth. "I have a whole new respect for every single person who works for me. I wanted to give them all a bonus but Winston talked me down."

"Yes, Winston would. Cathy was a bit tight with her money, and I imagine he would feel the same." He put a whole nacho in his mouth without dropping a bit of cheese. There wasn't even a smudge of salsa on his cheek.

"How about you?" I asked. "Did the nut-jobs come out?"

He was wearing a white polo shirt and jeans, and I noticed that there was a fairly nice stretch of fabric across his shoulders. He was in good shape, physically, all muscle and tan skin. I felt that ping again, and this time recognized it for what it was. Want. I wanted Scott.

He drank his beer straight from the bottle. "Oh, yeah. Lots of drunks on the road, drunks on the river, drunks pretty much everywhere. We also had the usual number of burned eyebrows and foreheads. A couple of fingers blown off. People never learn."

"Ouch."

"Exactly."

I looked around the Claw. "I think I like this place," I said.

"It grows on you. Lots of stuff does, up here. Life is a bit different here from other places. Things…take time."

"Well, I've got the rest of the summer."

"Have you thought about staying here?"

I looked at him, surprised. "You mean living at RiverCliffe permanently?"

He nodded.

"No, not really. I was going to take us back to Jersey, find a house, get some roots set back down."

"You could set roots down right here, you know. The schools are pretty good, you could be more hands-on at the inn, and your kids seem to like it here."

"I haven't thought about it. At all." This had always been just a summer vacation. I could not imagine myself actually living here.

"Do you think you'd miss all that big-city living?"

"Morris Plains is not exactly the big city." I looked at him, and couldn't tell if he was teasing me or not. "Do you? I mean, you had a taste of the Big Apple, but you came back."

"Yes, but I was born here. There was always something that brought me back to the river."

"It's the same river in Manhattan, you know."

He laughed and shook his head. "No, not really. Here, if you're quiet enough, and listen hard enough, you can still hear Hendrick Hudson and his crew playing nine-pins."

I froze, a nacho almost to my mouth. "What?"

"Rip Van Winkle? It was Hendrick Hudson who handed poor Rip Van Winkle the flagon that put him to sleep for twenty years."

"Oh, right. You are a man of many layers, Scott."

He grinned. "Most people are."

"So you hear them? The old Dutch founders, playing ninepins in their amphitheater?"

He raised an eyebrow. "Oh? So, you're a Washington Irving fan too?"

I felt a piece of onion caught between my teeth, and was trying to decide if I could work it out with my tongue, ignore it and never smile for the rest of the evening, or excuse myself and search for a toothpick. I poked a few times with my tongue before answering. "Not really, but I loved Rip Van Winkle. Poor guy, with his awful wife. Always felt bad about the dog though, you know?"

He nodded. "Yeah, I felt bad about that too. But yes, I do hear them. You can walk some of these woods and feel like you're the only person in the world, it's so quiet and still. There are some beautiful spots around here. Good for sitting and thinking."

I nodded, and thought about the bench in RiverCliffe Memorial Park, a perfect place to think. "Does everyone around here hear them? Hudson and his boys?"

He tilted his head. "No, I don't think so. But they hear other things. The Hudson Valley is famous for strange and inexplicable events."

Apparently this was the perfect moment for me to admit that I, too, heard voices from the past. I was sure that between Cathy and Serena, he had heard about the Cliffe women and their gift. If I told him what I'd experienced, would he accept it as calmly as everyone else around here did? I bit into a nacho, and the moment passed.

"Can I ask you something, Scott?"

He nodded. "Anything."

"Why did you ask me out?"

He tilted his head. "Really?"

I nodded. "Look, I was married for a long time and haven't dated since, and I'm pretty sure all the rules have changed. I'm just asking."

He sat back. "I asked you out because I thought you were a very attractive woman. You seemed smart and had a sense of humor. I found you…intriguing"

I raised my eyebrows. "No one has ever said *that* about me before. Big brownie points there."

He chuckled. "Now, why did you say yes?"

"Because I hadn't been on a date in twenty years, and you looked to be a great place to start. Maybe I'm wrong, but I don't think you're the sheriff who's evil and corrupt and in it for your own gain. I think you like helping people, and you seem to be a man with integrity. You're big and nice-looking, and I like that. I believe that there's a chemical reaction that can happen between two people, and I think it's happening between us. And I think you're kind, the type of man who wouldn't stomp all over a woman's heart on the way out the door."

He gave out a low whistle. "Man, your ex-husband really left marks, didn't he?"

I nodded. "Yes. On me and on my kids. So when I met you, and said yes, it was kind of a big leap of faith."

"How am I doing?"

I grinned. "Pretty good, actually. I have a feeling that you might be one of the good ones." I watched the muscles in his throat as he drank his beer. There were a few drops of beer on his lip, and as he licked them off, I felt a tightening in my chest, a purely physical reaction. I cleared my throat. "I also haven't had sex in, well…"

He nodded thoughtfully. "Just so you know, we can remedy that in about fourteen minutes. My place is just over the hill."

I was expecting a smart-ass comment to come rolling off my tongue. Instead, I said, "OK."

He looked a little stunned. "Really?"

I was a little stunned as well. "I'm not sure."

He cleared his throat and leaned closer to me, across the tiny table, pushing the half-empty plate of nachos to the side. "We are grown-ups."

"Yes, we are."

"And sex is pretty significant thing that happens between two people."

I was looking at his arms, the way the fine hair brushed back , the faint ripple of muscle under the skin. "Here's the thing," I said slowly. "I'm kind of in an odd place in my life right now. I'm here, at River-Cliffe, for the summer. I'm finally lifting my head up and looking around at my life and it's pretty good. But there are still things I'm a little gun-shy about. Like men."

He nodded. "That's understandable."

I leaned forward. "I think you're very attractive."

His eyes were looking straight into mine, and I saw them crinkle around the edges. "Why, thank you. I find you very attractive as well."

The glow that had been starting in my chest took a decidedly southward turn. I ran the tips of my fingers down the back of his hand. "If we did get together, would you be at all upset if it was purely…physical?"

His eyes were twinkling now. "Well, I'm usually not a wham-bam kinda guy, but since you are in that odd place, I think I could make an exception."

I smiled. "Fourteen minutes?"

He stood, the stool rocking back, almost crashing to the floor. He waved at the bartender. "Henry, on my tab," he called, reaching for my arm.

In the parking lot, he stopped. "Last chance for a graceful retreat."

I had to look way up. I had to stand on my toes to reach my arms around his neck. Once my mouth found his, the rest was easy. His arms tightened around me, and my feet left the ground. He wasn't being the polite gentleman suitor any more. His kiss was deep and demanding, and when I finally pulled away, I was breathless.

I had almost forgotten what it felt like to *want* someone on a very primal level: the racing heart, the pounding of blood in your ears, the deep ache in your groin.

"Yeah," I gasped. "Let's go."

I followed him along the unlit road for exactly fourteen minutes.

His condo was smallish, with lots of leather furniture. I caught a very quick look on the way to his bedroom. His king-sized bed was neatly made, so we just tumbled together on top of the quilt, peeling off clothes, taking our time. He had a condom in his nightstand, and I didn't feel at all embarrassed when he turned on the light. He was patient. He was tender. Were there fireworks? Enough. But more than that, he made me feel that what I wanted was more important than what he wanted.

And when we were done, and our breathing had slowed, he kissed the side of my neck.

"I think the chemical reaction thing is working just fine," he murmured.

I closed my eyes and smiled. "I think you're right."

I got home late, after midnight, and Lily was still up, watching television.

"Hey, everything okay?" I was feeling happy, the oh-my-that-felt-good kind of happy I hadn't felt in a long time.

She nodded.

"What time did Mia's dad come for her?"

Lily clicked off the television. "Her boyfriend came over."

"Oh? I didn't know she had a boyfriend. Is he nice?"

She shrugged. "Yeah, I guess. He wanted us to go visit the graveyard."

I stood very still, looking at her, all that happiness draining away. "And?"

She shrugged and looked down at her hands. "We went."

"You went? You left your brother and sister here alone?"

Her shoulders sagged and she rolled her eyes. "Mom, it's not like anything was going to happen. And if something did happen, Misha was working."

Misha worked the overnight shift during the week. He was responsible for answering any phone calls, dealing with guest issues, and doing the nightly audit. He also cleaned the lobby, swept the porches, replaced light bulbs, did a load or two of laundry…

"Misha is my employee, but he is not responsible for my children," I said coldly. "That was your job tonight. I even paid you for it."

She looked down at her hands again. "Don't you want to know what happened?" she asked, in a very small voice.

I felt a sudden chill and I sat beside her, grabbing both of her hands and shaking them. "Look at me," I said.

She did. Her eyes were wide and frightened.

"Okay. Tell me."

She took a deep breath. "Jordan was being a real jerk. We went in, and walked around for a few minutes. He had a flashlight."

"That's not too bad."

"He kept yelling for the ghosts to come out."

"He sounds like a real treasure."

"Nothing was happening," she whined. "I couldn't see or hear anyone, and Mia was all scared, and he said the whole thing was a big, stupid lie, and then he kicked a gravestone."

"And you let him? Lily, that graveyard is part of RiverCliffe, just like the barns and the house and the dock. Would you have let him kick a chair in the lobby?" I felt my anger rising, and I bit my lip to keep it in check. She was a kid, and Jordan was older, and a boy.

"So then, this guy came out and ran at me, yelling, and I screamed and ran away, and Mia screamed too, and Jordan fell," she mumbled.

"He fell? Was he hurt?"

She shook her head, looking miserable. "No. I mean, not really. He scraped his cheek."

I looked away from her, closed my eyes, and took a few long breaths. "Then what?"

"A guy was chasing us, Mom. He was angry and yelling and Mia and Jordan didn't see him."

I sat back. "Well, I imagine if someone kicked your gravestone, you'd be angry too. Now, what are you going to do about it?"

She brushed away a strand of hair from her cheek. "What do you mean?"

"Lily, honey, this is our life now. RiverCliffe. And part of all this good stuff, the river and the inn and Serena teaching you to cook...it's all great, but there's another side too. It was left to me, to us, because as women we have a gift, but we also have a responsibility to this place."

"I never wanted this," she hissed, her eyes glittering with anger. "Why should I be responsible?"

"If you feel this is all too much of a burden, then just stay out of the cemetery. It's that easy. Just understand that this is part of your past. Your...legacy."

"This is so stupid, Mom. I mean this is all because of your father? Who we never even met? And all this is dumped on us because of *his* stupid family?"

"So would you rather we never got this place, and that we were still back in Brooklyn? In Grandma's basement?"

She was silent, her fingers shredding the hem of her shorts.

"Everything has a cost, Lily," I said. I wanted to hug her. I wanted to smack her upside the head. I wanted to shake her until her teeth rattled.

"Stupid," she muttered.

"No, not stupid. Life."

I got up and went to into my bedroom. I sat on the edge of the bed until I heard her climb the stairs, then I went back into the living room and turned off the lights.

CHAPTER 8

The Kingston Mews nursing home looked a lot like Tara, the home of Scarlett O'Hara, in the movie version of *Gone With The Wind.* Several stories high, with soaring white pillars, it looked slightly out of place along the Hudson River, especially since I kept waiting for Mammy to stick her head out a window and yell for Scarlett to come in for supper.

Steve Guthrie was in a wheelchair, out under a sprawling maple, listening to a small, portable tape recorder. He was listening to an audio version of *Great Expectations,* and the narrator, I must say, was doing a terrific job. Bernie interrupted by calling out, and he turned his head in our direction, his hand reaching for the player, and turning it off.

"Bernie? That you?" he croaked.

He was small and bald, skin wrinkled and pale blue eyes that never stopped moving, as though still hoping to catch a glimpse of something, anything. Bernie bent down and kissed him on the cheek. "Yep, it's me. And Martha. And I've got Cathy's granddaughter with me. Risa." I felt a small rush of blood to my cheeks. Pride. I was Cathy's granddaughter, and here, in this place, that meant something.

He smiled, showing broad, white teeth, slightly crooked. "Martha? How the hell did Bernie manage to get you off the farm?"

Martha kissed him as well. "You make me sound like a hermit, Stevie."

"You are a hermit. And Risa?" He held out a hand in my general direction, and I grabbed it. His handshake was warm and strong.

"Pleased to meet you, Mr. Guthrie."

He waved that aside. "Stevie, please. You been up to the Claw?"

I nodded, felt like an idiot, and said, "Yes. Bernie took me up there my first week. Quite a place."

He smiled wistfully. "Yes. Spent the best years of my life behind that bar. Miss it every day." He moved his head slightly. "Bernie, I know you've secretly loved me all these years, but is there a reason for this here visit?"

Bernie glanced at me. "Actually, Risa here has a question for you."

He raised his white, bushy eyebrows in surprise. "Really?"

I swallowed. "Yes. I was curious about the biker who was killed, coming off the mountain."

His face changed slightly, looking confused, and I thought, no, he's forgotten it all, and I'm wasting my time. Then he nodded.

"Nice man," he said. "He'd been in before. Couple of times. He said he rode all the way up and down the Hudson River, all into Canada, six different times. I'd seen his bike, a huge, hulk of a thing. Harley, I'm pretty sure. Drank beer, played a mean game of pool. Got along with the boys. He wiped out just down the hill from the Claw. In fact, we all heard the crash and came out running, but all we could see was the flames."

I breathed out slowly. "Did you know his name?"

He shook his head. "Something biblical, I think. But his son's name was Henry. I remembered that. He and your father had a conversation, and the biker said his kid's name was Henry, and Billy said, hey, that's my middle name, so it kinda stuck in my memory. And I remember thinking the night he was killed that his son, his Henry would never know what happened to his daddy."

I turned cold. His son probably thought he'd been abandoned.

Having been abandoned myself, my heart twisted in pain. And Caleb...

"He met my father?"

Stevie made a choking kind of noise I took to be a laugh. "The Newsome boys spent a lot of time up at the Claw, 'fore they all died off or got locked away. Billy was a live one, I tell you what. Liked his whiskey. Polite drunk, he was. Not like his brothers. Lord, Martha, you know. Clay would tear up the place on a regular basis. But Billy was more interested in trying to bilk my customers with some fool con he was running."

I sighed. Of course. "So he was a regular? Billy, I mean."

Stevie shrugged. "When he was younger. He was only 'bout fifteen or so when he first started comin' round with his big brothers. We didn't ask for no I.D. back then. Once he took off and went down to the city, well, we saw less of him. But he liked to come in and tell us what he'd been up to. Bragging, mostly. When he married your ma, though, why, he was sure puffed up about that. Claimed he'd married the prettiest girl in New York City, and had the pictures to prove it. It was fellas like him that added real character to the Claw."

"I bet." I sighed again. "Well, thanks for the info." I looked at Bernie and Martha. "If you guys want to catch up, I'll wait back in the lobby."

I walked back into Kingston Mews and took out my phone and Googled Caleb Fielding. There was nothing. Then I Googled Henry Fielding, and got so many hits I'd be there for weeks looking through them all.

But, of course I started looking through all those names, stupidly thinking I'd find Caleb's son in the first ten minutes or so. I had the scenario perfectly planned in my head: I'd find the right Henry Fielding, get his address, and send a quick note telling him that his father had not walked away from him without a backward glance as my father had done. In the back of my mind was the niggling thought about how exactly I was going to explain all that, but then Martha and Bernie came and got me, and we drove across the river and back to RiverCliffe.

. . .

The Culinary Institute of America was a beautiful building set in a beautiful countryside, and the smells in the air were enough to make me want to buy a tent and pitch it, permanently, on their green and perfectly cut lawn.

The tour was interesting. All those bright young — and not-so-young—faces, pinched and earnest as they chopped and sautéed. There were classrooms, and labs, boring lectures on the science of gluten and food being transformed, like magic, before our eyes. Afterward, Scott and I sat and ate incredible peach pie with coffee so smooth and mellow I had a second cup, not caring that I'd probably be up all night. Then we walked to the river and sat and looked at the water.

"So now I want to go home and cook, and I'm a terrible cook. My children are never going to forgive you," I said.

He laughed. "Maybe I can cook for them instead?"

"Well, they're used to me, so the bar is set pretty low. You could probably win their lifelong gratitude by just not burning the mashed potatoes."

He stared. "You burned mashed potatoes? How is that even possible?"

I sighed. "To this day, I blame inferior cookware."

He laughed again. "And what do I have to do to gain *your* lifelong gratitude?"

I turned and met his eye. "Seriously? You can help me find a man named Henry Fielding."

He nodded. "Okay. Tell me about him. When was he born?"

"Before 1975."

He grimaced. "Where?"

"No idea."

"Oh, so this is an *easy* job."

"His parents are—were—Linda and Caleb Fielding. Caleb was from Texas. Served time. Was jailed in Detroit. You're not writing anything down."

"I have a good memory."

"I'm impressed."

"For example, I remember the first night we met, you asked me about a man named Caleb. Any connection?"

"Wow, I *am* impressed." Would now be the time to start the conversation about Caleb and Cathy and watching fireworks with a few generations of Cliffe relations all around me? I squinted at the sunlight. No. "There is, but can you trust me to explain it all later?"

"Sure." He nodded his head. "I'll see what I can find out."

HIs arm was resting on the back of the bench, and I was leaning against it. I felt a current of electricity, warm and vibrant, and it filled me with something exciting and new.

"So I want to thank you for the other night," I said.

I glanced up at him, and he grinned.

"No, thank *you*," he said.

I felt my smile break through. "I had a pretty good time."

"I was going to call you yesterday morning, but I didn't want to appear too needy. Or sex-starved."

I felt a giggle in my throat. When was the last time I giggled like a ten-year-old? "I've never done that before."

"Really? Well, congratulations. You did everything right."

The giggle burst through. "Ah, no, not *that*. I meant I've never gone to bed with a relative stranger before."

"Me neither. But think I've graduated from a relative stranger. Maybe just relatively strange?"

I laughed out loud. "Actually, you're one of the least strange men I've ever met. In fact, you're practically normal and decent."

He made a face. "Really? Normal? And *decent*? And I was trying so hard for mysterious and irresistible."

I leaned against him, and his arm slipped off the back of the bench to circle my shoulder.

"What are you thinking?" he asked.

"That life is not fair," I said.

"Damn," he said softly. "I was hoping you were thinking about me and a bearskin rug."

I burst out laughing. "That was earlier this morning."

"Oh, okay then. Good. At least it's crossed your mind." He kissed the side of my head, just where my hair was tumbling down around my temples. "What's not fair?"

I shrugged. "What we want and what we need. They're so different at times. It seems impossible to think about happiness, even when we can see it, just beyond our reach."

"It's all about priorities, Risa. What should come first?"

"Need. And I have what I need. For the first time in almost three years my kids seem happy. I have security now, and it's not dependent on another person. I have something that is just mine, something I can count on."

He nodded. "That sounds all good. So, what do you want? Besides me on a bearskin rug?"

I turned to face him, my hand reaching up to his cheek.

I wanted more nights with him, learning and exploring. He had awakened something in me that I'd forgotten—the simple pleasure of flesh on flesh. Our first time together had been patient and careful. Now, I wanted to see what we felt like without caution. But I didn't want to tell him that. It seemed too raw. So, instead I thought wildly for something—anything—else to say. "To be sure."

He narrowed his eyes. "That's not something," he said slowly, "that you can be given. That is something that needs to come from within."

I nodded. "I know. And that's unfair, too. I want someone to hand me a life without risk."

"That's what a child wants."

"Yes. And as child I never got that. My mother did everything for me, but it was always the two of us against the world. My father wasn't around to shoulder any of the burden, so I did. I was always afraid that I was going to do something to make our life harder. Like when we had to eat boxed mac and cheese for a week, or we had to turn off the heat upstairs to save oil. Not being able to buy something or do something or go somewhere... that was partly *my* fault. My life was always about walking a fine line, and terrified of falling."

I stopped abruptly. I hadn't planned to say so much. That was as bad as telling him that I just wanted sex for it's own sake. That was even worse.

"And now?" He turned and faced me, his eyes dark and serious. "Are you still afraid?"

"I'm getting better," I said slowly. In a flash I saw Caleb's face, and heard his voice. "I think I'm getting better, because now I see it was never the falling off I was afraid of. It was hitting the ground, and maybe getting hurt."

"I'll try, very hard, not to let you get hurt."

I believed him, and with that belief came a flicker of something new, yet familiar. I really liked this man. A lot. I kissed him, a light, butterfly kiss on his upper lip, then pulled back and away from him, letting the air cool the heat that had been building. We sat there for a while longer, not touching at all, until it was time to go home.

Lily had been on KidWatch, so I texted her to let her know I'd be bringing Scott and Chinese take-out home for dinner. She texted back to include Mia and Trent. I asked for requests, and got back a list so detailed it took me almost five minutes to place my order with ChinaOne.

Scott and I had mingled at Happy Hour. I was getting better at the small talk, and I was starting to enjoy myself with the guests. I knew I would never be up to Winston's standards, but I was coming along quite nicely, I thought. While Scott and I sipped wine, the kids dove in and ate practically everything. Luckily, I had stashed a few containers in the big walk-in in the inn's kitchen, so Scott and I did not starve. Winston had new figures from Larry the Leech, but I waved him off. Scott and I ate cold Chinese out of cartons while sitting on my tiny front stoop, overlooking the Hudson, talking until late. We spoke of small, common things—the summer heat, politics, our favorite places in Manhattan. Nothing else about us, about what was going to happen next. I thought we'd covered enough ground there for one day. What I did want was to take him back into my small bedroom, to try to figure out what other ways the two of us could fit together, but the glare of the television screen in the living room made that impossible.

By the time he left, Lily's guests were also gone. My three children were sitting together, watching television when I came in from wishing Scott a good night. They were lined up on the couch, looking very much like a small jury.

"What?" I asked. Was this about Scott and me? After all, this was the first man they had ever seen me with besides their father. Did their kid radar tell them we had had sex?

"So, we need to talk about the ghosts," Lily said. "Kira has told us all about her friend, and about the crowd during the fireworks. And as you know, I myself have …met one of them."

"Yeah, Mom, I was there during the fireworks, too. I didn't see nobody." Kevin groused.

"Anybody," I said automatically. I sat opposite them and sighed. "Sorry, Kev. This is apparently a girls-only gig."

"Why?" he asked, understandably indignant. In all of his twelve years, he had never been denied anything because of his sex.

I shrugged. "I didn't make the rules," I told him.

"So, what are the rules, exactly?" Lily asked.

I rubbed my palms together as I tried to line everything up in my head. "We can see and talk to the people in RiverCliffe Memorial Park. There are boundaries that they can't cross. They can appear to us any way they like, and they feel real. I mean, they feel solid. It's not like on TV, where you can put your hand through someone's chest."

Kevin looked crestfallen. "They don't float around, or take off their heads or anything?" he asked.

I shook my head. "No. Sorry."

He got off the couch and waved his hand, disgusted. "This is such a waste," he muttered, and slouched upstairs.

I moved into the space he'd vacated, right between my two girls, taking a hand from each, and holding tightly.

"This is not a terrible thing," I told them. "It's a…legacy."

"I think it's really great," Kira said, matter-of-factly. "It means that if you die, Mom, we can bury you over there and we'll still be able to see you every day."

I think my jaw unhinged completely. "Why, yes, you're right. I never thought of that."

Lily was still struggling a bit. "So, who's over there, exactly?"

"Well, your great-grandmother, and great-great, and most of the greats before that."

"And that guy who chased me? Who was he?" Lily asked.

I shook my head. "I don't know."

"That was mean, by the way," Kira said. "You should go over and apologize. Who was the lady sitting next to you, Mommy?"

"Cathy. Your great-grandmother."

"What was she like?" Kira asked.

"Nice. I liked her. You met her mom, Kira. Did you like her?"

Kira nodded. "Yes. And who was the man who sat next to you? Wasn't he there before? He waved to me, remember? The first time we came here?"

I nodded. "Yes. That's Caleb."

Lily looked troubled. "Do I have to go back in there?"

I shook my head. "You don't have to do anything you don't want to do. But can you tell me…why does this bother you so much? No one will hurt you, Lily."

Lily chewed her lower lip. "I read some of those diaries."

"And? What did you learn?"

"Those ghosts can read your mind," she said, looking down as she twisted her hands.

"I don't think they can, really. They stay connected to the people in their lives, and seem to know a great deal about *them*. They can see into your heart. Is that what you're afraid of?"

She reached up and pulled down her bun, her hair falling down around her face, hiding her eyes. "I don't like that. I don't want anyone to see inside me."

I felt tears start, and I stood quickly, walking over to the bookshelf and examining the long row of diaries like they were the most important things in the world. "Lily, are you afraid they'll judge you?" I felt so sad for her. What kind of person did she think she was that she didn't want anyone else to see? "Because I think that they're all beyond that." I turned and looked at my oldest daughter. What had she been keeping inside her that she thought was so ugly? "Whatever you're feeling about, say, your father, well…they will understand."

"Yeah, whatever."

"Lily, if you want to—"

"I'm *fine*, Mom," she said. I saw a familiar look in her eyes. She was shutting down. We were done here.

There was a silence. "Night, Mom." She put her hand on Kira's shoulder and steered her upstairs.

"Good night," I called faintly.

I looked around the empty room, then stood, walked outside, and stared across the cool darkness into the graveyard. I listened to the river, and the crickets, and the night birds.

My daughter was broken. Something was inside of her that made her feel…less. I knew that feeling. I'd grown up with it. It had taken me years to feel different. In fact, it had taken until RiverCliffe. I wondered if RiverCliffe could be the answer for her, too.

My night's sleep was dreamless.

Beth Calder arrived early Friday evening, just as Happy Hour was winding down. She came through the front door, pulling a bright red suitcase, with a Vera Bradley tote over one shoulder, and her trademark Birkin bag dangling from her left hand.

Winston swooped just as I saw her

"Welcome to RiverCliffe. Do you have a reservation?"

Beth towered over Winston. At five foot, eleven and a half, she would have turned heads even without the red hair, killer curves, or ga-zillion dollar purse.

"I'm staying with what's-her-name," she said, grinning as I walked up. "She swore I could have the Presidential suite, but I wanted to rough it instead."

Winston looked totally confused for a moment, then grinned. "Risa, you should have told me you were expecting a guest. We do have a Presidential suite, you know."

Beth dropped everything and hugged me. She smelled of Shalimar, a decidedly old-fashioned but classic scent, and cigarettes.

I pulled back. "I thought you quit!"

She rolled her eyes. "I thought I quit too, and then I a met a guy…" She grinned. "Boy, do I have a story for you."

I picked up her suitcase. "Yeah, well, as far as stories go, I bet I've got you beat. Winston, this is my good friend Beth Calder. She'll be staying with me, but can she get a card for breakfast and all that? Beth, this is Winston Talvert, who runs the show around here."

Winston picked up her Birkin and handed it to her, as though returning a newborn baby to the womb. "Pleased to meet you. Yes, of course, I'll get you a guest card that will give you access to our dining room, as well as the pool, stables, and dock."

"Dock? Oh, that sounds lovely. What I'd really like to do is sail. Can I do that?"

Winston grinned. "As a matter of fact, yes."

We all walked toward my apartment. "Kevin is learning, Beth," I told her. "Maybe you can take him out?"

"Of course. Stables? Not so much. Pool sounds good, and the dining room, although I was looking forward to Risa's cooking."

"Liar," I laughed. "Wait until you taste Serena's cooking. And she's teaching Lily, so at least one of my children will be able to serve a respectable meal."

We came through the living room, and Beth stopped, spun around, looking, then clapped her hands in delight. "Risa, this is yours? Oh, you lucky bird. I'm jealous."

"That's right," I said, dumping her suitcase on my bed and returning to the living room. "You're an antiques person."

She sighed happily, then leaned down to Winston. "I just bought a sack back Windsor chair. Original black paint. Boston, around 1820."

I could hear his gasp. "Original paint? Oh, God, was it signed?"

She sighed and shook her head. "Sadly, no."

I shook my head. "You and your antiques. Pictures of other people's dead relatives, and chairs you can't sit on."

She walked over to the multi-paned window over my kitchen table and touched the wavy glass. "Original?"

Winston nodded as he joined her. "Yes. Can you see the bubbles?"

"Oh, yes. Gorgeous."

"Wait until you see the flooring in the second floor back hallway. Pumpkin pine."

They sighed together. I came and stood between them. "Do you want to be alone?"

Winston shook himself and cleared his throat. "No, I need to help Serena clean up. Beth, it was a pleasure."

She took his hand in both of hers. "We'll talk," she whispered, and he left.

I watched him go and shook my head. "How did we become friends again?"

"You held my hair one night when I was puking on a rose-of-Sharon bush. Behind the library, I think."

"Oh, right. Well, the kids are at the pool, and they're dying to see you. Then I thought we'd go into town for something to eat, then a bit of drinking."

She was poking around my kitchen. "Sounds perfect. How are they, your kids? Do they like it here?"

"Yes, for the most part, they do. Of course, there are issues, mainly about their father, I think. He still hasn't managed to drive out here to see them, and I'm not sure if they even care anymore, which is a whole *other* thing. But they've each found their own little piece of RiverCliffe, and they've run with it." We walked out the back door toward the pool. The sun was still bright, and I could hear laughing and splashing.

"And you? Have you found your piece?"

"I own this place. I still have a hard time believing it sometimes, but, this," I opened my arms, "is mine. I'm doing the books, payroll, a little paperwork. I'm even learning to be social with my guests. It's not a terrible way to spend a summer."

"Yes, I saw you as I came in. Schmoozing. I didn't think that was in your DNA."

I shook my head. "You won't believe what's in my DNA. Hey, Lily, guys, look who's here!"

We drove across the river for burgers and ice cream. When we finally came back to RiverCliffe, my kids were worn out enough that I didn't have to chase them to bed. They stumbled upstairs and I fixed Beth and I drinks.

Beth liked her vodka, so I filled a shaker with ice, Grey Goose, and a smidge of vermouth. I grabbed an almost empty bottle of white wine, and we walked out to RiverCliffe Memorial Park and sat on my bench. I delicately sipped from the bottle while Beth poured a martini in the moonlight.

She took a drink and sighed. "This martini is perfect, and I must admit the view is spectacular. But why are we having our evening cocktail in a graveyard?"

"'You know those two men I told you I'd met? This is where one of them hangs out."

"Oh?" The moon was bright enough that I could see her eyebrow lift. "He's a mortician?"

"No. He's dead." I explained to her the Cliffe women, and their unusual relationship with the dead. She listened politely, poured herself another drink, and didn't say anything for quite a few minutes after I was done talking.

"Well," she said at last. "That's all very interesting. And since this is you, and not Fox News, I'm going to believe everything you say. So, you met this man, Caleb, and something clicked?"

"Yeah, pretty much."

"So, he's a pretty terrific guy, except for being dead?"

"That's it. We're…friends, I think. I've never had a guy who was just a friend before. And yes, he's dead, so friends is pretty much as far as things are going to go."

She exhaled loudly. "And here I thought I was going to have you astounded by my tale of Tony the Accountant and his ten-inch penis."

Unfortunately, I had a mouthful of white wine, which I sprayed all over the front of my shirt. "Seriously?"

She finished her drink and shook her head. "Yeah, but I think we should talk about you first." She picked up the shaker and poured again. "I may not make it back to the house. If I pass out, make sure your boy protects me from bears, okay?" She looked out over the river. "And there's another man?"

"Scott. Nice man. Very nice. Smart, funny, a bit outdoorsy for me, but a really good guy."

"And can you talk to him?"

"Yes." I sipped my wine so slowly it was getting warm.

"And? 'Cause I know you, and there's an 'and' in there somewhere."

"We had sex."

"Oh, my God! Yay for you. I was afraid things were going to dry up. So...how did that go?"

"It went pretty well. It went *really* well. And I have a feeling it could get a whole lot better."

She smacked my thigh with the palm of her hand. "There better not be a 'but' in here somewhere."

I shook my head. "No, there's not."

"Good. Risa, babe, you've been a wounded animal, cowering in your den, since Eddie left. I never liked Ed, by the way, but you know that, and it doesn't change the fact that you loved him. You thought you were going to spend the rest of your life with him, and he ended up being a miserable piece of crap and totally unworthy of you. So I got the part about hating men, mistrust, yadda, yadda...I'm glad you're getting over all that. And as happy as I am you've got the ghost of Caleb to bare your soul to, I'm even happier there's a living and breathing man you can bare the rest of yourself to."

I nodded. "I'm feeling pretty good about the whole situation, Beth. Now that I look back, sex was the best part of my marriage because in bed I felt in control. I was equal. It was the one place where I didn't feel like I had to ask permission or seek approval. I knew I was good and I felt a certain sense of power. It feels really nice to get that back again."

She squinted her eyes at me. "Is that what it's about with Scott? Power?"

"What? No." I shook my head. "Not at all. I just, well, I know this is nothing permanent, so I can just concentrate on enjoying myself. And enjoying him."

"Well, good. You deserve happy."

I leaned my head against her shoulder. "So do you."

"True. But right now I'd settle for Tony to have a personality besides the biggest schlong in the world. If wishes were horses…"

I nudged her with my elbow. "Really ten inches?"

"Oh, yeah. And he's only five-six, five-seven, tops. Hangs to his friggin' knees."

"Beth, please stop."

She drained her glass. "And you met your grandmother? Now, that is very cool."

"Yes. She was just lovely. It's so strange. It was always just Mom and I, and now I have a real family here. They're all dead, so there *is* that, but there's a connection. They're all here for me."

"Yeah," she giggled. "Just lying around."

"Oh, Beth, you've crossed over."

"Indeed I have. Can I start making dead people jokes?"

"Better than penis jokes."

"True. But just one, okay? Tony doesn't use have to use his left foot on the clutch when he's shifting gears."

"No."

"And he doesn't need a selfie-stick."

I stood up. "OK, we're done here."

She stood and swayed back and forth. "Risa, that river is beautiful."

"Yes, it is."

"This place is beautiful."

"Yes, Beth. We should go back now."

She looked around. "Is anyone here?" she said in an attempted whisper.

"No."

"You know what they call Tony when he's wearing swim trunks?"

"You're going to tell me no matter what, aren't you?"

"Elephant man."

She started to giggle again, and I joined her, and we stumbled out through the oaks, past the low stone wall, and back home.

As she aged, Beth got better about her drinking. Not smarter, exactly, just better at managing the day after. If I had downed three martinis in half an hour, I would have been paralyzed the next day. But Beth was up before I was.

I'd slept in the extra bed in Kevin's room, and when I stumbled downstairs her bed was empty and neatly made. By the time I made it out of the shower, she was in my living room, obviously having just returned from a run, dressed in baggy sweats and sleeveless t-shirt, with her hair pulled up and back off her neck.

"Hey," she said, slightly out of breath. "Great running here."

"God, Beth, how can you even walk?"

She flashed a grin. "Good genes. You know my mom is Irish. When's breakfast?"

"Now. Shower, and I'll meet you out there."

Lily was already in the dining room. Every time I saw her there I felt a little rush of pride, but was careful not to show it. Any sign of my approval could torpedo the whole situation.

Beth came in a few minutes later, with Kevin and Kira, and the three of them were seated. I waved hello and watched them together.

My kids loved Beth. She was so relaxed and happy around them. My heart twisted for her, knowing that she had been such an amazing mother to Erin. I watched as she talked to them, listening carefully, leaning in their direction, giving them her full attention. I gave them my full attention, but after all, I was only the mom…

As the dining room thinned out, Beth gathered quite a crowd. Serena and Lily both hung around, and at one point Winston came in, pulled a chair up, and sat.

What was he doing here on his day off? Planning something with Beth, obviously.

I grabbed a mug of coffee and hustled over.

"You are completely taking over my staff," I said to Beth. "Are you promising them a raise?"

She flashed a grin. "Just dazzling them with my unfettered charm and wit. Winston has a list of antique shops around, but I already promised Kevin here we'd go out in the sailboat."

I sipped my coffee, trying not to feel annoyed. Winston never gave me a list of antique shops. Of course, I'd never gushed over crackled glass, either.

Winston looked up at me. "It's supposed to rain tomorrow, and these shops will be open then, just later, probably. Beth could maybe check them out then?"

I could not ignore the wistful look in Beth's eyes. Trudging around, looking at dusty old furniture would be her idea of heaven, where I would just as soon stick a fork in my left eye.

"So, Winston, if you want, you could step in for me for the rest of the day. Beth and I could take the kids out on the river, then spend the afternoon draped over some wine by the pool. Then tomorrow, when it's raining, you can take her off to check out some of those places, and I'll stay by the desk."

He bounded up off the chair. "Really? I mean…" he glanced down at Beth, who just lit up like a Christmas tree.

"Yes, really. If Beth and I spend all day tomorrow with nothing to do but look at the rain, we'll both end up drunk and miserable. This way I get to enjoy this beautiful day, and tomorrow, Beth gets to prowl through the Hudson Valley's finest junk."

Beth raised an eyebrow. "Does this mean you'll come sailing with Kev and me?"

I rolled my eyes in mock surrender. "I guess. Next, you'll have me jogging."

She laughed. "I doubt it, but baby steps." She reached over and tugged Winston's pant leg. "What do you think? Can we do this in the rain?"

Winston grinned. "Yes, of course. Well, okay then, I guess I'm on duty. Risa, let me tell the desk we're switching, and I'll start clearing up tables."

I sat next to Kevin. "You won't take this opportunity to drown me, will you? I know you'd prefer Beth to me, and this could be a perfect chance."

He shoveled the last of his blueberry pancake into his mouth and chewed, thinking. "That doesn't sound as much of a good idea now. After all, you'll just end up buried next door, and you'll probably still figure out a way to tell me what to do."

"Kevin," Kira sing-songed. "Stop. I don't want Mommy to drown."

Beth patted my hand. "I'll take care, don't worry. What, you don't swim either?"

I sighed. "Brooklyn, remember?"

Beth snorted. "Me too, honey."

"Yeah, but your parents believed in fresh air and summer camp," I pointed out. "Marcie believed in bingo in church basements and afternoon matinees. If it wasn't for the Brooklyn Botanical, I would have spent my whole life thinking grass grew only on television."

I went and changed from my linen dress and put on a bathing suit and shorts, and met Beth, Kira and Kevin down at the dock.

I had seen the sailboat I'd bought for RiverCliffe, of course, when I'd been down at the dock, bringing Kevin his lunch or sitting with him, watching him practice tying knots. In my mind I'd imagined something slightly larger than a surfboard, with a sail. I'd been surprised that it was something considerable larger in real life, with a tall mast with two sails, and brightly colored life jackets thrown into the bottom of the boat, as well as a small outboard motor sticking out the back. Now, for the first time actually stepping into it, I was impressed to see it had room enough for a few people to sit comfortably.

"Do I want to know how much I paid for this?" I asked Wayne.

He grinned. "You'll be getting the bill in August. Right now, the boat is on probation. If it's not what we want, we can send it back upriver."

Kevin's head jerked up. "Mom. I love this boat. Can we keep it?"

Wayne, tall and very tanned, helped me into the boat, then handed over a giggling Kira.

"If we make it up and back without capsizing," I said, "we'll keep it. okay?"

We put on life jackets, I sprayed sunscreen over any exposed flesh I could find, and we were off.

It was a much different experience than the paddleboats in Central Park. It was like flying. Not that I'd ever actually spread my wings and taken flight, but when I closed my eyes, I could imagine myself, soaring, feeling totally free. I caught Kevin's eye.

"I'm kinda loving this," I yelled.

He grinned back, intent on his duties, holding a rope kind of thing, watching the sail move, and listening carefully to everything Beth told him to do.

We were out for almost two hours, and when we pulled back in to our dock, I was sold. "Is this getting much use by the guests?" I asked Wayne.

He nodded as he pulled Kira up and out of the boat.

"Maybe another one? Smaller?"

He grinned at me. "Will I be teaching you, too?" he asked.

"Maybe. Get me a price."

Kevin threw his arms around me. "Thanks Mom."

I hugged him back. He'd grown taller in the few weeks we'd been at RiverCliffe, and had lost enough weight that I'd had to buy him new jeans and shorts just that week. But what I noticed most about his body was the muscle and strength that hadn't been there before.

Kira jumped happily up and down on the deck. "If you buy Kevin a boat, then you have to buy me a pony."

"No, I don't. RiverCliffe didn't have a boat before. And we have plenty of horses. Good try, though."

Kevin stayed with Wayne, so Beth and Kira and I walked up and sat by the pool. It was a hot day, hazy and humid, and we spent lots of time in the water. When we finally came in for lunch, Kira gobbled down her tomato sandwich and announced a nap.

Beth watched her go upstairs. "Where's the vodka?"

"Beth, it's early," I protested. I'd had a wine spritzer out by the pool and felt like I was done for the day.

She grinned. "It's five o'clock somewhere."

When the two of us had our weekends together, we'd always spend time drinking, but there was something different about Beth this time. It wasn't just about a drink or two to relax. She seemed more...needy. I shook my head. "You're killing me here."

I checked my phone and found that my mother had called, twice, and that Scott sent a text, inviting all of us out for pizza.

"Hey," I called to Beth. "Feel like pizza?"

"Will there be wine?"

I laughed. "I'll make sure," and sent Scott a text back, asking when.

Then I called my mother, who answered on the third ring, cut me off before I could finish my hello, and informed me that my father, Billy Newsome, had tracked her down in Brooklyn, had just left her, and was on his way up to RiverCliffe.

CHAPTER 9

I stared into the phone. "What?"

Beth looked up from her martini making.

I sat down abruptly on the couch. "What did you say?"

"Your father was just here. I don't know how he found me, although maybe he just this week finally figured out how to use a friggin' computer. He stayed for about an hour. Tried to get me in the sack, complained about how messy the house was, and left. He said he was catching a train to Poughkeepsie tonight." I could hear her inhale. Obviously, an event such as this called for an additional cigarette. Maybe two. Or twelve.

"But—" But what? How did he look? Did he seem in good health? Was he sorry for leaving us and never sending a dime of support?

"I know. Believe me, Risa, honey, I know."

"Did you tell him you never divorced him?"

"No."

"Apparently, he's had three more wives since you."

"That snake. Although I'm not surprised. He loved his sack-time. It was the best part of our marriage."

I closed my eyes. "Ma, please."

"What? You're a grown woman. You know how it is."

"Maybe. But I don't want to know how it *was*." I chewed my lower lip, thinking. "I've met the local sheriff. I'm seeing him tonight. He's encountered Billy before, and knows how to handle him."

"Wait—what do you mean, you're *seeing* him tonight? Seeing as in *dating*? The sheriff? And why haven't you mentioned him before?"

"Really? You just drop this on my head and then ask me about who I'm *dating?*"

"Risa, honey, there's nothing you and I can say about your father that hasn't been already said. So, what else should I ask you about? Is he cute? How old, do you think? Married before?"

I propped my chin on the palm of my hand and rolled my eyes at Beth. She lifted the cocktail shaker, and her eyebrows. I nodded. I wasn't a big day drinker, but I had a feeling I was going to need a little something-something to get through this conversation. "His name is Scott Van Wyke, he's a bit older than me, tall and divorced. He's taking everyone out tonight."

"Everyone? Who's everyone? Is he already meeting your kids? God, Risa, how long has this been going on?"

"This is not an official ceremony or anything. Beth is here, and he's taking us out for pizza."

"He's meeting your kids and your best friend, and you haven't even *mentioned* him to me? Oh, my broken heart…"

"Ma!" I stood up, smacked myself on the top of my head, sat back down and took a deep breath. "Ma, it's not serious. I've only been here a few weeks. Yeesh, give me a break."

"What about your biker boy? Is he still in the picture?"

"Can we please talk about the fact that my father, whom had never been in the picture, is coming here tonight?"

"Whom? Well, excuse me Miss Grammar Police."

"Ma!" I shot up again. Beth handed me a martini, and I drank it all down in one gulp. Suddenly I felt as though the top of my head exploded outward, while at the same time the entire world sharpened, stilled, and settled quietly to the bottom of my brain.

Amazing.

I sat down. I was smiling. "You know what, let him come. I have law and order on my side, my best bud in the world is here, and I am the owner of RiverCliffe, so I can have him thrown out on his miserable ass if I want."

"Is that what you want?"

"He lied to you and he lied to his mother. In doing so, he really changed our lives. You don't know what we lost. I can't even begin to tell you, and it's his fault. What do you want me to do, invite him for tea and a nice long chat?"

"Do you need me? I could come up tomorrow."

"I got this, Ma. Why don't you come up in a couple of weeks, when Billy is gone, the dust has settled? Maybe for your birthday? We could have a great party for you here."

"I should come up there. You don't know Billy. You won't know what to do with him."

"I won't need to know what to do, Ma. I'll have him escorted off my property. Easy peasy."

She was quiet. I had to shut my eyes as the martini obviously kicked into phase two and I felt light-headed and slightly stupid. "I gotta go. I'll call you tomorrow night, and let you know how it all worked out. Bye, Ma. Love you."

I clicked off the phone, leaned back on the couch and said something fairly vulgar.

Beth sat beside me and took my hand. "Billy's coming here?"

I nodded. "He found my mother, paid her a visit, and he's on his way. My god, those things are amazing. No wonder you love drinking them. But I don't think I can feel my hands. How can you handle more than one?"

"Honey, like everything else, it's practice, practice, practice."

I looked at my phone, concentrated hard, and dialed Scott. "Hey, listen, thanks for the invite, but I may have to pass after all. Apparently, my father is on his way up here."

Silence. Then Scott cleared his throat. "Are you calling just to tell me, or are you asking me for help?"

The martini was making it a little hard to think clearly, but I knew the answer to that one. "I think I'd like your help."

"Is he coming by train?"

"Yes."

"Perfect. I can't prevent him from coming to RiverCliffe, but I can make sure he's escorted off before he makes it halfway across the lobby."

"Can you do that?"

"Sure. He'll have to take a cab from the station. I'll get a schedule, figure out when he might show up, and have someone waiting by the front door. I can't prevent him from going into RiverCliffe, but once he's inside, at your request, he can be removed."

The relief I felt was so immense I slumped further down into the couch. "Thank you."

"If you're that nervous, I can bring the pizza over there, and my well-used Monopoly game. Just be warned: I don't do pineapple pizza, and I take my Monopoly games very seriously."

"And how, exactly, did you know that my kids love to play Monopoly?"

He laughed. "My sources are everywhere." His voice softened. "You'll never have to see him, Risa. Not unless you want to."

"Well, I don't," I said, louder than necessary.

"Okay then, see you around six?"

I squinted at the read-out on the TV. Almost two. That would give me time to prepare myself for meeting—or not meeting— my father. It would also give me time to shake off the mind-numbing effects of the martini. "Scott, set it up. I'm making it official. I don't want him here."

"Done."

"And I'll see you tonight. Hey Scott?"

"Yes?"

"Beth will want wine."

"No problem."

"And thank you." I hung up and looked at Beth. "Now I need to get my brain back into some sort of order."

She nudged me with her elbow. "You really are going to have him thrown out? You're not even going to see him?"

My mouth felt very dry and I licked my lips. "I told you what he did to me, Beth. To mom and me, and Cathy. I hate him."

"You spent lots of years wanting to meet him. This might be your only chance."

I shook my head. "Maybe if I'd known all along, time would have tempered my feelings. But finding out the extent of his lies…it's too new, Beth. There's no scar tissue, just a big, open wound. No, I don't want to see him." I looked at her. "What I really want to do is feel my fingertips again."

She laughed. "Go on, then, and try to take a nap. I'll shower and handle the kids. I never knew you were such a lightweight."

"I didn't used to be. I'm out of practice. Divorce and living with your mother will do that to you."

"Now, see, those things would make me drink *more*."

I leaned forward and hugged her. "I love you. And I'm so glad you're here."

She patted me on the back. "I love you too, baby. Now, sleep this off."

I headed for my room. I couldn't face climbing the stairs to Kevin's room. As soon as my head hit the pillow, I was out.

I woke up, didn't have a killer headache, and went into the living room. The little house was empty. I took a quick shower, brushed the slightly mossy feeling off my teeth, and went into the inn.

Winston and MaryBeth, one of the housekeeping people, were huddled together when I entered the lobby. Winston waved me over.

"It would appear," he said in a low, serious voice, "that the Morgan's are stealing our towels. They've been here three days, and every morning the towels are missing."

Now, granted, the towels at RiverCliffe are large and thick, fluffy and white, and a joy to wrap up in after a nice, long shower. But worthy of theft?

"Seriously? They can afford to stay here for a week, but need to steal towels?" I shook my head. "How do you usually handle something like this?"

Winston sighed. "We usually don't."

I looked sideways at him. "You just let our guests steal from us?"

He looked uncomfortable. "Cathy always said it wasn't worth the bad juju."

"Bad juju? That's ridiculous. I won't have people stealing from us. What are you going to do?"

I saw his back stiffen as he squared his shoulders. "Nothing."

"Wrong answer, Winston."

"You said I could have free rein in running the inn," he hissed, his eyes bright.

"Yes, but not about something like this. Have they been here before?"

Winston shook his head, eyes still glittering. "No."

"Okay then. MaryBeth, stop giving them towels. If they complain to you, tell them to speak to Winston or me about it. Winston, if they come down, be outraged. Tell them that someone from the household staff must be stealing them. Tell them you're going to call the police right away and have the whole thing looked into. Make sure they know they'll be questioned as witnesses."

Winston's shoulders relaxed. "That's pretty good."

"Yeah, it is." I took a deep breath. "This is my inn now, Winston, and I've sat back and let you do what you want, but if and when I step up with something, I don't want an argument, got it?"

He nodded, and I saw Marybeth's lips twitch in a smile.

"So listen." I cleared my throat. "My father knows I'm here, and there's a really good chance he's coming. Maybe tonight."

MaryBeth ducked her head and slipped away. Winston set his jaw. "Okay."

"Scott knows. He'll be put off the property as soon as he steps in the lobby. But you'll be here, so I want you to be aware. If you see him and there's no deputy behind him, call me. Scott's bringing pizza."

Winston nodded. "Got it. From Scaletto's?"

"What?"

"The pizza. Is it from Scaletto's? I bet it is. Scott's a bit of a food snob. Lucky you. It beats the crap in town by a mile."

I sighed. Winston could switch moods faster than any person I'd ever met, and as much as I would have loved to talk pizza, I was starting to feel anxious. Billy probably knew all about the owner's apartment. What if he came directly there, and walked in with me and the kids sitting around the table, eating pizza? Scott, I'm sure, would handle it, but I'd see him, I'd have to talk to him, my kids would see him...

"I'll bring you out a slice. Just—" I stopped and chewed my lip. "If Billy shows up, call me. I don't want to see him, but, well..."

Winston nodded, his eyes sympathetic. "Sure, Risa. You've never met him, have you?"

I shook my head.

"No problem, then. I know what he looks like. I'll ring the house phone once, and then hang up."

I took a deep breath. "Thanks, Winston. Now, have you seen my kids?"

He nodded. "Beth went with all of them for a walk. I think they wanted to show her the barns. Kira seemed very excited about her chickens."

Good. My kids were safe. I walked over toward the barns, following the chatter and laughter.

We had cows at RiverCliffe, of course. Daniel milked them to make his cheese. I'd seen them standing out in the fields, and they all looked very pretty, but I chose to admire them from a distance. Apparently Beth wanted to get up close and personal, because she was standing in the doorway of the barn as the cows were moving in for the night, talking and patting them on their rather large and, to me, overwhelming back haunches. Kira, Kevin and Lily were all leaning against the fence, laughing, as Daniel tried to move the cows past her loving caresses.

I had a thought cross my mind, fleeting and terrifying, that she was drunk. Had she continued with her martinis after I'd taken my nap?

She looked up and waved happily. No, she wouldn't do that. Not with my kids. But…cows?

"Are you drunk?" I called out in a teasing tone, dreading her answer.

She stuck her tongue out at me. "Honey, to get this close to one of these, I need all my faculties razor sharp." She playfully swatted a particularly large, mostly black beauty on the rump and made her way to the fence. "How are you feeling?"

"Good," I said. "Scott should be here in a bit, guys. He's bringing pizza. Let's get back to the house, okay?"

"She didn't see my chickens yet," Kira whined.

Beth bent down and kissed the top of Kira's head. "Lead the way, sweetie. We got five minutes." Kira scampered away, Kevin and Beth behind. Lily stayed at the fence.

"Mom?"

"Yes?"

"So, Serena said she can put me on the payroll. I need working papers."

"Really? Wow, that's exciting. Okay. Let me check with her, and Winston, and take a look at where we are, budget-wise. I know we hire extra for the summer. And we'll get you papers." Serena wanted to hire her? I worked hard to keep the grin off my face. Serena was like a protective mother bear with her budget. If she wanted to add a new hire…

Lily scampered off after Beth. I stayed back and watched as Daniel got the last of his herd into the barn, and he closed the door behind him. I looked around the barnyard. There were the usual noises, and the ripple of giggling in the background. I looked over into the graveyard, serene and quiet in the setting sun.

I followed the noise of my children away from the barn.

Scott had to make two trips, the first time for three boxes of pizza, the second time for two bottles of wine and Monopoly.

I had a hard time restraining my children from diving in to the pizza. It smelled heavenly. When he came in the second time, Beth grabbed the bag with the wine.

"Scott, I love you already," she told him.

"What if I'm not Scott?" he asked, grinning.

"Well, tall handsome stranger, thanks for feeding us. And thanks for the wine." She flashed me a grin. "I like him."

I had to smile. "Yeah, me too." And I did. When he came through the door, I felt safe. Billy Newsome might be out there somewhere, trying to find me, but I felt like this man would protect me.

I'd never felt that before.

I grabbed two slices, put them on a plate, excused myself from the party and walked to the lobby.

Winston was working in our office. The front door had an alarm that flashed a light in the back office every time someone came in or left the building, so I knew he could be working and still know if Billy came in. I set the plate in front of him. He closed his eyes and inhaled, then sighed happily.

"Any man who brings you pizza like this is a keeper," he said, opening his eyes and reaching for a slice. He bit, chewed slowly, and swallowed with a smile. "Thank you."

"You're welcome. How are we doing?" He was looking over the next week's reservations.

"We're at eighty-seven percent, which is good. Not great, but we get walk-ins this time of year." He raised his eyebrows. "You want to talk business right now?"

"No. Enjoy your slices. I'll tell Scott you think he's a keeper."

He sighed. "Sadly, he plays for the wrong team. Can you ask him if he's got a gay brother?"

I laughed. "Sure. Later."

I walked back to the lobby, then went to the front door and looked out.

The entrance to RiverCliffe was actually a set of doors, almost ten feet tall, with gracefully arched glass and ornate brass knobs. I peered through the window. The river shimmered in the moonlight, but there was no movement. No yellow cabs pulling up front, discharging handsome Irishmen. No lone, bedraggled figure limping up the drive, battered suitcase in hand.

Good. Maybe he wouldn't show up after all. Maybe he was just playing my mother, trying to get a rise out of her. He'd been escorted off RiverCliffe before. Maybe he wouldn't bother trying again.

On the other hand, he was, if nothing else, an opportunist. I was here, the daughter he never knew, and he had no clue how I felt about him. He might very well imagine that I'd greet him with open arms.

If he did show up, and beat Scott's man to RiverCliffe, would Winston be enough to keep him at bay?

I should not have wasted my time worrying. We ate pizza, played cutthroat Monopoly until my son Kevin bought or won everything on the board, and drank wine. Beth drank most of it, and when she finally waved goodnight, she was swaying gracefully. Scott and I rinsed glasses and packed away the game in silence.

He sat on the couch and I curled up beside him.

"So, no company tonight."

I let out a deep breath. "Thankfully, no." I tilted up my head to him. "I really appreciate you coming here. I felt pretty safe tonight, knowing that if he did show up, you'd be there to help me. I had a thousand scenarios in my head, none of them great, but you were in most of them."

He kissed the side of my head. "I'm glad I could be here."

I turned my face toward him, my mouth meeting his. I wanted to show him I was grateful, but the kiss turned quickly into something more. I twisted and got to my knees and moved, straddling him on the couch. His arms went around my waist, pulling me in closer. Gratitude be damned. What I felt right then had nothing to do with being grateful. It was a simple lust, and I felt it growing in us both.

"It's amazing," I murmured. "I'm a woman who owns almost thirty beds, but I can't find one to use when I really want one." I pushed myself away from him and scrambled to the other side of the couch, waiting for my breathing to slow. My kids were upstairs. Beth was right in the next room. I simply could not do, in that moment, what I most wanted to do.

Scott's breath was coming in gasps. "There's always the back seat of my car."

I broke into a laugh and stood up. "I'd offer you a cold shower, but I'd only be tempted to join you."

He cleared his throat, ran his hands through his hair and stood. "I think I'll just take my Monopoly game and go."

We were about two feet apart, and I could feel the heat between us. "Good idea."

He grabbed the Monopoly game off the table and bent to give me a swift, hard kiss. I had to literally knot my fingers together behind my back to keep my hands off him. He went out the side door and I locked it behind him, feeling frustrated.

And elated. Being with him all evening, watching him with my kids and my best friend, and knowing that, if Billy Newsome came looking for me, he'd have to go through Scott first — it all added to a feeling that was starting to feel familiar. Like when I first met Ed, and there was that first rush of attraction, of wanting more. I was feeling that with Scott. Sure, there was a physical pull, but this feeling was…more.

I went upstairs, snuck into the bed next to sleeping Kevin and dreamed of Beth, drunk and running naked through the graveyard, Caleb chasing her. Then my father appeared, old and bent, his fingers curling as he pushed his open hand in front of me. I kept walking away from him, saying no, until I woke and it was morning and I felt like I'd had no sleep at all.

Billy Newsome walked into RiverCliffe House at two twenty on Sunday afternoon.

We were busy. He'd been there before, so maybe he remembered that Sunday was a heavy checkout/ check-in day. We had two couples waiting to check in, and another couple hanging around waiting for their room to be cleaned. I'd offered them a free glass of wine and had suggested they could sit on the porch or perhaps in the great room, but they instead chose to hover by the desk, checking their watches every five minutes. They were the Goodwin's, and they'd arrived just after one, and laughingly said they realized check-in time was officially three o'clock, but hoped they could sneak into their room early.

As it turned out, they could not. When told that, they stopped being so good-humored, but I had already learned the best way to avoid any direct confrontation with a guest was to smile and shrug. They had requested a specific type of room. They had been told when they made the reservation the room would be available at three. So... sorry, Mr. and Mrs. Goodwin. Gonna have to wait.

The other two couples were nicer and more patient, and, thankfully, their rooms were ready, so I was at the desk, pulling up their information, checking driver's licenses and getting signatures when I heard a rough voice, almost a whisper.

"My God, Theresa, you look just like your mother."

I looked up.

The first thing I saw were his eyes, and I felt a jolt of recognition. I was looking into Kevin's eyes. That's where my son had gotten the long, narrow shape, the deep blue color.

Then my brain pulled back and I saw the whole, the gray stubble of a beard, wrinkled forehead, and small, stained teeth behind a wide smile.

I felt an icy calm take over. I'd been ready for him last night. All the defenses had been in place, and he never showed. But that didn't mean he could waltz into RiverCliffe today without a fight. I turned to Trent, who was waiting to take luggage up to the rooms. "Trent, please call the sheriff's department and tell them we have a trespasser that needs to be removed at once."

He blinked a few times, looking surprised, but he was Bernie's grandson, so he just nodded and started to move.

"Hey, now, wait, wait." My father reached out and grabbed Trent's sleeve. "No need for that." He gestured toward me. "She's my kid. Everything's cool."

"Excuse me, but everything is *not* cool. Leave right now or I'll have you arrested. And let go of Trent. If you touch him again," I said, my voice cold and even, "I'll add assault charges to trespassing." He faltered, his hand dropping from Trent's arm. Trent hurried to the back office.

I was proud of myself, my quiet and even voice. No need for hysterics here, I thought. If I'd learned one thing over the past few weeks, it was never disturb the guests. I could go about my work, welcome these people to the inn, and maintain a careful distance from my father. In a few minutes, someone else would come and make sure he left. That was not my job. My job was to check in these people and make sure they felt welcome.

I smiled brightly at my guests. "Trent will be right back, and he'll show you to your rooms. Mr. and Mrs. Filipek, you're up first, I believe? Just sign here."

Mr. and Mrs. Filipek obviously thought that a show came with the room, because they didn't blink at the awkward and tense scene playing out before them. In fact, they avoided looking in my father's direction at all, and focused on a careful examination of the key card.

"All the doors to RiverCliffe House are locked at eleven," I explained, glancing at the second couple, the Roberson's, to include them in my spiel. I was also sure that Billy Newsome heard every word. "You can't get in without the card. Just use the same code you use to get into your room, and that will unlock the doors. Any questions?" Like, Why are you calling the sheriff, exactly? Trent popped into view just in time. He grabbed suitcases and headed toward the stairs. I turned to the Roberson's.

"And, if you could sign here. Trent will be right back, or you can head up to your room now, and he'll bring up your suitcases presently." The Roberson's had apparently been paying closer attention, because they practically ran away from the desk and up the stairs.

The Goodwin's looked from me to Billy, then back again. "He's your father? Shouldn't you show him a little more respect?" Mrs. Goodwin asked.

She was already on my short list for the day, and that pretty much tipped the scale. I was ready to call their room completely unfit for human habitation and send them to Holiday Inn down the highway.

"Ah, don't be too hard on her," Billy said, almost laughing. "We ain't very close." He leaned an elbow against the counter. "Where you folks from?"

At that moment the front screen doors slammed open and Martha charged in, Bernie trotting in her wake. Martha was a tall woman, and had at least six inches on my father, who, when he realized who she was, seemed to shrink even smaller.

"Martha, my dear gi—"

Martha leaned over him, her face like stone, and lifted her left arm, pointing to the front door. Billy swallowed meekly and skulked out, Martha and Bernie behind him.

I gasped. I hadn't realized that I hadn't been breathing properly until my lungs suddenly exploded. I felt a cold sweat on the back of my neck and I fell against the counter, filling my lungs. The Goodwin's withdrew without a word to the opposite end of the lobby, and I began the fast and frantic work of pulling myself together.

Luckily, there are plenty of things to do on a rainy Sunday afternoon in the Hudson Valley, so the lobby and great room were not cluttered with bored guests. It was a shame, really, because this farce seemed worthy of an audience. I swallowed a few times, kept my eyes closed until I felt steady and sane.

I could taste something in my mouth, ugly and metallic. Hate, I thought. This is what hate tastes like. He had walked in like he had a right to, had a right to my time and my energy, as though he was any other father stopping in to say hello, rather than a man who had left me, left my mother without so much as a backward glance. Not only that, he deliberately worked to keep us away from the help that would have been there for us, that could have made so much of a difference in our lives.

I opened my eyes, and the taste was still there on my tongue. I swallowed, and it hit my belly like a punch. It fed my anger and I felt strong and unafraid. I remembered what Cathy had said about anger and hate. She told me to use it. Well, my father was here, and it looked like we'd have something to say to each other after all. I needed all the anger and hate I could get.

I walked after my father onto the porch of RiverCliffe House.

The rain was falling, and the air was cool. I looked around the landscape, and it was pale and dreamy in the mist, almost surreal. Just the way I felt.

Billy was standing on the steps, just far enough down to be out of the shelter of the roofline, and the rain had drenched his head, the gray hair plastered to his scalp. Martha was completely dry and, being a step or two up, towered over him like a stoic avenging angel. All she needed was a sword and a set of wings.

"...dare you return here, you cowardly snake," she said, her voice like a stream of icy water tumbling over rough rock. "This poor child spent her whole life suffering from your selfishness, and you have the audacity to show up here like you deserve something?"

I must say, I was impressed. I hadn't heard Martha raise her voice above her usual monotone since I'd arrived.

"You're just lucky that lynching is frowned on around here, because I guarantee you that I could gather a willing crowd in about five minutes flat." Martha lifted her arm again and pointed farther down, to the highway. "Go. Remove yourself from this place. Because I hear the sheriff, and the next stop for you will be jail."

He looked at me, standing in the protection of the doorway. "Ah, now, Theresa, my own flesh and blood, you wouldn't put your only father in jail, now, would you?"

"Yes." I pulled myself up straighter. "In a heartbeat." I could hear the sirens now, off in the distance. Speaking to him wasn't hard at all, I marveled.

"Your mother told me what a good girl you were," he said, his voice sliding into a whine.

"I doubt that," I shot back. He was just an old man. "In fact, she probably told you what a bitch I could be."

His face changed, just a bit. "She did," he snarled. "I guess it was wishful thinking on my part that you didn't take after her."

"Thank God I didn't take after you," I said, my voice still steady. "You're a liar and a cheat. You kept me from my family, people who would have given me what you could not. You're a selfish man, Billy Newsome. You couldn't even share your wife and daughter with those who would have loved us." I could feel the blood pounding in my ears, but the words were steady and true. "My mother was an extraordinary woman, raising me alone, and I'm forever grateful for every single thing in me that takes after her," I said. Then I turned and went back inside. He had meant so many things for so many years. Now, finally seeing him, I realized that the only power he had was what I'd given him, and I easily swept that all away.

Trent was bounding down the stairs, and ran up anxiously. "Are you okay?"

I nodded. "Thanks for calling Bernie. She and Martha have things under control."

"Can I, like…" He shrugged. "Hold him? Just till the police get here?"

I almost choked on my laughter. "No, Trent, I think he's not going anywhere." The adrenalin was still racing through my body. Of course it was. But the hurt had washed away. I felt like I needed to run somewhere, jump up and down, do anything…the surge of anger I felt when I first saw him was disappearing. He was gone. It had been easy. I felt triumphant.

Serena came trotting through the dining room, Lily right behind her. My, the jungle drums were fast. Serena grabbed my shoulders and shook them. "Risa, you're white as a ghost. Are you okay?"

I nodded, and watched Lily walk slowly to the front doors and through them, out to the porch. She was looking for her grandfather, of course. She was curious. Why shouldn't she be? I didn't want to see him get in a cab and drive away, or get pushed into the back of a sheriff's car. I just wanted him gone.

"Where are Kev and Kira?" Serena asked.

I pulled my eyes from Lily and looked at Serena. "They're at Daniel's. Harry Potter movie marathon day."

She nodded. "Right. Okay then, that's good. That's very good." She dropped her hands from my shoulders and went to the front door, watching. "The sheriff is here. It's Gary, not Scott. But Billy is gone." She came back to me. "You want to go somewhere and just breathe?"

I nodded. "The Goodwin's here are waiting for 311; it should be ready any minute. There are five other check-ins, but they should be coming in later. Can I just take a few minutes?"

Serena nodded. "Of course. Trent and I got this."

I walked back through the lobby, silently thanking Cathy Newsome for the rigorous cross training of all her employees. Anyone, even MaryBeth, who was changing the sheets in room 311, could check-in guests, serve coffee, or clean the pool. I burst through the doorway of my house, sat on the couch and shut my eyes very tightly.

My father.

I needed to talk to someone. I needed to yell, scream, cry, rant, explain, question...

I bolted, leaving the door wide open, and ran to the rain, past the barns, and right through the break in the low stone wall.

It was raining harder, and I could barely see the river, but I stood, arms outstretched, my face lifted to the dark sky and tried to imagine all the bad feelings running down and away.

I opened my mouth. The rain tasted...soft. Cool. This is probably good for my skin, I thought, then started laughing. How ridiculous was that, to think about my skin? Then the laughing turned to crying and I dropped my arms and bent my head, and that's when I felt him, his arms around me, as he turned me and held me, and I sobbed into his shoulder in the rain.

He felt warm. How was that possible? My fuddled brain kept coming back to the fact that Caleb felt warm, and strong. How could a dead man feel warm?

I pushed away from him and tried to wipe my eyes, but the rain filled them. I grabbed his hand and led him back under the line of oaks, where the canopy allowed only drops through, and I could look at him, clear and focused.

"My father just showed up," I said. "I haven't seen him. Like, ever. And he just showed up at the front desk like it was the most normal thing in the world."

"I'm sorry."

I wiped my face. "Do you know about him? Billy?"

He nodded. "Cathy talked about him some. I met him, you know. Up at the Claw. A few times, actually. I liked him, but I knew he was trouble. He was a good listener, but he was always looking for a weakness." His jaw moved and bitterness crept into his voice. "I can't imagine having a kid and not being a part of their life."

I sniffed. "Tell me about Henry."

He raised one eyebrow. "You been checking me out?"

"I was curious," I said. "I have a right to be curious."

Caleb sighed and stuck his hands in the pocket of his jeans. "Henry was four when I left Linda. I always sent money, and I'd call him. I always made it back for his birthday. Linda wasn't…kind about things. She didn't want me to see him. She was back with her folks and I know it was hard." He shrugged. "They never wanted us to marry."

"And he never knew why you stopped calling?"

Caleb hung his head, and I could see his shoulders spasm. The pain was palpable, coming off of him like a wave, while my father had happily gone on with his life…

"I'm going to find him," I said to Caleb. "Henry. I'll find him for you. I'll tell him what happened. No one deserves to think they were just…left."

He threw back his head and ran his hands across his face. "And what, exactly, are you gonna tell him? That you met his dead daddy and wanted to set things right?" His eyes, when they met mine, were full of sadness. "Risa, what are you going to tell him?"

I reached out and grabbed his hand, holding it tightly in both of mine. "I'll tell him the truth, Caleb. If he thinks I'm crazy, fine. But I'll tell him you didn't just leave him." I gave his hand a shake. "At least he'll have been told."

"Thank you," he whispered. He brushed the damp hair away from my face. "You're going to catch something, standing out here in the rain. Go inside. Get warm."

I nodded. Oh, this man. He was my friend. He cared about what happened to me. I wanted him in my life, a real person I could talk to and depend on. Why couldn't I take him with me, beyond the boundaries of this place?

I turned and left him, walking through the oaks, when it occurred to me, like an unexpected shock, that I did have a man like that in my life. Scott, who had been willing to put himself between my father and me. To protect me. If I had run to Scott today, instead of out into the rain, he would have put his arms around me, and I could have found something more than just comfort there.

The lobby was empty and quiet. The Goodwin's had either been shown their room or decided to try their luck elsewhere, perhaps an inn with less of a floorshow. I didn't care.

I stopped to dry off my hair and change my drenched clothes, so I felt almost back to normal when I sidled up to Serena behind the desk.

"Lily okay?" I asked.

Serena's mouth twisted. "I think she was upset, to be honest. I think she wanted to talk to him."

I stared. "Why on earth would she want to talk to a man she'd never seen in her life?"

Serena shrugged. "He's her family." She looked uncomfortable. "When was the last time she saw her own father?"

"February," I said, slowly. "That was a long time ago." Ed hadn't proved himself to be much of a father in the past year. Was Lily looking, as I had, for some replacement? Did she think she'd find it in Billy Newsome?

Serena took a long breath. "Families are complicated things, Risa. Some are whole and fine, some are broken, some we make ourselves with whatever we have handy. But however it's put together, it's the thing that we always try to get back to. You may not think much of your ex-husband, but I bet your kids do."

I swallowed "You're right." We stood together, looking at the rain. "Are you and Daniel going to put together a family for those girls?"

Serena grew very still. "I don't think so," she said at last. "Suzanne was a force of nature, an amazing human being. I knew her, and loved her with all my heart, even as I wanted her husband more than anything in the world. Her girls loved her, too. Daniel, well, he's a man, and men need things. But those girls don't need the same things, and they're never going to need another momma."

"Would you be happy if things stayed just as they are?" I didn't know how things were, exactly, but I knew that Serena never spent the night at Daniel's, and that they were polite and impersonal to each other at the inn.

She shook her head slowly. "That's the thing, right? Today, right this moment, any time I spend with Daniel is enough. But tomorrow…who knows? We do change; I believe that strongly. We don't stay the same people from day to day, or year to year. And I may very well want more someday, no matter how happy I think I am right now. And right now, those girls won't let me any closer, and I can't do anything about it. No one can compete with a ghost." She shook herself. "And Scott has called here twice, said he couldn't reach you on your cell, and is worried about you." She waggled her finger in my face. "Don't you be hurting that man, boss. He's good enough for you, and you know it, so play this smart."

I nodded. "Yes, he is a good man," I said softly. "But I'm not staying, Serena. I'll be gone at the end of the summer."

She nudged me. "You don't have to be gone, you know. You can do whatever you like."

I looked down at her and I shook my head. "That's not part of the plan."

"Was meeting Scott part of the plan?"

I shook my head again, pulled out my cell phone and stared at it. I always turned off the ringer when I was behind the desk. There were three calls from him, actually. And two from my mother.

I sent him a quick text. *Im fine, working talk later*

He answered back at once. *Good. Billy asked to be driven to the Days Inn in Rhinebeck. He wanted to make sure you knew where he was. If you want to press charges tell me. Glad you're safe*

My mother would not be content with a text, so she'd have to wait.

I looked up at the sound of laughter. Trent was holding a large umbrella over the heads of two guests, and they all ran into the lobby together.

"Risa, this is Mr. and Mrs. White. I'll go back and get the luggage, if you can check them in?"

I put on my innkeeper face. "Of course, Mr. and Mrs. White. Welcome to RiverCliffe House. I'm Risa."

And the rest of the day just went on, like another, normal day.

CHAPTER 10

*S*unday nights were always busy in the dining room, so I did
not see much more of Lily. Beth and Winston came dripping through the door, loaded down with bulky packages wrapped in
brown paper and bags of take-out that smelled of curry and biryani.
Kevin and Kira had come in from Daniel's and went upstairs, but the
smell of food drew them both downstairs.

"Is that Indian food?" Kevin asked, peering into one of the bags. "I
didn't know we could get Indian food out here."

Winston smacked him playfully on the side of his head. "What do
you mean, 'out here'? We're barely a hundred miles from New York
City, not in the Yukon."

"I invited Winston to eat with us," Beth said, coming from the
bedroom, carrying a single package. "After all, he suggested Indian,
did the ordering, and paid for it."

"Well then, I guess it's okay," I said. "Thank you, Winston."

"Thank, you, Winston," my two children echoed.

Beth sat down with an exaggerated sigh and began opening
containers. "We hit seven shops and got soaking wet, but I got just
amazing things, and Winston here got a Parrish print that is just to die
for. And this is for you."

She handed me a slim package, wrapped in brown paper.

"A cookbook?" Kira asked hopefully.

I unwrapped it. It was plain brown leather, soft as butter. A diary. I looked at Beth and rolled my eyes. Beth grinned as she put some chutney on her rice. "And how was your day?"

I put the diary carefully on a shelf, went back to the table and sat. I cleared my throat. "Well, we had two walk-ins, so we're full up, except for one room with air-conditioning issues. There's one more couple due in tonight, but I'm sure they'll show. Oh, and yeah. Billy was here. Martha and Bernie escorted him off the property and into a police car, where he hitched a ride to Rhinebeck. He wanted me to know that. Why would he think I'd want to know where he was staying? What am I supposed to do, drive up there and have a drink with him?"

The silence was, as they say, deafening. I looked up from my samosas. "What?"

"He was here?" Kira asked, her voice rising like a fire siren. "Grandpa was here?"

I sat back. "Kira, why do you call him grandpa? And yes, he was here."

"What did he say?" Beth croaked.

"That I looked like my mother. Then while I was throwing him out, he defended me to a guest by telling them that we weren't, how did he put it? Close. Yeah, that was it. We weren't close. Like we only got together on birthdays or something."

Beth turned to Winston, glaring. "All those texts you were getting? The ones you said weren't important? I bet every single employee here was giving you the rundown, and you never said a word."

Winston turned bright pink. "It wasn't my news to spread," he mumbled.

"I would like to see him," Kevin said, shoveling food into his mouth. "I mean, how often do you meet your grandfather?"

"Never," I said. "Which is why I didn't introduce him around. He's ignored us all completely. Why would I treat him like family?"

"'Cause he's what we got," Kira said simply.

I looked at them, surprised, trying to see their reasoning. "This is not a nice man we're talking about here, okay? He's not a good person. Besides the fact that he left my mother to raise me without any emotional or financial support, he's also been in jail. Prison. Multiple incarcerations." I took a big gulp of my water and tried to cool myself down. "He's here because when his mother died, he didn't inherit anything. I did. And he's probably sniffing around for money, which he is *not* getting anyway, so why should I bother to see him. Why should any of us?"

"Well, maybe we should, just this once," Kevin suggested. "Before, you know, he's dead."

I opened my mouth, tried to think of something pithy and wise to say, then closed it. He was right, of course. I'd spent a large part of my life looking for this man, and now, at last, here he was. And he was old and, quite frankly, did not look so good. If he did die, and I never got a chance to speak to him, how would that feel?

"So, you two want the chance to meet him?" I asked.

They both nodded.

"So does your sister, I think," I said slowly. My kids wanted to meet him, to talk to him, despite my feelings on the subject. Nothing new there, really, but I felt a vague sense of betrayal, especially now, after meeting him and finding him totally unrepentant. Not once had he offered an apology or explanation Instead, he'd turned mean when I rebuffed him. All the more reason for me to not want to see him again.

I looked at Beth, who caught my eye then looked down, concentrating on her food. "What?"

She reached into another bag and brought forth, —surprise, surprise— a bottle of wine. "*I* think you should meet him, bring your kids, have a talk. You can set the rules, after all. Where, when, what to talk about. And if he gets out of hand, just leave. I doubt he'll come after you, not if he knows what kind of reception he'll get here."

Her too? She spent years knowing what I went through because of my father. Was she going to side with my kids, instead of understanding how I might be feeling?

"Really? Well, *I* think *you* drink too much." I stood up so fast my chair rocked back. I grabbed my phone off the table and walked out.

The dining room was full, and the noise filled the lobby and spilled out onto the wide front porch. The rain had stopped and now there was a mist, rising off the water that covered everything like a layer of shiny gray tulle. I flopped down into a rocking chair and called my mother.

"So, Mom, he was here," I said. "He said I looked like you, admitted we were not close, and was walked out and down to a waiting sheriff's car. He's staying locally, and he wanted me to know where. My kids want to meet him, and Beth said I should or I'll regret it."

"Sheriff's car? The same sheriff you're involved with that you deliberately never told me about?"

"Yeesh, really? That's what you've glommed on to? *He was here.* My father. Right in front of me, and I threw him out of my lobby and into the rain."

"And tell me, Risa, how did that make you feel?"

"Are you kidding me? Have you been watching Dr. Phil again?"

"Let me tell you what I've been thinking about for the past twenty-four hours. That he looked sick and worn out. He didn't have his spark. He's an old man with nothing. Did you hear me? He. Has. Nothing. We talked and he was very honest with me, although I have to admit he didn't mention his other wives, even after I told him we were never divorced. He was cranky and unpleasant, which is totally not his jam."

"His jam?" I echoed faintly.

"Billy was always a charmer, always working the crowd. Even with total strangers, he'd be on. He's a changed man."

"Yeah? Well, it doesn't sound like he's changed for the better."

"I think he has. I think he's realized he's at the end of his life with nothing to show for it, and he's trying to make amends."

"Or maybe he thinks he can get some easy cash from the daughter he's never met by playing the sympathy card."

She was silent for a moment. I could hear the soft inhale and could picture her, at the kitchen table, carefully taping the ash from her cigarette. "You may very well be right," she said at last. "He always was a good actor, and maybe this is just another part. But you didn't answer my question. When he was standing, there, in front of you and you told him to leave, how did you feel? Don't think about it. Just tell me."

"I felt sad," I blurted.

"Okay then. So what does that tell you?"

I sighed. "That my mother has been reading too many psychology books again?"

"I have, but that's not the point. The point is..?"

"I felt sad," I repeated dutifully.

"And?"

"And what? Ma, please. I called to get some advice, not a complete analysis."

"I think if your children want to see their grandfather, you should let them. After all, you don't have to speak to him if you don't want to, but it is not your place to deny those children the opportunity to meet Billy."

I took a breath. "You're right."

"Of course I'm right. Now, tell me, have you seen any dead people? What's that like? I've been dyin' over here."

I dropped the phone on my lap and threw my head back, staring at the pale blue ceiling of the porch.

"That bad?" Scott asked. He climbed the steps and sat in a wicker chair beside me.

I felt my heart jump and a smile came to my face. I was so glad to see him. Everything around me had been in steaming heaps of the past, and here he was, and it suddenly didn't matter any more. This man had nothing to do with my past, my father, my complicated relationship with my mother...none of it. He was, I felt in a flash, what my future might look like: warm and loving and safe.

I took the phone and shook it. "This is my mother, and she is crazy." I put the phone back to my ear. "Mom, thanks for the advice. I'll call you later, okay?"

I clicked off the phone and stared at it.

Scott reached over, gently took it from my hand, and set it on the small table between our chairs. "So, how was it?"

I locked my fingers together, and made the church and the steeple from my childhood. Then I held my hands up and aligned the little triangles just right, so I could see through them to the barely-there moon.

"I was angry," I said. "And it felt really good. Thanks to my mother, who is apparently acting as my analyst these days, I realize now that I also felt sad." I dropped my hands to my lap. "The kids want to meet him."

He leaned back. "I can imagine. And I bet they get along just great. He's probably a very romantic figure to them. After all, he never really caused them any pain, not like what their own father probably did. So here's this rascal of a grandfather, why wouldn't they want to meet him?" He reached over again, took my hand, and held it to his lips, kissing the palm of my hand gently. "If you want, I could take them over. You don't even have to be involved."

I stared at my hand, cradled gently in his. "You'd do that?"

"I like you, Risa. I like you quite a lot. Yes, I'd do that. Just say the word."

My throat felt full, and I was overwhelmed by his kindness, his willingness to help me. I brought his hand to my face, holding his palm against my cheek. "Word?"

He chuckled, and stood up, bringing me with him, and kissed me. It was a soft, comforting kiss, meant to heal and sooth. As I kissed him back, my desire for him came rushing in like water from a broken dam. Yes, I wanted the healing, but, once again, his touch made me wanting more.

"Any empty beds?" he asked, his voice rough.

I ran my hands down the front of his shirt, feeling the warm flesh beneath. "As a matter of fact, yes."

He looked down at me. "I'm beginning to think you want me just for my body," he said, his tone half-joking but his eyes deadly serious.

"I was beginning to think that too, " I said. "But it's more than that right now. " I buttoned and unbuttoned the top of his polo shirt. "Is that okay?"

"More is okay," he said. "More is fine."

He followed me back into the inn. I glanced around. "Jessie?" I called. "Is twelve empty?"

She stuck her head out of the back office. "Yes. The A/C is out, remember? He'll be here tomorrow."

I reached over and grabbed the keycard out of the slot. "I just need to check something."

If she had any questions as to why Scott followed me upstairs, she never asked. I opened the door on the second floor, and Scott slipped in behind me. I felt his hands on me as I turned the lock, pulling away my shirt leaving a trail of kisses down the back of my neck.

We weren't patient this time. We were not cautious. We pulled our clothes off in the gray, fading light. He dropped to the floor and pulled me to him. He tried to ease me onto my back but I pushed him away and climbed on top of him. It had been one hell of a day for me, and more than anything I wanted to lose myself, to find a way to shed any of the anger and hurt that was left in me. I closed my eyes, held his hands to my waist and rocked against him until all I could hear and feel was the bursting of my own heart. When we were done, I stayed on top of him, his arms around me, my head in the hollow of his shoulder.

"I'm glad you were here," I told him. "I needed this." I stopped and added, in a very small voice. "I needed you."

His arms tightened. "You should think about staying, Risa."

I slid off him and rolled onto the floor.

"You don't think I'm reason enough?" he asked. I could hear something in his voice I hadn't heard before, a wistfulness, a yearning.

"It's not that," I said. "It's not just me."

I closed my eyes. My father had come to RiverCliffe, and I'd told him to go, and I told him why. Now, just hours later, it didn't seem to matter at all. Because of Scott. And not, I realized, because of the sex. That had been good and cleansing. But the real healing, I knew, came from his heart, not his body. I heard the buzz of my phone and scrambled to find it in the pile of clothes. A text from Beth. They were looking for me. Was I okay?"

"Beth wants to know if I'm alright," I said.

I heard him sit up behind me, and felt a soft stroke down my back. "Are you?"

I nodded. "Yes. More that alright. I feel...clean. I feel safe." I gathered my clothes and began to put them on. We got dressed in silence. As I went to open the door I stood up and kissed him on the cheek.

"I'll think about it," I said softly.

He slipped out the door and was gone. I took a quick look around. The room looked empty and still. I closed the door behind me.

The next morning I woke up confused. I crept out of the twin bed next to Kevin, tiptoed downstairs, and made a cup of coffee.

I needed to sort things out.

First—RiverCliffe. Could I stay here? And if I did, would it be because of Scott, because of what we might become? Or should I step back and look at the bigger picture?

If we stayed, the kids would not have to move again. That was a huge plus, as I had not even been on Zillow or Realtor.com to see what kind of house I could afford in New Jersey. I had a perfectly good place to live in right here. True, the furniture was not worth saving, but there was enough space for us all in the apartment, not to mention all the wide, green space that lay outside the door.

Kira could stay with her beloved chickens. Kevin could stay on the river, tending the boats. His sour disposition had softened in the weeks we'd been here. He was less negative, less judgmental. He and Lily had almost stopped sniping at each other.

And Lily— we had reached some sort of truce in the past week or two. She stayed in the kitchen with Serena, or hung out with Trent and Mia. She cooked dinner a few nights a week and seemed to enjoy the praise and attention she garnered from us. She seemed content.

I wasn't sure how Winston would react to my staying on, but I also didn't care. I had proved to him—and myself—that I was an asset. I could easily take on more work and responsibility at the inn. After all, RiverCliffe was mine, and I had found I liked tending to its needs.

Second—Billy Newsome. Yes, my father had proved to be as big a scumbag as I'd always imagined. But, he was my father, the only one I'd ever have, and I at least owed it to my children to meet him and let them make up their own minds about him, and about what place they wanted him to take in their lives.

That called for a second cup of coffee.

Now—my love life. I finally had one. And it was looking pretty good.

My first attraction to Scott had been just physical. He set off all sorts of bells and whistles for me, and now I knew that if I wanted simple sexual satisfaction, he was definitely the go-to guy. But there was more to him, and his kind and genuine concern for my happiness was becoming more obvious. It wasn't just sex for him. He cared about what happened to me. He was unselfish in his actions. He wanted to protect me, and keep me safe, and that found a chord in me that rang long and true. I knew I could love him.

Maybe I already did.

Was that even possible after just a few short weeks? Did I really want to sit down and think long and hard about that just now?

No. I was happy and I was afraid if I started to analyze the situation too much, I'd find a way to spoil everything. I just wanted to keep this incredible feeling of joy.

I also wanted a third cup of coffee, but instead pulled another diary from my bookshelf. I checked the clock. It wasn't even six o'clock. Lily would be up and out in the next hour. Kevin and Kira were both usually out of the house by nine. Technically, I had to go to work, but, hey, I didn't have to. Beth and I could take a few horses and wander up the side of the mountain and talk a few things out.

That sounded like a good plan, so I opened the diary and started reading. I had discovered that reading them calmed me, let me think about something other than my own troubles, while letting me see deeper into the world that had become, quite unexpectedly, mine.

I could now hear the voices of the women in my head. Literally.

Each diary had a different style of writing, of course, but as I read, the voices I heard were not my own. Whatever magic or juju or hocus-pocus RiverCliffe held, it was seeping into my psyche.

This volume was Cora, Bea's sister, who I knew moved to New York City and was killed by a streetcar when she was just twenty-six. She was born at RiverCliffe, and had fallen in love there with a simple carpenter who would not leave Kingston, so she left him, in search of adventure. Her diary was not just about her life at RiverCliffe, but also New York in the twenties, flappers and illegal hooch, fast girls and dangerous gangsters.

"Who are you reading?" Lily asked.

I looked up. "Bea's sister, Cora. She was a flapper in Manhattan when that really meant something."

Lily sat down next to me. "What about working papers?"

"I have to go through the Board of Education, apparently, and they're on shortened hours during the summer. I'll try to go this week." I said.

She nodded. "Fine."

"So, Lily," I said, watching her closely, "do you want to meet your grandfather? I don't, but that doesn't mean you and Kira and Kevin can't have dinner with him."

She looked up, her eyes bright. "Yeah?"

"Sure, baby. Why not?"

"Thanks."

I almost expected a kiss, or at least a hug of gratitude, but, well, this *was* Lily.

"Okay, I gotta go," she said. "I'll tell Serena about the working papers thing, she may know about what to do, and… when can we see him?"

"Tonight. I'll call him."

She stood and left.

I heard a noise, and Beth was standing in the doorway, arms folded, looking smug.

"Good for you, Risa. Way to be a grown-up."

I put down the diary and rolled my eyes. "Is that what I was doing? God, I hate that."

She crossed the room and threw herself next to me on the couch. "Whatcha reading?"

"One of the RiverCliffe diaries. Cora. Cathy's aunt, who left the farm for the big city and met a tragic end."

"Did she see dead people too?"

"Yes, apparently, and she didn't like it. She did not spend much of her childhood playing among the gravestones, and I think that was one of the reasons she left. That, and the man she loved wouldn't take her away, so she left on her own."

"Speaking of men, how's Scott? I like him. A whole lot." She raised her eyebrows. "By the way, Jessie from the desk called looking for you last night. She mentioned that you and Scott had been…inspecting a room?"

I didn't even blush. "Hey, what's the point of having a zillion bedrooms if you can't use them whenever you want?"

"Was there rapture? Please, tell me there was rapture."

I shoved her to the other side of the couch. "Just stop. So, I'm thinking about staying here. At RiverCliffe. To live, instead of uprooting the kids and trying to find a house. It just seems like a good idea. I had thought today you and I could take a few horses out, wander the hills and talk. I might even tell you about my rapture. But maybe we could buy new furniture instead?"

She hauled herself up and made a cup of coffee. "Stay here? Really? Now, there's an idea, and it might not be a bad one."

"I haven't decided for sure, but I'm thinking about it."

"And is Scott the reason?"

I smiled. "One of them, for sure. I really like him too. But it just makes sense. This is not such a bad place to raise kids."

"True that. Even if you don't stay, this place could really use a facelift. And you need a new Keurig. This is way too slow."

"Maybe you're too impatient?"

She brought the coffee back and sat. "Do you really think I drink too much?"

Last night, after I came back, Winston was already gone, Lily was home, and Beth and the kids were all watching a movie. I joined them without comment, and she and I had both gone to bed early and without discussion.

I shrugged. "Yes, I do. I know that whenever we get together, we drink, and you were always better at it than me, but now…it's different. I don't think you drink for fun anymore. That kinda worries me, Beth. That's not a good thing for you to be doing."

She took a very long sip of her coffee, stared off to the left, took another long sip and looked at me. "I really don't like my life right now," she said. "I'm having sex with a jerk, but at least it's very expert sex so I feel *something* when we're together. My job is so boring, I hate it, I hate the people I work with, and my condo is too big and it's really ugly. So you're right, I don't drink for fun anymore."

I shut my eyes briefly. "Your condo is not ugly."

"You haven't seen it since I had it repainted. I swear to God, trendy gray sucks the life right out of a room."

"I never understood how you could stay there after Erin was killed," I said softly. "I would have thought the memories would have been too much."

"It was all I had, Risa. The memories. And now I've got this whole loft space that was hers that's just filled with junk and dust and—" She turned away again. "Did I mention I hate my job?"

"I would think that was an easy fix."

"Are you kidding? The number of unemployed lawyers in this state is staggering. I'm lucky to have a paycheck and benefits."

I heard noises above me. Kira and Kevin were up. "Things were so bad after Erin died, and I know I should have tried to spend more time with you," I said.

She shook her head. "You had your own family, Risa. You had your own kids. I was always so grateful every time you drove up to see me. It helped, it really did. Don't ever think you didn't do enough."

"I thought you were…better."

She sighed. "I was. I'll never be completely okay again, but I was getting better. But this past year has just been tough in other ways, and so everything just sucks. My life, my job, my condo, everything." She shook her head, then her whole body, like a horse shaking off rainwater. "Enough of that, please, or I'll start drinking again. Let's see if Kira wants to go shopping with us."

I took her lead. "Good idea. There has to be a Pottery Barn around here somewhere, right? "

"Pottery Barn?" She looked stricken. "With all the antique places around here? Oh, Risa, I saw a chaise yesterday, with this beautiful tapestry upholstery, that would be so perfect in here."

I shook my head and finished my coffee. "I have three kids, Beth. You can't watch a big-screen on a chaise. Good try, though." I grinned as Kira bounced down the stairs, Kevin following behind. "Hey, Kira, baby, want to go shopping with me and Beth? Maybe get a new couch?"

Kira lit up. "Can I get a new bed too? With a canopy? In pink?"

I laughed and hugged her, loving the feel of her small body against mine. "Pink? Really? Isn't that your sister's room too?"

"Yes, but she's not here."

"Good point, but still…so, would you guys want to have dinner with your grandfather tonight?"

Kevin actually didn't bite into his banana to answer. "Really?"

"Yes. You three. I'll call and take care of everything."

Kira frowned. "Why don't you want to come with us?"

Kevin sighed deeply and rolled his eyes. "Because, she's afraid if she spends too much time with him, she'll either kill him or decide she loves him. Don't you understand anything at all?"

I stared. When had Kevin become wise? Did that come with his newly developed muscles? His tanned shoulders? The bones jutting out from beneath his chubby cheeks?

"I understand lots," Kira yelled. "I understand that you're a fat dooty-head!"

"Enough," I warned.

Kevin grabbed another banana. "Wayne probably has lots for me to do, with the rain and all yesterday. When would we leave?"

How calm and mature he sounded. Not like a dooty-head at all. "I'll let you know. Kira, a bagel?"

She stuck her tongue out at Kevin's back as he left. "I'm gonna tell Haley I won't be able to help her today," she said, bolting for the door.

"Ask her if she wants to come," I called after her. "I'll buy her lunch." I looked at Beth who raised one eyebrow. I always wanted to be able to do that.

"Trust me," I told her. "I'd want to kill him."

"Whatever," Beth murmured, fixing another cup of coffee.

I went out to the front lobby, told Winston I would be away from my desk all morning, and looked up the number for the Days Inn at Rhinebeck.

There wasn't a Pottery Barn, as it turned out, but there was a Pier One, HomeGoods, Kirklands…we pretty much completely re-furnished my first floor in a little under three hours, leaving us plenty of time to find somewhere cool for lunch.

I invited Scott to join us. There was a giddy, silly feeling in the pit of my stomach, and when I thought about him, I wanted to smile. Beth watched me as I made the call, and must have seen the look on my face as we spoke, because when I hung up she shook her head.

"You've got it, girl," she said.

"Got what?" I asked, feigning innocence.

"It. And you've got it bad. Look at you, acting like you're in high school and the cute guy just passed you a note in biology." She smiled.

I just shook my head at her. But she was right.

I think he enjoyed little kids. He and Kira and Haley did not run out of things to talk about through the entire meal. I'd noticed that about him before, during Monopoly, that he paid just as much atten-tion to the children as the adults. He spoke to them calmly, not dumbing down at all, and gave their responses careful consideration, no matter how silly they seemed at the time.

Kira and Haley, for example, were trying to decide who would win if Batman and Superman were in a fight. Kira, because of Kevin and his exhaustive immersion in video games, had a bit of an information edge, but Haley must have done some research somewhere, because she made some pretty valid points. Scott listened gravely to both of their arguments, nodding and looking thoughtful, before finally siding with Haley because, after all, Superman *could* fly.

He even paid the check.

Beth draped her arm around his neck and kissed his cheek. "I do love a man in uniform. Thanks. Okay, girls, onward." She hustled them out toward the car.

I pulled on his sleeve. "I spoke to my father this morning. He's going to be at the McDonald's down from the Days Inn at six. Can you take my guys? If not, Beth's here, I mean—"

He held a finger to my lips. "Not a problem. You and Beth can enjoy a little together time before she goes, and I'll be the big bad wolf, keeping Billy in line."

Again I was struck by his kindness, his willingness to put himself between me and whatever might hurt me. I felt another giddy rush. It was not the intense physical desire I'd felt before. This was something new, and just as powerful. "My mother said he's old and has nothing."

"She's right."

"That doesn't mean I should change my opinion of him."

"No, it doesn't."

I leaned against him. The stiff khaki of his uniform shirt smelled fresh and faintly of starch. "Do you do your own laundry?"

"What?" He pulled back and looked down at me. "Laundry?"

"Yeah. I mean, that shirt is fairly impeccable. Do you iron it and everything?"

"No, I send them out."

"Oh, thank God for that. I don't think I could bear a man better at housework than I am."

"I like mopping floors best," he said, a sly smile playing across his lips. "You know, the way the Pine Sol smells, and the back and forth of the mop—"

I smacked his arm. "Okay, you can stop. Now I know I'm not good enough for you."

He turned me to him and his arms circled my shoulders loosely. "I think you're just fine."

I looked up at him, into those kind and pretty eyes. "Thank you for last night. I needed that. Well, you."

A smile played around his lips. "Hey, anytime. Seriously. Anytime at all. Just pick up the phone. Or yell, I'll hear you if you yell. Or…"

I laughed. At that moment I knew I had fallen in love with him, simply and stupidly. It had only been a few weeks, but I didn't care. I was a grown-up woman and I knew that whatever I was feeling was real, and that nothing else mattered if I could keep feeling this way.

"You have to go thwart crime," I told him, pushing him away.

He grinned. "Ah, yes." He slid into a W.C.Fields voice. "Thwarting crime. Yes, yes." He kissed me again and stepped back, and I walked out into the parking lot, squinting at the sun, as Kira and Haley waved goodbye.

Beth said she would cook. She wanted to mix us a few vodka and tonics, but we decided on seltzer and lime, which we drank at the inn, on the upstairs balcony, overlooking the grounds of RiverCliffe House and the river.

"I could spend all my days right here," she said, "looking at this view."

"Yes, it's pretty spectacular. What are we eating?"

"Serena gave me half a pie, Daniel gave me tomatoes and corn, Bernie gave me a handful of fresh herbs, and the guy who works here at night? Misha? He gave me two trout that he caught right after he got off work this morning. Cleaned them and everything. You're having an all RiverCliffe dinner."

"That sounds amazing. And thank you for doing the cooking. You know what I'd do with all that food."

She swirled her glass around, and the ice made a faint clinking sound. "Are you sure you don't want to go and meet him?"

"And say what, exactly? And do what? Listen to him make excuses?"

"There are no excuses, Risa. But aren't you even curious?"

"No."

"Liar. I spent too much time with you when all you wanted to do was find him and talk to him."

"I was lots younger then, Beth. I have other things in my life now that are way more important than Billy Newsome."

"He's your family."

"I have other family," I said. "I'm building a new family, right here in RiverCliffe. I used to think that if I could have his love, I'd be complete. Now I know I don't need him."

"Grown-up stuff again."

"Shut-up." There was a single sailboat on the river, with a bright yellow sail. "Too bad we couldn't go back on the river. That was fun."

"I'll be back. We'll do it again. Maybe I'll teach you?"

"Maybe. When could you come back?"

"Not until September."

"I'll be here."

"So, you've decided?"

"I think so. It just makes so much sense. And Scott…well, I think he and I are a pretty good idea too." I could see she was starting to swell up with a million questions, so I quickly deflected her. "What are you going to do about Tony and his amazing ten inches?"

She laughed. "Screw his brains out for a while longer, I guess. What else should I do?"

"*You* could move here."

She looked at me. "And do what?"

"Open a branch office of Hoover, Hoover and I Want Your Money."

She laughed. "Hoover, Murkowski and Swit."

"Whatever. Don't they have clients down this way?"

"I handle patents."

"You could do that from anywhere."

"You seem to think I'm so invaluable to the firm that I can write my own ticket."

"You're not?"

"No."

"Damn."

I had finished my drink. So had Beth. She was staring into her empty glass.

"If you stay here, I'll think about it," she said.

I nodded. "Fair enough. I think I hear my stomach growling."

"Ah. Is this your subtle way of saying you're hungry?"

"Yes."

"We could always take a drive and get McDonald's."

"Beth, please."

She stood, looked again at the river, and sighed. "Onward."

Scott brought the kids back a little after seven. Beth and I had just sat down, and the food smelled amazing, but when they came through the door, all thought of food slipped right out of my head. Between my heart doing little flips simply because Scott had walked into the room, and the fact that my children had just had dinner with my father, my emotions were so confused I wanted to smack myself on the side of the head to straighten myself out.

"Well?" I tried to sound casual, but my heart was pounding so hard, I think my voice was an octave higher. What if they liked him? What if they said they wanted to see more of him? I was still getting used to not thinking about what I would do and say if he came into my life. That was now done, and the weight off my mind was a new kind of freedom. What if my children dragged him back in?

"He was cool," Kevin said. "Can I go over to Daniel's? Jillian asked me."

I didn't even raise an eyebrow. "Course. Kira, honey, what did you think?"

She wrinkled her nose. "He smelled funny. And he kept wanting to give me a kiss."

I looked at Lily. "Oh?"

Lily exhaled loudly. "He did smell funny. Not BO bad, but, like, Grandma's friend who's taking all those pills? And Grandma says you can smell the medication the minute she walks in? That kind of bad. And he has really crappy teeth, and thinks he's funny."

"But he's not," Kira said. "He's not nearly as cool as I thought he'd be."

I had picked up my knife and fork and set them back down again about five times. "Oh?"

Scott cleared his throat. "Billy seemed to have a genuine interest in RiverCliffe."

"Yeah," I muttered. "I bet."

Beth got up and got another plate from the cupboard. "Scott, I know that your Big Mac was probably the best thing you ate all day, but would you like a bit of trout?"

His face lit up. "Trout? Why, yes, I'd love a bit of trout."

"There's pie," I said, to no one in particular. "Kevin, I bet the other half is in Jillian's fridge."

"'K," he said, heading for the door.

"Did you like him?" I asked. I'd been afraid to ask.

Kevin shrugged. "I guess. I mean, he's the only grandfather we have, so I guess he'll do."

The door slammed behind him, and Kira sat at the table with us, carefully eating her slice of peach pie. "Mommy, why don't we have two sets of grandparents like everyone else?"

Lily, slouched against the counter, answered. "Because our father is pretty old, and his parents are dead."

"He's not that old," I countered. "They just died young, is all."

"We haven't talked about Ed," Beth said. "How is he?"

"He's going to have a kid," Lily said, casually. "I can't believe it. He doesn't care anything about the ones he's already got, why would he want another one?"

I stared at my plate. "How do you know that, Lily?"

"We talk. You know that," she said. She put her plate in the sink. "I'm tired. I think I'll just be upstairs."

I picked up my knife and fork again and set it down. Ed was having another child, and Lily was right, he hadn't been such a diligent father the first time around. Was this his choice? I didn't think so.

After Kira had been born, he'd talked seriously about a vasectomy. Had meeting Alicia changed his mind? I shook the thought out of my head. He was not my concern any longer. I started to eat.

"This is delicious," Scott said. "Beth, you cooked this?"

Kira sighed. "If it's delicious, you can bet *Mom* didn't."

"Not nice," I mumbled.

"Yeah, but true. I'm going upstairs too," Kira said, sliding off her chair.

She pattered up the steps. The silence was not comfortable.

"Did you know?" Beth asked at last. "About Ed having another child?"

I shook my head and drank some water. It seemed that my throat felt suddenly very closed up. "No. I didn't know."

I didn't know. I hadn't been paying attention, either. I'd watched my children, seen their pain and anger, and not stepped up. I'd been so busy with my own issues I hadn't given enough thought to theirs. And Ed was part of that.

"This is my fault," I muttered.

"What is?" Scott asked, frowning.

"That my kids lives are falling apart."

Beth reached over and shook my shoulder. "First of all, their lives are not falling apart. Messy, maybe, but lots of kids' lives are messy. *Your* life is messy, but it's getting better. Theirs will too."

"You might want to drag their father into this a little more," Scott said. I looked up and found his eyes on my face, those kind, caring eyes. "You shouldn't be taking all this on yourself, you know."

I nodded. "I do know. I have to do something about that."

Scott smiled. "Maybe now that the situation with Billy is finally resolving itself, you'll have more energy for other mountains to climb."

I looked at him and something evened out inside me, even as I felt that tug of desire, tiny but persistent, deep in my gut.

He sat back. "On a completely different subject, I pulled up a few things for you. About Henry Fielding."

He reached into his pants pocket and pulled out a single folded sheet of paper. "He spent a lot of years in and out of trouble. In and out of jail. Got married, had a few kids, got divorced. He's been pretty straight for the past, oh, fifteen years. Lives with his mother now. He has a pretty successful online business. Solid citizen. He lives close. Connecticut."

I unfolded the paper. There wasn't much there. Just a few dry facts. "Thanks, Scott. I appreciate this."

Beth pushed her empty plate away. "What's this?"

"Just a little project," I said. "Pie?"

"Oh, yes, please," Scott said.

I put the paper carefully on the counter, smoothing it out with both hands, and began slicing into the pie. "So tell me about Billy," I said at last, placing a slice before Scott. I had to know. I didn't want to know, but if I was going to start running more interference in the lives of my kids, I needed as much information as I could get.

He thought before speaking. "He probably is sick. Lily was right about the smell, like the medication seeping out of his pores. And he was trying very hard to be funny and charming with the kids, but they were pretty unimpressed. He didn't say much to me, but tried to pump Lily for info on the inn, whether you were going to stay here. And about Marcie? Your mom? He was fishing."

Beth made a noise that could best be described as a delicate snort.

Scott was industriously shoveling pieces of pie into his mouth and spoke after swallowing. "He also said to tell you he'd be at the Days Inn till Friday."

"Yeah, well," I muttered. "So what?"

"Don't kill the messenger," he said softly.

"I'm sorry," I said. "I should be thanking you for all you did today. For me and my kids."

He maneuvered another piece of pie and chewed thoughtfully. "And for Caleb Fielding?" he asked.

Beth's eyes popped open, then she ducked her head and diligently ate more pie.

I cleared my throat. "Caleb Fielding is a man who was killed coming down from the Bear Claw, right before Christmas. He and his bike burned up, and Cathy buried him as a John Doe. I knew he had a son, and I wanted his son to know that his father didn't just, you know…"

"Abandon him?" Scott said. "That seems to be a recurring theme in your life."

"Well, maybe it is. I'm just trying to right a wrong here. I want Henry Fielding to know what happened."

"I see. If Caleb Fielding was buried as a John Doe, how do you know his name? And his son's name?" Scott sat back, looking interested. "Did he tell you himself?"

This was not the kind of secret I could keep, especially since he'd probably heard an earful from Cathy a long time ago. It was time to come clean. Besides, I could not love him if I didn't trust him. I nodded.

"Then all the stories are true?"

I nodded again. "Are you going to run away screaming?" I asked.

"Hey, I'm a cop. I've seen way scarier things than a pretty lady who can talk to dead people."

The relief I felt was palpable. I wasn't sure how he'd react, but I should have known. He was part of RiverCliffe, too. "I think you're a very good man," I told him.

"I try to be."

Beth stood, quickly took all the empty plates and scurried into the kitchen.

I leaned across the table and whispered. "And a pretty decent roll in the hay."

He grinned. "I try to please. You know, if you stay here at River-Cliffe, I know all sorts of tricks we could try."

I closed my eyes and squeezed them, hard. My plan had been to buy a house back in New Jersey. My plan…my plan…but RiverCliffe, and Scott Van Wyke, was better than any plan I could have imagined.

"I think I've decided. I still have to sound out the kids. I'll let you know."

He nodded again, and stood up, and I walked him out the door and around the inn to where his Suburban was parked in the side lot.

We stood there, together, and he cleared his throat.

"Since Beth is here, and the kids are settled in, we could drive out to my place and try one or two of those tricks right now."

I closed my eyes. I wanted that. Very much. But—

"It's Beth's last night."

"Right." He kissed me, then he kissed me again, and I wanted to wrap my whole body around him and take him down, right in the driveway. Instead, I pulled back., He shook his head sadly, got in his car, and drove away.

CHAPTER 11

*B*eth left the next morning. I wasn't sure who was sorrier to see her go, my kids, Winston or me. He stood next to me as she drove away, and I think there were tears in his eyes.

"I think I fell in love with your friend," he said.

I looked over at him. "Isn't she too…tall for you?"

He sighed. "We could have made it work." He sniffed. "Sex isn't everything, you know. I think we have a real connection."

"I told her she should move here."

"What a great idea," Winston said, smiling. "She could live with me until she got settled. She'd have quite a bit of a nest egg after she sold the condo. We'd have to put her things in storage until she found a place, but she could rent for a while. There's always something available in my complex."

"You must have had quite a time together Sunday."

"We did. God, if only she were a man…"

I poked him with my elbow. "Then *I* would have married her."

"Yes, well," he grinned. "Maybe, maybe not."

"She said she'd think about it if I decided to stay on here."

I glanced over. The smile was gone.

"Why would you do that?" he asked, his voice flat.

I shrugged. "Why not? It would save me from having to go out and find another place to live. The kids like it here."

"Of course they do. It's the summer," he said. "It's like camp."

I nodded. "That's true. But didn't you want to live at camp when you were a kid? Beth did."

He folded his arms across his chest. "I thought you were going to let me run things here, Risa."

I nodded. "I have, Winston. And I will continue to do so as long as I don't see anything that might hurt RiverCliffe. I think, though, that I could keep a much better eye on things here than from Jersey." I sighed. "Look, Winston, has my being here been a problem for you?"

He hesitated. "No, I guess not. But your being here makes me feel like at any moment, the other shoe could drop. That's an uncomfortable place to be."

"Cathy is happy I'm here," I said.

Winston let his arms drop to his side, and to my shock, his eyes filled with tears. "I wish I could see her again. I miss her terribly."

"I'll tell her that," I said. "Next time I see her."

He sniffed. "That's very unfair of you, playing the I-can-speak-to-her-and-you-can't card. Clever, yes, but unfair."

"I won't do it again, I promise. But the truth is, Winston, I do belong here."

We walked back into the lobby. It was after breakfast, and things were quiet. Lily was in the dining room alone, phone in hand. I watched her as she scrolled, her face alternately scowling or smirking. "I'll be right in," I told Winston, and went into the dining room, and sat across from her.

She looked up. "What?"

"Come to the cemetery with me."

She froze. "What for?"

"To talk. To think. It's the best place in the world for thinking."

Her scowl was fierce. "What do you have to think about?"

I sat across from her. "About maybe staying here. About getting your father up off his sorry ass and out here to see you guys. About what to do with your grandfather. Billy Newsome means nothing to me, but if he means something to you, we should do something about it."

"Wait. *Staying* here? You mean, not going back to Brooklyn or New Jersey, and just living here? All the time?"

I nodded. 'What do you think?"

She sat back slowly. "I don't know."

"See? That's something we can think about."

She looked at me through hooded eyes. "Do we have to go *there?*"

"I think it would be good. Besides, you have to apologize."

Her shoulders slumped. "To who? I haven't done anything."

"No, but your friend Jordan did."

"He's not *my* friend. And he and Mia aren't even talking anymore."

"That doesn't change anything that happened."

She was staring at the table, her fingers shredding the hem of the starched white linen tablecloth.

"Stop damaging the merchandise," I said gently.

She pulled her hands on to her lap. "Daddy isn't going to want to see us once he has a baby," she muttered.

"It's not just about what he wants," I told her. "If you want to see him, I'll make sure you see him, every weekend if you insist. I've got some very expensive papers that have some very specific details, and he's been ignoring them for too long. A new baby doesn't change anything."

"I need to think about it," she mumbled.

"Good. Then let's take a walk."

She glowered at me, but got up, stuffing her phone in the back pocket of her shorts. We walked together, through the gap in the low, stone wall, the cool oaks, and out into the sunshine.

"First, we need to make our apologies," I said. "Do you remember where you were?" I asked.

She shook her head. "It was dark. We were just wandering around."

I closed my eyes and breathed in deeply. The air here was always just a bit sweeter, it seemed. There was something in the air, not just the scent of the grass, but something else.

"Can you smell it?" I asked her.

"Smell what?"

I opened my eyes. "Never mind. I bet Cathy would know who you should talk to."

Lily moved closer. "You mean my grandmother? Is she, like, the gatekeeper?"

"That's one way on putting it," Cathy said gaily. "Gatekeeper. I kind of like that. You're Lily?"

My daughter turned around so quickly that she slipped a bit on the grass, and I reached out to steady her. She shook off my hand and pulled herself upright.

"I'm here to apologize." Lily said stiffly, her voice tight and high-pitched.

Cathy pushed a strand of hair off her forehead. "That's a very good thing. I know that Franklin was upset."

"Franklin?" Lily's voice was a bit stronger.

Cathy started walking down toward the river. "Yes, Franklin R. Hempstead. He was born in Rhinebeck, and would come down and work the farm. He loved it here. He died right after the war. Influenza. Lots of folks died from it that year. His mother buried him, right here." She stopped by a gravestone, a small gray marker, with a simple F. Hempstead engraved on it. But the stone was old and weathered, the marking barely legible.

"What war?" Lily asked.

"The Great War," Cathy answered. "World War One. He survived terrible things in the trenches."

"And he died of the flu?" Lily asked, her voice back to normal, and curious. As I watched her, I saw her posture begin to change. Her slumped shoulders drew back, and her back straightened.

"Not just any flu," Cathy said. "What killed Franklin killed thousands of folks. 1918." She flashed a smile. "Google it."

"Oh." Lily frowned. "So, he fought in France?"

Cathy nodded. "Yes. I'll tell him you were here."

Lily glanced around. "Why can't I see him now?"

"Because," Cathy said "he doesn't want to be seen. I know that some people think that when you die you find everlasting peace.

That's true for some of us. But for others there are scars that even death can't heal. Franklin saw and did things in France that even eternal rest can't erase."

Lily shifted from one foot to another, and she was frowning. "Then you aren't all happy once you die?"

"Not if you weren't happy when you were alive, Lily. A soul isn't something that's handed to you at the pearly gates, you know. Your soul is born with you. But it doesn't die with you." Cathy smiled. "Death is almost as complicated as life."

"Oh," Lily said. She looked disappointed. "So, why can I see only you?"

"Who else do you want to see?"

"I don't know. Kira said there were a bunch of people watching the fireworks."

Cathy smoothed back her hair again. "Your little sister is very open to us. I imagine she'll get to know us all."

"But I won't?" Lily asked.

Cathy's face softened. "Do you want to?"

"Can you read my mind?" Lily challenged.

I caught my breath. Could she? Could *they*?

Cathy shook her head. "I can see into your heart, Lily, and I see that you are angry and sad. I can see that you don't want to believe that there is something more to this world than what you've already accepted as part of your life. But that's okay, it really is. Can I read your mind? No, child. I wish I could, because then I would know *why* you're so hurt. And then maybe I could help you."

"My father doesn't love me anymore," Lily spat, her voice so cold that I stepped back. "Can you help me with *that*?"

I brought both of my hands to my mouth, clenched fists, and held my breath.

"You don't know that," Cathy said, calmly. "Most fathers don't stop loving their children. They just forget how important it is to show that love. Now my son, Billy, well, he just might be the exception to that, because he was born a selfish child and became a selfish man. But a good man just needs to be reminded." She shook her head. "So, no, I can't help you with that. I can't even help to try to talk you through your feelings. But your mother might. After all, she went through the same thing, didn't she? Have you ever asked *her* for help?"

My eyes were full of tears, so I could not see the look on Lily's face as she shook her head.

"I never thought of that," Lily said. She took a step closer to Cathy, and put out a hand, a quick touch on Cathy's arm. "Tell Franklin I'm sorry that my friend was such an asshole."

She stepped back, and I wiped my tears quickly and smiled brightly at her as she turned to me.

"Okay Mom, I'm going back. I'm going to hang out at the pool. With Mia. But this was a good idea." She turned abruptly and walked quickly back toward the inn.

I watched her, and felt Cathy beside me. "Thank you," I said.

I felt her quick hug. "Of course, dear. Are you alright?"

I nodded. "Yes. I am. I need to go and talk to Lily."

She nodded. "Yes, you do, but not now. Give her a bit of time to think about what she just said. Come, sit."

I walked to the bench and sat. She sat beside me. On my other side, another woman, younger than Cathy by at least twenty years, but with the same face and the same smile, slid next to me.

"This is my mother," Cathy said. "Bea. "

I smiled at her. "I was just reading about you. And Cora. Is Cora here?"

Bea shook her head. "Cora never wanted to be a part of any of this, and we honored her wishes, although I do miss her. It was good to see Lily. She may be coming around. You are, and that's good. But that little baby of yours, Kira? Where has she been? I think she's good enough to eat!"

Bea reminded me of a baby bird, all high energy and bright eyes. "Kira will be back, I'm sure. I just think I'd like to be with her when she comes."

Bea nodded her salt-and-pepper head several times. "Makes sense. You're a good mama."

I took a breath and looked around me. Here I was, sitting between two women, my grandmother and her mother, and I felt completely happy. These women were a part of me. My daughters were a part of them. Even Kevin, who would never see them or speak to them, belonged to them. This was another feeling new to me, this feeling of being a part of something bigger. Something more.

"Can I ask you ladies a question?"

Bea nodded so hard she practically bounced up and off the bench. "Anything."

"Why did Caleb appear to me?"

"Well, there are a few advantages, you know. Being dead." Cathy said slowly. "One is that we see people, truly see them, as they really are. Kira, for example. We all know her heart. Caleb, he saw your heart, Risa. He looked and saw and knew there was a connection. And he was right. I think the two of you are going to be friends for a very long time."

I looked away from her, down to the river. "I wish he were alive."

Bea chuckled. "So does he. The two of you would have been something special, I think."

Cathy took my hand. "There's something very comfortable about Caleb. He makes you feel like he could slip you right into his back pocket and take you along for the ride. But Caleb did not appear to you because you needed him. I think he needed you. He's been carrying a guilt in his heart so big that sometimes he can't even bear to lift his head. You could ease that, Risa. He could see that in you, like the mirror image of what was burning him up ever since he died. You'd been on the other side, hadn't you? That's why you want to find Henry for him."

I nodded. "Yes."

"It's a kind thing you're doing," Bea said. "Very kind."

I watched the river, and could make out Wayne and Kevin. They were putting one of the canoes into the water, handing over the life preservers, and pushing the canoe off the bank. Kevin laughed and I watched as Wayne put his arm around Kevin's shoulder. It was a sweet, fatherly gesture.

When I stood, the graveyard was empty. I walked back to the inn, detouring past the barns, walking slowly through Daniel's garden. The blueberry bushes were getting full, and I spent a few minutes carefully picking off only the fullest, bluest berries. With my hands full, I walked around the side of the inn, toward the front porch, just in time to see a black and white cab pull away from the front porch, leaving my mother standing on the porch, surrounded by suitcases, looking terribly pleased with herself.

"Ma?"

She turned and broke into a grin. "Risa! Love, why, this place is gorgeous! The brochure does not do it justice. I'd get a few new pics made up, though. And maybe, I don't know, get closer to the river?"

The inn? She wanted me to move the inn closer to the river? I felt the juice of the blueberries starting to run through my fingers, and realized my hands had involuntarily made a fist. "What are you doing here?"

As much as I loved my mother with all my heart, Brooklyn was her place. She hadn't left the borough in twenty years, not even to visit me in New Jersey. The fact that she showed up at RiverCliffe without telling me she was coming meant only one thing: she was here for a very specific reason, and she didn't want me to know what that reason was until it was too late for me to argue with her about it.

"After that ridiculous conversation we had about your father, I had to come. Where are the children? And that policeman? Is he here?"

Jessie came out smiling. "Welcome to RiverCliffe. Do you have a reservation?"

My mother drew herself up. "I'm Risa's mother. I don't need a reservation." Jessie grabbed two of mom's suitcases and followed her onto the lobby. I snagged the tote bag and the makeup case, and tried not to drip blueberry all over the polished hardwood floors.

Jessie snatched a small crystal bowl off a side table in the lobby and held it out to me. I dropped the smashed blueberries and shook out my hand.

"Why didn't you call?" I went around the front desk and

rummaged around for the paper towels stashed there. "This is really not a great time. Weren't you going to come for your birthday?"

Winston stuck his head out of the office door. "Risa?"

"Winston, this is my mother. Apparently, she's here for a visit."

Winston went into full Welcome to the Inn mode, sweeping around the desk and actually taking Mom's hand in both of his. "Mrs. Newsome, what a pleasure. We are so thrilled to have you!"

My mother reacted by going into her Queen Mother/Honored Guest mode. "Well, of course I had to see what my daughter was up to. RiverCliffe looks charming. Elegant. Not what I expected at all. And what is it that you do here, Winston?"

"He runs things, all the front desk stuff, reservations…he does it all," I explained, rubbing the purple juice from my fingers. "Jessie, can you take those back to my place?"

Jessie nodded, loaded the suitcases and the accompanying bags onto the luggage cart, and practically ran from the lobby.

Mom looked around. "Very classy, Risa. I guess I was expecting more of a… lodge."

"You saw the brochure, Ma. And what about getting closer to the river?"

She waved a hand. "Can't you do some Photoshop thing, bring the house right up to the riverbank?"

"But the house isn't *on* the riverbank."

She leaned in Winston's direction. "Just an exaggeration, Winston. An embellishment. I think it would do a lot for business."

Winston, bless him, was still smiling. "Business is just fine, Mrs. Newsome."

She patted his arm and sighed. "Actually, I'm Mrs. Harris, but it's too complicated to explain. Just Marcie, please. Lots of nice paintings, I see. And old furniture, how nice."

"They're antiques, Ma. Listen, why don't you come back: I'll show you where we live."

"What, you don't live here? I thought you'd have the Presidential Suite."

I took her elbow and tugged. "Yes, we do, but we save that for an actual president."

"I could use a drink, you know. The train was hot, and that cab ride…don't get me started."

"I wouldn't dream of it. I can get you some water, or seltzer…"

"How about something stronger?"

"Ma, it isn't even eleven."

"True, but I took an early train. I've been up since five. It's already been a very long day."

"I have something back in my kitchen. There's no bar here."

A look crossed her face that was part shock, part extreme disappointment. "Risa, no bar?"

Serena came out of the dining room, all smiles. Winston waved to her.

"Serena, can we get something nice and cold for Risa's mother?" Winston asked, his smile never cracking.

She made an about face and vanished.

Mom walked back to the double front door and nodded as she checked out the front sweep of lawn. "It is a nice view. Too bad about that road right there. Now, what about that nice policeman?"

I looked at Winston, praying he would see what I was up against and jump in. Marcie was trying to find me a man, and that was her at her most overbearing. What was I going to do with her?

"Scott is the sheriff, Marcie," he explained. "Of the whole county. It's a huge responsibility and, well, he can't just hang around here all day keeping your daughter company."

She turned back to us, and shot me the Look of Death. "See, this man here? He knows all about this Scott person. But me? Your own mother?" She shook her head. "I need to lie down."

Serena trotted back in with a tray, holding three glasses. She thrust her offerings at Mom.

"I wasn't sure what you were in the mood for," she said, somewhat breathlessly. "Here's some seltzer. Or iced tea. Or some plain water."

My mother smiled. "Now, this is service." She picked up the seltzer and drained the glass. "Risa, where do you live again?"

"The kids and I live back here. Winston, if you see any of my offspring, tell them their grandmother is here."

He bowed his head, the perfect picture of servitude. "Of course."

Mom reached out to pat Serena on the cheek. "You're very sweet. Thank you. And what do *you* do here?"

"She runs the entire kitchen and dining room," I explained.

"Really? She looks so young to have all that responsibility. But Risa, honey, if she takes care of the food, and he takes care of the rooms, what do you do? And by the way, this tray? Quite nice." She returned her empty glass. "Yes, classy."

I was trying to move my mother toward the back of the lobby, closer to the hallway that would eventually take her back to the apartment. It was a lot harder than it should have been.

I put my arm around her shoulder and pulled her firmly. "This way, Mom. I work the office too, and I help out in the dining room. I find things to keep me busy."

"She's invaluable, Marcie," Winston gushed. "Having Risa here has made all of our jobs easier."

She puffed up with pride. "She is something of a marvel, isn't she? So smart! Of course, she can't cook, but…"

"Ma," I practically yelled. "Come on. These people have work to do."

She waved over her shoulder as I maneuvered her down the hallway.

"Seriously, you should have let me know you were coming."

"I know how you hate surprises, and I'm sorry, but I had an impulse."

Another one of her "feelings". Oh well. "So what, exactly, prompted this impulse?"

"Your father, of course. He called me from that hotel he's staying at. Risa, you couldn't have given him a room? Anyway, he called me late last night. Told me about meeting the kids. He said you gave him the brush-off. I don't blame you, but Risa, he is your father."

I stopped, opened the door to the apartment, and let her in. As I closed the door, I took a deep breath and turned to her. We were eye-to-eye. "What the hell are you doing?"

"I'm arranging for you to meet with your father, that's what I'm doing. Of course, seeing the kids, and maybe a little pool time would be nice too. Is this it? God, Risa, so small! And more old furniture? We need to shop."

"Meet my father? I don't want to meet my father."

"Well, tough. He's sick and needs someone to take care of him. He'll probably come back to Brooklyn with me. But before that, the two of you need to meet and make peace. Now, that seltzer was fine and good, but I need a little something-something. And a cigarette. What? What's the look? Here, honey, stop looking so silly and get your mother some wine."

Lily cooked dinner for us that night. A small pot roast with baby carrots and rosemary potatoes. Everything was delicious. Too bad I could hardly eat. I was still doing a slow burn over my mother's pronounce-ment. He was moving back to Brooklyn? He needed someone to take care of him? And she wanted us to make peace? *Was she kidding?*

Mom was so proud. "Lily, thank God you're going to take after me in the cooking department. And little Serena taught you? Risa, I'm so relieved. Now, I know these children won't starve."

"Little Serena is a full grown woman," I said. "And I cooked for these children for a number of years before we moved in with you," I reminded her. "They didn't starve then."

She waved a hand. "Whatever. Now, Kevin wants to show me all the boats, and Kira wants me to see her chickens. But don't chickens sleep? Well, maybe the cows, then. Whatever. Should we come back here after my tour?"

I shook my head. "No. Martha and Bernie heard you'd arrived." Of course they did. I bet that news flashed around faster than a summer lightening storm. "Bernie sent a text, and they want to meet you. The kids will take you over there, and I'll meet you on their porch."

"And when do I meet the boyfriend?"

I sighed. "When the boyfriend has the time to come over here."

She made a face. "I would think he'd *make* time to meet your mother."

I lied smoothly. "I told you, it's nothing serious. God, we barely know each other. I've only been here, like, six weeks."

She shook her finger in my face. "It only took your father and I one night."

"Exactly. And look how well *that* turned out."

She sniffed. "The fact that your father was a hopeless criminal who couldn't keep a job or manage to stay out of jail had nothing to do with the fact that we were crazy about each other. Look at me, after all these years, he still makes my heart flutter, even though I know he's a charmer and a cheat. And after three other wives, who did he come to when he was sick and needed someone to care for him?"

"The most gullible woman on the planet?"

She shook her head sadly. "You, my poor dear, know nothing of love." She looked at my children's faces, all of them open-mouthed around the table. "Listen to me. A true love happens only once."

"Lily has a boyfriend," Kira offered.

"No, I don't," Lily snapped. "Trent is not my boyfriend. We barely kiss."

"Good." Mom said approvingly. "Keep it clean, Lily. Trust me. Once you get to know the pleasures of the flesh, it's very hard to keep your clothes on."

"Okay, Ma," I said loudly. "I think we're done here. Kira, help with the dishes? No, Lily, you cooked. We'll clean up. Just sit there and don't listen to Grandma."

"This is about the time of day I have my cigarette," Mom said, to no one in particular. "And maybe a little more wine."

"There are some lawn chairs out this door, Mom," I told her. "You can have a nice view of the river. And here, use this saucer."

"What, no ashtray? I know that smoking is politically incorrect, but for your mother?"

"If I knew you were coming," I said sweetly, "I would have been better prepared."

She held out her wine glass. I filled it halfway. She stood and strode out the door.

Kevin came up close. "How long is she staying?" he whispered.

"No idea."

He shook his head. "We've got a pretty good gig here, Mom," he said, his voice still low. "Don't let her talk you into doing something stupid."

I stared after him as he carried his plate to the sink.

"He's got a point," Lily said. "I like it here."

"What," I asked, "would you guys think of living here permanently?"

Kira threw herself at me and wrapped her arms around my waist. "I think that would make you the absolute best mommy ever."

I patted her head and smiled. "Why, thank you, honey. Kev, what do you think?"

He shrugged. His new jeans hugged his hips and the old t-shirt hung off his shoulders. "That would be okay, I guess. Beats Brooklyn."

I looked at Lily. She shrugged. "Sure. Why not?"

"Well then," I said. I was so surprised with myself I almost threw up my hands to take everything back. Snap decisions were not what I did. But this felt inevitable, so I just kept nodding my head. "We're staying. It's all good." And there, tucked in a small, secret corner of my brain, was Scott, and I just wanted to smile

Kevin shrugged. "Yeah, but Grandma, well, she might want us back in Brooklyn."

"Why?"

"To help her take care of Grandpa," Kira said, balancing all the forks on her small stack of plates. "Grandpa told us."

"Hold on." I stood, my hands up in the air, palms out. "Stop everything and tell me what he said. Exactly."

Kevin and Kira exchanged a look. Lily sighed. "He said that he was looking forward to being in our lives," she said. "He said something about living with us. In Brooklyn."

All the happy thoughts, even the Scott-happy thoughts, vanished. I marched out of the kitchen and over to my mother, sitting in the peaceful sunset, smoking.

"Ma, do you and my father have some sort of plan I should maybe know about?"

She shook her head. "Now, Risa, calm down."

"No, I will not calm down. My kids just told me that their grandpa was talking about living with them? In Brooklyn? What if I told you I've decided to stay here?"

"Here? In this place? I didn't know you were even thinking about something like that."

"Yeah, well, I was. Kinda. And the kids just said they liked the idea. So. We're staying here."

She shrugged. "You made an important decision like that just this minute? Risa, how is that even possible? Where are your lists of pros and cons? What about your endless planning?"

"Maybe I don't need lists anymore. Or plans. I've decided. I'll put the kids in school, change my address, everything."

She carefully rolled the tip of her cigarette around the edge of the saucer, shaping it to a fine point. "Well, I suppose that's all fine for you, but what about me? I'm not sure I'll be able to take care of him on my own," she said in a small voice.

"So you thought I'd pitch in? Just like that? Why, because I have money now? God, you're just as bad as he is."

"Don't you dare," she said sharply, looking up at me with narrowed eyes. "I gave you everything, and never asked for a thing in return. How could you say that to me?"

I took a breath and reined back my anger. "You're right. I apologize. But I do not feel like I have any responsibility to that man."

"That man is your father."

"You can call him that. I don't have to."

She sat and smoked, then sipped her wine. "He's dying."

"Everybody dies, Mom. That doesn't change who he's been for the past forty years. And it doesn't change my feelings toward him."

"Well, it should. You will regret this, Risa. If you let him die without making amends."

"I'm not letting him die. That's happening without me."

"You need to see him. Talk to him." Her face suddenly softened. "Please, Risa. As a favor to me."

Damn that woman anyway. I hung my head. "Fine. I'll see him. Tomorrow. We'll go over together, okay?"

She tamped out what was left of her cigarette and finished her wine. "Fine. Now, where are my grandbabies? We have chickens and boats to see."

I turned and went back to the house.

I stormed across to Bernie and Martha's porch. Bernie rose from her chair when she saw me, grabbed me by the shoulders, and guided me to a chair.

"Sit. Breathe."

I did. I closed my eyes and took long, steady breaths, until I felt my heart start to slow. I opened my eyes, and Bernie was crouched in front of me.

"So, how's your mama?"

"She's taking him back. He told her that he's sick, and she's going to care for him, and she seemed to think that I'm going to go back to Brooklyn with the kids and help her."

Bernie shrugged. "Do you want to do that?"

I shook my head. "No. I'm going to stay here. For good."

Bernie broke into a smile. "How nice. I was so hoping you'd stay. So just say no to your mother."

"I did."

"Then you're done."

"It's not that simple, Bernie."

She shook her head. "Of course it is, Risa. You are a grown-up woman with a family. Your priorities are determined by you and you alone. You want to stay at RiverCliffe, then stay."

I stared at my hands. "I'm going to see him tomorrow."

Bernie sat back on her heels. "Your idea?"

"No, but…mom asked. She *asked*."

She stood. "Hard to say no when your mom asks a favor, but it might not be a bad thing."

Martha came up behind Bernie and stared down at me. "Or you could say no to that, too."

I tried to smile. "I don't think I got a chance to thank you for running him off like that. It was a real pleasure to see."

Martha cracked a rare smile. "It wasn't just for you, Risa. I owed Cathy."

"I hope someday that you'll feel that much loyalty to me." I took a deep breath. "The kids are bringing her over, right after the tour. You wanted to meet her."

Martha sat back down. "Heard a whole lot about her, on and off over the years. 'Course we're curious."

"Well, she seems to be in rare form," I told them.

It was starting to get dark, and the fireflies were dancing. I had not grown up with fireflies, and when I moved to New Jersey, they seemed as enchanting to me as fairies. Here, in the quiet and peace of RiverCliffe, I could practically see their faces.

"Maybe they really are fairies," I said, then realized I had spoken out loud. Bernie and Martha were both looking at me strangely.

"Why couldn't they be?" I asked them. "I mean all sorts of things I never thought possible have happened since I moved here. My kids are happy, I've met friends, I've met a man…and then, of course, there's the cemetery full of family I never knew I had."

Martha rocked slowly. "My people have always believed in things that no one else could see. Belief should be a fluid thing, Risa. Never be afraid to change your mind about the world."

I grinned. "How New Age-y you sound, Martha."

She shook her head. "Not New Age at all. Just the opposite."

Bernie looked toward the barns. "Martha baked. Does Marcie like coffee in the evening?"

"She does, in fact."

"Or maybe Martha's plum wine?"

I turned and stared. "Martha, you make your own wine?"

She nodded solemnly. "Yep. Married into a family of bootleggers. I can make just about anything with the right ingredients and a few glass jars."

We sat in silence. Bernie could talk your ear off, but she was also good with saying nothing, and we waited for my mother.

Bernie heard them first. "They're coming. I'll get the cookies and some wine."

I stood and saw them, coming from the other side of the inn. Kevin must have walked her down the river a bit, and I had to smile at the thought of my Brooklyn born and bred mother trotting beside the Hudson River without a sidewalk in sight.

She was breathing heavily when they finally climbed the porch steps.

"This is quite wild country you have here," she gasped. She grabbed on to the back of a battered wicker chair.

"Mom, are you OK?" I said, rising.

She waved me back. "Of course, Risa. I'm used to walking for miles, you know that. But hills…" She looked at Martha who had stopped rocking and was sitting, still as stone. "I'm Marcie."

Martha stood, walked over, and swept my mother into her arms, hugging her tightly. I could see my mother's face, her eyes wide in surprise: then Mom's arms went around Martha's broad back, and they stood together in silence, until I heard my mother sniff as she pushed herself away.

"How silly," she muttered, rubbing her eyes with the back of her hand.

Kevin put his arms around her shoulders. "Yeah, Gram, that's just Martha. She kinda does that."

Bernie pushed her way out of the door. "Martha does what? Make people cry? Hey, honey, I'm Bernie. Kids, grab a cookie. Lily, there's juice back in the fridge for you kids if you want it. Marcie, for you I got something special." She held out her hand, and Mom shook it.

"Thank you, Bernie. Is that homemade?'

Martha sat down and began pouring. "Yep. Plum wine. From my

own trees, growing just out back." The wine looked thick and slightly syrupy, and when I sipped it, it slid down my throat like warm butter.

"Oh, my," Mom said.

Lily had come out with glasses and juice, and the kids sat on the steps, munching happily. The adults all drank their wine, very slowly.

"I must admit, this place is much more than I expected," Mom said. "The kids are really fitting in here. I never would have imagined. And you two ladies, well. Risa has told me all about you both." She cleared her throat. "And you both knew Billy?"

Bernie narrowed her eyes. "I hear he's sick, and you're going to be, what? Playing nursemaid? What is it, cancer? Heart? Cathy had heart trouble for years you know. That's what killed her."

Mom nodded. "Yes, it's his heart." I did not look at her as she spoke. "He's going to get weaker and less able to do for himself, and as his wife, well…"

"He left you," Martha said bluntly. "Left his daughter."

Mom nodded. "Yes."

"You're okay with that?" Martha asked.

Mom fluttered a hand. "Of course not. But…well, he's alone, and apparently, so am I." She waited, but no one felt it necessary to add anything.

Kira, her mouth full of cookie, finally said. "We can come and visit you, Grandma. Or you could move out here with us."

"I'm sure Grandma would not like to leave Brooklyn," I said smoothly, not wanting to give *that* idea any traction.

My mother reached over and poured herself another glass of wine. "Your mother is right, Kira, although I think it's very sweet of you to offer. You know I like my life just the way it is."

"Then why would you want Grandpa back?" Kevin asked.

I looked at Mom, eyebrows raised in anticipation.

"I told you," Mom said. "I still love him."

"More than your life?" Kevin asked.

Bernie cackled. "Well, now, that's a very deep question. What's the answer there, Marcie?"

Mom looked around at us, her eyes narrowing. "You all hate Billy, don't you?"

Martha shook her head. "Hate's a strong word. He behaved badly. Every single thing I saw him do was the wrong thing. I don't hate him. Never did, no matter what he told you. I just don't think he deserves any of you all."

"He doesn't," my mother said. "But I loved him once, with all of my heart and soul, and I never met anyone that even came close to taking his place. I'm old, getting older, and I'd do almost anything to try to get some of that back again."

The plum wine was making my ears buzz, but I heard every word she said. I also heard everything she didn't say; how the years of being on her own had taught her how to be strong, but she had never *wanted* to be strong. My mother had wanted to be prized, cared for, made to feel like a queen. Billy had given that to her. I never did. My kids never would.

Lily stood and announced she was going home, and Kevin and Kira followed. The adults sat a while longer, and talked weather, politics, the rising price of gas. All the things adults talk about when the truth is too close and too painful to hear.

I had thought that by the next morning I would change my mind and not go with my mother, but I found myself telling Winston I'd be gone for the morning, left Lily to organize her brother and sister, and drove Mom to Rhinebeck.

He was waiting for us in the small lobby. He was dressed in navy trousers and a short-sleeved, button-down white shirt, looking slightly formal. My mother, on the other hand, had dressed for a first date — white linen pants and a flattering red tunic, her hair and make-up perfect, gold dangling earrings and white kitten heels.

My father, when he saw her, took her in his arms and gave her a kiss, a long, deep kiss, and when he broke away from her, his face was shining.

He still loved her, I thought with a sudden start. As much as he could love anyone, he loved my mother, and it shone from his face and his eyes and he was not the least bit shy about it. He loved her, and was proud to be with her, and didn't care who knew it. How was a man like that capable of leaving her alone for forty years?

"Ah, Marcie my love, we still got it. If you hadn't thrown me out last Saturday, we could have had one hell of a weekend."

"If you hadn't criticized my housekeeping, you'd have had a much better chance."

He looked at me and spoke, like we were old friends, not father and daughter who had never had a full conversation in our lives. "You hear that? She says I criticized her housekeeping. You lived there! Tell me, were there a few things there not quite perfect?"

I couldn't help it. "My kids always said she could have her own segment on *Hoarders*."

He slapped his thigh. "Exactly! See, Marcie love, not just me."

My mother was glowing. "You're terrible." She looked around. "Where can we have coffee?"

He stepped aside and opened his arms, as though inviting us into his house. "There's a lovely little spot, just this way. Just a cafe, you understand, but clean. Nice people."

We sat in a booth, I on one side, my parents on the other. The waitress knew my father by name, flirted a bit until he introduced us all. "My family," he said proudly. "This young lady here is my gorgeous wife. Can you believe we married forty-five years ago? I know what you're thinking. She was a child bride. And this is my daughter, Theresa."

I saw it then, the complete disconnect. His eyes completely changed. I was his daughter, but I was never someone he loved. I was an accomplishment he was proud of.

The waitress simpered. "Oh, Billy, they're lovely." She leaned over me. "Your father is a real charmer. Now." She straightened. "Coffee all around? And who wants breakfast?"

I ordered French toast with extra bacon. I also wanted chocolate chip pancakes, grilled cheese and coconut cream pie, but managed to hold myself back.

"Mom says you're not well?" I asked. Classic conversation starter.

He patted the middle of his chest, obviously referencing his heart. "Yeah, had some tests, and it doesn't look too good."

"Sorry to hear that." I watched as a waitress walked by with a plate of pancakes. I wondered what would happen if I just reached out and took it from her hands. "And I guess you're going to need someone to, you know, look after you?"

He sighed and reached for Mom's hand, squeezing it. "Yes, I probably will. Things are not going to be getting any better."

"I see." I couldn't look at Mom. I couldn't look at him. I rearranged my silverware, took a big gulp of my coffee, and eyed the selection of syrups, with an eye to putting them into some kind of order. "And none of your other wives stepped up to the plate?"

I looked up then, and he almost looked uncomfortable. "Now, Theresa, that—"

"Risa." I said loudly. "I'm called Risa. You'd know that if you ever bothered to try to see me, even once in my almost forty years."

"Risa, honey…" My mother tried to touch my hand but I pulled away.

I stared at my father. "Why did you tell Mom that Cathy had died?"

He looked blank, eyes wide, then blinked. "What has that got to do with anything?"

"And you told your mother we were in California. She tried to find us. You knew she would, so you pointed her in the wrong direction. You even let her believe we shared her name. Why?"

He pulled his hand away from Mom's and laid them both in front of me, palms up. "Listen, kid—"

"I'm closing in on forty. Not so much a kid anymore."

"I know when your birthday is," he said, raising his voice.

"And you never thought to send a card? Not once in all those years? What, no postage stamps in prison?"

His eyes changed then. The warmth left, and they were cold and dead. "You know nothing about prison life," he said at last. "You know nothing about me."

"You're right," I said. I struggled to keep my voice even. "I know nothing about you. Except that you did not want us to be part of your family, so much so that we didn't even have the same name as them. Cathy would have welcomed us. Martha would have too. You lied so my mother wouldn't even try to reach out to them. And then you lied again to keep *your* mother from finding *us*. It's what you, do, Father dear. You lie to the people who love you. So why should I believe a word you say now?"

"Risa, I thought you were in California! You mom talked about it all the time!"

"I did, honey," Mom said.

The waitress appeared and set down the food. I stared at my plate. I felt sick to my stomach.

"Then how did you know where to find Mom in Brooklyn?" I had been starving just moments before, so I grabbed a slice of bacon and started to eat it. The hot grease hit my gut like lead. "Or did you always know where we were? You sent divorce papers. You knew where we were then. I bet that's it, isn't it? You always knew where to find us. You just chose not to."

His eyes narrowed even further. "You don't have a whole lot of respect for your father."

"No, I don't. Mom, aren't you even curious? Don't you want to know why, after all those years, he chose *now* to suddenly reach out and find you?"

My mother had a piece of toast in her hand, and she stared at it, then put it down.

"It is a good question, Billy. Why now? Because you're sick? Or because of Risa and all that money?" Her voice was soft, and I could hear her pain.

I pushed myself away from the table and stood. "I'm leaving now." I looked at my father. "I spent my whole life wanting to be part of something, a family, wanting to feel like I belonged somewhere. I always thought that if I ever found you, I would get that. But the truth is, you're the one who kept it from me for all those years. I don't need you to belong at RiverCliffe. I never needed you. And I don't need you now."

I left the cafe, barely seeing what was in front of me. I swept through the lobby and burst outside like a swimmer finally coming up for air. Tears broke through, angry tears that splashed my cheeks and turned the parking lot into a blur of color and sound.

I don't know how I found the car, but I did, and leaned against it, grateful for the hot hood burning through the back of my linen shorts, bringing the world back into focus.

I didn't have a tissue. Of course. I just stood and sniffed, wiping my eyes with the back of my hand.

When Mom appeared, she was carrying a large plastic bag. She opened the back door of the car and carefully placed her package on the floor. "I got our food to go," she said calmly. "After all, I'm the one who paid for it. If we hurry, we can get back to the inn before everything gets too cold. Nothing worse than cold breakfast." She opened the passenger side door. "Risa? Honey, you're the one with the keys. You maybe wanna get us back before I die from starvation?"

I don't know what it cost her to walk away. I never knew, because I never, in all the years that followed, asked. I just knew that, as always, she had put me first. I got into the car, backed out of the space, and turned onto the highway, heading back home.

CHAPTER 12

Mom and I ate our breakfast by the pool. The food was warm enough to be palatable, but I barely tasted anything. Then I went back to my office, back to work, and tried to forget the morning.

It was impossible, of course. I had just told my father off, and walked away from him without a pang of anger left. He had never been a father who left his beloved child. He never knew me, and never loved me. Everything I had imagined about him was false. Every wish had been based on pure fantasy. He was a stranger to me. Because of him, I had RiverCliffe, and I would always be grateful to him for that. And because of that gratitude, I would let him be a grandfather to my kids, if he wanted. But he was never again going to mean anything to me beyond that.

It was so liberating, I wanted to run down to the river and throw myself into the current, just to see where it would take me. Instead, I did the weekly payroll and adjusted September's work schedule to add in one extra employee. Me.

When I came out of my office around one, my mother was sitting in the lobby, her suitcases surrounding her, looking calm and serene.

"Mom? What's all this?"

She waved a hand. "I just decided that as lovely as this place is, it's not Park Slope, so I'm going back. I was going to ask the desk to call me a cab."

"What? But you just got here." I sat on a chair across from her. "Talk to me."

She sighed elaborately. "I thought, when I got here last night, that I would be spending the week getting to know Billy again, letting the kids get used to him, watching you get to know and love him. But… well, I still love him, and I always will, but you're right. He's a liar, and no measure of love can change that about a man. So, I'm going back home, and maybe I'll finally file those divorce papers, and see if Mr. Carruthers down the street wants anything from me beside coffee a few times a week."

"Mr. Carruthers?" I fought down a smile. "Isn't he a little old for you?"

She shrugged. "I always liked older men." Her eyes went past me, and her eyebrows went up. "Now, Risa, honey, why can't you meet someone like *him?*"

I turned and stood. Scott walked up and gave me a kiss on the cheek, and I felt a bubble of happiness rise up into my chest. His eyes twinkled at me, then he looked down at my mother.

"I heard there was a guest of honor," he said, smiling. "So of course I had to come by and say hello."

Mom went back into Honored Guest mode. "Why, hello. I'm Marcie." She held out her hand in the perfect position to have it kissed. Scott obliged.

"I'm Scott Van Wyke. Sheriff. Your daughter has not said enough about you."

Mom gave me the old, why-you-sly-dog look, and smiled back. "She hasn't said enough about *you*, either. Too bad I'm leaving. I can only imagine the kinds of conversations we could have."

I could imagine too, and had to hold myself back from racing to get the car keys.

"Leaving? Already? I'm surprised. The hospitality of RiverCliffe is legendary."

Boy, he was putting it on thick. I glanced at him, and he caught my eye and winked.

"Risa, I was going to ask you and your mother out tonight. Dinner. Looks like it will be just you and me?"

I smiled and nodded. "Why thank you, that would be lovely. Mom, are you sure?" After all, it would be rude of me to not at least *pretend* I'd love for the two of them to spend more time together, allowing her the chance to exhaust the poor man with questions designed to rate his marriageability.

I could see her giving it some real thought, but she needed the comfort of Park Slope right now. "Sorry. If I could catch an evening train, I'd stay, of course, but as it is, I've only got forty minutes."

"I can take her to the station," he offered.

I froze, torn.

On one hand, that would save me a trip, not take me away from going over next month's projections with Winston, and spare me the pure emotional torture that is saying good-bye to my mother, anywhere, anytime, but always worse with a large, unnamed audience.

On the other hand, did I really want the two to them together? Even for a fifteen-minute ride to the train station?

"Did you already say good-bye to the kids?" I asked her.

"Of course. I had to track Kira down in a barn. She was, I believe, shoveling horse manure with a child-sized pitchfork."

I grinned. "Yeah, she likes farm living. Okay, well, Scott that would be great. Thank you."

He managed to pick up and carry both suitcases and her tote bag without looking overburdened. Mom watched him walk out, then beamed at me.

"Oh, Risa, hold on to that one! Big, strong, handsome...why, he's perfect."

I sighed. "I'll try, Ma."

She stood and hugged me, and as she pulled away, her eyes were wet. "Give my best to the two lesbians."

"Sure."

"And your staff. They were all very nice to me."

"Okay. Listen, I'll be down in a few weeks to get the rest of my stuff. Please, no rummage sale?"

She rolled her eyes. "Risa, of course. Since you're going to stay here, I guess you'll need your things. Speaking of which, are you doing something with the furniture you have here in that apartment? Not for nothing, a little spruce up might be in order."

"New stuff is being delivered next week. I promise. I went shopping with Beth."

"Oh. Good. Beth has excellent taste."

We had walked through the lobby and down the steps, and Scott was standing next to his Suburban, large and black, with SHERIFF painted across the side.

Mom giggled as she accepted his help into the front seat. "I hope no one thinks I'm here on official business."

Scott slammed the door. "Not to worry, Marcie. I won't use the siren."

She looked disappointed as they rolled away, leaving me in front of RiverCliffe House, waving good-bye.

I called Ed from the office phone, so the caller ID would not encourage him to let me go directly to voicemail. "Ed, this is Risa. We need to talk."

"What can I do for you, Risa?"

"You can come and get the kids next week. I know you're working from home, and you told Lily your new place has a spare bedroom, so you can pick them up on Monday morning and let them stay for a few days. I'd suggest the weekend, but Lily and Kevin are both really busy on the weekends, so during the week is better."

I heard a sniff, and the noise he made when the smoke escaped his lips. "Not good timing, Risa."

I was so tired of his excuses I wanted to scream, shout, throw the phone across the room…"It never seems to be good timing, Ed. We have to make it the time."

A long, drawn-out breath. "So where is this bed-and-breakfast you're running now? Rhinebeck?"

"Close enough. They haven't seen you in over six months. I spent my whole life not knowing my father, and I'm not going to do that to my own kids."

"Risa, they know me."

"Yeah? I don't think Kira even remembers what you look like."

He was silent. "During the week? Jeez, Risa—"

"Okay, Ed. Here's the deal. You're coming to get the kids. You're coming next Monday, you're picking them up and letting them stay with you, and then you're bringing them back. And you're going to see them once a month from now on. Maybe you can stay here overnight or you can bring them back with you...I don't care. But you're going to do it." I was amazed how the words just flowed, without any of my usual angst over how he was going to react. I'd learned a few things about myself in the past weeks, the most important being that I did not have anything to fear from a man who did not like what I was saying. I had left my father without the power to make me feel less. I would do the same with Ed. "And I'll write to the judge, explain how my situation has changed, and say I don't need child support anymore. In fact, I'll insist that the kids will do better if you *keep* that money so you can spend it on them while they visit."

There was a long silence. In my mind's eye, I could see him, eyes narrowed, as he weighed the options.

"No child support at all?"

"Nope. None. Ever. I do not need your help raising these kids. I don't need your help for anything. But you will be in their lives. I know you're having another child, but you will not use that as an excuse to keep your distance from *these* children. Understand?"

Silence. I'm sure he didn't know what to make of this new person on the phone, the one that not only argued, but also refused to back down. I took a breath and threw out the last bit of enticement I had. "And if you do a good enough job, we can even re-write our agreement where you have to pay for college."

I heard the poof as he exhaled smoke. "Deal. Where is this place again?"

Lily did not want to miss work. I had gotten her working papers, and she was on the payroll, and already had a very complex budget worked out, her main goal being to earn enough money to buy a car. Kevin said he had work to do with Wayne. Kira did not want to sleep in a creepy house with her father's new wife.

"It's not a creepy house, Kira. It's a condo. It's fine. Kevin, I'm sure Wayne will be able to manage without you. He has for the past fifteen years. Lily, apparently next week is that big reunion thing, the whole inn is taken by one group, and Serena will be having buffet breakfasts while they're here. You'll be back in time for the weekend, when she'll need you again."

They were sitting in the living room, lined up on the couch, looking like they were waiting for the firing squad to lift their rifles. "Guys, this is your father. All you've done is moan about not seeing him enough. You're all going." I looked down at Kira, her eyes big and scared. "Kira, baby, you don't remember much about when your dad lived with us, but he was good to you. He was good to all of you. He loves you. You'll be fine."

"He left us," Kevin mumbled.

"He left me. You all were collateral damage, but we can do something about that now. This is not like when *my* father left, and chose to never see me again." I met Lily's eyes. "I will not let that happen to you."

She gave me a half smile.

"You're going to see your father, you're going to visit with him on a regular basis, and the subject is now closed." I looked at their faces, uncomfortable and closed. But I was right, I knew I was. They would get to know Ed again, and the remembered good times would come back, and they would start to build other memories, maybe with a new half-brother or –sister. They didn't have to love him uncondi- tionally. It was Ed's job, to earn back their trust and love. But my job was to make sure that nothing stood in the way, and I was going to do it as best I knew how.

There was a knock on the outside front door, and Scott stuck his head in. "Ready?"

Oh... "I forgot! Oh, Scott, I'm so sorry, the kids and I..."

He waved a hand. "No problem. Maybe I can come back later?"

Kira jumped off the couch. "You can have tacos with us," she offered.

Scott looked thoughtful. "What a lovely invitation. Risa?"

I glanced over as Kevin got up off the couch. "Kevin?"

He looked over surprised. "What? Sure, Sheriff. Tacos are one of the few things Mom doesn't mess up too bad."

Lily swept past us, her head shaking. "Just to be sure, let me do this. Do you mind ground turkey?" she asked Scott.

He shook his head. "Nope. Not at all."

"I can chop things," I called after Lily. I heard the sound of the cutting board hitting the counter top.

"I got this, " she answered. "Go take a walk or something."

I looked at them all. Kevin headed for the stairs. Kira had turned on the television. I looked at Scott "A walk?"

He nodded and we went out the door, and I reached for his hand, lacing his fingers in mine as we walked across the lawn and down to the river.

"Your mother is a character," Scott said. I could hear the smile on his voice

"Oh, no. What did she say? I'm going to be embarrassed, aren't I?"

He laughed. "She made a pretty convincing argument. If you'd been a car, I'd have driven you off the lot."

"Oh, I'm so sorry. She just...she measures success in husbands. I don't have one right now, so she can't imagine I'm doing anything else right."

"I liked her. She was funny and quite honest. She mentioned that she didn't think your ex-husband... Ed? She didn't think he was much good, as she put it, in the romantic arts, and hoped I was going to take a more liberal and mutually fulfilling approach."

I stopped dead in my tracks. "Oh, kill me now."

"At least she's looking out for *all* your interests," he said, reaching out for my hand again and tugging me back down the path. "I was almost going to assure her that I was giving that part of our relation- ship some very serious effort, but thought that might have been a bit much."

I had to laugh with him. "Yes, it might have."

We sat on one of the benches on the dock and watched the water.

"So, I guess Serena called and let you know she had arrived?"

"Yes, she did. She said you were surprised?"

"Shocked. But I should have expected her. She was following my father, after all."

"Yeah. Marcie mentioned that the visit didn't go so well." He glanced at me. "You okay?"

"Yes, as a matter of fact. It's a relief to know I will never again have to spend time or energy wondering about him." My words sounded flat and harsh. I cleared my throat. "Sometimes, it's better not to know."

He shook his head. "No, it's always better to know. But sometimes it's just better not to care."

"I'll take that. So now, I don't have to care about him anymore." I took a deep breath. "I've decided to stay at RiverCliffe. The kids are all okay with it. I even went out and bought new furniture."

"What?" I saw his face light up. "Really? Oh, Risa, that's great, just great."

He put his arms around me and I turned to him, into the circle of his arms and as he pulled me closer, my heart began to race, but I knew this time it wasn't just his physical closeness. Did his body draw me in? Yes, of course. But there was more. I felt so good to finally see it, finally feel it...I was in love with this man, this good and decent man who I knew would love me back.

"That's great, " he said again as we broke apart. "So, first things first. Did you get the kids in school?"

I shook my head. "No. I have to go back to Brooklyn and get all their records. I spoke to someone here at the Board of Ed, Abbie somebody?"

He nodded. "Yep. I know Abbie. I'll talk to her. I'm sure you don't have to go all the way back to Brooklyn. Which brings up another thing. Your minivan has about had it. You should really get yourself another car."

I nodded. "Yes, I do know. I was thinking a new SUV. I've always liked them."

His arm around me felt warm and safe. "We'll go this weekend, if you like. I can talk to Mike over at the Toyota dealership."

Serena had said he liked to swoop in and take over. She said that some women liked having everything done for them, and I saw, in a flash so clear and true that it almost blinded me: this would be my life with Scott. He was a man who took care of things. He would take care of my children and me. I also saw, just as clearly, what that would mean to my sudden and new-found freedom and me.

The surge of happiness was gone. "I don't need you to go to the car dealership with me, Scott." I heard the words as I said them, and they sounded ugly and ungrateful.

"Of course not, Risa, it's just—"

"And you don't have to talk to Abbie either. I can do these things for myself."

His arm around me loosened. "Of course you can, Risa."

"You're an all-or-nothing guy, remember?"

He nodded.

"So I need to know if you can love me and keep your distance at the same time. Because I love you, Scott. Or at least I'm falling in love with you. But here's the thing." I turned again to face him, my hand on the front of his shirt, my fingers cold against the warmth of his body. "I've loved two men in my life," I told him. "Billy and Ed. And I just now, this very week, finally got out from under the weight of that love. I finally learned that I didn't need them. I didn't need their love or approval or their kind word to be a strong person. I can stand up and say what I want and do what I want, and it feels amazing."

He was watching my face, and his eyes were warm and understanding. "I bet it does."

"I really want to get used to that feeling," I said. "I need to feel comfortable all by myself."

He took a long breath. "And you think that if you loved me, you couldn't do that?"

I shook my head. "No. I think if *you* loved *me* I couldn't do that."

He swallowed. "I do love you, Risa. I have, from that very first day. It hit me so hard I thought I'd never be able to breathe again. And I've done everything I could to make you love me. I've tried to help you, tried to do for you…"

I nodded. "I know you have. And it worked, Scott. I've never felt safe like this before. I've never felt so protected." Why was this happening now? Why was I just now finding a man I wanted to share everything with at a point in my life when I needed to do for myself? And he loved me. Deep in my own heart I'd known that, but hearing the words just brought even more pain. He loved me. He hadn't said those words lightly. Loving me, for a man like Scott, would be a deep and true thing, a lasting thing, an unbreakable thing. And loving me would mean standing in front of me to protect me, rather than beside me. My heart was swelling with knowing the cost of my words. "Will you be able to step back and let me fumble my way through on my own?"

He looked out over the river and shook his head slowly. "That's not the kind of person I am, Risa. I can't see someone I love struggle and not try to help."

"But I need to do that, Scott. I've just learned how and I need to keep on doing it. Not just for myself, but for my kids. I need to be strong for them. And with you around…"

"You'll lean on me instead of standing up for yourself."

I nodded. All he had to say was that he could step away from me. That he could love me without interference. That he could love me and watch me fall.

But he wouldn't say those words, because they would be a lie.

The swelling in my heart suddenly burst. "I don't know what to do, Scott. I don't want you to walk away from me."

There were tears in his eyes. "Risa, you know me. You know who and what I am. And you know that I love you. So you know what will happen if I don't walk away." He sighed. "I can't be the person you need, Risa. I can only be myself. I'm so sorry."

"Me too."

I heard Lily call from the back door. Dinner was ready.

"So, I guess maybe I'll just go back to my place," he said slowly.

I nodded. "That might be a good idea." I felt like I was falling, slowly, and I knew that when I hit bottom, my heart would shatter.

We stood and walked back together, across the road, and up the drive to RiverCliffe.

"This was such a bad time for us to happen," I said. I didn't want him to leave. I wanted him to stay and have tacos, then take me back to his place where we could stretch out in his big bed until there wasn't a drop of want or need or energy left in either of us. I wanted him to say again that he loved me, because I knew how much he meant it. I also knew what it would cost.

He put his arms around me and kissed the top of my head and drove away.

I went back to Brooklyn the same day Ed arrived to pick up the kids to take them back out to his place for an overnight. Just the two days before I'd traded in my minivan for a nice big Subaru Forester, and I headed south with a sense of purpose. I was going to pack up whatever was worth keeping of our former lives, and bring it up to fit into our fresh start.

Kira had made a list of stuffed animals, toys, and everything that was left in her closet. Lily wanted nothing. Kevin asked for the posters off his wall and all the sports equipment he had stashed up in my mother's attic.

With the furniture gone from the basement, the walls looked dark and drab. It was bigger than it had been with all of us crowded in, and I realized it could be a valuable space.

"Mom, what are you going to do with the basement now that we're gone?" I asked.

She sat back and gave me a look that said, are you kidding?

"I have stuff, Risa, that I had to crowd into my *other* rooms. Now I can put them back where they belong."

"Have you needed any of that stuff in the year and a half we lived here?"

She was sitting at her kitchen table, playing solitaire. She froze, one hand hovering over a queen, and glared. "Is there a point here somewhere?"

"Why don't I pay to have it painted, and have new windows put in? Get the bathroom redone. You could rent it out. Maybe even as an airbnb. Extra money, you know? Then you could quit the dog-walking."

She sniffed. "I love dog-walking."

"I know you do, Mom. But you complained last year of the cold. Wouldn't you like to give it up?"

She sniffed again. "Maybe. Let me think about it."

I drove to all three of my kids' schools, gathered their report cards and evaluations, and stuffed it in the tote bag with all the other paper fragments of my life that had remained in Brooklyn.

I went back to my mother's house, took one last look around, and then joined her on the front stoop as she had her cigarette. It was hot, no breeze, and the traffic from the street was very faint.

"Have you heard from him?" I asked.

She shook her head. "No." She flashed me a bright smile. "Guess he wasn't as sick as he thought he was."

"He made such a big show about meeting my kids. He fed them a whole line about how he wanted them to be with him. Same old BS."

She nodded. "Yes. Same old BS." She looked sideways at me. "So what about that nice policeman?"

"I've haven't seen him lately. We kind of—"

"Oh, Risa, how could you! He was so handsome and big and strong, and we had a very nice conversation in the car, you know, when he took me to the train? He even waited with me. A gentleman. What did you do?"

"I told him I loved him."

"Well, that was wonderful. But?"

"I told him I would lose too much if we stayed together."

She stared at me. "Now, why in the world would you say a thing like that?"

I'd been wondering the same thing, but was still sure I'd made the right choice. I felt myself getting better every day, surer of my decisions, more confident. Except, of course, around my mother, who, I had long ago acknowledged, would make me feel like a twelve year old any time we were together.

"Do you know, Mom, that for the first time since Ed left, I feel like the kids and I are living in a place that's really ours, that can't be taken away? I'm taking on more at the inn, and I'm running it the way I want to, and it's a real job. I'm earning my own money. I haven't done that since before Lily was born. This is the first time I've felt in charge of my own life. And you know why? Because I'm doing it alone. And as good a guy as Scott was, if I had kept him in my life, I wouldn't have been able to say that. He would have started doing things for me, too many things. You saw that, didn't you, when he took you to the train? All that kindness and caring, it's real. It's who he is. But I wouldn't have learned to stand on my own. I needed to be able to do that, Mom. That was more important."

She looked away from me, her lips in a tight line. She drew on her cigarette and let out a long trail of smoke. "I guess you've got a point. Me, I never wanted to stand on my own. I would have done anything to have Billy back, caring for me, taking away all the worries. But you, well, …" She looked at me and and waggled her cigarette. "He was a nice man. I feel bad about him. But what about that motorcycle fellow? You know, the one you met when you first got up there? Is he still around? " She raised her eyebrows. "Maybe?"

"He's a ghost."

Her mouth dropped open. "No."

"Yes. His name is Caleb Fielding and he was killed in a motorcycle crash."

She dropped her cigarette on the stoop as she grabbed both of my hands in hers. "So, you can see them? Talk to them?"

I nodded.

Her eyes filled with tears. "Oh, Risa, how wonderful."

I looked at our hands together and shook them. "Yes, it is."

"So maybe I'll go up there and you can introduce me?"

I laughed and shook my head. "Sorry. It doesn't work that way."

She drew back. "Maybe never before, but who knows? Spirits are very attuned to those who are sympathetic, you know. I bet they'll be falling over each other just to get a word in."

I laughed again. "Okay. I promise. Next time you're up, I'll take you to meet my mother-in-law."

Her eyebrows drew together sharply. "Really? You talk to her? After what she did?"

I closed my eyes and shook my head. "She didn't do anything, Mom. It was Billy. He did it all, the lies, the fake name...please, don't forget that. I know I won't."

She nodded and sniffed. "Yeah. A snake. But God, he was a charmer. And the love of my life."

I put my arm around her and gave her a quick squeeze. "I know."

I left with her promise to get someone in to convert the basement from a dark well of a place to something more hospitable. She was dry eyed as I left, and so was I. She was only two hours away, I kept telling myself, even though I knew that it was really a whole world away.

Kira loved her new school. She immediately made three new best friends. She also asked to take horseback riding lessons. Tim, who took care of the horses at the inn, as well as helping Daniel with the rest of the livestock, shook his head when I asked him. He didn't know much beyond walk and trot, he said, but he gave me a name and phone number, and soon she was set, with her tiny black helmet and scuffed ankle boots. She was going to ride in the Olympics, she told me. I believed her.

Kevin said he wanted to join the soccer team. I remembered life as a soccer mom: early morning practice, spending Saturdays baking in the sun or huddled under an umbrella in freezing rain. I had hated it all, even the most innocuous of tasks, like bringing the oranges to practice. I sighed and mentally kissed my weekends good-bye.

Lily hated all her teachers but admitted, grudgingly, to liking most of the kids in her classes. She wanted to take a baking class at the C.I.A. It cost almost as much as my freshman year at Brooklyn College. I said yes.

I took all the small victories.

And I missed Scott. Every single day.

Beth came back down again for a weekend. She and Winston shared another glorious day of antiquing. Kira and I took her on a long trail ride up into the hills, just as the leaves were turning. And she stayed an extra day, Monday, and we left right after the kids went school and headed east, to Bristol, Massachusetts.

The street where Henry Fielding lived was in an older development, large brick and stone homes on wide, green lots. I had called the night before, telling him who I was and that I had information about his father. Henry told me, very calmly, that his father had disappeared without a trace years ago, and he didn't even think about him anymore.

Since I knew better, I asked if I could come and see him anyway, and he said he'd be home.

When he opened the door, my heart almost stopped. He looked very much like Caleb, the same thick, dark hair that fell away from his forehead, the same smile, the same slim frame. He was taller, and his eyes were wide and blue, obviously, his mother's eyes.

"Yes?"

"I'm Risa. I called last night. And this is my friend, Beth"

He glanced past me and looked at Beth. He nodded, then shrugged, opened the door wider, and stepped aside to let us through.

We sat in a comfortable living room, slightly messy, with books spilling out of the built-in shelves and stacks of magazines. A woman sat by the fireplace, older but lovely, with white hair pulled off her face and back into a long braid that fell over her left shoulder and down. She had turquoise earrings that brought out the blue in her wide eyes, Henry's eyes. This was Linda, the country song about good love gone wrong.

"Caleb was killed in a crash," I said without preamble. "He was coming from a bar called the Bear Claw. It had turned cold, there was ice on the road, and he and his bike were burned beyond recognition." The words hurt as they came out, and I saw Linda's wide eyes turn dark with pain. "No one knew who he was, and no one stepped up to identify him, so he was buried as a John Doe in RiverCliffe Memorial Park." I looked at Henry Fielding. "Your father did not just abandon you." I stopped. What was I supposed to say next? "I thought it was important that you know."

Henry nodded a few times, glanced over at his mother, then at me. "How do you know this? How did you find this out?"

I had prepared my story very carefully. "The bartender at the Claw back then was a man named Stevie Guthrie. He actually remembered your father, and the details of the accident, but never knew your father's name. That's why, when it happened, no one could find a next of kin. But *my* father was also there, way back then, and talked to him. He knew your father's name. He knew your name. You see, my father *did* abandon me. And I just found him, just recently, and I asked him about your father, and he gave me the information I needed. I turned it over to a friend of mine in the sheriff's department, and he found you."

Linda spoke very quietly, the Texas panhandle still in her voice. "Why did you even try to find all this out?"

"I inherited a place called RiverCliffe, and when I did, I tried to find out everything I could. Caleb dying, right before Christmas, was something people still remembered. He just, I don't know, stuck with me, I guess." I looked back at Henry. "I know what it is to feel unloved. Your father loved you. He didn't just leave you."

Henry's eyes were clear and dry. "I've spent most of my life not

263

caring about Caleb Fielding one way or another, but I guess I'm glad you told me."

Linda stood, grabbed the back of the chair, and steadied herself. "I am very grateful," she said, louder than necessary. "I always knew he didn't just run away. He'd been done with running away. He ran from Texas, he ran from the draft, he tried to run his whole life. But when you were born, Henry, he said he found something to stay for. And even though we couldn't live together anymore, he tried to be a good father. He *was* a good father."

Henry shrugged. "You've been saying that for years, Mama."

"Because it's true," she shot back. "And here's the proof. What this lady says tells you that I've been right all along." She sank back into the chair, and quietly folded her hands together. "Thank you, Risa."

"You're welcome," I said, standing. "I have to go. Thank you for taking the time to see me."

We walked out quickly, and I pulled the car out of the drive and started back toward the interstate. I felt something start to shake in my core, and I pulled over to the side of the road, threw the car into Park, and closed my eyes, hands clutching the wheel.

He didn't believe me. He sat there and nodded and looked polite, but he didn't believe me.

"He thought I was crazy," I finally said, my breath coming in sobs. "It didn't make a bit of difference."

"Maybe not to him," Beth said quietly. "But she believed you, it made a big difference to her."

I opened my eyes and blinked back tears. And it would make a difference to Caleb. I pulled back out into the quiet street and headed for home.

When we got back to RiverCliffe, Beth put her suitcase in her car and gave me a long hug. "Do you miss him?" she asked.

I nodded. I missed Scott every day, a deep, sharp longing that tarried around my heart. She had not mentioned him until now, and I'd been grateful, because the pain was still too close.

"You can always try to work it out, you know," she said softly. "There's always a chance."

I shook my head and stepped away from her, forcing a smile. "Of course there is," I said.

She got into her car and drove off. She knew I wouldn't try. I had to move on.

Then I turned toward RiverCliffe Memorial Park.

I looked for him as I came through the trees, and he was sitting on our bench, staring at the river. I sat beside him and reached for his hand.

"I saw your son today, Caleb," I told him. "I saw Henry."

He turned to me, his eyes bright. "Really?"

"Yes. I told him what happened. How you were killed coming down off the mountain. How you never meant to leave him alone."

He blinked several times.

"Linda was with him," I said. "She's still lovely. She said she knew that you'd never have run away from your son. She said you had stopped running away."

He nodded to himself. "Yes, I finally had. And wouldn't you know that I'd end up somewhere like this, someplace I would never want to run away from, even if I could."

I bumped him with my shoulder. "Know what Bea said?"

He chuckled. "No, but I can imagine all sorts of things that Bea might of said."

"She said you and I would have been something special."

He tilted his head. "We are something special, Risa. We are everything that we can be. You are the woman who gave me the greatest gift a father could ask for. I knew, the moment you stepped onto holy ground, that you were the one to make a difference. I only hope I've given something back to you."

I took a deep breath. "Knowing you has been a gift, Caleb. A joy."

He narrowed his eyes. "But you're not happy, Risa. You're content. I can see that. You're in a good place, but there is no joy. You need someone in your life you can trust with your heart."

I shook my head. "No, Caleb. Giving your heart to someone is the best way to lose yourself. I've still got too many things to learn, and I need to learn those things alone."

He made a wry, clucking sound. "I didn't say anything about giving your heart to someone else. Only a fool does that. You always have to hold back a piece of yourself, that's how you stay true to who you are. You need to find someone you can *trust* with your heart. Someone who will hold it and cherish it as much as you do. And who will see that little bit you're holding back, and understand why."

I sat very still.

"Ah, darlin'," he said softly. "Did you find a man like that and let him slip away?"

I felt my throat close up and I thought back to all the times Scott had been willing to do for me, whatever I wanted, whatever I needed. He had proved from the very start that he was someone I could trust with my life. Could he have taken the same care of my heart?

I stood. "I gotta go."

"Well, sure, Risa, but—"

I grabbed him by the shoulders and gave him a quick, hard kiss on his cheek. "Thanks."

And then I walked, thinking hard, back to RiverCliffe.

It took me almost a week to get up the nerve, but I knew what I needed to do. And who I needed to talk to.

Serena was back in the walk-in freezer with Lily.

"Hey, gotta minute?" I called.

She scampered out, shivering, Lily right behind her. "God, I hate going in there. My biggest nightmare was always getting trapped in there. I made Cathy do something with the latch—"

"Serena. How's Scott?"

She narrowed her eyes. "Scott?"

"Yes. How is he?"

"Well, I don't know. Why?"

I raised my eyebrows. "You don't know? You talk to him every day."

She turned to my daughter and made a shooing motion with her hands. She watched until Lily was around the corner, then folded her arms across her chest. "I do not talk to him every day. Not for weeks now. He decided that he and I were still too close. He said he needed to stop being too over-protective. Muttered about all or nothing. At the time I figured it was because he decided that *you* were the one he was going to concentrate on. But since Winston seems to think the two of you have closed shop..." She shrugged her shoulders. "I have no idea what's going on." She sighed. "I told you he was a good man. Why did you run him off?"

"Because I'm an idiot?"

She made a face. "Yeah, well...but you're not an idiot now?"

"No. I'm probably just as big a fool as I was weeks ago. But at least now I *know* I've been a fool. Where would he be, do you think?"

She glanced at her watch. "Darts. Up at the Claw. Every Friday afternoon."

"Darts? Seriously?"

She grinned. "Boss, there's a whole lot to that man that will surprise you. Want me to keep an eye in the kids?"

I nodded. "Ed is coming to get them at six," I told her. "They're ready to go. Kira is at Daniel's, but—"

She waved her hand. "Go. Lily and I have got this."

"No, wait, Ed has to know that Kevin has a game tomorrow, and—"

"Do you really think your son cannot tell his own father he has a *game*? Go."

I drove up to the Bear Claw. The leaves had started turning, and the scenery was glorious, but I barely noticed. What was I going to say to him? I briefly thought about getting him drunk, seducing him in the back of his truck, and then seeing what would happen next, but the thought of trying to make love in a back seat at my age was too much.

The Claw wasn't too crowded, and most everyone was in one corner, around the dart game. I wasn't a big fan myself, so I hung back and watched for few minutes. Scott was out of uniform, in jeans and a flannel shirt, which only made him look even more of a lumberjack. His big shoulders moved easily under the soft fabric, and I remembered the strength in those arms, and the gentleness.

He saw me out of the corner of his eye at first, and turned slowly. The expression on his face did not change. He still smiled, but I could see his eyes darken.

"Hey, Risa. What are you doing here?"

I glanced around the room. Every single person was looking at me. I remembered what he said when we first met, how in a small town, everyone was a matchmaker, and how they'd been working on him for a while. They all probably knew that I'd broken it off with him. They all probably hated me for it.

I know I did.

"I'm at RiverCliffe now. Surely you'd heard?"

He nodded. "Yes, of course. But what are you doing *here*?"

I cleared my throat. "Can I talk to you for a second?"

He looked around at the group of men. "In the middle of a game here—"

"We can wait on the game," one of the men said quickly.

"Course we can," said another. "Besides, I need a beer."

Scott looked around again and shook his head, walking toward me, taking my arm in his hand and leading me to the other side of the bar.

"Is everything okay?" he asked.

I looked up into those beautiful blue eyes and stood on my toes, put my arms tight around his neck and kissed him.

I had not seen him in weeks. The last words I said to him hurt him. This could have gone very badly.

But his arms tightened around me, and he kissed me back, and the heat was still there, deep down, and when I finally drew back, I would have happily jumped into the nearest back seat around.

"I think I made a big mistake," I said, my words tumbling out as I watched his face. "I think that no matter how much you try to protect me, and keep me safe from whatever is out there you think will hurt me, you would still let me make my own way. You'd give me the space to do all the things I need to do to grow, and become better. I've never loved a man who would do that for me. But I think you would. Because you take care, Scott. And you'd figure out how to take care of me, even if it meant stepping back."

His eyes were wide and his mouth slightly open. He looked past me and I realized that the Bear Claw was completely silent, and that everyone in there had heard every word I said.

I swallowed. Please, dear God, let him speak. And soon, because I felt like melting into the floor.

"Hells, bell, Scott," someone called. "Say something to the lady!"

He ran his hands through his hair, and I felt a sick, sinking feeling. I'd waited too long. He realized I wasn't what he wanted after all. He'd met someone else.

"Risa, are you sure?"

I nodded.

His shoulders slumped and he closed his eyes. "Thank God, because I've been miserable these past weeks."

"And he has, too," someone called.

He lifted his head and the twinkle in his eye was back. "Sorry boys," he called, putting his arm around my shoulder. "I think I'm gonna have to forfeit this game."

We hurried out into the parking lot.

"Come down to RiverCliffe," I told him. "We need to talk."

He followed me down the narrow road in the darkness, and as we went into the apartment, he looked around approvingly "The place looks good. New stuff?"

"Yep. All new furniture. Even my bedroom. Wanna see?"

He grinned. "You bet. But can I ask you something first?"

I went into the kitchen and returned with two glasses and a bottle of wine. "Sure."

"Tell me about Caleb. I get that he's a ghost, but are you in love with him?"

I poured the wine. "Yes, he's a ghost. And no, I don't love him. If he had been a living, breathing person, then, I probably would have fallen. Hard. But I can figure out a worst case scenario when I see one."

"He means something to you?"

I closed my eyes for a moment. "Yes. There's a real connection. Maybe it's because he *is* a ghost. Cathy told me they could see inside, into the heart. He saw into mine, and he knew what I wanted." I looked up at Scott, his handsome, open face, into his kind and loving eyes. "He told me things I needed to hear. He told me I needed someone to trust with my heart. And when he explained what that meant, I knew he was talking about you."

He sipped his wine. "I'm still an all-or-nothing guy," he said.

"Serena tells me not so much anymore."

He made a motion with his head. "I'm trying."

"Well, that's good enough for me."

He looked down into his wine glass. "Are you certain I can give you what you need, Risa?"

I smiled. "Remember that day at the C.I.A.? I told you I had all that I need. I still do. But now it's about what I *want*. And I want you, Scott. I want to see if we can make something together."

"What about all that learning you still had to do?"

"If I'm any kind of reasonable human being, I'll spend the rest of my life learning. But I don't think you'll try to stop me. And if you try, I think I'm strong enough now to push back."

I motioned with my wine glass toward the bedroom. "You coming?"

I drew the curtains against the dark and pulled down the spread, and we crept beneath my new sheets, and afterward I brought some cheese and crackers to bed, and we ate and talked. Scott started a fire and we made love again, and when I woke in the morning, he was snoring gently, his body curved away from mine. I slipped out of bed without waking him.

As I walked through the living room, a small book of soft brown leather caught my eye. It was the diary that Beth had bought for me. I dug into my purse for a pen, settled on the couch, opened the first pristine page, and began to write. It was easy. I wrote about Caleb in long, unhurried sentences, until I had filled almost four pages.

I set the book aside. Later, I would write about Cathy and her sons. Martha and Bernie. My little Kira dancing among the gravestones. Lily and her anger. Hopefully, I would write about Scott, and our long years together. And one day, my words would be copied and bound and set upon a shelf.

I made myself some coffee and stepped outside, carrying a throw across my shoulders to guard against the chill. It was early, just dawn, and the sun was barely over the hills behind me as I sat in my lawn chair, coffee mug in hand, and watched as the river ran, silent and gleaming, as it had done for hundreds of years.

"Risa?"

Scott came and sat on the ground in front of me, leaning his broad back against my legs. "I love me a good river," he murmured.

I put my mug on the grass and wrapped my arms around Scott's neck, and set my chin on the top of his head, and together we watched the Hudson River turn to gold in the morning light.